THOMAS CRANE PUBLIC LIBRARY
QUINCY MA

CITY APPROPRIATION

PAST IMPERATIVE

ROUND ONE OF
THE GREAT GAME

DAVE DUNCAN

An AvoNova Book

William Morrow and Company, Inc.
New York

M‑H

2200

PAST IMPERATIVE: ROUND ONE OF THE GREAT GAME is an original publication of
Avon Books. This work has never before appeared in book form. This work is a novel. Any
similarity to actual persons or events is purely coincidental.

AVON BOOKS
A division of
The Hearst Corporation
1350 Avenue of the Americas
New York, New York 10019

Copyright © 1995 by Dave Duncan
Published by arrangement with the author
Library of Congress Catalog Card Number: 95-6181
ISBN: 0-688-14361-X

All rights reserved, which includes the right to reproduce this book or portions thereof in
any form whatsoever except as provided by the U.S. Copyright Law. For information address
Avon Books.

Library of Congress Cataloging in Publication Data:
Duncan, Dave, 1933–
    Past imperative : round one of the great game / Dave Duncan.
      p.   cm.
"An AvoNova book."
I. Title.
PR9199.3.D847P37   1995   95-6181
813'.54—dc20   CIP

First Morrow/AvoNova Printing: October 1995

AVONOVA TRADEMARK REG. U.S. PAT. OFF. AND IN OTHER COUNTRIES, MARCA REGISTRADA,
HECHO EN U.S.A.

Printed in the U.S.A.

QP   10   9   8   7   6   5   4   3   2

I see you stand like greyhounds in the slips,
Straining upon the start. The game's afoot.

SHAKESPEARE
Henry V, III, i

"Come, Watson, come!" he cried. "The game is afoot."

SIR ARTHUR CONAN DOYLE
The Return of Sherlock Holmes:
"Adventure of the Abbey Grange"

Hear all peoples, and rejoice all lands, for the slayer of Death comes, the Liberator, the son of Kameron Kisster. In the seven hundredth Festival, he shall come forth in the land of Suss. Naked and crying he shall come into the world and Eleal shall wash him. She shall clothe him and nurse him and comfort him. Be merry and give thanks; welcome this mercy and proclaim thine deliverance, for he will bring death to Death.

The Filoby Testament, 368

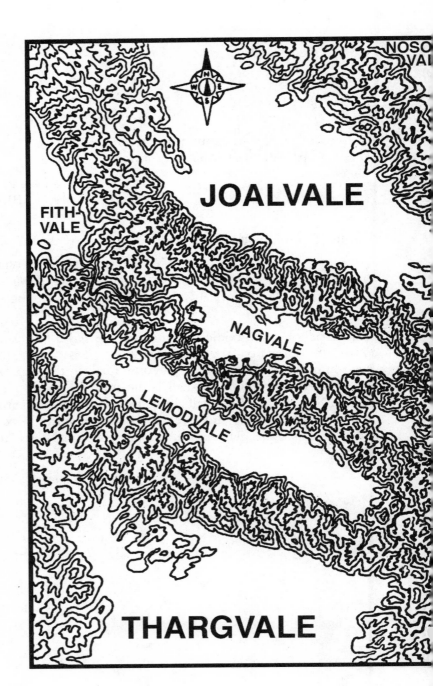

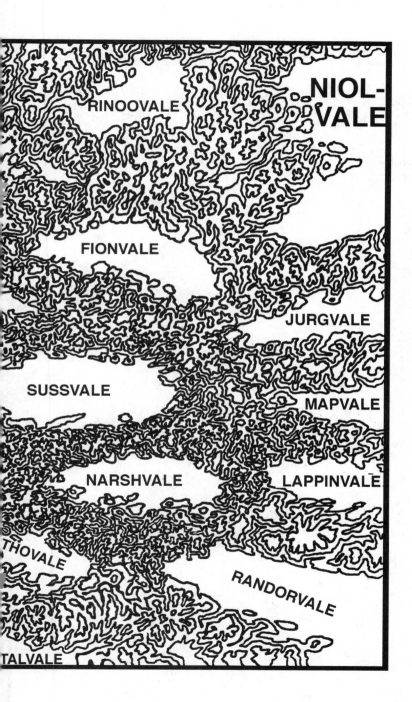

NIOL-
VALE

RINOOVALE

FIONVALE

JURGVALE

SUSSVALE

MAPVALE

NARSHVALE

LAPPINVALE

THOVALE

RANDORVALE

TALVALE

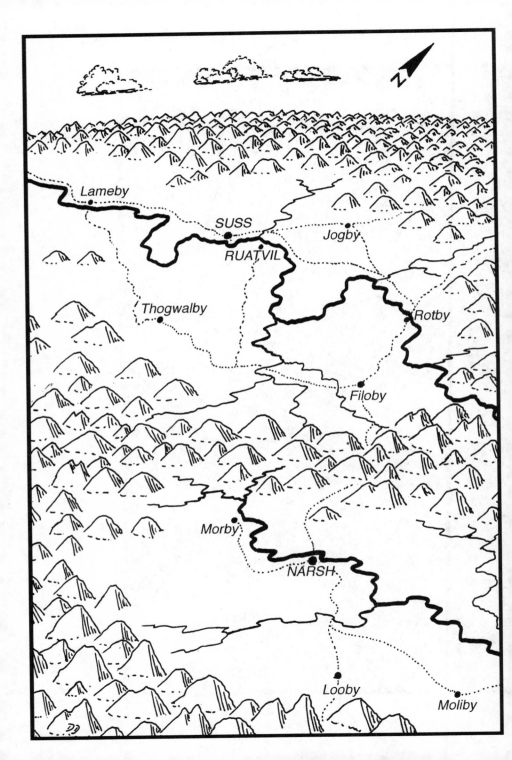

CONTENTS

TRANSLATOR'S NOTE

In Joalian and related dialects, a geographic name usually consists of a root modified by a prefix. English equivalents (for example Narshland, Narshvale, Narshia, etc.) fail to convey all the subtleties of the original. Joalian alone has twelve words to describe a mountain pass, depending on its difficulty, but no word for a mountain range.

The flora and fauna of the Vales are quite unrelated to terrestrial types, but convergent evolution has tended to fill similar ecological niches with species of similar appearance. Form follows function—a beetle is more or less a beetle anywhere, airborne species lay eggs so that they need not be burdened with immature young, and so on. To avoid overloading the reader's memory with names and the page with italics, I have either coined descriptive terms ("bellfruit") or assigned names on the basis of appearance. A rose is a rose is, sort of, a rose. The correspondence may be superficial; a "moa" is a bipedal mammal.

Time and distance have been converted to familiar units.

Spelling has been made as phonetic as possible, based on common English pronunciation. G is hard; c is used only in *ch*, *x* and *q* not at all.

Masculine gender words begin with hard consonants (b,d,g,k,p,t), feminine with vowels or aspirates (a,e,i,o,u,y,h), and neuter with soft consonants (f,j,l,m,n,r,s,th). Abstract concepts have their own declensions and begin with v,ch,w, or z.

Dissimilar vowels are pronounced separately, as if marked with a dieresis: *Eleal* is pronounced *El-eh-al*, not *Eleel*. Double vowels indicate a long sound: *aa* as in *late*, *ee* as in *feet*, *ii* as in *fight*, *oo* as in *goat*, *uu* as in *boot*.

The English word *candle* is pronounced *cand'l*. Joalian contains many such unvoiced vowels, which are indicated with an apostrophe. The initial consonant in *D'ward* would be stressed more than in English *dwarf*.

THE GODS

The five great gods of the Pentatheon are—

Visek The Supreme Parent is often regarded as male, but also as a triad: Father, Mother, and First Source. Visek may be spoken of in the singular or plural, as masculine, feminine, or abstract in ways that will not readily translate into English. The Light, the All-Knowing, the Father of Gods, etc., may take on attributes of other deities, such as wisdom, creation, justice. There are hints of monotheism in Visek worship. Except in Niol, where his main temple stands, Visek seems too remote and abstract a god to be truly popular with the masses. He is associated with the sun, fire, silver, and the color white.

His many avatars include **Chiol** (destiny) and **Wyseth** (the sun).

Eltiana The Lady is goddess of love, motherhood, passion, childbirth, crops, agriculture, transition. Her clergy wear red; her symbol is Ø and her main temple is at Randor. She is the only major deity to be directly identified with one of the four moons.

Her avatars include **Ois,** goddess of mountain passes.

Karzon The Man is the god of creation and destruction, and thus of war, strength, courage, virility, vengeance, pestilence, nature, and animal husbandry. His clergy wear green, his symbol is a hammer. His main temple is at Tharg and he is associated with the moon Trumb.

As **Zath** he is god of death, and hence the most feared of the gods. Then his color is black and his symbol a skull. Other avatars include **Garward** (strength), **Ken'th** (virility), and **Krak'th** (earthquakes).

Astina   The Maiden is goddess of purity, duty, justice, patron of warriors and athletes. Her clergy wear blue and her symbol is a five-pointed star. Her main sanctuary is at Joal. She is associated with Ysh, the blue moon.

     Her avatars include **Iilah** (athletes), **Irepit** (repentance), **Ysh** (constancy and duty), and **Ursula** (justice).

Tion   The Youth is god of art, beauty, science, knowledge, healing. His clergy wear yellow. His main temple is at Suss. The unpredictable yellow moon Kirb'l is identified with his avatar the god of humor.

     His avatars include **Ember'l** (drama), **Kirb'l** (the Joker), **Gunuu** (courage), **Yaela** (singing), and **Paa** (healing).

THE TRONG TROUPE

Trong Impresario

Ambria Impresario, Trong's second wife

K'linpor Actor, Trong's son

Halma Actor, K'linpor's wife

Uthiam Piper, Ambria's daughter

Golfren Piper, Uthiam's husband

Yama Actor, Ambria's cousin

Dolm Actor, Yama's husband

Piol Poet, brother of Ambria's first husband

Gartol Costumer, Trong's cousin

Olimmiar Dancer, Halma's sister

Klip Trumpeter, Gartol's stepbrother

Eleal Singer, an orphan

OVERTURE

1

THE SUMMER OF 1914 WAS THE FINEST IN LIVING MEMORY.
All over Europe the sun shone, day after day, from a sky without
a cloud. Holidaymakers traveled as they wished across a continent at peace, reveling in green woods and clean, warm seas.
They crossed national borders unimpeded. Almost no one noticed the storm building on the political horizon; even newspapers mostly ignored it. The war struck with the suddenness
of an avalanche and carried everything away.

There was never to be another summer like it.

Toward the end of June in that year the Greek steamship *Her-
mes,* preparing to depart from Port Said and having a vacant
stateroom, embarked at short notice a gentleman whose name
was entered in the log as Colonel Julius Creighton. He was
polite and aloof and inscrutable. During the crossing of the
Mediterranean, he remained extremely reticent about both himself and his business. He was without question an English *milord,*
but beyond that obvious deduction, neither the officers nor the
other passengers were able to progress. Everyone was intrigued
when he chose to disembark at Cattaro, in Montenegro, which
was not on the road to anywhere. The English, they agreed,
were crazy. They would all have been considerably more surprised had they been able to follow his subsequent travels.

He set foot on European soil on the twenty-eighth of June,
which by coincidence was the day Archduke Francis Ferdi-
nand's death in Sarajevo opened the first crack of the collapse

that was to bring down the whole world. The Montenegro border was less than fifty miles from Sarajevo. The reader is therefore cautioned that Colonel Creighton had absolutely nothing to do with the assassination.

He progressed rapidly north and east, traveling mainly on horseback through wild country, until he reached the vicinity of Belgrade. In a wagon in a wood, he was granted audience by a gypsy *voivode,* whose authority transcended national borders.

Creighton continued eastward and spent a night as guest of a certain count of ancient lineage, lord of a picturesque castle in Transylvania. In Vienna he met with several people, including a woman reputed to be the most skilled courtesan in Austria, with the fairest body in Europe, but the substance of their meeting was unrelated to such matters.

By the fifteenth of July he had reached St. Petersburg. Although the Russian capital was racked by workers' strikes, he succeeded in spending several hours talking with a monk celebrated for both his holiness and his political connections.

On the twenty-third, when Austria issued its ultimatum to Serbia, Colonel Creighton arrived in Paris, having wasted a couple of days in a cave in the Black Forest. Paris was in the throes of the Caillaux scandal, but he ignored that, conferring with two artists and a newspaper editor. He also took an overnight train south to Marseilles to visit Fort St. Jean, European Headquarters of the Foreign Legion. He spent most of his time there in the chapel, then returned to the capital.

On July 28, when Austria declared war on Serbia, he obtained a berth on the next boat train to London—a surprising feat, considering the near-panic in the Gare du Nord.

On reaching England, he completely disappeared.

2

EDWARD ARRIVED IN GREYFRIARS ON THE 4.15 FROM London. It was the Saturday of August Bank Holiday weekend, and the little station was almost deserted. Paris had been in panic. London was a riot of trippers fighting their way out of town, heading for the seaside. Greyfriars was its usual sleepy country self.

He emerged from the station, bag in hand, to find the Bodgley Rolls at the curb, with Bagpipe himself at the wheel.

Edward said, "Damned good of you to put me up, Bodgley," and climbed in.

Bagpipe said, "Good to see you, old man. Care to go for a spin?" He was trying not to swallow his ears at being allowed to drive the Rolls.

So Timothy Bodgley drove Edward Exeter home to Greyfriars Grange by a somewhat roundabout route, but took care that they arrived in decent time to get ready for dinner. Edward thanked Mrs. Bodgley for taking him in at such short notice— and at his own request, of course, but that part of it was too painful to mention. She insisted he was always welcome.

Then there was a gap. This is a common result of head injuries.

He retained no record at all of the next hour. After that came a few scattered images of dinner itself, random pages saved from a lost book. His most vivid recollection was to be of his own intense embarrassment at being in blazer and flannels, like a stray dog that had wandered into the thoroughbred kennel. One of his cases had been stolen in Paris, and he had had no time to hire evening clothes on his dash through London. He had had no English money, either, and the banks were closed on Saturdays.

The nine or ten faces around the table remained only a blur. The Bodgleys themselves, of course, he knew well: Bagpipe and his parents—the large and booming Mrs. Bodgley, and the peppery general with his very red face and white mustache. There was a Major Someone, an ex-India type. There was a Dowager Lady Somebody and the vicar. And others. The scraps of conversation he did remember were all about the imminence of war. The major explained at length how easily the French and the Russians between them would roll up the Boche. Everyone agreed it would all be over by Christmas.

Later, when the ladies had withdrawn and left the men to the port and cigars, the talk was of the need to teach the Germans a damned good lesson, and which regiment Edward Exeter and Timothy Bodgley should join, and how lucky they were to be young enough to serve.

The evening concluded with patriotic songs around the piano, and everyone turned in early because the general was scheduled to read the lesson in church the next morning.

Later still, Edward sprawled on the window seat in his room while Bagpipe in pajamas and dressing gown sat on the chair, and the two of them nattered away like old times in the junior dorm. Bagpipe raved about the book he was reading, *The Lost World,* and promised to lend it to Edward as soon as he had finished. They reminisced about their schooldays, amused to discover that a mere week away had already wreathed Fallow in a haze of nostalgia. They returned to the subject of the war, and Bagpipe waxed bitter.

"Me enlist? It's not meant, old man. Won't pass the medical. Not Pygmalion likely!" Even as he said it, his lungs sounded like a dying cat. He had asthma; he had never been able to run even the length of cricket pitch without turning blue, but he was a straight enough chap in spite of it. He would miss the war, and Edward was at a loss to know how to comfort him, although he babbled nonsense about valuable alternatives, like intelligence work.

Then Bagpipe shrugged it off and tried to hide his chagrin. "What say we go down and raid the larder, like old times?"

Edward must have agreed, although he retained no recollection of doing so. A trivial boyish prank like that should have been beneath their dignity, but perhaps it suited the mood of unreality that had so suddenly descended upon their lives. They had emerged from the ordered, cloistered discipline of school into a world poised on the brink of madness.

The kitchen was in the oldest part of the Grange, a vast stone barn of echoes and monumental furniture and unsettling, unexplained shadows. There, for Edward Exeter, reality ended altogether.

After that there were just a few confused frozen images, like blurred photographs in newspapers, or line drawings in the *Illustrated London News*. There was a girl screaming, her screams reverberating in that cavernous stone scullery. She had wild eyes and hair that hung down in long ringlets. There was a knife. There was blood—a porcelain sink with blood pouring into it. He retained a very foggy memory of people beating on the door, trying to get in, and of himself fending off the knife-wielding maniac with the aid of a wooden chair. There was a terrible pain in his leg.

Then darkness and nightmare.

ᵍᵉᵗᵉᵗ 3 ᵗᵒᵗᵒ

IT WAS THE HOUR BEFORE DAWN. A GALE LEFT OVER FROM winter rolled clouds through the sky, continually veiling or unveiling the moons, so that sometimes the narrow streets were inky as coal cellars, and at others a man could read the storekeepers' signs creaking to and fro in the wind. Over the slate rooftops, far behind the chimneys, the ice-capped peaks of Narshwall glimmered like teeth with black tongues of cloudshadow lolling over them.

Dragon claws scratching on cobblestones betrayed the progress of a watchman, riding slowly along Straight Way, making his rounds. It was a living, if not a very lucrative one, nor especially prestigious. It was a cursed cold living on a night like this, and his thoughts were mainly of the snug, wife-warmed bed awaiting him at sunrise. He wore a metal-and-leather helmet and a steel breastplate over a layer of fur and two of wool. He switched his lantern from one hand to the other, feeling its warmth even through his gloves. He was in more danger of freezing his fingers than of meeting with trouble at night in Narsh.

Narsh was a peaceable place, but long ago the city fathers had decreed a curfew, so someone must uphold it. Illicit love affairs were the main cause of curfew-breaking, but most nights the watchman met not a single soul. Any evildoers that might be skulking around heard his dragon approach or saw his light and took cover until he had gone. The ban applied only to persons on foot, of course. It excluded dragon riders and coaches, and thus it did not restrict the city fathers or their friends.

Scritch, Scritch, went the dragon's claws. The wind rattled shutters and moaned in high eaves. Total blackness enveloped Straight Way, except where the watchman's lantern cast an uncertain beam on doors and the gaping mouths of alleys. Through a momentary gap in the clouds he caught a glimpse of the fourth moon, Eltiana, a gory red star in the east. He thought a silent prayer—his usual prayer to the Lady, emphasizing the undesirability of her sending further progeny to swell the household he must feed on his meager pay.

Then great green Trumb soared into view, as if springing out from ambush, his mighty half disk illuminating the town, highlighting the spires of the Lady's temple . . . and revealing a double line of people shuffling along the street just ahead of the watchman. For a moment he was struck speechless. Then he barked a command to speed his mount: *"Varch!"*

The dragon was perhaps also surprised, for it was accustomed to amble the night streets at a comfortable *Zaib* and had probably not been required to go faster in many years. After a brief pause, as if it were trying to recall the training of its youth, it increased its pace obediently, and the night watch of Narsh bore down upon the lawbreakers.

There were about a dozen of them, arranged roughly by height, from a tall couple up front to a child trailing at the rear. They all bore bulky packs. The watchman rode past them, shining his lantern on them, heading for the leaders. They were not residents, he concluded, for few of them were clad in the all-enveloping Narshian furs. Most of them were hunched and shivering. Strangers! Curfew breakers!

He drew ahead, spoke orders to his dragon, and came to a halt, barring their way. They stopped. Many of them lowered their burdens to the ground with evident relief. They peered up at him. He peered back down at them with all the majesty of the law.

The law's majesty was not as awe-inspiring as he would have liked. The dragon was not much of a dragon. Its scales were so worn and scuffed where the stirrups had rubbed at them over the years that it had been double-docked—the pommel plate removed so that the saddle could be placed farther forward than was normal, or truly comfortable. Its rider was thus seated on a slight slope and could not lean back in comfort against the baggage plate.

The dragon studied the malefactors with as much interest as the watchman, while puffing pearly clouds for the wind to disperse. Its eyes glowed pale green. Ferocious as dragons seemed, they were the gentlest of beasts, and most people knew that. The watchman was not quite certain what he was supposed to do when faced with a dozen lawbreakers at once, and half of them women.

He said, "Ho!" Then he added, "Identify yourselves!"

The leader was a tall man in a flowing robe that swirled continuously in the wind. So did his white patriarchal beard. When he doffed his hat and bowed, he revealed a bald pate surrounded by a mane of long white locks, and the wind began playing with them also. Nonetheless, he was a striking figure under the green moonlight, and his voice rang out with the sonority of a peal of bells.

"I am Trong Impresario and these are my associates in the troupe that bears my name—singers, musicians, actors, wandering players, seeking only to serve the Lord of Art."

Wandering beggars, more like, but the watchman recalled that he had seen a playbill outside the Shearing Shed a couple of days ago.

"You are abroad before first light, and such is forbidden!"

The Trong man swung around to regard the east. With dramatic suddenness, he threw out a long arm. "Behold, sir! Already the dewy dawn blushes to look upon the deeds of night!" He spoke with a Joalian accent, but that did not mean he could see the horizon through a two-story building.

"Forgive us if we have offended!" proclaimed his companion. She was almost as tall as he, and her voice seemed even more resonant, carrying a hint of clashing steel. It was not as readily identifiable, but certainly not homely Narshian. " 'First light' is not a precise term. We are strangers and may have misconstrued your local usage."

The watchman could not imagine why anyone would waste good money going to hear this rabble of outlanders recite poetry or even sing, if that was what they did. It seemed very un-Narshian behavior, but if anyone attended those performances, they would be the wealthier citizens—and their wives, of course. To make trouble for this band of tattered beggars might possibly land him in disfavor with important persons.

"State your business!" he demanded, to give himself time to think.

"We proceed," Trong declaimed, "to the temple to make sacrifice. Our wandering feet lead us onward to the Festival of Holy Tion in Suss, and we would seek the favor of Ois before hazarding fearsome Rilepass."

Ah! In his youth, the watchman had attended the Festival of Tion a few times. He had competed in the boxing contests until his face became so battered that he had been refused admittance. Of course a troupe of actors would be heading that way at this time of year, and no one in his right mind would venture a mammoth ride over Rilepass without making an offering at the temple. As goddess of passes, Ois was liable to drop avalanches on travelers who displeased her.

He cast another quick look at the sky and again saw the red moon peering through a narrow gap in the clouds. Ois was an avatar of the Lady, Eltiana, who was not only one of the Five, but also specifically identified with the red moon. She was watching him to see what he was going to do. She might disapprove of him harassing pilgrims on their way to worship one of her manifestations. He had best let these vagabonds proceed about their business.

"You should have waited until daybreak!"

The woman spoke up quickly. "But our need to reach Suss is urgent. You must know that this is the seven hundredth festival, and very special. There are many like us, seeking passage, and the lines are long this year. Our impatience was inspired by our piety, Watchman."

It was true that Narsh had seen an unusual number of festival-goers passing through in the last fortnight, although the watchman's wife had told him that the normal contingent of artists, athletes, and cripples was much the same. Surplus priests and priestesses were to blame.

"Go in peace," he proclaimed, moving his dragon out of the way. "But next time observe the law more strictly."

They heaved their packs higher on their shoulders and tramped off in unhappy silence.

Trumb dipped into cloud again and the street darkened. The last the watchman saw of the actors as they faded out was the child at the rear. Stooped under her bulky pack, she walked with a marked limp. He could guess why that one was going to the Tion Festival.

ACT I

TRAGEDY

4

MURDER! IT NEVER BLEEDING RAINED BUT IT BLOODY poured.

Carruthers had taken his family to Harrogate, Robinson was hiking in Scotland, Hardy had broken his pelvis, and Newlands was in bed with acute appendicitis. Meaning Mister Muggins Leatherdale was left running the whole shop. Meaning simple Inspector Leatherdale, just six months short of retirement, poor sod, was now expected to do the work of a superintendent, a deputy superintendent, a squad of detective inspectors, and earn not a ha'penny more for it.

On top of all that there had been threats of civil war in Ireland last week and real war breaking out all over Europe now—the Boche and the Russkis at each other's throats already and the Frogs mobilizing—with resultant official warnings to look out for all sorts of un-English activities, like riots and marches. Half the force was away on holiday.

And now a murder, the first in the county in twenty years. Not just your drunken brawl in a pub, charge reduced to manslaughter. Not just some sordid backstreet quarrel over a woman, oh no! Nothing so simple for poor Muggins Leatherdale. No, the chief constable's own son murdered in the chief constable's own house and the Old Man himself two-thirds off his rocker with grief and shock.

Howzat for pouring?

Bloody Noah's Flood!

★　　★　　★

The bells of St. George's were pealing as the big car purred through Bishops Wallop. Leaning back on the leather cushions with his bowler on his lap, Leatherdale heard them with a strange sense of unreality. He'd been routed out of bed at midnight and his eyelids felt thick as muffins. Shameful. He was getting too old to be a real copper.

The sun was baking hot already, a perfect Bank Holiday weekend in a perfect summer. War and murder and insanity, and yet the bells of Bishops Wallop pealed as they always had. They had rung like that when Leatherdale was a boy, spending holidays with his grandparents in a cottage whose thatched roof and ceilings had seemed uncomfortably low even then. The tenor bell had sounded a tiny fraction flat in those days, and it did now. It had probably seemed that way to Richard the Lionheart.

Church bells were still ringing as he was whisked through Sternbridge, and he wondered what his grandfather would have said to that miracle. Or his father, for that matter. Toffed out in their Sunday best, the worthy folk ambled along the street to worship, very much as their forebears had done for centuries. Dogs barked to repel the intruder and probably thought their efforts successful, for the motor accelerated as it left the village and raced up the hill beyond. It must have been doing forty when it reached the long avenue of beeches and chestnuts.

He watched the great canopy of summer foliage rushing overhead as the vehicle traversed the green tunnel. All his life he had gone to work on his bike, in uniform. On his bike he would be able to hear the thrushes and the woodpeckers and see butterflies working the hedgerows, but he had asked the chauffeur to lower the black leather hood so he could enjoy the breeze, scented with thyme and clover. England in August! The hayfields were deserted today, their crop half cut. Down in the bottoms horses swished their tails at flies. Everywhere he looked, the hazy skyline was ornamented with church spires and towers rising over the trees. Once he could have named them all and probably still could if he had a moment to think—St. Peter's in Button Bent, St. Alban's in Cranley . . . Norman, High Gothic, Perpendicular. For a thousand years, every Englishman had dwelt within walking distance of a church.

He had pulled out his watch before he realized that the bells had just told him the time. Elsie would be pulling out the stops in St. Wilfred's about now. He was going to be early for his appointment.

This jaunt was all a waste of time anyway. Leatherdale had a corpse and a killer and an open-and-shut case. The motive might not be obvious to nice-thinking folks, but a copper knew about the seamy side of life. Such things could happen even in drowsy little Greyfriars, where a runaway horse was a month's excitement. They happened; they just weren't talked about. This jaunt to Fallow had been Mrs. Bodgley's idea and the Old Man had been ready to agree to anything. So Leatherdale got a ride in a Rolls Royce. He yawned.

Fallow? He had passed the gates a few times, never been inside. It was outside his manor. Outside his ken, too—educational establishment for young gentlemen. Snob factory. Fallow boys would show up around Greyfriars sometimes, on day outings with their parents, like tailors' dummies in their school uniform, top hat and tails, each one like every other one. All speaking alike with the *proper* accent and polite as Chinese mandarins, all of 'em.

He'd thought to quiz the police doctor about Fallow, but the answer had been very much what he'd expected. A highly respected public school, Watkins had said. Not Eton or Harrow, of course. Second eleven, but probably about the best in the second eleven. Has a very solid relationship with the Colonial Office. Turns out the men who run the Empire—something of a specialty of the house, you might say. A chap'll bump into Old Fallovians all over the globe, in just about every Crown Colony everywhere. Running them, of course. White Man's Burden, palm and pine, and all that.

Dear Mrs. Bodgley could not imagine anything on God's

green earth that would turn a tailor's dummy, right-spoken, frightfully polite Fallow boy into a savage killer. Or her equally well-mannered son into a victim.

But Leatherdale could. Not nice. Not nice at all!

⟿ 5 ⟿

T HE SKY WAS GROWING LIGHTER AS THE TRONG TROUPE approached the temple. They were still arrayed in approximate order of size, although that was not a conscious arrangement. Trong Impresario led the way, like some peripatetic monument, with the statuesque Ambria at his side. Last of all came little Eleal Singer. The wind was still just as bitter and boisterous, whirling scattered snowflakes along the canyon of the street.

Hobbling under the weight of her pack, Eleal was immediately behind Klip and Olimmiar. She hated Narshvale. It was her least favorite of all the lands the troupe visited each year. Narshvale was cold, with leaden skies always seeming just about to spill snow. In Narsh itself the streets stank, because of the coal the Narshians burned to warm their ugly stone houses— grimy stone with roofs of black slate. The people stank, too, probably because they didn't wash their clothes. You couldn't wash llama fleece, it wouldn't dry before next winter.

She especially disliked the temple and Ois, its goddess, although of course no one would ever say such a thing out loud. Ambria probably felt the same way, because she always told Eleal to wait outside. If the old hussy thought Eleal did not know what went on in there, then she was sorely misinformed. In some of the villages the troupe played, they all had to share the same sleeping room. Eleal knew perfectly well what happened in the dark, under the covers. Uthiam and Golfren did it a lot, because they'd been married less than a year. K'linpor Actor and Halma did it too, and Dolm Actor and Yama, but not as often. Even Trong and Ambria did it sometimes. Everyone had to pretend not to hear, and nobody ever mentioned it, although when one couple started it, they often set off others.

They were married and did it because they wanted to and must like it. What happened in the temple of Ois was different. It involved money, and was supposed to be a sacrifice to the goddess, but no other god or goddess that Eleal knew of demanded that. She often wondered how the priestesses felt about it. She'd even asked Uthiam once if that was what the men did on their annual visit. Uthiam had become indignant and said of course not, Trong Impresario would never allow them to, not even the bachelors.

"You mean it's wrong?" Eleal had asked, very sweetly.

"Certainly not!" Uthiam had declared, one must not presume to judge what the gods decree. She had turned very pink and changed the subject.

Up front, Trong and Ambria had rounded the corner. They would stop at the temple door for everyone else to catch up, and then Ambria would order Eleal to wait outside. Well, Eleal saw no reason why she should walk all that way and then back again with this heavy pack. She was not going to wait outside and freeze to death—she had other plans!

Checking that Uthiam and Dolm were still talking and paying no attention to her, she ducked into a doorway and made herself as flat as paint.

She felt breathless and her heart was thumping faster than usual. She had eaten no breakfast, yet there was a tight feeling in her insides. The annual mammoth ride over Rilepass always affected her like this. The summit was very scary, with huge masses of ice and snow liable to break off and crash down. Sometimes even a surefooted mammoth could slip and fall miles down, into a gorge. It was very exciting.

Everyone sacrificed to Ois before crossing Rilepass. On the

other hand, the goddess was not likely to worry very much about one twelve-year-old girl, and even the goddess couldn't drop an avalanche on her without also dropping it on all the other people riding in the same howdah. Eleal was going to go and pray to Tion instead. She had some very special prayers to make.

She risked a glance around the corner, but Dolm and Uthiam were still in sight, and a few of the others also. She pulled back into her hiding place, grateful to be out of the wind, puffing on the tip of her nose to warm it.

Some big cities boasted several temples, but even towns like Narsh that had only one temple would also have at least one shrine to each member of the Pentatheon, either in person or to an aspect. Ois was an aspect of Eltiana, the Lady in her role as custodian of passes. Narsh also had a shrine to Kirb'l, the Joker, and the Joker was an aspect of Tion, the Youth.

It was very curious that the dour Narshians should have chosen that particular Tion persona to be his local representative. Narshians had less humor than any people she knew. Whereas most people never left the land they were born in, Eleal was very well traveled. The troupe visited seven of the Vales on their annual circuit. This year they had spent half a fortnight in Narsh. They had staged the comedy three times and the tragedy four times, without taking in enough to pay for the groceries, so Ambria said. Mill owners and ranchers, she grumbled—the meanest people in the world. They certainly had no sense of humor, so why should they honor the Joker so?

Piol Poet said that humor was the highest form of art, because it made people rejoice. He was joking when he said so.

Another glance showed Eleal that the coast was now clear. She left the alcove and hurried back the way she had come, her mismatched boots going *clip, clop, clip, clop.* Some of the locals were emerging now, as dawn approached, all bundled up in their smelly fleeces and furs. Miserable troglodytes! Trong Impresario had been stupendous as Trastos, especially when he was dying, but Narsh had just sat on its hands.

Piol had written speaking parts for Eleal into both plays this

year, small ones. She played a gods' messenger in the tragedy—
she sang offstage, of course—and a young herald in the comedy,
where she could use the staff to hide her limp. So she had played
Narsh for the first time in her life, being received with wild
indifference. Her curtain calls and standing ovations had totaled
zero, exactly. In Lappin her acting had won applause one night;
her singing in the masque always did. Tonight she would play
in Sussland. Sussvale was a warmer, nicer place and did not stink
of coal smoke. The Sussians would clap for her.

She turned a corner. Fortunately, there seemed to be a law
everywhere that holy places must bunch together. The shrines
in Narsh all adjoined the back wall of the Lady's temple, like
chicks huddled under a hen's wing. There was one for Visek
the Parent, one for Karzon the Man, one for Astina the Maiden,
and the Youth's was at the far end of the street. What all the
other buildings were, she did not know. Priests' houses, perhaps.

Clip, clop, clip, clop . . .

She would not have much time. She had her prayers all
planned. First she would ask the god to see her safely to his
Festival, of course—just in case Ois took offense. Then she
would pray for her friends, that the troupe might win the drama
contest, Piol Poet for the play itself, and others for their individual performances. It was a bad year when the Trong Troupe
did not collect at least three roses. Especially she must pray for
Uthiam, who had been practicing *Ironfaib's Polemic* for months
and could still bring tears to Eleal's eyes with it. Uthiam was
married now. Next year she would either be the wrong shape
or have a baby to look after.

Not far to go. *Clip, clop . . .* She was panting, sweating in her
llama fleece coat, despite the icy wind. She slowed down a little.
If she were too much out of breath, she would not be able to
sing for the god.

And the last prayer . . . It was not so very much to ask. The
Youth was god of art, and therefore the god most favored by
actors. He was also god of beauty, which was why ugly or deformed people could not enter his Festival. And he was god of
healing. Every year, at the closing ceremonies, he would grant

at least one miracle cure to some fortunate pilgrim. Was it so much to ask that Eleal Singer's leg be made whole, so that in future years she, too, could enter his festival and sing for his glory?

The shrine was marked by an archway, painted yellow. Heaving her pack higher on her aching shoulders, Eleal limped inside.

She had never considered that there might be someone else there.

The shrine was a smallish, squarish room, lit by the doorway and some high windows. It contained only a low altar for offerings, with two tall candlesticks—which she strongly suspected were not real gold—and a large frog, carved out of yellow stone. She had come here many times. She thought that the god of beauty ought to have arranged for a more esthetic shrine, but she supposed its simplicity was sort of artistic . . . if you liked sheds. The frog was one of the Youth's symbols, associated especially with Kirb'l, who was not only the Joker but also the golden moon, the one that did not behave like the other moons. So the frog itself was all right. It was the leer on its face and its skewed eyes that secretly annoyed her.

The man annoyed her much more. He was tiny and bent, and without his voluminous fur robe he would be tinier still. He was busily sweeping the floor with a scrawny broom, raising clouds of dust for the wind to stir.

Seeing her shadow, perhaps, he stopped his sweeping and turned around to peer at her. Inside his hood, all that showed was a face with a million wrinkles and eyes that did not look in the same direction. He must be even older than Piol Poet.

"Blessings upon you, missy!" he slobbered, leering at her cheerfully with toothless gums.

All she could think of to say was, "I came to pray to the god!" Which was obvious, of course.

"And make an offering, I hope? My breakfast, I hope?" He rolled one eye in the direction of her pack.

To her disgust, she saw a hem of dirty yellow protruding from under his furs. This rag doll must be the resident priest. She had never seen him here before, or even wondered who tended the shrine and removed each day's offerings. So she could not just ask him to leave. She did not want a nosy old priest eavesdropping on her prayers. And the only real offering she might give was a single copper coin, which she had not intended to give.

Still, she had come and had best get on with her business so she could run back to the temple door and wait for the others. Or perhaps she could just meet them out at the mammoth pens.

"I was planning to sing for the god."

The old man sighed, although his toothless grin did not fade. "Then I must enjoy your song. It will be a lighter breakfast than yesterday's, although probably more memorable. That's the best you can do?" he added wistfully.

She was nettled, as any true artist would be by such an attitude. He was making fun of her. "Music is my profession!"

He pursed his lips in wonder and turned to lean the broom in a corner. "May your offering be worthy of the god. What is your name, child?"

"Eleal Singer."

"*Who?*" The old man spun around with surprising agility. Both his eyes had opened very wide, although only one was looking at her. "You are *Eleal?* But where is the Daughter?"

She had been just about to wriggle out of her pack straps. This inexplicable reaction made her pause. "What daughter?"

The priest took a step toward her, anxiously rubbing his hands. His fingers were twisted, white with cold. "The Daughter of Irepit, of course! Don't you know about the prophecy? Don't you realize that you are in terrible danger? There is a reaper in town! You are so much younger than I expected!" Still babbling, he followed Eleal as she backed away. His wrinkles writhed in anguish. "Surely death will seek you out to break the chain! Who is looking after you, child? Your father? Parents?"

She had no parents, but she was not about to explain that to this crazy old man with his ravings of reapers and danger and chains and daughters of Irepit, whoever she might be. He was more than a few seats short of a full house. Someone had shuffled his script.

"Thank you for the warning," she said. Her retreat had brought her to the door. "I'll go and look after that right away!" She turned and ran, pack and all. *Clipclopclipclopclip . . .*

⟨⟨⟨ 6 ⟩⟩⟩

THE BIG CAR PURRED IN THROUGH THE GATES OF FALLOW. Leatherdale peered out sourly at the ivy-shrouded Gothic buildings, the shady elms, the central lawn basking in the sunshine. He'd played billiards on worse. The Gothic was of the Railway Nabob variety, but pleasantly aged now—best part of a century, at a guess. Pretty soon it would class as old, even by English standards. He wondered what it cost a man to send his son to a place like this, even as a day boy. If you had to ask, you couldn't afford it.

Had Elsie given him a son, the boy would have followed his father's footsteps through Parish Boys' School in Greyfriars. He'd have learned the Three R's and been gone at fourteen, most likely. Not for him the inside track of a public school— classical education, university entrance, front of the queue when the posh jobs were handed out. This was where the bosses came from, the officers, the cabinet ministers, the men who ran the Empire. The Old Boys' Network began here, at the snob factory.

The car glided to a stop in front of an imposing doorway, flanked by steps. There was no drawbridge or portcullis, but the architecture implied that there should be. The morning was magically peaceful, with doves cooing somewhere and a few faint clicks and puffings from the engine.

"Tudor House, sir," said the chauffeur, opening the door. He must know, having driven the Young Master here often enough.

Leatherdale stepped down. "Shan't be more than twenty minutes, I expect, but you've got time to go find a cuppa round the back if you want."

A respectful smile thawed the man's professional inscrutability. "Why, I'd trust 'em with my life, sir! But I'll stay here."

Eight boys had condensed out of the summer morning to examine the car. They ranged in height from not much over four feet to not much less than six. They wore toppers and tails and not one hand was in a pocket. They were standing back, carefully not crowding close enough to the machine to provoke its guardian, murmuring technical details without raising their voices: "Guff! She'll do more'n that . . . " "Bags more'n thirty horsepower!"

These unfortunates must be boarders with no homes to go to, residing at Fallow over the summer holidays. Lordie, what would it cost even to clothe a boy here? On a Sunday morning, Leatherdale would have expected them to be marched off to church parade. Then he realized that the tallest boy was Oriental and three of the others various shades of brown. Perhaps none of them were Christians. Rather startled by that possibility, he set off up the steps.

"Inspector Leatherdale?" The speaker was standing in the doorway, a bearded, paunchy man with a marked resemblance to the late King Edward.

Who else would it be, coming to ruin a perfect summer Sunday?

"Mr. Jones?"

Jones was staring past his visitor at the thousand-guinea motor. Perhaps his query had not been totally inane. Policemen did not normally travel in quite such style.

★   ★   ★

The hallway was dim and baronial, so full of silence that it seemed to echo with it, smelling of polish and chalk, exercise books and blotting paper. Marble stairs flanked by iron railings led up to mysterious heights. The room to which the visitor was led was equally institutional, furnished with aging armchairs and an ingrained reek of pipe smoke. Despite the windows open at the top, the air was stuffy and dead. Stern portraits of elderly gentlemen peered down disapprovingly between bookshelves, and the linoleum by the door was dangerously worn.

"Masters' common room," Jones explained quite needlessly. "May I offer you some tea, Inspector?"

Leatherdale declined the tea and accepted a chair with his back to the windows. It was more comfortable than it looked, and much too comfortable for a man who had been granted only two hours' sleep.

Jones took a chair opposite, first removing a copy of the *Times*, which he brandished to demonstrate indignation. "Seen this morning's news? The Prussian rogues have invaded Luxembourg! And declared war on Russia. Belgium, Holland, Sweden—all mobilizing. Bounders!"

"Bad business," Leatherdale agreed.

"The Kaiser's a maniac! Doesn't he realize that we mean what we say? England's made it perfectly plain, hasn't it, for years, that if Luxembourg or Belgium is invaded, then we'll have to fight? Don't the blighters understand that our word is our bond? That they're going to bring the British Empire in against them?" He slapped the paper down angrily. "May as well get it over with, I suppose. The Hun has made it pretty clear that he plans to smash France and Russia first and then deal with us later."

Leatherdale made sounds of assent. Jones's resemblance to the late king was astonishing, except that he wore pince-nez, which flashed in the light from the window. From lifetime habit Leatherdale quantified his estimates—middle fifties, five-foot-eight or -nine, weight close to fourteen stone, well dressed, hair brown turning gray at the temples, full beard likewise.

"I mean we have no choice, have we?" Jones persisted. "When a chap already has the world's biggest army and keeps adding to it, and then his neighbors justifiably start to get alarmed and add a few guns of their own and the Germans scream that they're being encircled . . ." Having apparently lost the thread of his sentence, he scowled into silence and leaned back to regard his visitor. "Madmen!" he added. "Huns!"

His accent was pure Oxbridge, a long way from the mining valleys of his ancestors, the sort of drawl that always carried hints of arrogance, whether intentional or not. He wore a brown suit of good Harris tweed and a pair of stout brogues—and also an entirely inappropriate old boy tie. Leatherdale decided he resented that tie. Whatever school or university or regiment it represented, it was around that shiny white collar at the moment only to impress him.

"I shan't keep you from your ramble any longer than I have to, Mr. Jones." He pulled out his notebook. "I need some background information. To be specific, I need to see the personal files on two of your boys. Technically old boys, now, I believe."

"I'm frightfully sorry, Inspector, but that will not be possible." Jones blinked solemnly. Was he enjoying himself baiting the rustic policeman? Or was he merely the chicken left in charge of the farm, scared to do anything at all while the watchdogs took their holidays at the seaside?

"This is not a matter of cribbing apples, Mr. Jones." Did he think Leatherdale had nothing better to do on summer Sundays?

The master tapped his beard with the tips of his steepled fingers. "I do not doubt that the matter is important. I should be happy to assist you in any way I can, but the filing cabinets are locked and I have no keys."

Without question, his first priority would be to protect the school's reputation. He could have been picked out as a schoolmaster a furlong off. He had the diffident, mannered speech, the air of tight control, and even the curious blunting of masculinity that sometimes showed in men who must constantly guard their tongues. Clergymen had it also. He was a book whose pages were becoming yellow and dog-eared, the binding threadbare and gilt lettering worn. It would open to predictable pages.

Now he reached for the arms of his chair, as if to pull himself out of it and end the interview. "I do wish you had mentioned documents when you telephoned, Inspector. I could have saved you the journey. You only said you wanted information, and you will recall that I did explain that the Head will not be back until Thursday at the earliest, and any statements really ought to come from him. I am just *in loco magistri,* you might say, not authorized to comment at all." The pince-nez glinted.

He was not a material witness, who must be played like a ten-pound salmon on a five-pound line. Far from it—he was just a watchdog that could be brought to heel. Yet the man could help, if he would. Juries hated to convict without being shown a motive. Jones could clarify the motive in this case. Which one was the pouncer—the killer or the victim? Or both?

Leatherdale decided to try a couple more drops of honey before applying vinegar. "Now, if I may have your full name, sir?"

"David Jones. French master."

How many hundreds of boys had been processed into speaking French with that accent? "You have been here how long?"

"Ten—no, eleven years now. Before that—"

"Not necessary, sir. I just wanted to know how well you are acquainted with the boys in question."

The fancy spectacles shone white and inscrutable. "I am not sure that I might not be in breach of confidence were I to discuss any of our pupils without the Head's authorization or perhaps the advice of a solicitor, Inspector."

Yes, he was enjoying himself.

"The keys to the filing cabinets? Who has them?"

"The Head, of course. Dr. Gibbs."

"And the duplicate set? There must be a duplicate set?"

"I don't know. I certainly don't know where they are, if they exist."

"Mr. Jones, the matter cannot wait until Thursday. How may I get in touch with the Headmaster?"

A gold tooth flashed as Jones smiled. "I don't think you can, Inspector. He was on his way to Crete to visit Evans's dig. He has four senior boys with him, and two more are on their way to join him—or they were. Dr. Gibbs and his companions got as far as Greece. With the present turmoil, I suspect their journey home may take longer than expected."

Leatherdale favored him for a moment with a blandly thoughtful expression. Then he said, "Technically the board of governors would have overall authority over the premises?"

Jones flinched. "I suppose they must, but the board have always—"

"In a sense, sir, you and I work for the same man. General Bodgley is not only chairman of your board, but also my chief constable. I should perhaps have brought a note from him, but I assumed you would cooperate without it."

"Cooperate? I assure you—"

"Actually that is his car and chauffeur outside. Perhaps if we can reach him by telephone . . ."

The watchdog was in full retreat already. "Inspector, er, Leatherdale, I assure you that I am trying my best! I do not know where the keys to the cabinets are kept. I do not know exactly where the Head is. I can show you his telegram, but it was dispatched from some railway station in Austria and will not help you. The bursar is touring in Switzerland. If General Bodgley does not have a duplicate set of keys, and I would not expect him to, then I cannot imagine who else does." Jones clawed at his beard with his left hand.

"Dr. Gibbs does not employ a secretary?"

"Paddling at Blackpool, I believe. This is August Bank Holiday weekend, Inspector! England is closed. However, if any Fallow boy is in trouble, then of course I am more than ready to assist your inquiries in any way I can."

Better. Leatherdale nodded. "I just need information about a couple of them, that's all."

"Their names?"

"Edward George Exeter?"

Jones stiffened. "Exeter? Oh, Lord! You don't mean they got caught up in the Balkan imbroglio, too?"

"Nothing to do with the Balkans that I know of, sir."

"But Exeter and Smedley were on their way to join Dr. Gibbs. The two I mentioned."

"They were forced to cancel. They returned home from Paris."

"Well that's a relief! A great relief! I was quite concerned about them and I—" Jones's smile vanished as fast as it had come. "You mean there's been an accident?"

"No, sir."

This time the shock was obvious. "Exeter is in *trouble?*"

"What can you tell me about him, sir?"

The teacher drew a deep breath. "Exeter was house prefect in his final year! An excellent boy in every way. He was here in Tudor! I was his housemaster, Inspector, so I know him well. Exeter would be almost the last boy I would expect to fall afoul of the law! That is the case, isn't it? You're telling me that he is being investigated by the British police?"

"I am afraid that is the case."

Looking stunned, Jones pulled a linen handkerchief from his pocket and dabbed his forehead. His distress and astonishment seemed quite genuine. "I mean, he has definitely not just met with an accident or something?"

"Too early to say, sir. No charges have been laid as yet, but at the moment the situation does look grave."

"God bless my soul!" Jones sprawled back in his chair. "Exeter? I nominated him for my house prefect, Inspector, and he performed every bit as well as I expected. I cannot give you a higher character reference than that—cannot give any boy a higher recommendation. You did not say that . . . I mean, I have notes of my own on boys in Tudor. I shall gladly make them available." Again he moved as if to rise, although now it was an obvious effort.

"Later, sir, I shall appreciate seeing them. Meanwhile, tell me what you know of him. His character, his background. His family, particularly."

Jones sank back again, fumbling with his handkerchief. He paused for a moment to gather thoughts, then spoke without looking up. "Leadership, Inspector. Leadership is our product.

They come here as children. They leave as young men. Rather innocent young men by the world's standards, I suppose, but well molded to take their place in the service of the Empire. Many a lad has walked out of here and in three or four years been running a chunk of country somewhere half the size of England—dictator, judge, soldier, engineer, tax collector, policeman, all rolled into one. Not for power, not for money, but purely out of a sense of duty!"

Leatherdale waited.

Jones's glasses glittered. "Latin and Greek and all that—none of it really matters. It isn't what you know that matters in this world, it's what you are! *Esse non sapere*—school motto. We teach them honor, honesty, and fair play. They take it from there. Not all of them, of course, not by a long shot. But the best ones are as good as you'll find anywhere. I'd have classed Exeter with the best." He looked across defiantly at the policeman.

Mrs. Bodgley had said very much the same.

"Some specifics, if you please."

Jones stuffed the handkerchief back in his trouser pocket. "Edward Exeter? Born in British East Africa—in '96, I suppose. Came here when he was about twelve. Left officially a week ago. Good pupil, credit to the school. Turned down a chance to play for the county this summer."

He paused then. Still Leatherdale waited, sensing better game on its way.

"Exeter's had more than his share of tragedy already. I'm sure you recall the Nyagatha affair?"

"Vaguely."

"Exeter's father was the district officer. He and his wife were among the dead. They were due to go on leave within days."

"The general mentioned something about it. He was, er, rather vague." That was an understatement of elephantine proportions.

Jones pulled a face. "You'd best look up the official report if you're interested. The whole thing was just one of those senseless episodes of bloodshed that seem to be the inevitable price of progress. Less than ten years ago that whole area was just uncharted bush, you know. Barbarism is still very close below the surface. The trouble did not even originate in Exeter's district. Some disaffected warriors of a neighboring tribe—Meru, or some name like that—outlaws, hungry, raiding for food . . . massacre, atrocities, followed by retribution. So history rolls along, leaving a few more gravestones by the roadway to be mourned for a generation." Mr. Jones sighed at the folly of mankind.

"How old would Exeter have been, then, sir?"

"Sixteen."

"He was here, in Fallow? How did he take it?"

"Oh, really! How do you think? He was shattered, of course. The news came in on a weekend and no one in Whitehall bothered to notify him. The first he knew was when the newspapers arrived on Monday morning. He hadn't seen his parents in four years, and was looking forward to a reunion that summer."

"No brothers or sisters?"

Jones sighed again. "None. He made a wonderful recovery. Tremendous pluck. His marks hardly dipped. And then, just as he seemed to be over the worst of it, the board of inquiry report came out and opened all the wounds again."

"Spell the name of that place, sir, if you please. And the exact date, or as close as you can recall?" Leatherdale knew he was getting full cooperation now. He felt no satisfaction from so easy a victory. "How did it open the wounds, sir?"

"Well, it opened wounds for Exeter." Jones removed his pince-nez and wiped them on his tie. He dabbed one eye surreptitiously with a knuckle. "His father was cleared of any blame in the atrocity itself. As I said, the perpetrators were just a band of malcontents wandering off the reserve. But Exeter was severely criticized for not maintaining a garrison of trained native troops handy to defend the post. Young Exeter will tell you— and I can almost sympathize with his views—that his father was being condemned for being too good at his job. If he'd been a worse governor and ruled by terror as some of them do, then he would have had protection to hand! Another of the ironies of history, mm? But Exeter has already passed through the Valley of Shadows, young as he is."

"And his legal guardian?"

Jones replaced his glasses and peered incredulously. "Why do you need to ask? Can't he speak for himself? Is he missing?"

"No, sir." Leatherdale flipped back a couple of pages. " 'Concussion, compound fracture of the right leg, extensive minor contusions.' He was just starting to come around when I left."

"Good God!" Jones paused, as if shocked by his own profanity, then added, "His guardian is his uncle, the Reverend Roland Exeter, director of the Lighthouse Missionary Society."

He spoke as if everyone knew the Reverend Dr. Exeter, and admittedly Leatherdale had heard of him. He did not reveal that he had already spoken with the holy gentleman on the telephone early that morning, nor that it had taken the Reverend Exeter's housekeeper considerable time to persuade him even to come to the phone. When he had come, he had explained at length that his religious beliefs forbade him to travel on Sundays—no, not even to visit an injured nephew involved in a murder case.

"Exeter also corresponded with a chap in the Colonial Office," Jones said, frowning. "I have his name and address somewhere, I'm sure. A Mr. Oldcastle, as I recall. In such cases, His Majesty's Government takes an interest, of course, and quite rightly so."

"No other relatives?"

"Only a cousin, so far as I know."

Leatherdale's antennae quivered, but he said, "Family friends?"

"None I have ever heard mentioned."

"Does the name 'Jumbo' mean anything to you, Mr. Jones?"

"Common nickname, that's all. We have a Jumbo Little in Fourth Form."

"No. Tell me about the cousin."

"Miss Alice Prescott. I have her address also, I believe."

"They are close?"

Jones forced a thin smile of acknowledgment. "Exeter went to her twenty-first a couple of months ago. Until she reached her majority, they were both wards of their reverend uncle. I have not met the lady for several years, but I believe the young man is seriously smitten. I do not know how she feels about him. He is three years her junior and they are first cousins."

"I shall see she is informed, sir."

"Thank you. I'm sure Exeter will be grateful, and if she is anything like he thinks she is, she will respond."

A good housemaster was much more than a jailer. Leatherdale raised his estimation of David Jones. In the case of at least one of his charges, he had obviously won trust and friendship.

"Tell me of the boy himself, sir."

"Solid!" Jones thought for a moment. "Fair athlete, but not exceptional, except at cricket. There he was one of the best fast bowlers we've had for some time. A bit of a loner, especially since the tragedy, but popular despite that. He made an excellent prefect. Born leader—kept the youngsters in line and never raised his voice. They worshiped him. Damnably weak in maths—can't seem to see the point of 'em. A real flair for languages. Walked off with the medals in Greek and German and came close in Latin, too. More competition in French," he added vaguely.

This sort of stuff would be deadly in court.

"So he has left school. What are his ambitions, can you say?"

Jones hesitated. "If I know Exeter, then he's panting to get into uniform like all the others. Teach the Hun a lesson, by Jingo!"

"And if there's no mobilization?"

"He was going up to Cambridge. Looks like he has his choice of two or three colleges—there is money in the family for that sort of thing."

"To follow in his father's footsteps? Colonial Office?"

Pause. "Oh, no. Modern languages."

Leatherdale made a note. The witness was holding something back. Probably young Exeter resented the organization that had condemned his father for being too good at his job. His ambitions could hardly be relevant to the murder, though.

Motive? Leatherdale wanted the motive. What turned a model public schoolboy into a savage killer?

"No family on his mother's side?"

"Exeter himself knows of none. She was a New Zealander."

"Of European stock?"

Jones laughed contemptuously. "You're looking for a touch of the tar brush, Inspector? I admit he has black hair, and he takes a good tan, but those eyes! Blue as they come. Looks Cornish, I'd say."

Nettled in spite of himself, Leatherdale said, "I didn't see his eyes, sir. They were closed." He shrugged and took up his quest again. "What of his private life? Any wild oats in his background?"

The French master had aged several years since he sat down. The condescension had long since faded from his manner, but that remark brought an angry flush to his cheek. "I have already given you my appraisal of Exeter. He is a young English gentleman."

"A direct answer, if you please, Mr. Jones."

Jones snorted. "Boys in public school have no private life. What happens in the holidays is beyond my ken, but I should doubt it very much, in his case. Schools such as Fallow are a great deal more celibate than any monastery the church ever knew. I told you—I think Master Exeter has his heart set on his cousin. I simply cannot imagine his being promiscuous."

Reluctantly, Leatherdale noted the reply. "Forgive this next question, but it must be asked. How about, 'The love that dares not breathe its name'?"

"No! Any hint of that in Fallow is cause for immediate sacking—boys or masters!" Jones glared for a moment, then sighed. "Of course it is always a potential problem in any all-male community. Some otherwise exemplary schools . . . you know, I'm sure. We are not naive. We watch for it. We haven't had a case in several years. Cold baths and constant vigilance, Inspector!"

"Not Exeter?"

"Absolutely not."

He seemed to be sincere. He might not be quite as shrewd a judge of his charges as he believed. A storm of passion of one sort or another was the only credible motive in the case. Leatherdale toyed with his pen for a moment, wondering if there was anything more he need ask about Exeter. The housemaster's enthusiasm for the boy was worrisome. However misplaced, it would go down well with a jury.

When he looked up, Jones seemed to brace himself in his chair. "And the other boy you are interested in, Inspector? Smedley, I suppose?"

"Timothy Fitzjohn Bodgley."

"What?" Jones could not have displayed greater shock had he been informed that he had been chosen to tutor the Prince of Wales in Hebrew. "Explain!"

"At the moment the details are confidential, Mr. Jones. It missed the Sunday papers, but some of it will most certainly be in tomorrow's."

The master moaned. "For God's sake tell me! This is awful!"

"First your comments on young Bodgley, if you please. Was he also in your house?"

"Yes he was. He and Exeter were close chums as juniors and the friendship lasted—they don't always, of course. It's less on Exeter's side than Bodgley's, I'd say. Exeter is more, er, self-sufficient." Jones began polishing his glasses again, gazing blankly meanwhile, as if he could not see without them. "Bodgley's a delicate boy. He is frequently troubled by asthma. This has kept him back in games . . . He was known as Bagpipe."

"His father is an Old Etonian." Leatherdale did not mention that he had researched his chief constable in that worthy gentleman's own copy of *Who's Who*.

Jones smiled faintly at nothing. Then he replaced his spectacles and seemed to come back to life. "You are wondering why he did not send his own son there? Because of the asthma. Fallow is closer to home than Eton. Or are you wondering why our chairman is not an Old Fallovian? That's a matter of politics—money and influence, Inspector. And if you are wonder-

ing whether young Bodgley was of better family than most of
our boys, the answer to that is yes. The blood runs blue in the
Bodgley veins. His future in the Empire, if any, will be at the
level of British resident, far above the district officerships to
which Exeter might aspire. Foreign Office and *corps diplomatique*
would be more his field. He's a bit spoiled, pampered and over-
sheltered, and inclined to feel sorry for himself. I might just be
persuaded that he had been led into wrongdoing by an older,
stronger character—which I would not believe of Exeter—but
basically he's a fine young man, and I am convinced that whatever you suspect these two of, your information is incorrect."

He tried to smile, but the result was grotesque. "There! I
have been completely frank, have I not? Now will you inform
me of the trouble they appear to be in? Less than a week ago I
saw my young friends walk out into a world that looked ready
to throw itself at their feet. I asked Exeter to sacrifice a glass of
retsina to Poseidon in my name. Now you tell me he is back in
this country and under suspicion of wrongdoing."

"I can tell you a little." Leatherdale did not close his notebook. "The preliminaries you already know. When Smedley's
parents called him back from Paris, Exeter returned also. He
apparently found himself with nowhere to go, but he had a
standing invitation to visit Greyfriars Grange. . . . Where did he
normally spend his holidays, when his parents were alive?"

"Here," Jones said quietly. "He has lived at Fallow since he
was twelve, except for a few odd breaks, such as OTC camp or
school outings or visiting his friends. Many of our boys are children of parents living overseas. Other parents will often take
pity on their sons' chums in such case—invite them to stay over
Christmas, for example."

"Never with his uncle?"

"Rarely. I gathered that the experience was always mutually
unpleasant."

Leatherdale made a note. "And as an old boy, he could not
just return to Fallow?"

Jones shook his head sadly. "Inspector! He had just *left school!*
Don't you remember how huge that milestone loomed in your

own life? Even if the alternative was his friend's charity . . . The raven had been released from the ark!"

Interesting point, Leatherdale thought. The youth must have been in an agitated state of mind. His uncle had been surprised to learn he was back in England.

"Exeter telegraphed to the Bodgleys from Paris and was accepted. He arrived yesterday." Watching carefully, he continued. "I can outline the statement released to the newspapers. General Bodgley's household at Greyfriars Grange was awakened shortly after midnight this morning by the sound of an altercation in the kitchen quarters. Investigation revealed Mr. Edward George Exeter injured and unconscious, and the mortal remains of Mr. Timothy Fitzjohn Bodgley. Foul play is suspected."

"Good God!" All the color drained from Jones's face, leaving a parchment marred by brown age spots. He licked his lips and even his tongue seemed pale. "Dead! How?"

"The nature of his injuries is not being released, sir."

"Inspector! I have known these boys for years. They are my friends and my life's work and until last week they were my wards!"

Leatherdale decided to trust him. It might prove to be an indiscretion, but he was in charge of the investigation. He had the right to make his own mistakes. "In strict confidence, then, sir? I do not wish the press to get its hands on this."

Jones licked his lips. "I may tell Dr. Gibbs when he returns?"

"That would be in order. Exeter fell or was thrown down the cellar steps. He sustained the injuries I mentioned. Bodgley had been stabbed to death with a carving knife."

Jones's mouth moved for a while before he croaked, "Just the two of them there?"

"That is implied in the official statement. I cannot say any more, sir."

"But why in Heaven? . . ."

"Motive? A good question. Why should two young men raid a kitchen at that time of night? Since the cellar is used to store the general's wine, we might speculate that they were after more than a cup of tea."

"I suppose some such prank is not impossible," Jones admitted hoarsely.

"If it was a prank, it rapidly became something else." Leatherdale waited hopefully, but if Jones guessed what he wanted to hear, he did not oblige. Pity. Leatherdale was curious to know which one of the two had started the hanky-panky and which had resisted. In spite of his considerable advantage in height and weight, Exeter's only possible defense was self-defense. It would not get him off or even reduce the charge to manslaughter, but it might wring a recommendation of mercy out of a sympathetic jury.

He closed his notebook. He had an open-and-shut case. He had failed to uncover a motive, but the Crown was not obliged to establish motive. At the next assizes, learned counsel would explain to the jury how Exeter had stabbed his friend and then, in a panicky attempt to flee from the scene of the crime, had fallen down the cellar steps.

The defense would drag in the vague reports of a woman screaming—they would not be able to explain her disappearance through doors bolted on the inside. They were welcome to propose that Bodgley had thrown his guest into the cellar and subsequently thrust a steel carving knife in his own back so hard that he had nailed himself to a teak draining board.

The jury would deliberate and then the judge would don the black cap to order Edward George Exeter hanged by the neck.

Suddenly Leatherdale was seized by a frightful desire to yawn. It was time to go. He could do no more good at Fallow, if indeed he had done any good at all. He should be grateful for a rare opportunity—the thrill of a murder investigation without the tedious follow-up, for it would all be taken out of his hands by tomorrow at the latest. He had everything he needed to brief Scotland Yard when the Old Man came to his senses. Even if the Old Man didn't, Robinson should be back by then, if he could find his way through Bank Holiday traffic.

A telephone rang somewhere in the distance.

"That is probably the press already," he said wearily. "I advise you not to say anything at all." He levered himself out of the chair. "If you will look out for those notes you mentioned, sir?"

Jones stayed where he was, staring up at his visitor as if felled by shock. When he spoke, though, it was obvious that he had been thinking hard. "The general's son was murdered in his own house and yet he, as chief constable, is titular head of the investigation? Is he not placed in an impossible situation, Inspector?"

"Awkward, sir. I expect he will call in Scotland Yard in due course."

When he came to his senses, he would—or when he was allowed to, for Leatherdale had a strong suspicion that the formidable Mrs. Bodgley was meddling in police business.

"The Home Secretary may have something to say when he hears of it, I shouldn't wonder," Jones said drily. His eyes were invisible behind white reflections again. The instant Leatherdale left the building, David Jones would be on the phone to some senior members of the board of governors.

"Not up to me to question orders, sir."

The two men stared at each other.

"I don't envy you, Inspector," the schoolmaster said softly.

Leatherdale sensed the offer of the Old Boys' Network. "We all do our duty as best we can, sir."

Jones scratched his beard. "Normally, of course, the Home Secretary's sacred weekend would never be disturbed by anything as petty as willful homicide. But I'm afraid times are not normal. The Cabinet is in almost continuous session because of the crisis. On a weekend? Incredible! On August Bank Holiday weekend in particular? Epochal! It may take a little time for Whitehall to catch up on routine matters, you realize?"

Leatherdale had not even thought of that. What the damned Frogs and Huns and Wops got up to on the Continent was their business, and he hoped His Majesty's Government would keep the country out of it. Let them all kill one another off, as far as he was concerned. But he realized that this snotty French master had made a good point. If Bodgley continued to behave like an idiot, then London might not crack the whip over him as fast as it normally would.

"I expect you're right, sir. Now—"

"If you had evidence of an intruder, you would not have come here today!"

"I really am not at liberty to comment further, sir."

Why was the schoolmaster smirking?

"Are you familiar with our burglary, Inspector?"

"*Your* burglary, Mr. Jones?"

"At Whitsun there was a burglary—here, in Tudor House. Any criminal who attempts a break-in where there are a hundred sets of young lungs available to sound the alarm is excessively rash, wouldn't you say, Inspector? Besides, what could there be worth stealing beyond the odd illicit packet of Gold Flake?"

Behind the spectacles, Jones's eyes were gleaming bright.

Leatherdale felt a hint of uneasiness. "I fail to see how this is relevant, sir." A break-in at Fallow would not have been reported to Greyfriars—wrong county.

Jones showed his teeth in a snarl of frustration. "Perhaps not. Yet the coincidence . . . I believe—" His smile vanished as if a new idea had struck him. He sprang to his feet with surprising agility. "Inspector, where is Exeter now?" he demanded shrilly.

"Albert Memorial Hospital in Greyfriars."

"Under guard, Inspector? You said no charges had been laid, but you do have someone there to guard him, don't you?"

7

STILL THINKING *CRAZY OLD MAN!* ELEAL SINGER LIMPED OUT through the city gate. How could she possibly be in danger? Why should death seek her out?

Here in the open, the wind blew like an avalanche. She pulled her hat down firmly and wished she did not keep thinking about avalanches. The low sun shone on a scene of hubbub and bustle. Traders were erecting stalls; ranchers were arriving with herds of llamas, brought down from Narshslope for sale. In the distance stood the ominous, ice-cloaked peaks of Narshwall. From them the land descended in bare hills and grassy ridges to the plain of Narshflat. Narshwater was the color of dirty milk, its banks still bearing grubby remnants of winter ice floes among the reeds.

A wide space of muddy grass separated the river from the city. Here the mammoths were kept during the summer and fall, when the pass was open. Here the farmers and herders came to trade. Most cities would hold festivals and games on a common like this, although Eleal doubted that the dour folk of Narsh were capable of appreciating either, any more than they appreciated theater.

Soon she was clear of the market and could see the mammoths, a dozen great gray-brown mountains with tusks. They would step over the puny rail fence around them with no trouble, so it must be intended more to keep people out than mammoths in. Mammoths were bigger and stronger than anything, and their little eyes gleamed with intelligence. As she hurried through slower-moving knots of people, one of the bulls curled up his trunk and trumpeted. She decided to take that as a welcome.

But the crowds! She had never seen so many people here before, milling around the rickety flight of steps where the travelers paid their fares and mounted. She scanned the group urgently. If everyone she could see was hoping to leave today, then there would simply not be room! A dozen mammoths and ten or twelve passengers per howdah meant . . . meant . . . well, not enough seats to empty the meadow, certainly. Where was the troupe? Loading had not yet begun, so they could not have left yet, but where were they?

Not everyone was there because of the mammoths, though. A troop of men drilled with pikes, another squad practiced archery. She also noticed a camp of three or four tents and a small herd of dragons. They were too far off for her to be sure, but that was probably T'lin Dragontrader's outfit. T'lin was her special friend. He trekked around the Vales with his herd, so she often ran into him, but this year she had not seen him since winter, in Jurgland. It was a pity she would not have time to speak with him before the mammoths left, because she had information for him.

The first mammoth was plodding over to the steps to load. The old mahout astride its neck looked like a doll, he was so high. There was still no sign of the rest of the troupe. Eleal began to feel seriously worried. Had they waited for her at the temple? Had they sent someone back to the hostel to look for her?

The seven hundredth Festival of Tion was attracting a far larger attendance than usual. All about her, people were making weepy farewells, issuing instructions and warnings. A surprising number were priests and monks, their colored gowns peeking out from under drab llama fleece robes added for warmth. Some were merchants, accompanied by bearers to carry their wares and even by armed guards. Others were athletes, large young men heading for the festival, receiving last-minute instructions from the fathers or uncles or friends who had trained them. She noted the usual cripples and invalids and blind people, going to seek a miracle. The remainder, men and women, could be assumed to be just pilgrims.

She squirmed through the crowd, hampered by her pack and her limp.

"Eleal!"

She spun around with a gasp of relief. It was Uthiam Piper—all alone, and without her pack. Uthiam was Ambria's daughter. She was eighteen, and the most *beautiful* actor: her looks, her voice, her grace. At the moment she looked cold as ice in her woolen robe, but she was still beautiful—and so welcome!

"You little chump! Where did you get to?"

"Oh . . ." Eleal said airily. "I went to pray to Kirb'l." Then she realized that she hadn't. "Where is everyone? What's keeping them? So many people—"

"And more to come! The temple is packed."

"But the festival starts on Thighday!" And this was Ankleday! "If we don't—"

"The portents were bad!"

"Huh?"

Uthiam's face was grave. She bent to whisper, for the crowd had closed in around them. "Trong Impresario offered a white cockerel as usual. When the priests went to read its entrails, they discovered that it had no liver."

That was ridiculous! How could a cockerel not have a liver? What a terrible omen! Eleal's vision of a journey over Rilepass today suddenly dimmed. The goddess must be very displeased about something.

"So what is happening?"

"We have to wait until the priests have dealt with all the others. We shall have to offer a greater sacrifice."

The look on Uthiam's face gave Eleal cold shivers. "You don't mean . . ."

"Oh, no! At least, I don't think so." She obviously wasn't sure, though. "The priests suggested a dragon foal."

Eleal gasped. "Ambria will have a foaming fit!" A dragon foal would cost more money than the troupe would take in in weeks. This was going to be a very expensive day. Hard times for the troupe meant thin eating.

Uthiam smiled. "But they'll probably settle for an alpaca."

Old Ambria was still going to have a fit. Even an alpaca would cost several nights' take, especially the take in tightfisted Narsh, but the big woman would bridle her tongue for fear of upsetting the goddess further.

"We may not get away today," Uthiam said, straightening. "I'd better go back to the temple." Obviously the prospect did not please her.

"Me too?"

"No need for you to come. Wait here, just in case. I think I saw T'lin Dragontrader, didn't I?"

"Who?" Eleal demanded. Her friendship with T'lin was supposed to be a secret. Uthiam's amused expression indicated that she knew that and it wasn't. But Eleal would have time to visit with T'lin. She could wander around . . . Then she recalled the crazy priest's warning that she was in danger.

"Uthiam, isn't Irepit goddess of something? What's a Daughter of Irepit?"

Uthiam looked understandably surprised. "They're a sect of nuns—down in Nosokvale, I think. They—"

"Rinoovale," said a croaky voice, "not Nosokvale."

Eleal spun around angrily. "Eavesdropping is a sin!"

Uthiam's hand thumped the side of her head so hard she staggered. That was unfair—she had only been repeating what Ambria had told her lots of times.

The woman who had spoken was a nun, her flowing woolen garb conspicuous amid the leather-draped multitude. Whatever height she might once have had was now lost in a stoop and a hump, so she stood barely taller than Eleal. Her face was dominated by a long thin nose that seemed to be the only part of it not crumpled in wrinkles—it was red, with a shiny drop at the end of it, while her cheeks were an antique yellow, although the cold had added a purplish tint to them. Her hair and neck were hidden by a wimple, which, like her habit, had once been blue, although now both were threadbare and almost colorless.

She was blinking at Eleal with eyes that likewise seemed faded to a colorless, blurry gray; they were watering copiously in the icy wind.

"Forgive her, holy lady," Uthiam said. "She is a wayward brat." She shook Eleal's shoulder. "Apologize!"

"The follies of youth are easily forgiven!" the woman muttered. Her pale moist eyes were still fixed intently on Eleal, whose ears were ringing. "In the Blue Scriptures, the *Book of Alyath,* it is written, 'Time is the gods' wages.' Is that why the young, whose life is most enjoyable, should be so eager to see it pass, while the old, who have lost most of their capacity for joy, savor every moment?" She blinked more, apparently waiting for an answer.

A naked sword hung at her side, its point almost touching the ground.

"M-mother?" Eleal said, staring at that incongruous weapon.

"Sister," said the nun. "Sister Ahn." Her lips were almost as blue as her eyes, yet she seemed unaware of the cold. She turned her watery gaze on Uthiam. "Is it not wonderful how many are heeding the prophecies?"

"Prophecies, Sister?" Uthiam spoke loudly also.

The sword was a real weapon, a really-truly shiny blade, and it bore no speck of rust. Yet now Eleal noticed the woman's right hand resting on a staff. It also was blue, and the fingers were so twisted that they probably could not grasp a hilt firmly enough to draw. Just looking at this shivering crone made her feel cold.

Blue was the color of Astina, the Maiden, who was goddess of lots of things: justice and soldiers and athletes, among others. That might explain the sword, but why should Astina be goddess of soldiers, when the Man was god of war? And why athletes? They should be the concern of the Youth—who ever heard of a female athlete? The universe ought to be more logical, and an armed geriatric nun was carrying things altogether too far.

"The seven hundredth festival!" Sister Ahn suddenly smiled, revealing a few yellow pegs of teeth. "Great wonders are foretold. Praise to the god. But should we not approach the young man selling tickets?"

However well-intentioned, the old woman's smile was quite the most gruesome Eleal could ever recall seeing. Her accent was unfamiliar, but perhaps that was because her speech was smeared by lack of teeth.

Uthiam was studying the nun with an oddly wary expression. "We are waiting on friends to join us, Sister. May the Lady bless your journey."

"Ah." The old woman sighed. "Ask rather that the Maiden grant you safe return. Many who see the wonders will not carry word of them home." Muttering to herself, she tottered away, leaning on her staff, the point of her sword almost trailing on the grass. Understandably, the crowd eased open to let her through.

"Don't wander too far," Uthiam said. "And stay out of trouble for once." She turned and pushed off through the mob.

Eleal decided she might as well go and see T'lin Dragontrader.

A DOZEN OR SO CITY CHILDREN LURKED AROUND THE dragons, being ordered away by two men shouting in clipped Fionian accents. T'lin himself stood by the tents, talking with two more of his assistants.

Dragontrader was a big man with a monstrous copper beard. His face was roughened and scarred by weather and he usually sported a showy sword and outrageously bright clothes. In Narshvale, he bundled up in llama hide like everyone else, but his boots were dyed blue, his leggings yellow, and a green scabbard hung out from under his red coat. Above all that he wore a black turban. Undoubtedly he would have a white shirt or something on underneath—no god in the Pentatheon would ever be able to complain of being neglected by T'lin. He seemed almost as large as one of his dragons.

As Eleal approached, his eyes flickered over her with no sign of recognition, but almost at once he clapped one of his companions on the shoulder, ending the discussion. He stalked away in amongst the dragons, pulling a rag from his pocket. Eleal doubled around the herd to approach from the other side, glad that he had not been trading with a customer.

A few of the great shiny beasts were standing, munching at bales of hay, flapping their frills up and down softly in pleasure. Most had lain down to chew their cud, but the fences of horny plates along their backs rose higher than her head and concealed her admirably. The long scaly necks stood up like palm trees. She caught glimpses of Dragontrader's turban and worked her way in his direction.

She loved dragons. That was how she had met T'lin—hanging around his herd. Sometimes he had only five or six, sometimes forty or more. Today she thought about fifteen or twenty, so he might be either buying or selling. When she was young she had toyed with dreams of marrying T'lin and being with the dragons all the time. They looked so ferocious and they were so gentle. They smelled good, and they spoke in funny belching noises. As she went by them, she trailed fingers over the shiny scales, admiring the play of light on them. Bright green eyes watched her under heavy browridges, jewels in caves. In darkness, dragon eyes actually glowed.

She made out Starlight and detoured to greet him, T'lin's own mount. No dragon was ever a real black, but Starlight was what was called deep twilight, and the twinkle of light on his scales had given him his name. He truly resembled a starry night. The two long frills that extended back from his neck were magnificent, longer than any others she had ever seen, like small wings. He lowered his head to snuffle and belch hay scent quietly at her. She liked to think he remembered her, but that was probably just wishful thinking.

T'lin was standing beside one of the cud-chewers, a five- or six-year male of the color called Osby slate, a sort of blue-gray. It was not yet docked, the long crest of plates standing unbroken along its back. The big beast purred softly as T'lin busily polished its flank with his rag. He bent over as if to examine its claws. Then he squatted down on his heels and grinned at Eleal through his bush of beard. His face was still not very much lower than hers. They were quite private here, between the Osby slate and a glacier blue female. They were also sheltered from the wind.

"And how is the Beloved of Tion, the Friend of the Gods, the great singer?"

"She is very well, thank you," Eleal said politely.

He looked oddly weary for so early in the day. Perhaps he had been traveling all night. She noticed a small gold ring in his left ear and wondered if that was new, for she could not recall seeing it before. How odd! And why only one ear?

"How is the goddess-impersonating business?" he asked.

"Slow, in Narsh at least. Tonight we shall meet with more fitting recognition. The citizens of Sussia appreciate art. If the gods will," she added.

T'lin snorted loudly. That was a habit of his. She suspected he had picked it up from listening to his dragons' belchings.

"You do not care for the worthy burghers of Narsh? You prefer that maniac rabble in Sussland?" He shook his big head in disbelief. "They are born mad and then go crazy."

Eleal racked her brains. "Narshians are so mean they won't even give you a cold." She had been practicing repartee recently, and thought that remark showed it.

T'lin's green eyes twinkled. "Sussians don't know an assembly from a riot!"

She went on the attack. "How is the dragon-rustling business?"

T'lin covered his face with his big rough hands and wailed.

"As the gods are my witness, the child wrongs me! No more honest trader ever crossed a pass."

That remark reminded her of the troupe's problem and stopped her from indulging in more banter.

"I have some information for you," she said.

T'lin's shaggy red eyebrows shot up. "I await it eagerly. You are an invaluable source of information to aid a poor honest man in wresting a living."

He was joking of course, but his quick green eyes had noted her worry. Probably very little Eleal told him was ever news to him. Sometimes the troupe played in rich people's houses, and even in rulers' houses, and then she might hear or see things he could not learn elsewhere. Everything else was mere gossip or obvious to any sharp eye, although he never said so. He was curious about all sorts of things: the chatter in the forum or bazaar, the price of foodstuffs, the lives of the rich, the grumbles of the poor, the edicts of the gods, the crops, the roads.

"When I buy a dragon," T'lin had told her once, "I do not just look at its claws. I look at every scale, every tooth. I look in its eyes and its ears. Sometimes very small things can tell me very important things, especially if they can be added together, yes? Now, a young dragon with his saddle plate already docked but no wear on his claws and no girth marks on his scales—do you know what those mean, Avatar of Astina? Why, it means that he has never done much work, does it not? So he has been a lucky young dragon, yes? Or he has a problem, maybe. A bad temper, maybe. Now when I come to a land to trade, I do not just ask the going price of dragons, because no one would tell me. Well, they would tell me, but I would not believe them. No, I look at everything in that land—in the whole vale, every-thing! Finally I decide what the price of dragons should be, and whether I want to buy or sell there."

Then he would smile triumphantly and stroke his copper beard, and she could never tell if he spoke seriously or in jest.

When Eleal Singer reported to T'lin Dragontrader, therefore, she reported everything she could think of. He never said he already knew something, he never said that anything did not interest him. When she had finished, he would pick out an item or two from her list and ask for details, but she never knew which topics he would choose, or whether he was really any more interested in those than the others or was just being a good trader. His face never changed expression by as much as one red beard hair.

At the end, he would reward her. When she had been little, the reward had been a ride on a dragon, but now he gave her money—sometimes only a few coppers, once a whole Joalian silver star, but he would rarely tell her what she had said to earn it. Sometimes he would comment that she had reported well, or that she should have observed this or that, things she had missed.

She had learned how to note Things That May Interest T'lin as she went about her life. She had learned how to remember them and keep them organized in her head. Actors were good at memorizing, of course.

She took a deep breath and began with the floods in Mapland. Then she described the riot in Lappin with six people killed and two houses burned, and the unusual number of monks and priests on Fandorpass—all colors, white, red, blues, yellows, greens—and how there were as many waiting to get on the mammoths, although he would have noticed that for himself. She mentioned the magistrate who had died here in Narsh and the assembly to be held next Headday to elect his replacement. That reminded her . . . "I am told there is a reaper in town!"

The glacier blue female belched thunderously and turned its long neck to stare at her reprovingly, as if she had made that disgraceful noise.

"There's a lot of Thargians in the city," she finished proudly. "I've heard them talking. They were trying to disguise their voices, but we theater people are very attuned to accents. There were two blue monks at the show two nights ago, and three well-dressed women last night, although I only heard one of those speak. I heard two young men in the baker's. There was a fat man with a local merchant and his wife I've seen before. And I overheard a white priest in the street. They were all trying to speak Joalian-style, and the men had beards, but I'm sure they were all from Thargia. Well, from somewhere in Thargdom, anyway." She thought quickly for a minute, and said, "That's all."

During her whole recital T'lin had just stared at her, motionless as a statue, balanced on his toes. She would not be his only informant in Narsh. Often she had seen him talking with people who could not be customers—children, beggars, priests. Most of them must be locals; she was probably the only one who traveled as he did. Once or twice he had remarked on that. Residents knew a lot, he had said, but travelers who came rarely saw changes better and noticed differences between places.

Now he took his rag and began to polish the Osby slate dragon thoughtfully. The monster purred. A dragon purr was an awesome sepulchral sound, like a hollow metal shell full of bluebottles.

"Men die all the time," T'lin murmured. "Not every unexpected death is caused by a reaper."

"But some are!"

"And not all Thargians are spies."

"Then why do they try to disguise their voices?"

He shrugged. "What set off the riot in Lappinvale?"

"Followers of D'mit'ri Karzon attacked a house they said was being used by worshipers of the Prime. The house was burned and six people killed. The governor did not punish anyone," she added. That should intrigue him. The Thargians usually kept very strict order in lands they ruled, although Thargland itself was said to be a rowdy place.

After a moment T'lin said, "In Lappin there is a temple to Zoan, the god of truth, who is an aspect of Visek, the Prime. Why should the whites need to worship him in a house instead of the temple? And why should Karzon followers care anyway?"

"That was what I heard."

He scratched his beard thoughtfully. "Are you sure it was the Parent they were supposed to be worshiping? Tell me the exact words you heard."

T'lin Dragontrader had never admitted before, as far as she

could remember, that anything she had told him was news to him. She felt rather excited, wondering how much he would pay her this time. She closed her eyes and thought very hard. Then she looked at him again.

"The One?"

"Are you sure or are you guessing?"

"Mostly guessing," she admitted.

His eyes were like hard green stones. "What do you know of the One?"

"Well . . . Usually it means Visek, the Parent, the Source. Or one of his aspects, like Zoan."

"Blessed are the avatars of Visek, father and mother of gods, blessed be his name. You said 'usually'? Who else is the One?"

"Dunno." Theology was confusing, and not something she had ever known T'lin to show an interest in before.

Now he polished the dragon in silence until Eleal began to fidget.

"There is a god whose real name is never mentioned," he said solemnly. "He is called the One True God, or the Undivided."

"Visek."

The dragon trader shook his head. "The Parent was not called the One like that until this other came. Other gods do not approve of the Undivided. He has few followers in Lappin, I expect. Fewer now, you tell me. He has no shrine or temple there."

Eleal nodded, perplexed by his sudden interest in gods. Probably it was a blind anyway, for he suddenly changed the subject.

"These Thargian visitors? Can you describe any of them so I would know them? Any squints or cauliflower ears?"

"Of course not! What sort of a spy would he be? But the fat one I saw with the locals . . . the local was Gaspak Ironmonger. He's thought to have a slight chance of being the new magistrate and if he supports the Joalians instead of the Thargians—"

T'lin chuckled and rose to his feet. "Did you ever hear of the chicken farmer who bought a leopard to rid his land of foxes?"

"No," she said, bewildered.

"Joalians are the foxes."

"Oh! And the Thargians are leopards?"

Dragontrader laughed. He fumbled in a pocket. "Indeed, you are a mountain of useful knowledge, Beloved of Tion. Here!"

She held out her hands and he sprinkled silver into them without bothering to count it. She gasped in delight at this shower of riches.

"Well done, Leading Lady of the World," T'lin said. "Give my love to Suss."

"If we can get there . . . T'lin! Dragons can go over mountains!"

"Yes," he said warily.

"Then, since the mammoths are so busy this year, and we *need* to get there more than, oh, a merchant say, or a priest—I mean, our art is important! I was just wondering . . ." She saw a glint in his eyes.

"Yes, I could put you and your friends on my dragons and be a ferryman, but I wouldn't get away with it twice. Do you know who owns those mammoths, Aspect of Astina?" He bared his teeth. "The temple of Ois! And the priests would not appreciate competition. They would have my trading license canceled."

"Oh."

"Yes. So you stick to acting! Good fortune at the festival."

How could he be so tactless? Did he not know the rules? "I have decided my art is not yet mature enough for me to enter."

T'lin shrugged. "Well, good luck in Sussland, anyway."

9

THE STRAPS OF HER PACK WERE CUTTING THROUGH EVEN
her heavy fleece clothes as she trudged back to the mammoths
across the muddy meadow. *Squish, squash, squish, squash . . .* Her
hip hurt, and she could feel a stitch starting in her side.

As she neared the loading point, the line of mammoths was
already moving out, the leaders wading across the river. One
last shaggy bull stood by the stair, and he raised his trunk to
trumpet, perhaps calling on the others to wait for him. The
loading had gone quickly. There had not been time for the
others to complete another sacrifice in the temple; Uthiam Piper
had known where Eleal was; they would not have left without
her. Another night in miserable cold Narsh!

When she reached the crowd squashed in around the steps,
she could see no sign of the troupe. She began squeezing her
way through, ignoring angry protests about what the world was
coming to and the usual mutters that children had no respect
for their elders these days.

She could not see the huckster, but she heard voices raised in
frantic competition as the customers bid for seats in the last
howdah. Even if T'lin had given her enough money for a
ticket—and it sounded as if the offers were being made in
gold—she could not just go on by herself. Not without telling
the others. It would have been a good idea to send her on ahead,
though, because Gartol Costumer had left two days ago to make
arrangements for a performance in Filoby tonight. He would
wonder what had happened. A missed show meant patrons dis-

55

appointed and more money lost. What a disastrous day!

The festival started in three more days! To miss the festival would be a tragedy.

Then she thought of even worse disaster. Ois was goddess of all passes. Suppose she would not turn aside her anger, and the troupe was stuck in horrible Narshvale forever? Even Fandorpass could be dangerous.

Something poked hard in her back. "Child!" said a sharp voice.

She wriggled around in the crush, and discovered the ancient blue nun peering at her accusingly. It was her staff that had done the poking.

"Is your name Eleal?"

"Yes! Do you have a message for me?"

"Oh, no!" Sister Ahn's long nose seemed redder than ever, her faded eyes even moister. "But that explains why we keep meeting."

"Do you know if my friends have left?"

"Friends?" She shook her head sadly. "Oh, your friends are irrelevant, child. You are the only one mentioned."

Suddenly the crowd moved like leaves in the wind. The two men in front of Eleal backed up so fast she was almost knocked over. She staggered, recovered, and found that she and the blue nun were alone in an empty space, looking across at the huckster. He was a beefy, red-faced young man, and there was an expression of comical astonishment on his pudgy features.

"Well, that helps," Sister Ahn murmured, almost inaudibly. "Come, child." She leaned a twisted hand on Eleal's shoulder and pushed with surprising firmness.

Eleal resisted. "I can't go without my friends!"

"You are the one who matters!" the nun snapped. "Is it not written, *Eleal shall be the first temptation?*"

"Written?" The crazy old priest had mumbled something about a prophecy. "Written where? Written what?"

"If you do not know, then it is probably destined that you shall not know. Come!"

She pushed harder. Peering down nervously to make sure the

unsheathed sword was not about to cut her off at the ankles, Eleal found herself being propelled toward the huckster. She looked up suddenly as he uttered a wail of horror.

A man had come forward to the base of the steps—probably a man, possibly a tall woman. He was swathed in a heavy robe, like a monk's, keeping his head bent so the hood would hide his face. He was black, all black. Even the cord around his waist was black. The hand that reached out to offer a coin to the huckster wore a black glove.

The huckster dropped his satchel with a loud jangle and leaped back, colliding with the mammoth's leg. He tried to speak and made no sound at all. His eyes bulged; his face had gone comically pale. Trong Impresario himself could not have depicted terror more convincingly.

Again the black-robed stranger tried to offer payment. Again the huckster refused it, sidling away farther, clearly determined not to let that fateful hand come close to him. With a shrug the dark monk turned to the steps and proceeded to climb slowly up to the howdah. The mahout stared down in horror as this sinister passenger made his approach.

The crowd was scattering in sullen silence, many of them running.

"Truly the gods reward those who have faith," proclaimed the blue nun. "Come, my dear, let us see what the price of a seat is now." She hobbled forward on her staff, urging Eleal along also, but she had taken only a couple of steps before the huckster grabbed up the satchel he had dropped, dived through under the mammoth, and took to his heels as if Zath himself were after him.

"Wait!" cried the nun, but the wind swept the word away. The black monk had taken his seat. Nine seats around him remained empty. The stairs were empty.

"You can go now if you want," Eleal said. Her mouth was dry, but surely the man in black could not be what she suspected he was.

"We must both go, for so it is written, but we cannot go

until we have *paid,*" Sister Ahn wailed. "And now that young man who sells the tickets has departed."

She sounded confused. She was probably crazy. On the other hand, the rest of the world did not seem to be much saner. One man had been given a seat at no charge and no one else except Sister Ahn seemed willing to share the howdah with him, although the seats were now available for free. How to explain that miracle? In tightfisted Narsh, too! The mahout had eased himself up the mammoth's neck until he was almost sitting on its head, as far from the solitary passenger as he could get.

"Perhaps that driver up there will negotiate a price," Sister Ahn muttered, but at that moment he spoke to the mammoth, and the big beast rolled forward.

Eleal looked around despairingly, but the onlookers were leaving. She was alone with the old woman. No one else had been willing to ride with the man in black. What else could he be? "Was that a reaper?"

Sister Ahn was still staring after the departing mammoth, apparently at a loss. She glanced at Eleal in bleary surprise. "He is a holy one, a servant of Zath. Yes, what they call a reaper."

Eleal's heart turned a cartwheel, her knees wobbled violently, and something seemed to squeeze her throat shut. "I've never seen a reaper before," she croaked. "In daylight?" Reapers were never discussed, or at least only in whispers—or croaks. But the mad old priest had mentioned him.

The nun chuckled. "You certainly wouldn't be able to see him in the dark, my dear!" she said, her good humor apparently restored. "And why not in daylight? He's only human. He must do something between sunrise and sunset."

That was even worse! "You mean he goes around in *disguise?*"

"He doesn't normally wear his habit, no. You can see the effect it has." The old woman shook her head disapprovingly. "No one would sit beside him."

"You would have?"

All the innumerable wrinkles around Sister Ahn's mouth puckered up in one of her gruesome smiles, although her watery eyes gave it an incongruous sadness. She raised her long nose so she could look down it. "Why not? If he wanted to gather my soul for Zath now, he could have done so. I am sure he can run much faster than I. In the Green Scriptures, Canto 2578, it is written, *"All gods play dice, but Zath's never lose."*

The worst part of this insanity was that she had expected Eleal to accompany her. "Then why did you not go?"

"Because I had not paid, of course. We children of Irepit are not permitted to accept charity. Everything must be paid for somehow—a story, or a lesson, usually. I had offered to give lessons on the journey, but the young man refused my bid." Her eyes were wandering even more than before, and she seemed puzzled that her companion did not understand. "When the other offers were withdrawn, I hoped he would reconsider."

The reaper must have been present in the crowd earlier. When the ticket price became unreasonable, he had donned his robe and revealed his avocation. Eleal shivered.

"What is a reaper doing here?"

"Earning his living by day, I expect," Sister Ahn said offhandedly, uninterested in reapers. "Gathering souls by night."

Eleal looked up at the sky apprehensively. The big moon would be setting about now, but the sky was cloudy. Trumb had not eclipsed for at least a fortnight; he must be about due.

> *When the green man turns to black,*
> *Then the reaper fills his sack.*

Which did not mean he didn't fill it other nights also.

In the distance the mammoth plodded into Narshwater, and across, and out the far side, gradually catching up with the others and dwindling into the distance. The tiny black figure sat alone with nine empty seats around him. Soon he became hard to see . . . Why was the reaper traveling to Sussland? Who had earned the enmity of Zath? Trumb must start eclipsing again soon. Where was the troupe? Should she go to the temple?

Worried, shivering in the icy wind, she glanced around the meadow. It seemed almost deserted without the mammoths, although there were llamas and dragons in the distance, and market stalls set up near the city gate. The other team would arrive tonight from Sussvale. The pen stood deserted, a flimsy rail fence around a patch of mud and mammoth dung. Klip Trumpeter was sitting on his pack with his head in his hands and his back to her. Apparently he had missed the reaper drama altogether!

Eleal hurried over to him at her fastest skip: *clop!clip!* . . . *clop!clip!* . . .

Apart from her, Klip was the youngest member of the troupe. He had played women's parts last year. Now he couldn't and he wasn't ready for men's, so he worked mostly as a roustabout. His pimples were as many as the stars and his opinion of himself as both man and musician was as high. Olimmiar, who was a couple of months older, considered him still only a boy. Golfren Piper would not perform with him. Why had he come? And why alone?

"Did you see who—"

He looked up. She recoiled at the pallor of his face. "What's wrong?"

"The alpaca," he said hoarsely.

"What about it?" She saw that Klip had lost three years somewhere since dawn. The arrogant self-styled musician was just a frightened boy now, and the change scared her.

"It was beautiful, Eleal, beautiful! All white and silky! Not a dark hair on it. Not a scratch on its hooves. Ambria paid five Joalian stars for it!"

Five! "And?"

Trumpeter's face crumpled as if he wanted to weep. "And its insides were all rotten. Black, and foul. Horrible. The stench filled the whole temple."

Eleal was already trembling with cold. Fear was no help. First a crazy priest, then an even crazier nun, then a reaper, and now this! She dropped her pack beside Klip and sat down, tucking her hands into her sleeves. At least the reaper had left town.

"What have we done to anger the Lady so?"

Klip's tongue moved over his lips. His acne showed as ugly purple blemishes on his ashen cheeks. "The Lady herself, or just Ois? We don't know. The priests say . . . Have you ever been to her temple?"

"No."

"That may be it. None of us worship at the temple here, except when we are about to leave. It may not have been enough."

Eleal felt sick. "And?"

Klip swallowed hard. "Now we have to make amends."

"All of us?"

"The women. Ambria tried to get Olimmiar excused, saying she was only fifteen and a maiden. The priests just said that made her service specially potent." Trumpeter groaned and buried his face in his hands. He mumbled something that might have been, "Meaning they can charge more."

Eleal waited . . . and waited. She could count the thumps of her heart. Finally she had to ask.

"Me too?"

He looked around sharply; she saw that the wind had filled his eyes with tears also. "No, no! Oh, I'm sorry, Eleal! I should have said! No, not you! Ambria asked, but the priests said no, not if the Lady has not blessed you yet and made you a woman."

She felt a rush of relief and despised herself for it. The others' sacrifice would lift the Lady's anger and she would not have contributed. She did not want to, but neither did they.

"Maybe next year?" Klip smiled sourly.

"Maybe," she said uneasily. It was certainly possible. Many girls received the Lady's blessing at thirteen or even earlier. She was oh-so-glad it was not this year, though! "So what do we do now?"

"Go back to the hostel and wait until their service is complete."

"You mean it may take a long time?"

"That's up to the priests, to decide when the goddess is appeased. Days, maybe."

Tion's Festival began in three days!

Klip rose suddenly and lifted the two packs. Eleal reached for hers and he moved it out of her reach.

"I can manage!" she shouted.

"I want the exercise," he said gruffly. "I'm trying to make my shoulders stronger."

She detested people taking pity on her because of her leg, but she decided to believe him and let him take both packs. As they began to walk, she concluded Klip Trumpeter was not so bad after all.

"I'll let you into a secret," she said. "If you promise not to repeat it. A couple of days ago Olimmiar remarked how big and muscular you were getting. You mustn't tell her I said so!"

He glanced down at her with a wan smile. "I won't tell her because I don't believe a word of it."

"Well it's true!"

"No it isn't."

Eleal sniffed and tossed her head. She had only been trying to cheer him up. The least he could have done was pretend to believe her. Just for that, she wouldn't tell him that she had overheard Trong say he would make a good actor one day.

They trudged in silence toward the gate. Then Trumpeter said miserably, "I think it was Uthiam all the time!"

"What was?"

"The priests asked for her specially."

"By name? They knew her name?"

"The one who played Herinia two nights ago, they said— was she there? It was all a plot, Eleal! Don't you see? Some rich man saw her as Herinia and coveted her. He prayed to the Lady, and offered gold, and she granted his prayer! The priests had been instructed."

"Klip!" She put a hand on his sleeve. "You mustn't say such things about the Lady!"

He glowered at her. "I'll say them about Ois, then, even if

she is a goddess! They took Uthiam away from the others—so they could send word to the man that she was available now, see? And he could be first. Uthiam's the sweetest, most beautiful—"

"Yes, she is. But—"

"Golfren was going crazy! He offered ninety-four stars if he could be the man to lie with her, the only man. Ninety-four!"

Ninety-four stars? That was a fortune! Eleal had long wondered why Golfren wore a money belt, which he probably thought no one except Uthiam knew about. "How could a wandering troubadour like Golfren Piper ever have collected so much money?"

"Dunno. I think he was planning to offer it to Tion in Suss to grant victory to Uthiam in the festival!"

"The priests refused?"

"They said husbands didn't count. I thought he was going to *hit* them!"

"Oh, Klip! Poor Golfren!"

Poor Uthiam!

Suddenly Trumpeter stopped and threw down one of the packs, so he could wipe his nose on his sleeve. He glared at Eleal with red-rimmed eyes. "I'll see you back at the hostel!"

She nodded sadly and limped away among the market stalls and the people.

10

As she reached the cluster of traders' stalls by the gate, Eleal realized that she was very hungry. She felt she should not be thinking of personal comfort when her friends were making so terrible a penance, but she had not eaten since the previous evening—and she no longer had Rilepass to look forward to. She wandered in among the fleece-wrapped servants and housewives, inspecting the wares. Mostly the offerings were of vegetables, for these were farmers' stalls. Eventually a savory scent drew her and she discovered a booth dispensing meat pies.

T'lin had given her money, of course, but she wanted to keep that. Many women were crowding around that table, competing for the trader's attention. Eleal moved in close at one end, and knelt as if to tie a lace. A moment later, as a customer clinked coins in payment, a small hand made a deft grab between two bulky customers. A pie vanished from the display.

Gleefully clutching her prize close to her, Eleal rose and walked away. When she reached a safe distance, she produced her loot and simultaneously bumped into a tiny woman in blue.

"This is kind of you, my child," Sister Ahn said, taking the pie in her twisted fingers. "It is long since I last ate. My, this smells delicious!" Her eyes were faded, watery, and filmed by age. They were also quite free of guile.

After a brief pang of annoyance, Eleal decided to be magnanimous. To feed this batty old crone would be meritorious. The Maiden would notice and might intercede with the Lady to turn aside her anger. And there were lots more pies where that one had come from.

"Oh, you are welcome, Sister! You really ought to be taking better care of yourself. A good llama fleece coat is what you need. Do you have somewhere warm to sleep?"

"I cannot accept charity," the nun mumbled, gazing longingly at the pie she held. "It is written, *Everything has its price.*"

"Payment is not necessary. One of my business ventures proved unexpectedly profitable this morning, so I can easily afford it."

The old woman still appeared frozen in her skimpy wool habit, and still unaware of the fact. The tip of her nose was turning white. "Here is what we shall do," she said, looking around vaguely, as if in search of a table and chairs. "We shall share this and I shall explain to you about the reaper. Take care of it for a moment." She returned the booty while she settled herself on the grass—an awkward procedure for which she leaned on her staff with one hand and adjusted the sword with the other, so as not to cut herself. Eleal wondered why the wind did not blow her over.

"Well, I do have pressing business engagements," she said, dropping to the ground. "But I admit I should like to know about the reaper and why you journey to Suss and why you carry a sword and several other things."

Sister Ahn took the pie in her grotesquely warped fingers, broke it in half, murmuring a grace, and then offered Eleal the larger piece. It was rich and juicy and delicious, still faintly warm from the oven.

"So you are Eleal!" she said, chewing vigorously. "Younger than I expected. What trade do you follow?"

"Eleal Singer. Actually I am more of an actor now, but we have so many Actors in the troupe that it seemed wise—"

The nun frowned. "What do you act?"

"Both tragedy and comedy. And I sing in—"

"What," Sister Ahn demanded, removing a piece of gristle from the mouth, "is the difference?"

Carefully not showing how shocked she was by the old woman's ignorance, Eleal explained. "Comedies are just about people. Tragedies have gods in them. People too, of—"

"Mmph! You portray goddesses?"

"Sometimes. I mean, I shall when I am tall enough."

"Then you must learn how goddesses think. You will travel to the festival tomorrow?"

Eleal told of the cockerel and the alpaca. When she started to explain what the other women in the troupe were doing, she felt nauseated and stopped eating.

Sister Ahn continued to work on the pie with her few teeth. The skin of her cheeks was like crepe, with all the underlying flesh underneath wasted away. A wisp of pure white hair had escaped from under her headcloth.

"Their penance may last a long time," she mumbled with her mouth full, "and the festival is soon. You will have to go without them."

"I can't! I mustn't!"

The nun waved a hand dismissively. "It has been foreseen that you will. You can't fight destiny. History awaits you."

"I am *not* going to leave Narsh without my friends! I must stand by them in their hour of distress."

The nun pursed her already shriveled lips. "Your religious education has been woefully neglected. Why 'distress'?"

"It seems so horrible!"

"Oh it is. That is why it is valuable. Have you not been taught that everything has a purpose? The purpose of life is to learn obedience to the gods."

"Of course." Eleal forced herself to take another bite of pie. She did not want to think about what was happening in the Lady's temple. Before she could ask about the sword and the reaper instead, the lecture resumed.

"The gods made us to serve them." Sister Ahn wiped gravy from her chin with a gnarled hand. "In this world we learn to do their will. When we have completed our apprenticeship, Zath gathers us to their judgment, to serve in whatever manner we have shown ourselves best fit for. In the Red Scriptures, the *Book of Eemeth,* it is written, *Among the heavens and the constellations thereof shall they be set, lighting the world as the lesser gods."*

Eleal had never understood the attraction of being hung in the sky like laundry for all eternity.

"To do what we want is easy," the nun said, still chewing. "To do what the gods want may not be. The reaper upset you, and a deal of other people also, but he worships Zath as Zath commands him. To take life is a sin for most of us. To obey the dictate of a god is never sin. A reaper can slay with a touch of his hand, but only because Zath has given him that power. Likely the god gave him other powers also, to help him in his unhappy task. He must put the god's gifts to their intended use. What for you or me would be murder is for him both a sacrament and a duty."

Eleal shivered. "And the Lady?"

"Likewise. To offer your body to a man for money would be a crime most foul. To do so as a sacrifice to the Lady when she commands it is a holy, precious thing. Obedience is all."

The faded gray eyes turned from Eleal to stare blankly across the windy meadow. "I have never lain with a man. I have never killed anyone. That does not make me better than those who do such things in holy service. I am sworn to obey another goddess in other ways, that is all."

A troop of armed citizens went striding past, returning from their drill. They all seemed to glance sideways at Eleal's odd companion, and she realized that no other passersby had come as close. Apparently a Daughter of Irepit was to be avoided— not given as wide a berth as a reaper would merit, but wide enough to remind Eleal of Uthiam's wary expression when she faced this cryptic crone.

"What goddess? Irepit? Is she an avatar of the Maiden?"

"Of course—Astina in her aspect as goddess of repentance. A stern goddess! Not as stern as Ursula, her aspect of justice, but—"

"Why drag that sword around if you don't use it?"

The old woman smiled her gruesome smile happily. "Because

the Holy Irepit has so commanded, of course. It is a reminder and a burden, a burden I bear gladly."

"A reminder of what?"

"A reminder of mortality and obedience." She pointed a bony finger at Eleal's right boot, with its two-inch sole. "You also bear a burden, child."

"Not willingly!" Eleal was annoyed to feel her face flushing.

"But perhaps the gods had their reasons for laying it upon you."

It was very impolite to discuss people's infirmities. The sword was not the same thing at all.

"Swords are valuable! Suppose some man covets it and threatens to kill you for it?"

The nun shrugged her narrow shoulders. "Then I refuse and he kills me. If he takes it without killing me, then I must kill myself in penance for whatever evil he may someday do with it. I said it was a burden."

"You may never use it?"

"Only in ritual. Some of my sisters have frozen to death rather than profane their swords by chopping wood with them."

"Well!" Eleal said crossly. "You tell me that everything has a purpose. Obviously the purpose of a sword is to kill people, er, men, I mean."

"Oh, I never said it had not killed people!" The nun patted the hilt of the weapon lovingly. "It has belonged to my order for a long time, so I expect it has been the death of many."

That made no sense at all. The woman was as crazy as the equally ancient priest who had first mentioned her. The two of them must be in cahoots somehow. Feeling very uneasy, Eleal scrambled to her feet.

"To endure without complaint, to obey without question," Sister Ahn said, as if unaware of the movement, "this is what life is for. It is written in the *Book of Shajug* how holy P'ter, having ruled over the Thargians for tenscore years and seven—"

"Why are you traveling to Suss?"

The nun sighed. "The play was written long ago. By your definition it is a tragedy, for the gods are involved. There is a part in this play for one of my order. I deemed . . . I was deemed the most expendable."

"And me? You knew my name!"

"Your part is written also."

"Namely?"

Sister Ahn peered up awkwardly at this impertinent young questioner. Tears were trickling down her cheeks. "So many questions! In the Blue Scriptures, the *Book of Alyath,* we read, *Ask not lest the answer displease you; seek not lest you become lost; knock and you may open a dangerous door."*

Crazy as a drunken bat!

"I really must be off!" Eleal said royally. "Business, you know. I do wish you would find yourself some warmer garments. Now, pray excuse me."

She stalked away. She half expected to hear an order that she stay and listen to more, but it did not come.

~~~ 11 ~~~

SUNDAY NEVER REALLY EXISTED FOR EDWARD EXETER. From time to time the pain in his leg would solidify out of the fog and he would open his eyes and see the mess of bandages and ropes and discover that he could not move. His head throbbed. He faded in and faded out. Often he would try to turn over and again be balked by those ropes and that leg stuck up in the air. He was vaguely aware of nurses coming around at intervals and talking to him. As soon as he grunted a few words, they would go away satisfied. Sometimes they tucked thermometers under his tongue and scolded when he went to sleep and dropped them. There was a nasty business with a bottle, too.

Often the world was filled with silent music, sometimes music soaring like a Puccini aria, sometimes funny music, like a Gilbert and Sullivan patter song, although he heard no words.

Once or twice he noted the drab brown walls and the stink of carbolic and ether. Then he would deduce yet again that he must be in a hospital and therefore was being cared for and could safely drift off again. At other times he thought he was back in Paris and reflected that Smedley's uncle kept jolly hard beds. Once he had a memory of pain and streaming blood; he started to cry out then. Someone came and jabbed a needle in him and the music returned.

A voice he knew spoke his name, very far away. His eyelids were heavy as coffin lids, but he forced them open and saw Alice.

"I'm dead, aren't I?" His tongue was too thick, his lips too stiff.

"Not very."

"Then why am I seeing angels?"

She squeezed his hand. "How do you feel?"

"Not quite as good as usual."

"You'll be better tomorrow, they say."

He blinked to try and make his eyes work correctly. There was an electric light up there. "What time is it?"

"Evening. Sunday evening. You had a bang on the head. I told them there wasn't much brain there to start with."

He tried to say, "Tell me you love me and I'll die happy." He wasn't sure if he managed to. They woke him later to give him a back rub, but Alice had gone.

12

ELEAL HAD BEEN WANDERING AIMLESSLY AROUND THE city's dreary gray streets until eventually her feet brought her into the temple quarter. The house of Ois was easily the tallest building in town, but no less ugly than any of the others. She did not want to visit that! Old Sister Ahn might describe what was happening there as a great and holy sacrifice, but Eleal still felt that it was degradation, and she would not witness her friends' shame.

Then she recalled the silver in her pocket. She was the only member of the troupe who had not made an offering that day, unless half a pie to a nun counted. She decided she would go to Tion's shrine and sacrifice some money there. If the crazy old priest was still there, she could reassure him that she was obviously in no danger and the reaper had left town anyway.

But why just the Youth? Why not visit all the shrines? She could pray to the Parent for comfort and the Maiden for justice and even to the Man for courage. She could ask them all to intercede with the Lady. She headed for the street behind the temple. The area was busy now, full of hurrying Narshian troglodytes.

She had often come along this street, so she knew the first shrine was Visek's, although she had never entered it before. Its imposing archway, which must once have been white, was now a grubby drab color and the faded sun symbol of the mother and father of gods was barely visible. She walked in boldly, to the small and shadowy courtyard, overgrown with somber trees and roofed by black branches and gray sky. The walls were smeared with lichen. Faint scents of stale incense cloyed the air. There was no one else present.

The statue of the Father opposite the entrance was crude, spattered with bird droppings and shedding flakes of white paint like dandruff. It depicted a stern, bearded man wearing a crown and long robes. The contorted Narshian script on the plinth was obscured by moss, but the god had only one eye and one ear, in his aspect as Chiol, god of destiny. She hoped he had his one ear turned her way now, to hear her prayer. Chiol had a very splendid temple in Joal, which she had seen but never visited— she never had problems with destiny.

She knelt before the figure. To pray to the All-Knowing, one should wear something white. Well, the inside of her fleece coat was *sort-of* white, so that was all right. She pulled out two of the silver coins Dragontrader had given her, unable to see what they were in the gloom.

There were other offerings lying on the plinth: a few coppers, two jars and a bottle, a cold leg of goose with flies crawling on it, a hank of wool, and a string of beads, which was probably somebody's most precious thing. She resisted a temptation to open the jars and sniff at the contents. She laid the silver beside them.

She bowed her head and repeated a prayer from the White Scriptures: "Father of Gods, Mother of Mortals, Giver of Truth, grant us comfort in our sorrows and forgive us our sins."

That was very appropriate, she thought, and in a moment she did feel better. Surprisingly better—but then she had never offered silver to a god before. She murmured the first thanksgiving she thought of; it was from the Blue Scriptures, but that would not matter.

Eleal limped out cheerfully, into a swirl of snow.

White flakes danced around in the streets, sticking only to people, it seemed, and not settling on the ground. They made it hard to see where she was going. Tugging her collar tighter, she set off between the hurrying pedestrians, the carts, and wagons.

The high wall continued, marked by unwelcoming doors. Trees poked over the top in places, suggesting private gardens. The next shrine was Karzon's, in his aspect of Krak'th, god of earthquakes. She had rarely prayed to the Man before, and certainly never to Krak'th. She had no more problems with earthquakes than she did with destiny.

The afternoon was drawing to a close already; she was cold and weary. Her hip hurt. Blinking into the snowflakes, she saw a familiar figure stalking toward her. Anyone could recognize Dolm Actor at a distance by his height and rolling gait. Normally, of course, she would run to him. Dolm was a gangly, cheerful man, almost as tall as Trong Impresario, but much younger. He had a wonderful voice, although he moved poorly and his gestures were graceless. She could just remember when Dolm had been young enough to play the Youth. Now he usually portrayed the Man when the troupe performed tragedies, lovers or warriors in the comedies.

But Dolm would not be cheerful today, with Yama sacrificing in the temple. Dolm was very probably doing what she was doing—making a pilgrimage to all the shrines of Narsh—and in that case he was heading for Karzon's, as she was. She did not want Dolm to listen to her prayers.

She did not think she was wicked enough to listen to his. It wouldn't be easy to arrange, anyway. She stepped behind a parked wagon to let him go in unmolested. As he came closer, she decided that there was something strange about the way he was behaving. He passed by without seeing her, and without entering the shrine.

Curiosity is a sin, Ambria Impresario scolded.

Curiosity is a great talent, T'lin Dragontrader said.

So Eleal watched, and in a few minutes she decided that her hunch was correct, and Dolm Actor was being furtive. She stepped out from behind the cart and followed, keeping close to a rumbling wagon of bales. He walked faster than the yaks plodded, but every few minutes he would pause and look behind him.

He was tall and she was small. She could be a lot more in-

conspicuous than he could, and on a gloomy afternoon in a riot
of snowflakes, she could be downright invisible.

Perhaps he was going to Chiol's shrine, to begin there, as she
had. Why should he make such a mystery of it, though?

Without warning, Dolm vanished. Eleal caught a brief
glimpse of a closing door. She stamped her heavy boot with
annoyance.

Curiosity howled in frustration. Like her, Dolm visited Narsh
only once a year, and briefly, yet he had obviously known exactly which door he wanted. As it was just a spread of timber
in a featureless stone wall, with no name or marker on it, he
must have been here before. The wall was too high to climb,
even had she dared try such a thing in a busy street. Shrubbery
protruded over the top, so there was a garden beyond. It might
be a back gate to the temple, or else another courtyard, like
Chiol's shrine.

Another courtyard, *next* to Chiol's shrine!

Without pausing to think, Eleal sprinted back to the archway
and through, into the gloomy shrine. There was still nobody
there. Without a word of apology to the god, she hurried to
the sidewall. Cursing her cumbersome boot and her heavy Narshian fleece, she scrambled up a tree until she could peek over.

Below her lay a larger courtyard, enclosed by high mossy
walls, overgrown with old trees and gangly shrubs. It had an air
of neglect and decay about it, as if no one ever came. It was
another shrine, although never in her life had she heard of a
sacred place being kept secret. Despite the snow swirling in the
air, she had a clear view across the wet cobbles to the god.

The figure was so lifelike that it stopped her breath. She had
never seen finer, even in the grandest temples. It was larger than
mortal, wrought in bronze, a male in a loincloth. The Youth
was usually shown nude and Karzon fully clad, but this must be
the Man, for he was a heavyset mature adult, not a slim-waisted
adolescent. Besides, he bore a skull in one hand and a hammer
in the other. He was also weathered to a muddy green, and
green was the color of Karzon, the Man. He stood in a sort of
thicket of implements that stuck up around his feet: a spade, a

sword, a scythe, a shepherd's crook, and other attributes of his many aspects. All of those were also of green bronze, except the sword, which was red with rust—she hoped it was rust.

That was no minor local god. That must be Karzon himself, god of creation and destruction. She had never been to his temple because it was in Tharg. So the Man had two shrines in Narsh—a public one to Krak'th and a private one of his own. Curious!

Then she saw Dolm, sitting on the ground below her, bare to the waist. While she watched, he hauled off his leggings and stood up, wearing nothing except a black cloth tied around his loins. He was visibly shivering as the snow settled on his shoulders and the prominent bald spot on top of his head, but the fact that he had stripped off everything except that one mono-colored garment meant that he was about to perform some special ritual sacred to one god. Black meant *Zath* Karzon, the Man's avatar as god of death.

She wanted to vanish, but mad curiosity froze her to her perch on the branch. Even if Dolm looked up, he would not notice her face peering at him through the foliage. Yet outsiders prying into secret rites were asking for very serious trouble. Trouble from *Zath?*

And *Dolm?*

Dolm Actor, her friend?

Piol Poet would never eat fish. Ambria belonged to a women's cult that she would never discuss, and recently had begun taking Uthiam along to meetings, whenever they could get away. Eleal had overheard them talking about it when they did not know she was listening, but she had not learned much more than that it had something to do with Ember'l, who was goddess of drama, avatar of Tion in Jurg. Probably many people had sworn special allegiance to some particular god or goddess. A twelve-year-old was not likely to be told about such private matters.

Oh, Dolm!

Soldiers always wore something black. Many other men did—but an actor? An actor worshiping *Zath?*

She stared in disbelief as that lanky, bony man strode forward to stand before the god and raise his lean arms in supplication. He was almost as tall as the idol. She did not recognize the words he began to chant—they sounded Thargian, but not a dialect she recognized.

It was a complex ritual. Dolm turned around several times—he had an extremely hairy chest, Dolm. He dropped to his knees and touched his face to the ground. He sprang up, legs astride, and recited something else. He touched his toes, crouched, rose, bowed, in careful sequence, chanting softly all the time in his sonorous actor's voice. He dropped on hands and knees and barked three times like a dog. And finally he wriggled forward on his belly to the base of the plinth. Eleal shivered at the thought of all that cold, wet stone, and snow.

Dolm Actor rose to his knees, and grasped the sword with his left hand. It came free of the plinth easily. He recited another formula and kissed the rusty blade. He stretched out his right arm, laying his hand at the god's feet, palm upward. For the first time his voice faltered and he seemed to hesitate. Then he slashed down at his wrist as if trying to sever it completely.

He cried out, dropping the sword. A torrent of blood spilled from the cut arteries.

Eleal's hair rose straight up, or at least felt as if it did.

Steadying the wounded arm with his left hand, Dolm lifted it so the red fountain of his own life's blood gushed down upon his own balding head. The injured hand hung limp and useless.

That last obscenity snapped the spell that had rooted Eleal. This was no normal worship! This was no little clique of gossipy women muttering secret prayers. This was some arcane invocation. Hiding from Dolm Actor was child's play, but she could not hide from the god of death if he came in person.

Teeth chattering, she slithered wildly downward through the branches until she collapsed on the leaf-strewn ground. Then she sprang to her feet and fled.

ACT II

MYSTERY

✤ 13 ✤

THE NEW HOTEL IN GREYFRIARS WAS A GLOOMY VICTO-
rian structure of red brick, a short walk from the High Street,
flanked by *Robinson & Son Drapers* on one side and *Wimpole Bros.
Chemists* on the other. Its prices were reasonable—four shillings
and sixpence for bed and breakfast. It was convenient to the
station and much favored by commercial travelers. On Bank
Holiday weekend, it was as vivacious as the inside of a sealed
tomb. No games of auction bridge would liven its Residents'
Lounge this evening. Very few pairs of shoes would be set outside its bedroom doors tonight for Boots to polish before morning.

The entrance hall was dark, but still stuffy from the day's heat.
Permanent odors of yeast and stale cigar smoke lingered amid
the aspidistras drooping in the windows and the horsehair sofas
flanking the dead hearth. Walls and woodwork were a uniform,
sad brown; the elaborate plaster ceiling was stained to the color
of old tea. As the revolving door hissed to a stop behind her,
Alice Prescott mentally prepared for a few hours of dread boredom before she could sleep. Her room would still be hot, and
it overlooked the shunting yard. The bed was surely the lumpiest south of the Humber.

The West Country could never be as unbearable as London,
but she longed to reach her room and shed a few clothes. Africa
had been hotter, but in the Colonies a woman was not required
to wrap herself in *quite* such absurd creations of Oriental silk
underskirts and ankle-length cotton voile gowns and broad silk

sashes. Or, if she were, then she would not be expected to spend an afternoon trudging around a county town.

Her plumed hat was going to come off before anything else did.

Most Sunday evenings in Greyfriars would offer nothing whatsoever in the way of entertainment except Divine Service at St. Michael and All Angels'. Today, however, there had been an impromptu meeting in the park, which had provided some unexpected excitement. Mr. Asquith, God Bless Him, had been three-cheered several times, the Kaiser had been loudly booed. The mayor had spoken a few words about the Empire on Which the Sun Never Sets and England Expecting Every Man to Do His Duty. A hastily gathered band from the Boys' Brigade had played some martial music, and everyone had sung "Land of Hope and Glory" and "God Save the King." Then the crowd had quietly dissolved, slinking away as if ashamed of having displayed emotion in public.

Alice headed for the desk to collect her room key. She could see it dangling on the board with the others, well out of reach. There was no message in her pigeonhole, and no news was good news because the only people who knew where she was staying were the hospital and the police.

She hoped D'Arcy had found the note she had left for him in the sitting room—at times he could be quite astonishingly unperceptive, blind as a mole. She teased him about that. She had left another note on the pillow: "See note on mantelpiece." She wondered what he had done this morning without her. Perhaps this Sunday he had actually gone to church! She would send a telegram to his chambers in the morning. Unless Edward took a grave turn for the worse, she absolutely must get back to town tomorrow.

The clerk was not in evidence. Before she could lift the little brass bell thoughtfully placed on the desk for just such an emergency, a man spoke from the far end of the hall.

"Miss Prescott?"

She jumped and turned.

He must have been sitting in the corner armchair. Now he

had risen. He was large, portly, dressed like a banker in his Sunday best, waistcoat and gold watch chain.

"I am she."

He nodded and walked over to her, taking his time, carrying his bowler. She closed her fingers on the bell. His hair was thinning, his graying mustache turned up in points like the Kaiser's.

"Inspector Leatherdale of the County Constabulary, Miss Prescott. Wonder if I might have a word with you?"

Alice released the bell. Her heart was behaving disgracefully. "Of course, Inspector. I hope you can inform me what has transpired. I did inquire at the station, but the officer there was most uncommunicative."

The policeman nodded, as if that was to be expected. He gestured to the heavy sofas by the fireplace. "There are some gentlemen in the Residents' Lounge, ma'am. This should be private enough."

She led the way over there and perched carefully on an edge, keeping her back straight as a musket. The cushion sagged so low that her knees tilted uncomfortably to the side. She stood her parasol upright against the arm and removed her gloves. Leatherdale pulled up the creases of his trouser legs at the knees in thrifty middle-class fashion, then settled deeply into the sofa beside hers. He produced a notebook and fountain pen.

He looked annoyingly comfortable. She hoped she appeared more composed than she felt, because she felt like a felon caught red-handed, which was ridiculous. Dear Uncle Roland would consider her sense of guilt very fitting if he knew of it and knew what caused it. He could not know, of course, but absence of evidence would never lead him to doubt. He had been convinced of her depravity as soon as she moved out on her own, and that had been long before she met D'Arcy. Immorality was not a criminal offense. It just felt like it at the moment.

"Now, Inspector! I understand that—"

"Your full name, please, ma'am. For the record."

He took charge of the conversation so effectively that she found herself waiting in obsequious silence while he wrote down every answer. What did her age have to do with Edward's accident? Or her address? Or that she had been born in India, raised in British East Africa, was self-supporting, taught piano?

"Edward George Exeter is your first cousin?"

"He is. He is also seriously injured, Inspector. I was told he fell down some stairs, but I have yet to learn—"

The inspector looked up with eyes as cold and penetrating as the iceberg that sank the *Titanic*. "We do not know how he came to fall down those stairs, Miss Prescott. That is something we hope to establish when he is well enough to answer questions."

"You mean it was not an accident?"

"What happened to Exeter may or may not have been an accident. The other young man involved was stabbed to death. I can tell you, though, that there seems to have been no one else present at the time. As of this date your cousin has not been charged, but he is an obvious suspect in a clear case of murder."

The ensuing silence had the impact of bells. Stabbed to death? Murder?

Edward? She felt herself opening and closing her mouth like a fish.

The questions began to roll again. She did not hear them, and yet she could hear her voice answering them.

"Anything I can do to help . . . caught the first train . . . uncle's housekeeper sent me a telegram . . . very fond, extremely fond of Edward . . . more like brother and sister . . ."

It was unbelievable. Edward would never murder anyone! Murder was something that happened in the slums of Limehouse. Murder was Jack the Ripper or Dr. Crippen, not Edward! There had been some horrible mistake.

She must have said so, because the inspector was nodding understandably. "I know how you must feel," he said, and suddenly he seemed avuncular and less intimidating. "Between ourselves, I am much inclined to agree with you, Miss Prescott. Your cousin seems like a very promising young man, well thought of, of good family . . ."

He must have asked, or she had volunteered, because she

discovered that she was telling him all about their family, and about herself.

". . . other sahibs fled town when the cholera arrived. My parents were both doctors, though . . . sent me away and they stayed . . . I don't remember them at all . . . mother had two brothers. I was sent off to Kenya on the mail boat, like a parcel. Uncle Cameron, Aunt Rona . . . like parents to me . . ."

She was telling of Africa, the only childhood she could recall . . . Why should the policeman care about that? Yet he was still making notes, apparently managing to keep up with the story pouring out of her.

"And you came Home when exactly?"

"In 1906. Edward followed in '08, when he was twelve."

"You do not live with your uncle now, though?"

"I am of age, Inspector."

"But you have lived on your own for some time?" he asked, watching her shrewdly under bushy gray brows.

She took a deep breath. She knew the conclusions men drew when a woman lived on her own. That those conclusions were now true in her case made them no less unfair. They would have been there had she never met D'Arcy. There had been no one before D'Arcy.

"Uncle Roland is not an easy man to live with."

"Your cousin shares that opinion?"

To describe Edward's opinions of Holy Roly could not help, although they were starting to look appallingly accurate. "The relationship is cool on both sides. It was all right at first, but since Aunt Griselda died, my uncle has become . . . well, difficult."

The inspector nodded thoughtfully and studied his notebook for a moment. Hooves and wheels clattered past the windows.

"Exeter rarely stayed with his uncle, even in holiday time?"

"My uncle goes out of town a lot. He . . . He tends to distrust young people. He preferred not to leave us in the care of the servants. I was more fortunate. My father was survived by two elderly maiden aunts. I mostly spent my summers with them in Bournemouth." The Misses Prescott had been reluctant to put up with their great-niece. They had had no use for an adolescent boy about the house, a boy unrelated to them.

"So he lived year-round at Fallow?"

"Not completely. Friends would often invite him to visit during the holidays. He has been to the Continent several times, France and Germany, staying with families to learn the language. The school arranges such things."

The more she could tell about Edward the better, surely? Then the police would see how absurd it was to suspect him of anything.

"You know, I don't believe Edward has ever told a lie in his life, Inspector? He—"

The policeman donned his fatherly smile. "Your family seems to have been very dedicated to the Empire, Miss Prescott. Let me see if I have them pegged correctly. Mr. Cameron Exeter, Edward's father, was a district officer in British East Africa. Dr. Roland Exeter was a missionary in the South Pacific for the Lighthouse Missionary Society, of which he is now director. Your mother, Mrs. Mildred Prescott, was a doctor in India?"

Alice laughed for the first time. "I think we all have guilty consciences. My great-grandfather was a nabob. He made a fortune in India. Loot, Edward calls it."

Leatherdale made another note. "Your family has money still, then?"

"Some, Inspector. We are by no means wealthy, though."

That might be more true than she meant it to be. More and more it looked as if Edward was right and Holy Roly had poured the whole lot into his blessed Missionary Society. She had not seen a penny of her inheritance yet. But surely that scrap of dirty family laundry was irrelevant? Surely this whole family history was irrelevant?

The policeman did not seem to think so. Was he truly on Edward's side as he had claimed, or was he somehow trying to trap her into saying something she should not? But what on earth could she reveal that would be damaging? Nothing!

"Your uncle, the Reverend Roland Exeter, is an elderly man?"

"In his seventies, yes."

"Seventy-two, actually," Leatherdale said offhandedly. "Born in 1842. And your mother?"

Puzzled and oddly uneasy now, Alice said, "I'd have to work it out. She was thirty-eight when I was born. I can't recall why I know even that much."

Leatherdale scribbled. "So 1855 or '56. And Roland in '42. How about Cameron?"

"I don't know. I never saw them after I left Africa, remember. But he must have been much younger."

The bushy brows flickered upward. "According to *Who's Who,* your uncle Roland was the second son—meaning Cameron was the oldest child."

She smiled and shook her head. "I'm quite sure he wasn't! I remember how shocked I was at how old Uncle Roland was when I met him. Perhaps it's a misprint?"

"Possibly." The inspector seemed to change the subject. "It seems odd that your adoptive parents never came Home on leave. District officers are usually granted leave every two years or so, aren't they?"

"I don't know. Yes, I suppose so. Nyagatha is very remote. It was even more remote in those days." That seemed irrelevant, somehow. All the Empire was remote.

"Your cousin Edward. Last week he was on his way to Crete. When he had to cancel his plans—when he came back to England—why did he come to Greyfriars?"

"I'm not sure."

"Did he get in touch with you?'

Alice shook her head. "He dropped me a postcard on his way through London. I am not on the telephone, you know. He just said the trip was off and he was coming here, to stay with General and Mrs. Bodgley."

"He did not wish to stay with his uncle," Leatherdale said. "Why not with you?"

She felt herself blushing, but it would not matter. "I could not put him up!"

"Why not?"

Her cheeks felt warmer yet. "Really, Inspector! If the highly respectable ladies who employ me were to hear that a *young man* had been seen entering and leaving my flat, then they would never allow me across their doorsteps again! They would not let me near their pianos, let alone their children!"

Which was true, but not the real reason. What if Edward had stumbled on something of D'Arcy's lying around? His dressing gown, for example? Edward was a romantic. It would kill him.

"You are on good terms, though?"

"Oh, yes! I told you, I regard him as a brother."

"And what are his feelings toward you?"

She turned and stared at the empty fireplace. "You had best direct that question to him, Inspector."

"Murder is no respecter of privacy, Miss Prescott!"

She turned to him in horror. "Heavens! You don't mean I am going to find myself pilloried in the gutter press? *The News of the World?*" If the reporters ever scented a scandal as well as a murder and dragged D'Arcy in, his career would be completely ruined. His wife was a vindictive bitch.

The big man shrugged. "In normal times I expect you would. I believe the Kaiser will save you in this instance."

"Well, that is certainly a relief!"

"So will you answer my question, ma'am?"

"My cousin believes he is in love with me."

"Believes?"

She turned again to the fireplace. "Edward has led a very sheltered life, and in many ways an extremely lonely one. He last saw his parents when he was twelve. They died in very horrible circumstances four years later. I was the only person he could turn to. I am three years older, which is a lot at that age. Some of his letters were heartbreaking!"

And just when the pain was easing, Cameron's reputation had been stamped into the mud by the board of inquiry. For Edward, that had been a toboggan trip through Hell.

She forced herself to meet the policeman's steady stare. "I am literally the only girl he knows! Can't you see? Edward has a romantic Celtic streak to him. He believes he is in love with me. Now he has left school . . . in a few months . . . when he has had a chance to meet other girls . . .''

Edward would not meet many girls if he had to spend those next few months in jail.

14

ABOUT THE ONLY GOOD THING AMBRIA IMPRESARIO EVER found to say about Narsh—and Eleal agreed with her on this— was that it had a very good hostel. True, it was shabby and none too clean, like the rest of the city, but it was located conveniently close to the shearing barn where the plays were performed. It provided innumerable poky rooms, and it was never busy so early in the spring, when the troupe needed it. There was no embarrassing pretending to be asleep when the troupe played Narsh.

Snow was starting to pile up in alleys and the light was failing when Eleal at last found her way back there—thinking gloomily that they should all be down in warm Filoby by now, getting ready for the evening's performance.

She was still very shaky from her narrow escape, but no terrible gods had come after her. Dolm Actor himself might have bled to death, if his rites had failed. He would have been in too much pain to notice any noise she had made in leaving, and the snow had not been lying then, so she should have left no tracks.

Now that she had recovered from her fright, she felt angry, which was strange. Perhaps she should feel sorry for Dolm, who served so terrible a god, but she couldn't feel sorry. Murdering people was wrong, no matter what old Sister Ahn might say.

Dolm had deceived her all her life, and she just felt angry.

She wondered what T'lin Dragontrader would say when she told him about that bizarre performance. He would believe her. To mention it to anyone else was unthinkable—even if Dolm Actor never returned, the troupe would not credit her story. She would be the only one who would ever know what had happened to him.

The hostel was a welcome sight in the dusk. There was no smoke rising from the chimney, though, as she had hoped there would be by now. She found the key in its usual cranny under the step. The door opened into the big communal kitchen that took up most of the ground floor, big enough and high enough to house a family of mammoths. Another door led out to toilets and washrooms; a wooden stair against one wall led up to sleeping rooms above.

She stood for a while, sniffing the familiar smells of ancient cooking and old tallow, listening to wind rattling the casements and whining in the eaves. There seemed to be no one else in the familiar old warren. She decided she would take off her coat first, comb her hair, and then kindle a fire to heat up wash water. She felt limp and sore from a long day. Only a llama should be expected to spend so long inside a heavy fleece.

She set off up the staircase that clung to the high, raw-stone wall. From long habit, she stepped on the ends of the treads. Ambria was always accusing her of sneaking, but she hated the sound of her uneven gait and had learned to move quietly in consequence. *Our Lady Mouse,* Golfren called her sometimes.

In some cities the troupe slept in one big room, while in Jurg they stayed in the king's house. The Narsh hostel lay somewhere between those two extremes. It was so large and so empty at this time of year that Eleal had a room all to herself, not having to share with Olimmiar. She walked down the long corridor, turned the corner, and saw her pack lying abandoned by Klip Trumpeter's door. Muscle building only went so far, obviously.

As she stooped to lift it, she detected a faint rasping coming from the room itself. The door was ajar, but whatever was making that odd noise was not visible through the crack.

One of the really nice things about the Narsh hostel was the size of its keyholes. Trumpeter was standing with his back to her, stripped to his breechclout as Dolm Actor had been. But Klip was not engaged in any arcane holy ritual. The cloth was white, anyway, although not as white as it should have been. He had a brick in each hand, and he was swinging them up and down, up and down. His bony back and shoulders gleamed with sweat, and the noise was his panting. He sounded almost ready to collapse.

He was really serious about those muscles! Perhaps he had believed her little lie after all? She sensed interesting opportunities for teasing—she might mention bricks at supper and smile at him innocently. That would make Trumpeter's face glow like one big all-over pimple.

Amused, Eleal took up her pack and tiptoed off along the corridor. Then she came to another open door, and her heart jumped into her mouth and stayed there.

This was Yama and Dolm's room. Like the others, it contained no furniture except a straw pallet, but their packs were lying there. Someone must have brought all the baggage back. Shivering with a sort of sick excitement, Eleal stared at this deadly opportunity.

When she had been little, she had found people's packs absolutely irresistible. There was always something interesting in them! Once she had found a hand-tinted print of a naked woman in K'linpor Actor's, and had produced it at lunch for everyone to admire. That had been a painful experience all round.

She had grown more discreet after that, but about two years ago Ambria had caught her going through Trong's pack and had taken a belt to her. That had really hurt. And then Ambria had said that Eleal Singer was nothing but a stray fledgling and the troupe had no duty to care for her and feed her and if she was ever caught prying like that again, she would be thrown out on the street where she belonged. That had hurt even more.

Since then, she had mostly managed to resist personal packs. They were a bad habit.

This, however, was different! This was important.

This was crazy—the man served Zath.

He was almost certainly dead, victim of his own clumsiness in botching a ritual. If he wasn't, there might be evidence in that baggage that would convince the others.

There was no one else in the building except muscle-man Klip, and he was busy.

All packs looked much alike. Whoever had brought the baggage back could easily have made a mistake. About three heartbeats after that last thought, Eleal Singer was limping along the corridor carrying Dolm Actor's pack instead of her own. It was very little heavier.

Panting like a cat, she laid it on her pallet, then spared a moment to lock and bolt her door.

Her hands trembled so much that she could hardly manage the buckles. Gasping for breath, she began hauling out clothes, spare boots, a printed book containing extracts from the Green and the Blue Scriptures, a couple of manuscript copies of plays— this year's repertoire. A makeup kit. A wig that ought to be in the prop box and had probably been left over after last night's performance. And a little bag of dream pods—well! Ambria Impresario would be very interested to know about them.

When Eleal had taken out everything, she looked for secret pockets like those in Golfren and Klip's packs. This one was a little trickier to figure out, but she managed it. It contained exactly what she had feared, a black garment. She did not even dare pull it out to inspect it. She had no need to. It was bulky enough.

A door banged, and voices came drifting up from downstairs. Almost retching with terror, Eleal began stuffing everything back in what she hoped was the right order, making a frantic muddle.

Curiosity is a sin!

Curiosity is a great talent, but this time that talent had worked too well.

Only a reaper would ever dress all in black. Sister Ahn had said, murder was both a sacrament and a duty for reapers. She had not mentioned whether their powers included the ability to know when someone had been ransacking their packs.

With her hair combed, wearing her shawl over her warmer dress, Eleal approached the stairs. She was an actor, wasn't she, sort of? Very well, she must act as if she still believed that Dolm was just an innocent, none too talented, actor. Holding her head high, she began to pick her way carefully down the stairs, holding the banister.

Then she saw that she had no need to act. Only Piol Poet and Golfren Piper had returned, and they were in no state to be an audience. Dull evening light struggled through high barred windows to show plank tables and the black iron range. The big kitchen was as bleak and cold as the streets outside. If there was no snow on the flagstone floor, Eleal could imagine it just by looking at Golfren Piper's face.

Wizened little Piol Poet knelt at the grate, trying to start a fire and producing nothing but smoke. He was the oldest of them all, but practical and helpful, a quiet soul who never said an unkind word. His wife had died years ago, so he was less intensely involved than the others in today's disaster.

Golfren Piper had perched on a stool and was gazing sickly at some empty, cobwebby shelves as if the end of the world had come and gone and left him behind. His pale blue eyes flicked round to look at Eleal, though. He raised eyebrows inquiringly. She nodded reassuringly. He forced a faint smile of approval and looked away again. She liked Golfren. He was slim and fair and would have been well suited to playing gods had he not been so wooden on stage that he resembled a tree with rheumatism. Piol wrote walk-on parts for him, but his main value to the troupe was as a musician and as Uthiam's husband.

Klip Trumpeter was probably still upstairs, giving himself a rubdown. Gartol Costumer had gone on ahead to Suss and would soon be wondering what had happened to everyone. That left three men unaccounted for, including Dolm Actor.

Eleal tried to muffle an immense sigh of relief. She dallied for a moment with the idea of racing back upstairs to rearrange

Dolm's pack better. Then she decided someone might come to investigate, and Dolm himself might still return any minute anyway—she could not be certain he had died.

She sat down on a chair and looked around, being calm as the Mother on the Rainbow Throne in *The Judgment of Apharos.*

"You feeling all right?" Golfren asked, frowning.

"Yes. Yes, quite all right. Er, where's everybody?"

He shrugged. "Don't know. Trong and K'linpor went to consult their brothers. Dolm and Trumpeter—"

"I'm here," Klip said, clattering down the stairs, rubbing his hair with a grubby towel. "What brothers?"

Golfren pulled a face. "Local lodge of the Tion Fellowship. Forget I mentioned it."

Klip glanced thoughtfully at Eleal and then asked, "Any news from the temple?"

Golfren shook his head mournfully.

Piol rose stiffly from the range, where faint flickers of light showed success. He scowled at his hands and took the towel from Klip to wipe them. The murderous silence was broken by thumping of boots on the stoop. The door creaked open, swirling snowflakes, sucking smoke from the range. Trong Impresario slunk in. His son followed, closing the door with an angry bang.

As always, Trong bore the haggard, tragic expression to be expected of a man who died two hundred times a year. Usually he walked tall, a rawboned giant with a mane of long silver locks and beard, striding through the world without deigning to notice it, his mind far away among divine wonders of poetry and fate. Tonight he shuffled across the room in silence and crumpled onto a chair like a wrecked wagon, gangling limbs awry. That was not the way he depicted sorrow on stage, but it was more evocative.

K'linpor Actor looked nothing like his father. He was round-faced and pudgy—a fair actor, except that his voice lacked power. K'linpor was also a surprisingly agile acrobat in the masques. He sat down by the table and laid his head on his arms in utter dejection. He would be thinking of Halma, of course.

Their marriage was even more recent than Golfren and Uthiam's.

"What news, sir?" Golfren inquired.

Trong shook his head without looking up. "None." His voice had lost its usual resonance. "It's just us, apparently. They have heard no word of the Lady banning others."

"Nothing they can do?"

"Pray. They will sacrifice a yak this evening on our behalf."

Silence fell. Eleal wondered who "they" were. Important, rich citizens, apparently, if they could afford to donate a yak. And was it to be sacrificed to the Lady, or to Tion?

Dolm Actor had offered a lot more than that to his chosen deity.

Trong roused himself with a sudden surge. The big man straightened and glared around in his god aspect.

"We have a free night before us. It is a fortuitous opportunity to rehearse the *Varilian*. The child can stand in for Uthiam—"

K'linpor raised his face slightly. "Father, you are talking *dung.*" He laid his head back on his arms.

Trong looked shocked, then slowly melted back to his former desolated posture and stared at the floor.

Men without women . . . The range was crackling cheerfully, gushing smoke. Eleal pulled herself away from awful thoughts of reapers. She stood up, marched across, and flicked a lever.

"It helps to open the flue first!"

Old Piol scratched at the silver stubble on his jowl. He smiled and started to say something; it became an attack of coughing.

Eyes stinging, Eleal moved away from the range. "We must eat," she said in her best goddess voice, because that was what Ambria would say. "I don't feel like it either," she told the disgusted expression all around, "but we should. The markets will close soon."

"She's right," Golfren said, rising. "You will be our keeper tonight, Eleal. I'll come with you."

"I'll get my coat . . ."

Boots thumped on the step outside. Heads turned.

The door flew open, swirling snow and smoke and cold air. Dolm Actor swept in with a basket on his arm. He slammed the door and glanced around with an inquiring grin.

Eleal looked down quickly at the greasy flagstones, unable to meet his eyes. Invoking Zath! Self-mutilation! Black gown in pack! *Reaper!* She scurried back to her seat by the table and hunched herself very small, trying to hide her shaking.

Dolm's resonant voice rang out, reverberating in the big room. "Well, you're a glum lot! Nobody thought about food, I suppose?"

K'linpor straightened up, soft face flushing. "Where have you been?"

There was a momentary silence. Eleal did not glance up, frightened that Dolm might be watching her.

"Me? I went back to the temple."

Golfren roared, *"What?"* and stepped backward, knocking over his stool with a crash.

"I didn't see any of our ladies there, if that's what's worrying you," Dolm said soothingly. He stepped to the table beside Eleal and laid his basket on it. He was so close that she could smell the wet leather of his coat.

"I did what we should have all done . . . except Klip Trumpeter maybe. Yet, why not him, too? He's a staunch young man now. I dropped some of my own hard-earned silver in the bowl, and I made sacrifice to the Lady."

Liar! Eleal thought. *Liar! Liar!*

Trong bellowed, *"No!"* in a voice that seemed to shake the house. His craggy features flamed red.

"Yes," Dolm said calmly. "I saw it as my duty. I chose the oldest, ugliest woman I could find. She was immensely grateful."

"That is utterly foul!" Golfren Piper yelled.

"It was a holy ritual! Do you criticize the goddess?"

Silence. Eleal stole a glance at Golfren. He was as red as Trong—redder even, because his face was fair-skinned and clean-shaven. His knuckles were white. She wondered if there was about to be a fight.

Yes, she thought, it was foul. She thought of Dolm's long, hairy limbs and body, and she shivered. Goddess or not, it was foul to make a woman submit to that against her will.

"Well?" Dolm Actor inquired.

Piper growled, "No."

"Wise! The woman in question had been assigned a penance. I did not ask for what, naturally." Dolm was always a cheerful, almost boisterous person, but now he sounded exuberant, excited. Eleal wondered if he had been drinking, but she could not smell wine on him, only the wet leather.

Dolm laughed. "She had been waiting there every day for two fortnights, she told me. Of course she was grateful! I trust the Lady approved. It wasn't my most enjoyable experience, I admit, but I did my duty in a spirit of proper humility, with prayer."

Golfren muttered an obscenity and turned his back.

"I find I cannot disapprove under the circumstances," Trong Impresario declaimed with obvious reluctance.

"Good!"

Eleal was still shaking, hoping no one would notice, too terrified to move, still staring at the disgustingly dirty floor. Dolm was lying! No matter how brief the remainder of his horrible ritual had been, there had not been time for him to recover and go to the temple and then visit the markets and come back here. He had not been running, or he would be puffing. Running? Lying with a woman? After losing so much blood? He had been soaked in blood while she watched, and more blood still pumping out of him.

"Furthermore," Dolm said, "we all . . ."

Alerted by the silence, Eleal glanced up.

He had sensed something wrong. He raised his head as if sniffing. He looked slowly around the big room, studying each face in turn. Finally he dropped his eyes to hers.

Then he smiled, and the recognition in his dark eyes was

obvious—fond reproof. *He knew!* He knew she knew. She was the one.

Slowly, agonizingly slowly, Dolm reached down with his left hand to scratch his right, which rested on the handle of the basket beside her. His sleeve slid back. She could see his bony, hairy wrist. There was no mark on it, no scar, no bandage . . . No bloodstains, even!

She looked up again at his face.

No blood on it, no blood in his hair—and the hair combed over his bald pate was lank, showing no sign that it had been recently washed.

He was still smiling, like a snow cat.

"This must have been a difficult day for you, child!" he said softly. "Are you feeling all right?"

She started to turn her head away and his hand shot out to grasp her chin. The touch of a reaper!

Eleal screamed and leaped away from him. She hurtled across the room and threw herself against Golfren Piper, hugging him fiercely. She needed Ambria, but he would have to do. Everyone seemed to shout, "What?" at the same moment.

Golfren put his arms around her and lifted her bodily, as if she were a child. He muttered soothing noises. "Yes, she's had a very hard day!" he said.

The door flew open with a crash and Ambria Impresario made an Entrance.

ᘓᕐᕐ 15 ᕐᓇᖅ

AMBRIA WAS AN IMPOSING WOMAN ON THE MOST TRIVIAL occasion. She could peel a tuber dramatically or ladle gruel with majesty. These days the heavy breasts sagged and the hair was dyed, but no more convincing goddess had ever trod the boards, and she blazed with authority in that kitchen doorway. Taller than most men, deep-voiced, big-boned, she had been known to silence a hall of drunken miners with a single gesture. Now one arm was extended shoulder high from hurling open the door; her hood was back, letting her dark hair flow to her waist, framing aquiline features normally pale, ashen in her present distress. The snow-mottled cloak hung to her boots, making her seem taller than ever.

"We are all here." Her voice rang through the vast room. "We are all unharmed, save a few bruises." She swung aside in a swirl of leather to let the others enter.

The men cried out in joy. Uthiam Piper ran in, heading for Golfren, who dropped Eleal instantly. She caught a brief glimpse of a livid welt on Uthiam's cheek before it was hidden in an embrace.

Yama Actor ran to Dolm; Halma to K'linpor. Olimmiar stepped inside last, holding a rag over one eye. She stopped beside Ambria and stood with face lowered. Trong rose, moved one foot forward a pace, and spread his arms in welcome.

Ambria swung the door halfway closed and halted it there. "Hold!" Her deep voice boomed like a thunderclap, silencing everyone. "There is no need for us all to repeat the sordid details. I shall tell the tale." Her compelling eyes raked the room in challenge. Everyone watched; no one spoke. The door remained half closed.

"We did as we were bidden." The spectacular voice dropped to a lower register. "We offered ourselves in the service of the Lady. A man came to each of us—"

"Three," Olimmiar said with a sob.

Ambria enveloped her in a powerful arm and pulled her close without looking down. "Each of us was accepted, then. Not one of the men was able to . . ." She drew a deep breath. " . . . complete the holy ritual. The goddess refused our sacrifice."

"You mean they were all *impotent?*" Dolm Actor barked.

Ambria slammed the door so the building shook. Everyone jumped. "Yes," she admitted. "The priests are deeply concerned, naturally. But none of you husbands need worry about, er, consequences."

"That's insane!" Dolm said, and suddenly laughed shrilly. Everyone glared at him, even Eleal. "And three tried with Olimmiar, one after the other?" His eyes flicked inquiringly to Uthiam.

"Two."

"So a total of eight—"

"We need not discuss sordid trivia," Ambria Impresario proclaimed. She strode majestically across the big chamber toward Trong, one hand extended, the other sweeping Olimmiar Dancer along beside her. "Some of the men became violent in their distress, but the priests stopped them before there was any serious damage. Now you know. The matter is closed." She stepped into her husband's embrace.

"No it's not!" Dolm was grinning and quite unabashed by her anger. Eleal had never seen any member of the troupe defy Ambria openly like that, but then Dolm had been bubbling like a kettle since he came in, and a reaper certainly need not fear an aging female actor.

Ambria whirled around in wrath. Olimmiar looked up in

astonishment, revealing a puffy swelling around her eye. K'linpor's mouth was hanging open.

"It's a miracle!" Dolm jeered. "A holy miracle! Of course we
must discuss it. Were they all old, fat factory owners?"

Ambria's ivory cheeks flamed scarlet in a way Eleal would
never have believed possible. "No they were not!" Echoes rang.
"In my case, as I remained unchosen, the priests went out and
found a twenty-year-old quarry worker who has already fa-
thered two children. Does that satisfy your prurient curiosity,
Dolm Actor?"

He sniggered. "Did it yours? Well, now what happens? Are
we free to depart from Narsh, as Ois has apparently no use for
us?"

The big woman seemed to shrink slightly. "No. We are summoned to the temple at dawn. The priests will seek an oracle
to discover the Lady's will."

Even Dolm Actor flinched.

There was a moment's silence, and then he said softly, "All
of us?"

"All of us."

Everyone turned to look at Eleal Singer.

When times were good, the troupe was one big happy family.
When times were otherwise, which was more frequent, it was
still one big family, and rarely too unhappy. Everyone was related to everyone else in some contorted fashion. Old Piol Poet
was the brother of Ambria's first husband and thus Uthiam's
uncle. Even Klip Trumpeter was a stepbrother of Gartol Costumer, who was Trong Impresario's cousin. Everyone was family except Eleal Singer. Although she could recall no trace of
her life before the troupe took her in, she was the outsider, the
waif, the stray.

Normally she never thought about that distinction. Certainly
nobody ever mentioned it, not even Olimmiar at her most catty.
That evening Eleal could smell it. She was the only one who
had not been to the temple of the Lady. She was the last hope.
All other efforts had failed, so in the morning they would take

her there and she would be unmasked as the cause of the trouble. It was obvious.

Perhaps Sister Ahn's lunatic babbling had been true, and the gods were staging some great cosmic tragedy that involved little Eleal Singer.

Wives clung to husbands. Olimmiar Dancer had attached herself to Halma, her sister. Old Piol fussed around, preparing a meal in tactful silence. Trumpeter soon went up to his room and came down muffled in llama fleece. He announced briefly that he was going out for a walk, and vanished rapidly through the door into a near-blizzard, followed by a puzzled frown from Ambria, a glare of outrage from Trong, and a sardonic smile from Dolm. Young Klip knew an opportunity when he was handed one.

He might be heading for a disappointment, though—he did not know that Dolm had been lying about going back to the temple.

Every time Eleal risked a glance in Dolm's direction, he was directing his sardonic smile at her. She wondered about her chances of living through the night. No one ever spoke of reapers; to denounce one was probably suicide. To denounce Dolm Actor would be an act of rank madness. The others would just assume that the stressful day had unhinged her mind—he was Ambria's cousin's husband, one of the family! The only evidence Eleal could hope to produce was that black garment hidden in his pack and she was certain that it would have gone elsewhere by now. Even if it could be produced, he could always claim that it was an old stage costume and then accuse her of having stolen something.

Maybe it *was* only an old costume, although she could not imagine any audience tolerating a play with a reaper in it. Maybe she had imagined the loathsome ritual. Maybe she had gone crazy.

As the evening dragged on in quiet confidential whispers, she realized that everyone was planning to head off to be alone very early. Actors were night birds by profession, but tonight wives wanted to be alone with husbands and husbands wanted to be alone with wives.

Larger and larger in her mind grew an image of her cubicle door, with its heavy lock and its thick iron bolt. Not even a reaper was going to break through those without waking everybody!

Then Dolm himself stretched his long arms overhead and yawned.

Eleal realized that she must leave before he did, or she might find him waiting for her in her room.

"G'night!" she snapped, jumping to her feet.

She scampered across the room to the stairs—*Clip, clop.*

"I'm very sleepy," she explained, racing up them two at a time.

Clip, clop . . . "See you in the morning," she shouted back as she tore along the corridor.

She dashed into her room—took a hurried glance around to make sure it was unoccupied—closed the door. It creaked loudly, but at the last minute she slowed it so it would not slam. She turned the key gently, wrestled the bolt over, and flopped down on the floor, panting as if she had run over Rilepass carrying a mammoth.

The window was barred. The walls were solid stone, the floor and ceiling thick planks. If anywhere was safe from a reaper, this was it. As an afterthought, she took the big key out and tucked it in her pack. She stuffed a sock into the keyhole.

Preparing for bed was never a lengthy process in chilly Narsh. She donned her woolly nightgown, rolled up her second-best dress to be a pillow, and laid her llama fleece coat on the pallet as a cover. Then she knelt and took hold of her amulet to say her prayers.

The amulet was a little golden frog that Ambria had given her a long time ago, as soon as she could be trusted not to swallow it. It looked like gold, but it left green stains on her chest. It seemed a very frail defense against the god of death, whom she had probably offended mightily by spying on his sacred ritual.

The wind rattled the casement hungrily. Her usual prayers seemed grievously inadequate this night. She extemporized a long addition, addressed to Kirb'l Tion, asking for his aid in letting the troupe travel to the Tion Festival in safety. Shivering with cold, then, she whispered an apology to the Man for spying on holy ceremony in his shrine. After all, the shrine itself had not been specifically dedicated to *Zath* . . . she could not speak that name.

At last she snuggled in under the heavy fleece. Cockerel with no liver, alpaca white outside and black inside, a reaper on a mammoth and another in the troupe, men stricken impotent by the Lady . . . She would not be able to sleep a wink!

But she did.

ᶓᶉᶈ 16 ᶇᶈᶏᶓ

NIGHTS IN HOSPITALS ARE MUCH LONGER THAN DAYS. EDward Exeter had discovered this truth during his first term at Fallow, when the unfamiliar diseases of England had made him a frequent patient in the san. He rediscovered it in Albert Memorial.

A nurse came around with a light, checking on people.

"Where am I?" he asked.

She told him.

"What happened?"

"You had an accident. Do you want another needle?"

"No. I'm all right." He did not like the silent music the drugs brought.

"Try to sleep," she said, and went away.

Trouble was, he seemed to have been sleeping for weeks. The shock was wearing off, he decided. His leg lashed him with a sickening beat of pain, he was stiff with staying in the same position so long. He kept trying to remember, and when he did remember, he didn't want to. His recollections were very patchy and most of them must be nightmares.

When he did sleep, he was tormented by those same nightmares. He would wake up in a state of shivering funk, soaked with sweat and remember nothing of what had so frightened him. For the first time he began to wonder what on earth he had done to himself. Not playing rugby at this time of year. Train accident? There was a bandage around his head and his leg was in splints.

Yet the strangest dream that came in that endless night was amazingly sharp and memorable, so that in the morning he was to wonder whether it had really been a dream at all.

Light was shining in the door, and the room was a mass of confusing shadows. This time he seemed to have just wakened naturally, not frightened. His leg throbbed with a regular pulse that seemed to go all the way through him. He studied the ropes holding it up and then turned his head on the pillow. There was a window there with no curtains, and the sky outside was black. He rolled his head over to the other side to look up at the man standing there.

"Behold the limpid orbs," the man said, "reflecting the sense within, the very turning of the soul. Prithee, then, this maiming of thy shin, it does not pain thee o'ermuch?"

Edward said, "It's not too bad, sir." It wasn't, really.

"To dissemble thus becomes thee more than honesty."

The visitor was an odd little man—quite old, with a fuzz of silver curls and a wrinkled, puckish face, clean-shaven. He was stooped, so his face stuck out in front of him. His overcoat had a very old-fashioned Astrakhan collar and seemed slightly too large for him. He was holding an equally antique beaver hat in one hand and a walking stick with a silver handle in the other.

"We have not come into acquaintance beforetimes although ink in veritable tides has flowed between us. I am your worship's servant, Jonathan Oldcastle." He bowed, clutching the topper to his heart.

"Mr. Oldcastle!" Edward said. "You're . . . You're not what I expected, sir." In the way of dreams, Mr. Oldcastle's appearance seemed perfectly acceptable for an officer in His Majesty's Colonial Office. Yet none of the letters he had written to Edward in the past two years had read like Mosley Minor's atrocious efforts to extemporize Shakespeare.

The little man chuckled, beaming. "I fain perfect attainments beyond expectation. This council needs be consummated with dispatch. Pray you, Master Exeter, being curt and speedy in response, advise me what befell, what savage circumstance contrived this havoc upon thy person and thy fortunes. Discover to me the monument of thy memory that we may invent what absences the dickens may have wiped thereof."

He had a broad accent, which Edward could not place, and his speech would certainly have been unintelligible had this not all been a dream.

"I don't remember much, sir. I went . . . I went to the Grange, sir, didn't I? To stay with Bagpipe."

Mr. Oldcastle nodded. "I so surmise."

"Just for a few days. They said they didn't mind, and I was welcome. I'm planning to enlist as soon as mobilization starts of course, but until then . . ."

There hadn't been anywhere else to go. Words caught in his throat and he was afraid he was going to start piping his eye.

"Comfort thyself!" Oldcastle said soothingly. "I think someone approaches. Tarry a moment."

Edward must have drifted off to sleep again, because he jumped when Oldcastle said, "Now, my stalwart? What else lurks in thy recollection?"

"Dinner? I didn't have any proper togs. It's all very vague, sir."

Mr. Oldcastle breathed on the silver head of his cane and wiped it on his sleeve. "And after that?"

"We turned in. The general was going to be reading the lesson in church next morning."

"Yes?"

A curious smell of mothballs was overpowering even the ever-present stink of carbolic.

"Then Bagpipe came and said did I feel like some tuck, and why didn't we raid the larder."

"And you did. And what then befell?"

Screaming? Long curly hair? Porcelain sink. . . .

"Nothing!" Edward said quickly. "Nothing! I can't remember."

"Be not vexed," Mr. Oldcastle said, matter-of-factly. "Oftentimes a wounding of the head will ruptures cause upon the spirit withall. Thou cannot fare hence upon the morrow, good young coz. Dost peradventure know by rote the speech of bold King Harry before Harfleur?"

" 'Once more into the breach,' you mean, sir?"

"The same."

"I should. I played the king when Sixth Form did *Henry V* last Christmas."

"Be it that, then. No bardic fancy ever better nailed the spirit of a man. Now mark me well. Here are you well cosseted and I shall set a palliation about thee, but if thy foes evade my artifice and so distrain thee, do thou declaim that particular poesy. Wilt keep this admonition in thy heart?"

"Yes, sir, I'll remember," Edward said solemnly. In the way of dreams, the instructions seemed very important and logical.

"I wish thee good fortune, Master Exeter."

"Goodnight, Mr. Oldcastle. I'm very pleased to have met you at last, sir."

He slept better after that.

17

A CLICK FROM THE BOLT WAKENED ELEAL. THE LOCK turned, making much less noise than it had for her. In utter darkness, all she could see was the window, a lopsided patch of not-quite light, distorted by clinging snow. Yet somehow there was enough light for her to know how the door swung open, with not a hint of its usual squeak.

He glided in, blacker than black, making no sound. The door closed, equally silent. Moving like smoke, he approached. He stopped at her feet and she supposed he was looking down at her, but she could see no face, no eyes, only a pillar of darker dark.

All she could hear was her heart.

"You saw." It was a whisper, but even a whisper had resonance when it came from Dolm Actor.

The words were not a question and she was incapable of answering anyway.

"Normally that would seal your fate in itself," said the whisper.

Normally? Was there a shimmer of hope there? Would she die of terror before she found out?

Obviously he knew she was awake. "You are an incredible little snoop. I always wondered if you would ransack my pack one day. I would have known, of course. It is given to us to know when we are detected. Then I should have had to send your soul to my master. I hoped it would not be like that, Eleal

Singer. We do have feelings, you know. We are not monsters. We mourn the necessity."

Pause.

Not quite a chuckle . . . yet when the deadly soft voice spoke again, it held a hint of amusement. "I thought I was the problem, you see. I thought it was my master's print on my heart that had displeased the Lady. Yes, my master is he whom you call Zath—the Unconquerable, the Last Victor. I reported to my master, as you saw, seeking guidance. I was told that it is you who are the problem, not me."

She wanted to scream, *Why me?* and her mouth was as dry as ashes. Her nails were digging into her palms and her insides were melting to jelly. Her teeth continued to chatter.

"The *Filoby Testament* . . . but you will not have heard of that. Never mind. The gods have decreed, Eleal Singer, that you shall not journey to Sussland. That is all. Your presence there might change the world. I was instructed to ensure it does not happen."

She thought of the priest and Sister Ahn. She could not even scream.

The reaper sighed. "Please believe, the necessity distressed me. I am not evil. I am not vindictive. I honor my master with the gift of souls—that is all. True, he grants me great rapture when I perform this service, but I would rather offer strangers, really I would."

Dolm, who was always so jovial . . .

The reaper moved. Without exactly seeing, she knew that he had knelt down at her side—within reach.

She could not hear him breathing. Did he breathe when he was being a reaper?

"But here tonight I learned that it will not be necessary. Holy Ois knows who you are and how to stop you. She has the matter in hand. I was told I need not meddle within her domain. In the morning she will do what she wills, whatever that may be. You will not be journeying to Sussland."

That did sound like Eleal Singer was not going to die now.

The morning could look after itself.

"Is there anyone you wish to die?" the reaper inquired softly.

Eleal's teeth chattered.

"Well?" he asked. "Answer!"

She stuttered, "N-n-no!"

"Pity. Because if you wish to see someone die, Eleal Singer, then you need only tell that person that I am a reaper. I shall know, and they will die. Is that clear?"

She nodded in the dark, and knew he knew that.

"If by any chance Holy Ois does allow you to go to Suss, then of course I shall have to act." Dolm sighed, and floated erect again. "And I must go and act now. Act? Actor?" He chuckled drily, as Dolm did when he was about to make a joke. "Ironic, is it not? That rare performance you saw had but one spectator, yet she does not have to pay. Others must pay, strangers must pay. An expensive performance! He will want two at least, perhaps three if they are not young. Sleep well, little spy."

The blackness drifted toward the door. Then it stopped.

"I only came," said a whisper more definitely in Dolm's usual offhand tone, "because I thought your remarkable curiosity had earned an explanation."

The door opened, closed. The bolt slid. The lock shut.

Eleal drew great sobbing breaths of icy air. She was going to live through the night. Compared to that, nothing else mattered, not even her wet bed.

✒❧ 18 ❧✒

PATIENTS WERE WAKENED AT SIX O'CLOCK SO THEY COULD be washed and fed and have their beds made before the doctors' rounds. Shaving in bed was bad enough, but other things were worse. Bedpans were the utter end.

The nurse wanted to give Edward another needle, but he refused it, preferring to put up with the pain, rather than have porridge for brains.

She was quite pretty, in a chubby sort of way, with a Home Counties accent and a brusque manner. She would tell him nothing except he'd had an accident and Doctor Stanford would explain. His dream kept coming back to him and the memories he'd had in his dream—he could remember remembering them, sort of. Bagpipe was in there somewhere.

He was in hospital, in Greyfriars. He still could remember almost nothing after those awful images of dinner and him with no evening dress. After dinner . . . nothing, just fog. And nightmares.

He was worried about Bagpipe. He asked about him, Timothy Bodgley.

"No one by that name in the hospital," the nurse said, and then just kept repeating that Doctor Stanford would explain. She wouldn't even say how she was so certain that there was no one by that name in the hospital when she had not even gone to check. She did admit that this was Monday, and visiting hours were from two till four. "You've got a fine collection of stitches under that bandage," she added, changing the subject clumsily, "but your hair should hide most of the scar."

"You mean it won't spoil my striking good looks?" he asked facetiously, and was shaken when she blushed.

He surprised himself by eating the greasy ham and eggs he was given for breakfast. The tea was cold, but he drank it. He had a private room, and that worried him. He had a broken leg—a badly broken leg—and that worried him even more. He could not enlist with a broken leg, so he might be going to miss the war. Everyone agreed it would be over by Christmas.

He asked for a newspaper to find out what was happening in the crisis, and the nurse said that was up to the doctor.

He was left alone for a long time, then. Eventually a desiccated, graying man in a white coat marched in holding a clipboard. He had a stethoscope protruding from one pocket. Right behind him came Matron, armored in starch, statuesque as Michelangelo's *Moses.*

"Doctor Stanford, Mr. Exeter," she said.

"How are we this morning?" The doctor looked up from the clipboard with an appraising glance.

"Not bad, sir. Worried."

The doctor frowned. "What's this about you refusing a needle?"

"It doesn't hurt too much, sir," Edward lied.

"Oh, doesn't it? You can overdo the stiff-upper-lip business, young fellah. Still, I'll leave it up to you."

A few questions established that the only real problem was the leg. The many-colored patches Edward had discovered on his hips and arms were dismissed brusquely. Eyes and ears, fingertips on his wrist and a beastly cold stethoscope on his chest . . .

The doctor changed the bandage on Edward's head. "Eighteen stitches," he said admiringly. "Most of the scar won't show unless you want to try a Prussian haircut." He scribbled on the clipboard and handed it to Matron. "Get the blanks filled in now he's conscious, will you?"

He stuffed his hands in the pocket of his white coat. "You have a badly broken leg, Exeter, as I'm sure you know by now.

In a day or two we'll take off the splints and see if we can put it in a cast. Depends on the swelling, and so on. We may have to load you in an ambulance and take you to have it x-rayed, but we hope that won't be necessary. You're a healthy young chap; it should heal with no permanent damage. In a year you'll have forgotten all about it. For the time being, though, you have to endure the traction."

"How soon can I enlist?"

Stanford shrugged. "Three months."

"May I see a paper?"

"If you take it in small doses. Don't persist if you get a headache. Anything else you need?"

"I'd like to know how I got here."

"Ah! How much can you remember?"

"Very little, sir. Greyfriars Grange? Bagp . . . Timothy?"

The look in the doctor's eye told him before the man said it. "He wasn't as lucky as you."

The ham and eggs rose and then subsided. Edward swallowed hard a few times and then said, "How?"

"He was murdered."

"Murdered? Who by?"

"Don't know yet. Do you feel up to answering some questions for the police?"

"I'll try. I don't remember very—"

In strode a large, heavyset man. He must have been waiting by the door. He was dressed like a banker, but he had *Roberto* written all over him, and the look of a man who might have been a first-rate rugby fullback. Getting a ball past him would be like swimming up Victoria Falls, even now, with a staunch bow window stretching the links of his watch chain. His mustache spread out like the horns on a Cape buffalo, turning up in points at the end.

"Five minutes, no more," the doctor said.

The policeman nodded without a glance at him. The doctor departed. Matron followed him to the door, but in a way that suggested she was not going far.

"Inspector Leatherdale, Mr. Exeter." He pulled up the chair.

"I am not asking for a formal statement. You do not need to tell me anything, but I would appreciate hearing what you can recall of the events which led to your injuries."

Edward told what he could, mostly while studying the way the inspector's hair was combed over his bald spot. His memories were so patchy that he thought he must sound like an absolute ass.

"That's the lot, sir. Er . . ."

"Take your time. Even vague impressions may be helpful to us."

"Crumpets? Crumpets and strawberry jam on a deal table."

"Why crumpets at your age? Why not raid the sherry?"

Edward started to smile and then remembered Bagpipe. "We tried that three years ago and were sick as dogs. It was a tradition, that's all." Never again, Bagpipe!

"Anything else you recall?"

"A woman with long curly hair?"

The rozzer's face was as unmoving as a gargoyle's. "What color hair?"

"Dark brown, I think. It hung in ringlets, sort of a Gypsy look. Very pale face."

"Where did you see her? What was she doing?"

Edward shook his head on the pillow. "Screaming, I think. Or shouting."

"What was she wearing?"

"Don't remember, sir."

"But this might have been hours earlier, and you don't know where?"

"Yes. No. Yes it might have been and no I don't know why I remember her."

"What more?"

"A . . . A porcelain sink turning red, scarlet. Blood running into a sink. A *stream* of blood." He felt a rush of nausea and bit his lip. He was shaking—lying flat on his back and shaking like a stupid kid!

Leatherdale studied him for a minute, and then rose. "Thank

you. We shall require a formal statement as soon as you are up to it."

"Bodgley's dead?"

The massive head nodded. "You fell down some steps. He was stabbed."

"And you think I did it?"

Inspector Leatherdale went very still, and yet seemed to fill the room with menace. "Why should I think that, Mr. Exeter?" he asked softly.

"Private room, sir. You said I didn't need to tell you anything. Nobody would answer my questions."

The man smiled with his mouth but not with his eyes. "No other reason?"

"I didn't!" Edward yelled.

"Five minutes are up, sir," Matron said, sailing in like a dreadnought, clipboard ready and fountain pen poised. "Your full name and date of birth, Mr. Exeter?"

"Edward George Exeter . . ."

The inspector moved the chair back to where it had been without taking his eyes off Edward.

"C. of E.?" Matron said, writing busily.

"Agnostic."

She looked up with a Medusa stare of disapproval. "Shall I just put, 'Protestant'?"

Edward was certainly not going to support any organization that tolerated Holy Roly as one of its advocates. The Nyagatha horrors had been provoked by meddling, addle-headed missionaries, and that was another reason.

"No, ma'am. Agnostic."

She wrote unwillingly. "Diseases?"

He listed what he could recall—malaria and dysentery in Africa, and all the usual English ones he'd caught when he came Home: mumps, measles, whooping cough, chicken pox.

Then he saw that the policeman was still standing in the doorway, watching him.

"You want to ask me some more questions, Inspector?"

"No. Not now. We'll take a statement later, sir." His mouth smiled again. "Normally I would ask you to keep yourself available, but I don't expect you'll be going anywhere for a day or two."

ᔷᔩ 19 ᔦᔩᔨ

A BLEAK DAWN WAS BREAKING, BUT EVEN THE BEGGARS were still asleep, huddled in doorways and corners under their dusting of snow. Somewhere back in the temple precincts doomed cockerels screamed defiance at the coming day. The troupe had assembled as instructed, and they were the day's first business for the temple.

Inside the long hall, night had not yet ended. Even the many candles glittering upon the altar before Ois could not brighten that big, cold place. Off to the sides, in the shadows, a few fainter glows showed where lamps burned under some of the innumerable arches. Those few bright alcoves amid so much dark somehow reminded Eleal of Sister Ahn's scattered teeth.

Shivering with cold and apprehension, she knelt between Trong and Ambria, seeking comfort from their huge solidity—although even Ambria seemed cowed today. The floor was cold and hard on the knees. They knelt in a circle, all of them except the missing Gartol Costumer; twelve counting Eleal. She had been placed with her back to the door, facing almost straight at the goddess. She clutched a gold coin, the first real gold she had ever held. The cold of the floor was seeping into her bones.

In the center of the circle stood a silver bowl, containing a feather, two eggs, and a white pebble. The priests had placed them there with great ceremony to begin the ritual.

The image of the Lady was the largest Eleal had ever seen, but it was a picture, not a statue. It filled the end wall, the full height of the temple, crafted from shiny white tiles, but her nipples gleamed scarlet, like rubies. Darker tones shadowed her belly and the undersides of her great breasts; her face was barely visible in the high darkness. At her feet an old man warbled holy writ in continuous monotone. In time he would be relieved by another, and another, until the entire Red Scripture had been pronounced. Then they would begin at the beginning again. So it had always been. He was not always audible, but he never stopped.

A half dozen or so priests had chanted a service to the Lady. Now a drummer began a low, menacing rhythm while a new group executed a strange, posturing dance. They were all young, obviously, and their shaven heads showed that they were priests, despite their curious close-fitting garments, which left arms and shins bare. In the candlelight the cloth seemed almost black, but it was red, in honor of the Lady. Eleal was fascinated by their ritual, very measured and deliberate, more like stylized gymnastics than any dance she had ever seen.

One of the illuminated alcoves blinked in the corner of her eye. Then a second. She leaned back slightly to see. A man was walking along the wall, followed by a priestess. He obscured another lamp, and stopped. A woman rose beyond him, apparently from a seat inside the alcove. She opened her robe. He walked on and she sat down again—unwanted, rejected. Eleal shuddered, tasting a sourness rising in her throat. Ambria hissed angrily and she turned her face back to the ceremony.

In a moment, though, the man progressed to where she could see him without moving her head. Her eyes insisted on straying in his direction. She watched how he found a woman he fancied and paid the priestess. The priestess walked away, he entered the alcove and began to undress.

The acrobatics ended in a flurry of drum strokes. Again Eleal returned her attention to where it belonged. A priest approached and gestured; the actors scrambled to their feet. There was a pause. She felt even smaller now, standing between tall Ambria and taller Trong. She studied the goddess to keep her mind off what was happening in that alcove. The Lady was emerging from darkness as daylight began to seep in through the high windows. The stone face bore a curious expression, eyes almost closed, scarlet lips parted, a hint of tongue showing. It was not a merciful face. It gave no clue why a mighty goddess should be so wroth at little Eleal Singer.

Drums thundered, making her jump. They sank into an irregular, disturbing beat.

"State your age first . . . ."

A priest and a priestess had entered the circle and placed themselves in front of Golfren. The voice, however, came from outside, from an older man standing behind him, muttering instructions. Then Golfren spoke, his voice higher-pitched than usual:

"I am twenty-six years old, my name is Golfren Piper. I am married and childless. I revere the Lady and beseech her to have mercy upon me." A coin clinked.

The priest behind the little priestess put a hand on her shoulder and guided her along to stand before the next supplicant.

"I am twenty years old, my name is K'linpor Actor. I am married and childless. I revere the Lady and beseech her to have mercy upon me." Another clink.

Eleal caught a glimpse of the older priest, the one on the outside. His red robe was sumptuously embroidered and begemmed, it bulged over his belly. He carried a lit taper in a soft, plump hand, light gleaming like wax on his shaven head and doughy jowls, sparkling on his jeweled fingers.

The priestess was very young, little more than a child, yet her head, too, was shaven. A cord around her neck supported a golden vase, dangling between her small breasts. She was barefoot, seemingly wearing only her robe—and that was so thin that the bumps of her nipples showed through it. She must be frozen.

The priest behind her was a large youth, one of the gymnasts, still breathing hard from his exertions. His hairy shins and forearms contrasted oddly with the shiny smoothness of his head and face.

"I am forty-five years old, my name is Ambria Impresario." Ambria's splendid voice was hoarse and uncertain this grim morning. "I am . . . I have been married twice, Father . . ."

The outside priest muttered questions, directions. The little priestess turned and began to walk away. The young priest grabbed her arm and pulled her back. When he released her, she stayed where she had been put, like a chair, but her hands and head twitched oddly.

Eleal clenched her fists against her thighs to stop them shaking. She was next after Ambria. She felt the gold coin sticky on her palm.

"I am forty-five years old, my name is Ambria Impresario. I am widowed and remarried and have borne one child. I revere the Lady and beseech her to have mercy upon me."

Suddenly the priestess started to laugh. The young priest behind her grabbed her shoulders and shook her until she stopped. Then he pulled her along to stand in front of Eleal. Her eyes were vacant, her jaw slack. Drool shone on her chin and darkened the bodice of her robe.

The priest outside the circle had arrived also. Eleal sensed him at her back and caught a whiff of a scent like lilac.

An actor must not falter over such simple lines: "I am twelve years old," she said clearly, "my name is Eleal Singer. I am unmar—"

"If you are a virgin, then you must specify."

Her teeth chattered briefly. She swallowed. "I am twelve years old, my name—"

A thunderstorm rumble from Trong drowned her out. "Her true name is not Singer but Impresario. She is my granddaughter."

Eleal cried, *"What?"* very shrilly. The sound seemed to soar like a bat up into the dark recesses of the roof. The drums rumbled.

The priest made an irritated sound. "Explain. Quickly!"

"I had a daughter," Trong growled, staring fixedly up at the goddess. "She shamed herself, and then died. I have reared the bastard in obedience to holy scripture. Her name is Eleal Impresario."

His face was hidden from Eleal's vantage by his silver mane. She looked up at Ambria in disbelief. Ambria nodded, smiling sadly.

Again the idiot priestess started to laugh. Her husky keeper shook her, but she continued. He shook her harder—viciously, like a floor mat, her head lolling back and forth, the gold vase thumping to and fro on its cord. He finally managed to stop the fit, but he retained a hold on her after that.

The older priest was sounding annoyed at the interruptions to his ritual, but was obviously determined to proceed in proper form. "Name her by the father's trade."

"I don't know it!" Trong growled, sounding as if this disclosure was hurting him badly. He was so upright himself, it was hard to imagine him having raised a wanton child.

"Your daughter would not name the man?"

"She could not! She disappeared for a fortnight. When we found her, her wits had gone and the damage was done. She never spoke a rational word after."

The priest grunted. "Use the Impresario name."

Eleal was one of the family! But joy was debased by a surge of anger. Why had they never told her so? Why had Ambria once threatened to throw her out as a stray?

"Make your appeal!" the priest snapped.

Eleal pulled her wits together and spoke the words rapidly. "I am twelve years old, my name is Eleal Impresario. I am a virgin. I revere the Lady and beseech her to have mercy upon me." She dropped her coin in the vase and was surprised to hear it plop into liquid.

The moronic priestess sniggered, her eyes moving vaguely and somehow wrongly. Her muscular attendant looked seriously worried now. She hung limp as a towel in his grip. He moved to dangle her in front of Trong. The drumbeat was growing faster, urgent.

Eleal Impresario? That did not sound right! She would continue to call herself Eleal Singer. After all, her singing brought her wages—token wages, perhaps, but real copper money. Trong Impresario's granddaughter! Why had he never told her? It wasn't her fault her mother had been wicked! What of her mother? What had she been called? Had she been an actor? Beautiful? Ugly? How old when she died? How had she died?

Eleal glanced around at the others, wondering if any of them had known this secret. Surely K'linpor must have! He was avoiding her eye, watching the priest and priestess working their way around the circle. *Uncle* K'linpor!

"I am sixty-five years old, my name is Piol Poet . . ."

The whole temple was emerging from night now as the high windows began to shine. Luridly tinted carvings covered every surface. Walls and pillars were mantled in gods and flowers of painted stone, the floor was bright mosaic, dominated by the Ø symbol of the Lady. Reds and greens, ivory and gold leaf . . . Eleal had never guessed there could be so much riotous color in drab Narsh. Perhaps all the color in Narshvale had flowed into this holy place.

A flicker of movement caught her eye. The solitary male worshiper had emerged from the alcove and was heading for the door, his sacrifice completed. The woman appeared also, fastening her robe, hurrying after him. Was she heading home to husband and family, and had she been performing a penance or merely offering sacrifice to win the Lady's favor?

"I am thirty-three years old, my name is Dolm Actor . . ." The reaper contributed his coin, then flashed a triumphant smile across at Eleal. How many souls had he gathered to Zath since leaving her room?

Eleal looked away quickly, and watched a line of red-robed priestesses filing in from some unknown doorway. Each took up station in an alcove. Early-rising worshipers were appearing also, peering curiously at the ceremony in progress.

The drums thundered and stopped. At the Lady's feet, the hoarse recitation became audible again. Supporting the priestess's deadweight, the young priest lowered her until she was sitting on the floor. He knelt at her side. Steadying her with one brawny arm, he lifted the vase to her lips.

"Join hands!" commanded the fat man. Eleal's hands were grabbed by Ambria and Trong. The drums started again. The young priest forced the girl's head back and tilted the vase— enough for her to drink, not enough to spill the coins. Scarlet fluid dribbled over both of them, but she coughed and choked, apparently taking some of it in her mouth. Satisfied, he lifted the loop over her head and passed the vessel out to a waiting hand. Then he dragged her to the center of the circle and left her there, lying like a corpse alongside the silver bowl. He stood back and watched intently.

Many more priests and priestesses had surrounded the troupe. They began to chant—softly at first, rapidly growing louder. Blurred by their own echoes, the words were an archaic form of classic Joalian. Eleal gathered only that they praised the Lady and beseeched her to vouchsafe guidance. The beat was capricious, unsettling. Her heart thumped painfully.

The little priestess had begun to twitch. The singing surged higher. She screamed. She beat her fists on the floor. Louder and faster went the drums. She thrashed as if in pain, yet her face was flushed. The silver bowl went clattering across the floor, splashing eggs. She paused, lifted her head, and looked around the circle that confined her, madness in every move, every twist of her face. Her hands clawed at her robe and ripped it off, revealing a willowy, wasted body, flushed and sweating.

Without warning she was on her feet, lurching at Eleal, hands clawing for her, eyes burning with hatred. Eleal tried to leap back; Trong and Ambria staggered but did not release her. The priest caught the maniac just in time and tried to haul her back to the center, but she fought him in frenzy, screaming and frothing. Amazingly, it became a real fight. The priest was as tall as Trong, young and husky; she was a scrawny stripling half his size with limbs like spade handles, but in moments she had bitten and mauled him, shredded his robe and opened bloody tracks on his face with her nails. Twice she almost broke free altogether, heading for Eleal, twice he caught her in time. He was trying to restrain her without doing hurt; she had no such scruples. They fell to the floor and struggled more there. The drums and singing echoed deafeningly.

In another bewildering change, she cried out and went rigid, head back, limbs spread, sprawling over her opponent. The man threw her off and backed away on hands and knees, bleeding and gasping as if he had been wrestling bear cats.

Her eyes flicked open. *"Athu!"* she roared, in a voice as deep and resonant as Trong's—an impossible voice for that child-sized body. The drumming and singing stopped instantly. *"Athu impo'el ignif!"*

It was the voice of the oracle. Outside the circle, priests began scribbling on parchment as the words of the goddess reverberated through the temple. Again the dialect was too archaic for Eleal to follow. She thought she heard her name a few times, but then she thought she heard several names she knew, and probably none of them was intended. The priests seemed to make sense of the torrent, though, for their pens moved rapidly.

It died away into animal gurgles and stopped. A drum tapped. The singing resumed, a triumphant paean of thanks and praise.

Red-robed priestesses pushed in to attend the unconscious oracle. The circle fell apart. Wives and husbands embraced in relief at the end of the ordeal. Trong released Eleal's hand. Ambria hauled her close and hugged her fiercely. In a moment she felt wetness. Bewildered, she looked up and realized that the big woman was weeping.

20

IT WAS OBVIOUS WHY THE TEMPLE RARELY ASKED THE LADY for an oracle. The little priestess had been carried off, wrapped in a blanket. Her burly guardian had limped out, clutching a rag to his bleeding face and leaning on a friend. A young boy had brought a bucket and knelt to wash stains from the floor.

The richly adorned priest with the big belly was chuckling as he pawed over a group of parchments, discussing them with other elderly priests and priestesses. They all seemed pleased.

The troupe stood apart, huddled together, waiting to hear what the goddess had decreed. Eleal clung tight to Ambria's big hand and tried not to see Dolm Actor's patronizing sneer.

Then the fat priest waddled over to them, still clutching the records. "The Lady has been most generous!" he boomed. "I have never seen clearer, more explicit directions."

There was a worried pause. "Tell us!" Ambria said.

"Just the two of them, I think." He checked one page against another. "Yes, just two. The one named Uthiam Piper?"

Uthiam whimpered. Golfren's arm tightened around her.

"Three fortnights' service, it would seem," said the fat man. He shrugged his pillowed shoulders. "Not as severe a penance as I would have expected, really."

Uthiam's cheeks were ashen. She raised her chin defiantly. "I have to whore here for forty-two days?"

Shocked, the priest raised his shaven brows. "Sacrifice!"

"For what?"

"For your sins and your friends' sins, naturally. They are free to go—except one, of course. One remains. I am sure you made out that much. It is a small price to win so much favor and forgiveness, for yourself and your loved ones. Many women learn to enjoy it." He leered slyly.

He had eyes like a pig's.

Little Piol Piper cleared his throat. "I thought—" He stopped. He was the scholar. If any of the laity had understood those ancient words, it would be Piol.

"You thought what?"

The old man clawed at his silvery, stubbly beard. "I thought an alternative was offered?"

The priest nodded, his dewlaps flapping. "But not a reasonable alternative for a band of wandering players, I am sure."

"How much?" Golfren yelped. His fair-skinned face was paler than any.

The fat man sighed. "One hundred Joalian stars."

"Ninety-four, you mean! You know we have that much!"

The priest pursed his thick lips sadly. "You cannot bargain with a goddess, actor."

"But I was to give that money to Tion that he might favor my wife in the festival."

"Your wife will not be attending the festival this year. She will be serving the goddess, here in the temple. The mammoth herders who risk their lives daily in the pass will certainly not be rash enough to offend Holy Ois." His fat smirk left no doubt that the men would be advised of the danger.

Golfren looked close to tears. "That gold was my father's farm and his father's before him! And we only have ninety-four."

Everyone looked at Ambria, Uthiam's mother.

Her hand in Eleal's was sweating. Her voice was hoarse: "If we make up the difference, Holy One, it will leave us penniless. The fare to Suss is reputedly higher this year than it has ever been. We are poor artists, Father! Our expenses are heavy. The festival is our only hope of recouping our fortunes so that we may eat next winter. Will the Lady ruin us?"

The priest's eyes narrowed inside their bulwarks of lard, appraising her. "If you travel with the Lady's blessing," he said reluctantly, "I believe the temple could arrange passage for you." It was indeed possible to bargain.

"Today! The festival begins tomorrow. We must travel today!" Hints of the old Ambria were emerging.

"One hundred stars and you go today," the priest agreed.

Ambria sighed her relief. "And the other one?"

"Mm?" He chuckled and consulted the parchments again, comparing them. "Oh, yes. Eleal Singer . . . or Eleal Impresario . . . the goddess called her something else . . . No matter. She must remain. Must enter the service of Great Ois."

Somehow Eleal had expected this. She shivered. She felt Ambria's hand tighten on hers.

"There is no ransom for her?" Piol demanded.

The fat man scowled. "Ransom? Watch your tongue, actor!" He looked around suspiciously. "Are you offering one?"

"You have taken every copper mite we possess!" Ambria shouted.

"Ah!" He shook his head sadly and consulted the scripts again. "In any case, we are given no choice in her case." He glanced at Trong, who was projecting utter despair. "The, er, misadventure occurred in Jurg?"

"Yes," the big man muttered, showing no surprise.

"Of course!" The priest chuckled, shaking his head in mock disapproval. "Mighty Ken'th again! But the Lady is a jealous goddess! She demands the child." He glanced around the group. "Come, you are being let off lightly! A hundred stars and the girl."

Eleal also looked around. No one would meet her eye except Dolm Actor, who wore a distinctly I-told-you-so sneer.

"She will be well cared for," the priest said. "Trained in the Lady's service. It will be an easier, more rewarding life than you can offer her." He waited, and no one replied. "In a couple of years . . . But you know that."

Getting no response, he beckoned with his fat soft fingers,

summoning a woman almost as large as himself. "Take this one and guard her closely. Farewells would be inappropriate," he added.

Ambria released Eleal's hand.

21

INSPECTOR LEATHERDALE HAD LEFT A MAN OUTSIDE THE door, as Edward soon realized. Conversations came along the hallway, stopped while they should have been going by, and then resumed again in the distance. Beds and carts slowed and squeaked as they were navigated around the obstacle. Perhaps the jailer had been there all the time, but he was one more indication that Edward was a murder suspect. As the guard could hardly be intended to prevent the criminal escaping, he must be hoping to eavesdrop on conversations. There was no other conceivable reason to waste a policeman's day, was there?

The room was depressingly square. The walls were brown up to about shoulder height, where there was a frieze of brown tiles; above that the plaster was beige. Having nothing better to do, Edward catalogued his assets. Item, one brass bed with bedclothes, pillow, and overhead frame. Item, one chair, wicker-backed, hard. Item, one bedside cupboard in red mahogany. Item, one small chest of drawers to match . . . one bellpull just barely within reach . . . one iron bed table on wheels, with a flip-up mirror . . . one wicker wastepaper basket . . . . He had a jug of tepid water, a tumbler, an ashtray, and a kidney-shaped metal dish suitable for planting crocus bulbs. The cupboard contained a bedpan and a heavy glass bottle with a towel around it. Robinson Crusoe would have been ecstatic.

A distant church tower was the only thing visible outside. The window was open as wide as it would go, but no air seemed to be coming in—it couldn't be this hot outdoors, surely? What a summer this had been!

So he had left school at last and in little over a week become prime suspect in a friend's murder. He thought of Tiger, the school cat, and how he had liked to sit under the tree where the robins nested, waiting for the fledglings—two fledglings.

Poor old Bagpipe! He'd never had a fair shake with his wheezing. And now this. There'd have to be an inquest, of course. How would their classmates take the news? How many would believe Edward Exeter capable of such a crime? He decided they would judge by the evidence, just as he would. At least this was England and he would be tried by British Justice. It wasn't as if he must deal with Frenchies, who made you prove yourself innocent. British Justice was the best in the world, and it did not make mistakes.

At least, he did not think it did. Trouble was, he had no idea what the case against him might be. Could he possibly have gone insane, a sort of Doctor Exeter and Mr. Hyde? Was that why he couldn't remember? Lunatics were not hanged, they were shut up in Broadmoor and quite right, too! If he had a Hyde half who went around stabbing people, then his Exeter half would have to be locked up also.

The bobby had treated him with kid gloves, and that was a rum go. A mere witness would be quizzed much harder than that—especially a witness who couldn't remember anything. He was a minor and an invalid, and the policeman had been very careful and respectful so that he could not be accused of bullying. Edward could recall much worse wiggings from Flora-Dora Ferguson, the maths master. Leatherdale must be absolutely sure his case was watertight, so he was in no special hurry to hear what the suspect might testify.

At that point in his brooding, Edward heard a familiar voice raised in the corridor and thought, *No! Please no!* Visiting hours began at two o'clock and it couldn't possibly be even nine in the morning, and yet he knew that voice. He also knew its owner would not be blocked by any hospital rule in Greyfriars, nor by any matron, no matter how intimidating. Nor even by a uniformed constable from the sound of it.

"Gabriel Heyhoe, don't be absurd. You've known me all your life. I dried your eyes when you wet your pants at King Edward's coronation parade. If you want to prowl through this bouquet in search of hacksaws, then go ahead, but meanwhile stand aside."

Mrs. Bodgley swept into the room like Boadicea sacking Londinium. She was large and loud. She overawed, and yet normally she somehow combined a booming jollity with as much majesty as Queen Mary herself. She had been the star attraction at Speech Day for as long as Edward could remember and the boys of Fallow worshiped her.

Today she swung a familiar battered suitcase effortlessly in one hand, and she was dressed all in black from her shoes to her hat. A black glove threw back her veil.

"Edward, poor chap! How are you feeling?"

"Fine. Oh, Mrs. Bodgley, I am so sorry!"

Warning beacons flamed in her eyes, as a policeman loomed in the doorway behind her, his helmet almost touching the lintel. "What exactly do you mean by that statement, Edward?"

"I mean I'm sorry to hear the tragic news about Timothy, of course."

"That's what I thought you meant, but you must learn to guard your speech more carefully at present!" She towered above him, peering over her ample black bosom as Big Ben looks down on the Houses of Parliament. "The remark might have been construed as an apology. I brought your things. Your money I extracted and gave to Matron. I put the receipt for it in your wallet. And I brought this book for you. Here."

He stuttered thanks as she thrust the book at him. "But—"

"Timothy was enj . . . said it was the best book he had ever read, and I thought you would need something to pass the time. No, don't bother thanking me. I'm sure he would have wanted you to have it. And apart from that I had better not stay and chatter or Constable Heyhoe here will suspect me of perverting the course of justice. I want you to know that we—I mean I—do not for one moment believe that you had anything whatsoever to do with what happened and nothing will ever convince me otherwise. I for one know that there was a woman's voice in that cacophony, even if the general . . . but we must *not* discuss details of the case, Edward. Furthermore, I intend to see that you have the best legal advice available and if there is any need for money for your defense, should things come to that unhappy pass, then it will be forthcoming. I have already so instructed my solicitor, Mr. Babcock of Nutall, Nutall, & Shoe. So you are not to worry, and Doctor Stanford assures me that your leg can be expected to mend with no lasting ill effects."

He opened his mouth and she plunged ahead before he could say a word.

"Timothy always spoke very well of you, and the few times we have met I have been greatly impressed with you, Edward. I know that your housemaster and Dr. Gibbs rated you highly and I trust their judgment—most of the time and certainly in this. So do not fret. The whole terrible affair will be solved, I am quite sure. Now we must not say another word on the matter!"

With a grim smile, she swirled around and flowed out of the room, the policeman backing ahead of her. Edward looked down at the book he was holding, and it was a blur.

A nurse entered, bearing a vase of dahlias that had probably been growing in the grounds of Greyfriars Grange less than an hour ago. She lifted the suitcase from the floor onto the bed.

"If you want to go through this and take out whatever you need, sir, then I'll take it away. Matron does not approve of luggage lying around in rooms."

He muttered a response without looking. The book was *The Lost World*, by Sir Arthur Conan Doyle.

He opened it at random and a bookmark fell out.

ᕦᕤ22ᕥᕣ

TWO FLIGHTS UP, THE PRIESTESS WAS PUFFING AND LEAN-
ing a sweaty hand on Eleal's shoulder. They turned along another corridor smelling of incense and soap and stale cooking.
Eleal was too numb for fear or sorrow. Mostly she felt a sense
of loss: loss of her friends, her newfound family, loss of liberty,
loss of career, loss even of her pack, which had been refused
her. The distant chanting had died away into silence as if she
were sinking into the ground, away from the living world. She
reached an open door and was pushed inside.

The room was poky and plain, seemingly clean enough despite its musty smell. Bare stone formed the walls, bare boards
the floor and ceiling. It contained a fresh-looking pallet, a chair,
a little table, a copy of the Red Scriptures, nothing more. A
beam of sunlight angled in through a small window, seeming
only to emphasize the shadows. No lamp, no fireplace.

The priestess released her captive then and sank down gladly
on the chair, which creaked—the bulges of her sweat-patched
robe suggested a large body. She wiped a sleeve across her forehead. Her hair was hidden under her scarlet headcloth; her face
was saggy, padded with chins and rolls of fat, and yet Eleal
thought it was the hardest face she had ever seen.

"My name is Ylla. You address me as 'Mother.' "

Eleal said nothing.

Ylla's smile would have curdled milk. "Kneel down and kiss
my shoe."

Eleal backed away. "No!"

"Good!" The smile broadened. "We shall make that the test, then, shall we? When you are ready to obey—when you cannot take any more—tell me you are ready to kiss my shoe. Then we shall know that we have broken your spirit. We shall both know. You are entering upon a life of unquestioning obedience."

She waited for a reply. Not getting one, she narrowed her eyes. "We can try a whipping now if you want."

"What about Ken'th?"

Ylla laughed loudly, as if she had been waiting for the question. "Boys and old men pray to Ken'th. Men perform his sacrament willingly enough, but few would be seen dead near his temple!"

Few women went near his temple either, for Ken'th was god of virility. "Is he my father?"

"Perhaps. The goddess hinted at it. And it would fit with what your grandfather said. Women taken by a god aren't much use afterward."

That much Eleal knew from the old tales—Ken'th and Ismathon, Karzon and Harrjora. When the god withdrew his interest, the woman died of unrequited love. How strange that Piol Poet had never used either of those two great romances as the basis of a play! (She would never see a Piol play again.)

How strange to hear Trong described as her grandfather!

There was no hint of sympathy in the priestess's stony face. "But don't think that makes you special. A mortal's child is a mortal, nothing more."

Usually less, according to common belief. To call a man *godspawn* was about the worst insult possible. It implied he was a liar, a wastrel, and a bastard, and his mother had been as bad.

Eleal thought of Karzon's shrine and that powerful, potent bronze figure. Ken'th also was the Man. What if she prayed to Karzon? She did not even know her mother's name.

"If you are thinking of appealing to him," Ylla said contemptuously, "then save your breath. Gods sire bantlings like mortal men spit. I suggest you don't mention it. You are an acolyte in the service of Holy Ois, and older than most, so I must explain a few things."

She folded her plump hands in her lap. "We get many unwanted girls, usually much younger than you, but most of us are temple bred. My mother was a priestess here, and her mother before her. For eight generations we have served the Lady."

"And your father?"

"A worshiper." Ylla showed her teeth. "A hundred worshipers. Don't try to lord it over me for that, godspawn. In a year or two the Lady will bless you. You will be consecrated by priests, then, and thereafter you will serve her that same way. You will regard it as a great honor."

"No I won't!"

The fat priestess laughed, flesh rippling under her robe. "Oh, but you will! When properly instructed, you will be eager to begin. I am forty-five years old. I have borne eight children to her honor and I think I am about to bear another. You also, in your time."

They would have to chain her to the bed, Eleal thought. She would rather starve in a gutter. She said nothing, just stared at the floor.

"Why do you limp?"

"My right leg is shorter than the other."

"I can see that. Why? Were you born like that?"

"I fell out a window when I was a baby."

"Stupid of you. But it won't matter. It won't show when you're on your back, will it?"

Eleal gritted her teeth.

"I asked you a question, slut!"

"No it won't."

"Mother."

"Mother."

Ylla sighed. "You will begin your service by plucking chickens. By this time next year, you will be able to pluck chickens in your sleep. Scrubbing floors, washing clothes . . . good, honest labor to purify the soul. Normally we should start with your oath of obedience. However—"

She frowned. "However, in your case the Lady gave explicit instructions."

"What sort of instructions?"

"Mother."

"What sort of instructions, Mother?"

"That for the next fortnight you are to be kept under the strictest confinement. I don't know if we can even take you to the altar for the oath—I'll ask. And guards on the door!" The old hag looked both annoyed and puzzled by that.

"The *Filoby Testament!*"

Ylla stared. "What of it?"

Eleal had blurted out the name without thinking and wished she hadn't. "It mentions me."

The woman snorted disbelievingly. "And who told you that?"

"A reaper."

Ylla surged to her feet, astonishingly fast for her size. Her thick hand took Eleal in the face so hard she stumbled and fell prostrate on the pallet, her head ringing from the blow and a taste of blood in her mouth.

"For that you can fast a day," Ylla said, stamping out, slamming the door. Bolts clicked.

The room faced east, offering a fine view of the slate roofs of Narsh. The wall beneath it was sheer, and although the stonework was rough and crumbly, Eleal had no hope of being able to climb down it. It was quite high enough to break her legs. Upward offered no hope either, for her cell was a full story below the cornice—they had thought of that.

Below her lay a paved courtyard, part of the temple complex, enclosed by a row of large houses in high-walled grounds. She could see through the gaps to the street beyond, where people went about their business, enjoying freedom. She could even see parts of the city wall, Narshwater, farms, grasslands. If she leaned out as far as she dared, she could just see the meadow with the mammoth pen.

To north and south Narshflat became Narshslope, rising to

join the mountains of Narshwall. She had a fine view down the length of Narshvale. Indeed she thought she could see to the end of it, where sky and plain and mountains all converged. It was a small land and a barren one. She wondered why Joalia and Thargia would bother to quarrel over it.

Later she saw the mammoth train leave and even thought she heard faint trumpeting. She was too far away to make out the people. The mammoths themselves were small as ants, but she hung over the sill for a long time, watching them go.

Farewell Ambria! Farewell Grandfather Trong, you cold, proud man! Farewell Uthiam and Golfren—and good luck in the festival! May Tion keep you.

Remember me.

If she listened at the door, she could hear her guards muttering outside, but she could not make out the words. A choir of students practiced for a while in the courtyard below.

Not long after noon, Ylla returned, bringing some burly assistance in case it might be needed. She made Eleal strip, and gave her a red robe too large for her, a skimpy blanket, a jug of warm water, and a pungent bucket. She even confiscated Eleal's boots, leaving her a pair of sandals instead. Eleal stooped to pleading over that—walking was much harder for her without her special boots. The priestess seemed pleased by the pleading, but refused to change her mind.

Then she departed, taking everything Eleal had been wearing when she entered the temple, even her Tion locket, and leaving her a sack of chickens to pluck—eviscerated sacrifices, caked with blood and already stiff.

The rest of the day went by in boredom, fear, anger, and despair in various mixtures. The prisoner raged at her split lip, the goddess, the priestess, the fat priest, the chickens and all their feathers, Dolm the reaper, the *Filoby Testament*—whatever that was—her unknown father, her unknown mother, Trong and Ambria for deserting her and betraying her and lying to her. She refused to open the book of scripture. She seriously considered throwing it out the window, then decided that such an act of open defiance would merely provide an excuse to whip her. By late afternoon she knew that whippings would not be necessary. A few days of this confinement and she would be willing to kiss every shoe in the temple.

A year of it and she would be ready for the naked men in the alcoves.

ꝑꝑ 23 ꝑꝑ

THE DAHLIAS WERE MERELY THE LEADERS OF A PARADE OF flowers that staggered Edward. They came from his old house-master Ginger Jones on his own behalf, with another on behalf of all the masters, from the president of the Old Boys' Club, from Alice, and from a dozen separate friends. The word must have spread across all England, and he could not imagine how much money had been spent on trunk calls. The nurses teased him about all the sweethearts he must have. They set vases on the dresser and then ranked them along the wall he could see best, turning the drab brown room into a greenhouse. He could hardly bear to look at them. It was Bagpipe who needed the flowers, wasn't it?

Somewhere in that floral parade, someone smuggled in a copy of the *Times*. He suspected the plump nurse with the London accent, but he wasn't sure. It was just lying there on his bed when he looked.

Mr. Winston Churchill had ordered the fleet mobilized. Some holiday excursion trains had been canceled. France and Russia were preparing for war with Germany, and there had been shooting at border points. He found his own name, but there was nothing there that he did not already know. In normal times the yellow press would make a sensation out of such a story, a general's son murdered under his own roof by a house-guest, complete with nudge-nudge hints about public school pals. Just now the war news was sensation enough, but the press might be one more reason why there was a policeman outside his door.

The *Times* made his eyes swim, so he stopped reading for a while. He had just picked up *The Lost World* when he heard another voice he recognized, and all his muscles tensed. Had he not been tethered he might have rolled under the bed or jumped out the window. As it was, he tucked his book under the covers in case it might be snatched away from him, then waited for a second visitor who would not be restrained until formal visiting hours.

The Reverend Roland Exeter was a cadaverous man, invariably dressed in black ecclesiastical robes. His elongated form was reminiscent of something painted by El Greco in one of his darkest moods, or a tortured saint in some Medieval church carving—a resemblance aided by his natural tonsure of silver hair, a homegrown halo. His face was the face of a melancholy, self-righteous horse, with a raucous, braying voice to match. Celebrated preacher and lecturer, Holy Roly was probably better known than the Archbishop of Canterbury. Alice called him the Black Death.

He strode into the room clutching a Bible to his chest with both arms. He came to a halt and regarded his nephew dolefully.

"Good morning, sir," Edward said. "Kind of you to come."

"I see it as my Christian duty to call sinners to repentance, however heinous their transgressions."

"Caught the early train from Paddington, did you?"

"Edward, Edward! Even now the Lord will not turn his face from you if you sincerely repent."

"Repent of what, sir, exactly?"

Holy Roly's eyes glittered. He was probably convinced of his ward's guilt, but he was not fool enough to prejudge the criminal matter with a policeman listening outside the door. "Of folly and pride and willful disbelief, of course."

There had been no need for him to come all the way to Greyfriars to deliver the sermon again. He could have written another of his interminable ranting letters.

"I don't feel up to discussing such solemn matters at the moment, sir." Edward's fists were clenched so hard they hurt, but he had tucked them under the sheet. This was not going to work. The two Exeters had exchanged barely a dozen friendly words in the two years since his parents died. Fortunately, the guv'nor's will had stipulated that Edward be allowed to complete his education at Fallow, or Roly might well have pulled him out. Roly had had no choice there, but his idea of pocket money for a public school senior had been five shillings per term, probably less than any junior in the place received.

Also fortunately, Mr. Oldcastle had provided generously and regularly. Edward was resolved to have his affairs audited as soon as he reached his majority, for he strongly suspected that his parents' money had long ago vanished into the bottomless pit of the Lighthouse Missionary Society. Meanwhile he must endure his minority for almost another three years.

Holy Roly's wrinkles had twisted into an expression of mawkish pity. "You see that you have thrown it all away, don't you?"

"Thrown all what away, sir?"

"All the advantages you were given. You don't imagine Cambridge will accept you now, do you?"

"I understood that every Englishman was innocent until proven guilty."

"Then you are a fool. Even if you do not get your neck snapped on the scaffold, all doors are closed to you now."

There might be a hint of truth in what the old bigot was saying, but he was obviously enjoying himself, preparing to heap hellfire on an immobilized sinner. His voice descended to an even more melancholy range. "Edward, will you pray with me?"

"No, sir. I have told you before that I will not add hypocrisy to my shortcomings."

His uncle came closer, opening the Bible. "Will you at least hear the Word of God?"

"I should prefer not, sir, if you don't mind." Edward began to sweat. Normally at this point he excused himself as politely as possible and left the room, but now he was trapped and the bounder knew it. That might be the main reason he had come.

"Consider your sins, Edward! Consider the sad fate of the young friend you led into evil—"

"Sir?" That was too much!

"The First Epistle of Paul to the Corinthians," Roly announced, opening the Bible, "beginning at the thirteenth chapter." His voice began to drone like an organ.

Blackened sepulchre! He had not come to ask after his nephew's health, or to ask what really happened, or what he could do to help, or to display faith in his innocence. He had come to gloat. He had been predicting Edward's perdition since the day they met and now believed it had happened even sooner than expected. He had to come and drool over it.

How could two brothers have been so unalike?

Edward closed his eyes and thought about Africa.

He thought of Nyagatha, high in the foothills of Mount Kenya, amid forest and gorges, glowing with eternal sunshine, as if in retrospect the rainy seasons had been suspended for the duration of his childhood. He savored again the huge dry vistas of Africa under the empty sky, the velvet tropical nights when the stars roamed just above the treetops like clouds of diamond dust. He saw the dusty compound with the Union Jack hanging limp in the baking heat, scavenging chickens, listless dogs, laughing native children in the village. He recalled the guv'nor handing out medicines in the sanitarium; the mater teaching school in the shade of the veranda to a score of wriggling black youngsters and three or four whites; tribal elders arriving after treks of days or weeks to conclave in the black shadow of the euphorbia trees and listen solemnly to Bwana's advice or judgment; visiting Englishmen passing through the district, drinking gin and tonic at sundown and amusing themselves by talking to the boy, the future builder of Empire. It had all seemed quite natural—was not this how all white people grew up?

Above all he remembered the leggy, bony girl in pigtails, who bossed him and all the other children of every color—who chose the games they would play and the places they would visit and the things they must do and the things they must not do, and with whom he never argued. He remembered again his horror when she had to go Home, to England, to the mystical ancestral homeland her parents had left before her birth.

"Edward?"

Hospital and pain returned. "I beg your pardon, sir. What did you say?"

Holy Roly closed his eyes in sorrow. "Why can you not see that prayer and repentance are your only hope of salvation, Edward? He will make allowance for your doubts. *Lord I believe; help thou mine unbelief!*"

His sepulchral, ivy-coated bleating was probably comforting the ward next door. It was giving his nephew prickly heat.

"I appreciate your kindness in coming all this way to see me, sir."

Hints were wasted on Uncle Roland.

"Edward, Edward! Your father was a misguided apostate and look where it got him!"

Edward tried to sit up and his leg exploded in flame. He sank back on the pillow, streaming sweat.

"Good-*bye*, sir!" he said through clenched teeth. The pain was making him nauseated. "Thank you for coming."

A flush of anger showed in the sallow cheeks. Roly slammed the bible shut. "Do you still not see? *Exodus*, chapter twenty-one, the fifth verse: *Thou shalt not bow down thyself to them, nor serve them: for I the Lord thy God am a jealous God, visiting the iniquity of the fathers upon the children unto the third and fourth generation of them that hate me.*"

"I never quite saw that as fair play, somehow," Edward said, wondering what insanity was boiling inside the old maniac now. "Bowing down to what?"

"Idols! False gods! The Father of Evil! Your father was a disgrace to his country and his calling and his race! Read what the board of inquiry wrote about him, how he betrayed the innocent savages placed in his care—"

"Innocent savages? They were innocent until you Bible-bangers got to work on them! My parents would be alive today if a bunch of meddling missionaries—"

"Your father turned away the Word of God and frustrated the laws of his own people and sold his soul to the Devil!"

That did it. *"Out!"* Edward screamed, hauling on the bell-pull. "Go away or I shall throw things at you."

"I warned him that the Lord would not be mocked!"

"Nurse! Constable! Matron!"

"Wherefore, seeing we are encompassed about . . ." declaimed his uncle, rolling his eyes up to inspect the electric lighting.

The lanky policeman appeared in the doorway. Footsteps were hurrying along the corridor.

"Get this maniac out of here!" Edward yelled.

". . . sin which does so easily beset . . ."

"Nurse! Matron! He's driving me as mad as he is. He's insulting my parents."

"And it is also written—"

"He's preaching sedition. Remove him!" To emphasize the point, Edward grabbed up the kidney-shaped dish and hurled it, aimed to bounce off the book his uncle was again clutching to his breast. It was unfortunate that at that moment the old man started to turn. The dish, in cricket parlance, broke to leg. As Matron steamed into the room, a loud shattering announced that Edward had bowled a vase.

She impaled him with a glance of steel. "What is the meaning of this?"

"He insulted my father. . . ."

Too late the expression on Holy Roly's cadaverous face registered. Edward could not call back the words, nor the act itself.

He had resorted to violence!

Matron spoke again and he did not hear her; he did not see an ample, whaleboned lady in a stiff white cap and starched uniform. He saw instead the crown prosecutor in black silk and wig. He heard himself being forced to admit to the jury the damning answer he had just given, and he heard the question that would follow as surely as night must follow day:

"Do you remember discussing your father with Timothy Bodgley?"

24

THE SUSPECT HAD TRAVELED TO PARIS AND BACK WITH Julian Smedley, who was therefore an obvious witness. The Smedleys resided at "Nanjipor," Raglan Crescent, Chichester, and Leatherdale could justify another drive in that spiffy motorcar General Bodgley had placed at his disposal.

"Nanjipor" was a terrace house. It had an imposing facade fronted by a garden of roses, begonias, and boxwood topiary hedges. From the outside, therefore, it was identical to all the other houses in its row. The interior was suffocatingly hot and resembled a museum of Oriental art—wicker chairs, gaudy rugs, brass tables, lacquer screens in front of the fireplaces, idols with innumerable arms, hideously garish china vases, ebony elephants. The English had always been great collectors.

A chambermaid ushered Leatherdale into a parlor whose heavy curtains had been drawn, leaving the room so dark that the furnishings were barely visible. There he met Julian Smedley.

For Bank Holiday, young Smedley wore flannel trousers with a knife-edge crease, a brass-buttoned blazer, and what must obviously be an Old Fallovian tie—he was too young to lay claim to be an Old-Anything-Else. His shoes shone like black mirrors. He sat very stiffly on the edge of a hard chair, his hands folded in his lap, staring owlishly at his visitor. He added, "sir," to every statement he uttered. He gave his age as seventeen; he did not look it.

A certain amount of reticence could be expected in anyone who found himself involved in a very nasty murder case and Smedley was probably shy at the best of times. He might have been more forthcoming had Leatherdale been able to speak with him alone.

His father was present and had a right to be, as the boy was a minor. Sir Thomas Smedley was ex-India, a large, loud, and domineering man. He apologized for not being at his best: "Just recovering from a touch of the old malaria, you know." He certainly did not look well—he was sweating profusely and his hands trembled. Tropical diseases were something else the English collected while bringing enlightenment to the backward races of the world.

Sir Thomas had offered sherry and biscuits, which were declined. He had thereupon opened the interview with a ten-minute diatribe against the Germans: "Blustering bullies, you know. Always have been. Stand up to them and they crawl, try to be reasonable and they brag and threaten. Absolutely no idea how to handle natives, none at all. Made a botch of their colonies, all of them. Thoroughly hated, everywhere. Southwest Africa, Cameroons, East Africa—it's always the same with the Boche. The Hottentots taught them a thing or two, back in '06, you know. Never did get the whole story there. Now they think they can make a botch of Europe. Might is Right, they say. Well, they've got a surprise coming. Russians'll be in Berlin by Christmas, if the French don't beat them to it."

And so on.

When Leatherdale forced the conversation around to his case, Sir Thomas glowered and shivered, listening as his son confirmed the story. Then the father came in again, explaining why he had sent the telegram to Paris ordering Julian home, stressing his vision and common sense in doing so.

With his companion recalled and the Continent bursting into flames, with the strong possibility that he might be unable to join up with the rest of the party, young Exeter had chosen to return to England also. Any other decision would have demonstrated very bad judgment. Sir Thomas gave no hint, however, that he had offered hospitality to his son's friend, suddenly at a loose end. Had young Julian thought to do so? If not, why not? If he had, why had Exeter chosen the embarrassing alternative of an appeal to the Bodgleys' charity? While Leatherdale was considering how to ask those questions, he put another:

"What was Exeter's state of mind?"

"State of mind, sir?" The boy blinked like an idiot.

"Was he disappointed?"

"At first, sir. But eager to get his own back, of course—sir."

Leatherdale felt the thrill of a hound scenting its prey. "His own back on *who?*"

"On the Germans, sir. We're going to enlist together, sir."

Red herring.

Sir Thomas uttered a snort of potent scorn.

"Exeter has broken his leg," Leatherdale said. "It will be some time . . ."

The scorn registered. The lack of invitation clicked into place also. He confirmed some times and dates while he shaped his questions, then turned to the father. "You know Exeter, Sir Thomas?"

"Believe Julian introduced him last Speech Day."

There was strong disapproval there. That was the first indication Leatherdale had found that the entire world did not approve wholeheartedly of Edward Exeter. Another quarry had broken cover.

"How would you judge him, sir?"

Smedley Senior drummed his fingers on the arm of his chair. Suddenly he was being cautious. "Can't say I know the boy well enough to pass an opinion, Inspector."

That might well be true, but it did not mean that Sir Thomas did not have an opinion, and it would be based on something, however inadmissible it might be as evidence.

"His housemaster speaks very highly of him," Leatherdale said.

Sir Thomas made a *Hrumph!* noise.

"You thought enough of him to approve him as your son's companion on a trip across Europe."

Hrumph! again. "Well, they were chums." Father eyed son with a See-How-Wrong-You-Were? expression. "It was only for a few days, till they joined Dr. Gibbs and the others . . ."

Leatherdale waited.

Again Sir Thomas cleared his throat. "Must admit I have nothing against the boy himself. Deucedly good bowler. He may be straight enough. Guilty until proved innocent, what? I've seen Fallow work wonders. There was a young Jew boy there in my time . . . Well, that's another story."

Another silence. Leatherdale knew the road now.

"Do you know his *family* at all, Sir Thomas?"

"Only by reputation."

"And that is?"

"Well the Nyagatha affair, of course."

"Tragic?"

"Damned scandal! Read the board of inquiry report, Inspector!"

"I intend to. Can you give me the main points, though?"

That was all the encouragement Sir Thomas required. "Shocking! If Exeter had survived, he'd have been drummed out of the Service. Lucky not to be thrown in the clink. A band of malcontents wanders out of the jungle and burns a Government Station? White women raped and murdered! Children! Not a single survivor. Shameful! If Exeter had maintained a proper force of guards as he should, damned business would never have happened. Disgraceful! And there was all sorts of other dirt came out, too."

"Such as?"

"His overall performance. Aims and motivations. The man had absolutely *gone native*, Inspector! Tribal barbarities that had been stamped out in other districts had been allowed to persist. Witch doctors and such abominations. Roads that should have been built had not been. Missionaries and developers had been discouraged—virtually thrown out, in some cases. The commissioners were extremely critical. Gave his superiors a very stiff wigging for not having kept a better eye on him."

In the shadowed room, Sir Thomas's glare was as ferocious as any of the sinister idols'. His son was staring at the floor, fists clenched, saying nothing. His back was still ramrod-stiff.

So young Exeter had perhaps spent his childhood in unusually primitive surroundings, even by Colonial standards. That was not evidence. But it did help explain a certain curious document that Leatherdale had found in the suspect's luggage.

"Mr. Smedley?" Leatherdale said gently.

Julian looked up nervously. "Sir?"

"Did Edward Exeter ever express any ambition to follow in his father's footsteps? In the Colonial Office, I mean?"

Sir Thomas snorted. "They wouldn't touch another Exeter with a forty-foot pole."

"Hardly fair to the boy, sir?"

The invalid shivered and produced a linen handkerchief to dab his beaded forehead. "There are some names you don't want around on files to remind people, Inspector! Have you any further questions to put to my son?"

"Just one, I think. What do you think of Edward Exeter, Mr. Smedley?"

Julian glanced briefly at his father and seemed to make an effort to sit up even straighter, which was not physically possible.

"He's white!" he said defiantly. "A regular brick!"

ᵜᵜ 25 ᵜᵜ

SLOWER THAN A PLAGUE OF SNAILS CRAWLED THE HOSPI-
tal minutes. Lunch lay in Edward's stomach like a battleship's
anchor: pea soup, mutton stew, suet pudding, lumpy custard.
He was trying, with very little success, to write a sympathy letter
to the Bodgleys.

Amid his foggy memories of his visit to the Grange, he
had a clear vision of old Bagpipe cursing the asthma that
would keep him out of the war—and now here he was himself, flat on his back with his bloody leg in pieces. Three
months! It would be all over by then, and even if it wasn't,
then all his chums would be three months ahead of him.
What bloody awful luck!

Not quite as bloody as Bagpipe's of course. . . . His birthday
present from Alice had been a handsome leather writing case,
which fortunately had not been pilfered in Paris. It bore his
initials in gold and had pockets for envelopes and stamps and
unanswered correspondence. Abandoning the Bodgley letter, he
pulled out two well-thumbed sheets that he had stored away in
one of those pockets. He knew the text by heart now, but he
read it all over again. Then he set to work copying it out, word
for word.

It was dated the day of the Nyagatha massacre, and the writing
was his father's.

145

My dear Jumbo,

It was with both surprise and of course delight that Mrs. Exeter and I welcomed Maclean to our abode last night. Although conditions have improved vastly over the last few years, his journey from the Valley of the Kings was as arduous as might be expected. Had he been delayed only another three days at Mombasa, I fear he would have missed us here altogether. Indeed, delivery of this letter cannot precede by more than a week our personal arrival Home. Needless to say, the tidings he brought concerning your own crossing were equally agreeable to us. Without implying that any incentive beyond that of being reunited with our son and adopted daughter is necessary to motivate us to visit the Old Country, your presence there and the resulting prospects of riotous revelry in your company are a joyous prospect!

Who was Jumbo? Who was Maclean? The casualties of the massacre had included a "Soames Maclean, Esq., of Surrey," but the board of inquiry report had given no explanation of who he was, or what he had been doing at Nyagatha, except to describe him as a visitor. Just an old friend? Nothing odd about that. But then the letter turned strange.

Your new interpretation, of which Maclean has advised me, I find very convincing and in no small measure disturbing! You are to be congratulated on perceiving something that should have been perfectly obvious to all of us and me in particular, but of course was not. (He was named after Mrs. Exeter's father!) Unfortunately, in this case insight, which should promote increase in understanding and alleviation of apprehension, has tended rather to promote proliferation of enigmas!

The only person Edward knew who had been named after his grandfather was himself, but why should that matter to Jumbo, whoever Jumbo was? The letter then mentioned him directly.

While friendship, gratitude, and personal respect all incline me to acquiesce, dear Jumbo, the awesome responsibilities of fatherhood dissuade me from permitting a personal interview. The boy is not yet old enough to understand the implications. Rest assured that he will be fully informed before the critical date, and while he will still be very young even then, the decision will be his alone. We have given the Kent group strict instructions not to reveal his whereabouts to anyone at all. You will understand that no personal slight is intended.

His mother agrees with me wholeheartedly in this. Perhaps we are being overcautious, but we both feel "better safe than sorry"!

You will be relieved to hear that I am still strongly in favor of breaking the chain. Soapy has been trying to convert me with all his customary eloquence, but so far without success.

Five days ago, in the middle of the Champs Élysées, Edward had realized that a man named Soames Maclean might very likely be known as "Soapy" behind his back, especially if he were noted for his eloquence.

I still disapprove of turning a world upside down. The effects of good intentions are well-known and my work here has merely hardened my conviction that paving with better intentions only makes the road descend more slowly. One cannot take away half of a culture and expect the remainder to thrive. I have at least kept out the worst of the busybodies and preserved as many of the indigenous customs as I dare.

For example, I have not prohibited warfare among the young men of Nyagatha, although all the other districts banned it at once. It is not war as the Europeans understand war, nor is it done for slavery or conquest. It is a ritual combat with shields and clubs that rarely results in serious injury to the men themselves and never harms women and children. It is very little rougher than a county rugby match, and it is the basis of their whole concept of manhood. In neighboring districts, the culture has virtually collapsed without it.

I doubt that information concerning my irregular activities can much longer be kept from the local powers in London. I shall be

*severely criticized, but that is of no consequence. I hope and believe
that we have softened the inevitable blow.*

*As for religion, I need not tell you of the dangers of tampering
there! Even a bad faith, if it provides stability, may be better than
the turmoil . . .*

There it stopped, in mid-sentence. His last words.

*Criticized? Oh, guv'nor, how they criticized you! They tore your
corpse to shreds in their elegant Whitehall meeting rooms. They hung
your parts on bridges for the world to mock.*

Three days after those words had been written, a white-faced
boy had been hastily summoned to the Head's study at Fallow,
but not before he had seen the morning papers. The telegram
from London had arrived a couple of hours later. That had been
bad enough. Much worse had been the letters from the dead
that had trickled in over the next two months, full of cheerful
plans for the journey Home and the family reunion. Every week
another ship would dock and the wound would be reopened
before it had even had a chance to scab. A year later, when a
thin crust had begun to form so that his heart was not always a
stone and he could even smile again without feeling guilty—
then that awful board of inquiry report had started him bleeding
all over again.

And a couple of months after that, even, some idiot, well-
meaning, thoughtless lawyer had forwarded a box of his parents'
possessions that had somehow survived the fire. Fortunately,
Holy Roly had forgotten to mention them. They had lain in
his attic until a week ago. Edward had stopped a night in Kensington on his way to Paris, dropping off all the gear he had
accumulated at Fallow. Only then had he discovered that box,
and in it that extraordinary letter.

What did it all mean? Who was Jumbo? What was the Valley
of the Kings? Mr. Oldcastle of the Colonial Office lived in
Kent—was he somehow related to the Kent group mentioned?
The only person who might be able to answer any of those
questions was Mr. Oldcastle himself. Now he had time on his

hands, Edward was going to send him a copy of the letter. The original he would keep forever, his father's last words.

A patter of feet and rush of voices in the corridor announced the start of visiting hours. Alice would be prompt, she always was. Edward put away his writing and crossed his fingers. How exactly did one bait breath? . . .

Alice had been the first good thing he had seen in England, come to Southampton to meet him, a poised young lady of fifteen standing on the docks with her aunt Griselda—Roland had been too busy to leave town. Edward had met him that evening and they had disliked each other on sight. Dislike had flowered rapidly to mutual contempt. Alice and Griselda had probably kept the frightened twelve-year-old from madness or suicide in his first few weeks of that strangely green, soggy, solid England, full of mists and pale faces.

He had gone up to Fallow in the autumn, and what had been a nightmare of alienation and homesickness for all the other new boys had been a blessed release for him. That winter Griselda had faded away altogether, a mousy, kindly woman unable to withstand her famous, fanatical, power-crazy husband. Roland had grown steadily worse ever since, shriller, more eccentric, more bigoted.

Alice had been an absent relation, rarely seen, but her letters and Edward's had flashed across England in a single day, not to be compared to the twelve-week round trip to Kenya, and he had been grateful for her and to her. Whenever the loneliness had overflowed, he had written to Alice, and two days later her replies had arrived, full of stern comfort and practical advice.

The years had crept by. In retrospect, he should have informed his parents how things stood between him and the Reverend Roland, but it would have seemed like tattling, so he never had. He had given no thought to words like *tragedy, probate, executor.* . . . Plans for the family reunion had been seeded, nourished, cultivated—and ultimately blasted by that inexplicable massacre just days before the Exeters were due to leave

Nyagatha. The ship that should have brought them Home had brought details of their deaths.

Even before the disaster, Roland Exeter had displayed a driving ambition to convert his niece and nephew to his own brand of religious fervor. His brother's will had named him guardian of the orphaned boy and the twice-orphaned girl, and he had reacted like a missionary given a personal gift of two cannibals to win from the darkness.

Alice had left school by then. Her uncle had expected her to remain and keep house in the dread Kensington mausoleum which was home to both him and his Lighthouse Missionary Society. When she had moved out and set up her own establishment, he had denounced her as a scarlet woman, damned to hellfire for eternity. That was Roly's standard way of expressing disapproval.

Edward had remained at Fallow, but there he had raised the banner of liberty and manned the barricades, a staunch upholder of his father's skepticism, fighting his guerrilla war at long distance. He had not set foot in a church since the Nyagatha memorial service.

The corridors had gone quiet again. Was she not coming? Had she been forced to return to London, or had he merely dreamed her presence yesterday?

Were I a praying man, I should pray now.

Most girls made him squirm and shuffle and stutter. With Alice he could just stand and smile for hours. His face ached after being with her, just from smiling.

He had not seen her since her birthday. He had obtained a somewhat irregular exeat to attend the celebration—irregular in that his guardian had neither requested it nor known of it. Ginger Jones had stuck his neck out there, but the shrewd old housemaster had known for years how the wind blew.

The three years' age difference had dwindled now. In Africa it had represented the gulf between big child and small child. In England between boy and young woman. Now she was twenty-one, but he was a man in all but legal status. He was five feet, eleven and three-quarters inches tall.

In the spring he had even grown a mustache. It had not been wholly satisfactory, and Alice had obviously not thought much of it, so he had shaved it off when he got back to Fallow. The principle was what mattered.

Feminine heels clicked in the now-silent corridor. He held his breath.

Alice walked in. The sun came out and birds sang. She could always do that to rooms now, even drab brown hospital rooms.

She walked straight to the bed and for an intoxicating moment he wondered if she would kiss him, but she raised her eyebrows archly and handed him a string shopping bag full of books. He laid them on the bed.

She dressed very well, considering her limited means. She was wearing dove gray, to match her eyes—masses of striped cotton, from wrists to ankles, with a broad sash around her waist. Heaven knew what else ladies wore underneath. She must be cooked on a day like this, and yet she did not seem so. She removed her rose-bedecked hat, laying it and her parasol on the foot of the bed. Then she pulled up the chair. Her eyes were assessing him.

He realized that he had been staring at her like a stuffed stag. "Thank you for coming."

"I had to promise we will not discuss the case." She flicked a thumb at the open door and mimed someone writing. "You are much better!" She smiled. "I'm glad."

"Actually the treatment of choice in such cases is a kiss."

"No, that's a discredited superstition. Kisses overexcite the patient."

"They are good for the heart and stimulate the circulation."

"I'm sure they do. Seriously, how are you feeling?"

"Bored."

"Doesn't your leg hurt?"

"Throbs a bit once in a while. No, I'm in tip-top shape."

"You shaved off your mustache!"

"Actually that gale in early June did for it."

Alice glanced over the floral display with appreciation. "Impressive! Are all of them from barristers and solicitors or are some of them personal?"

She was not conventionally beautiful. Her hair was a non-descript brown, although bright and shiny. Her teeth were possibly on the large side, her nose might have been better had it been a thirty-second of an inch shorter. Overall, her face could almost be described as horsey—although not safely in Edward's hearing—but she had poise and humor and he would rather gaze at her than any woman in the world.

"Has Uncle been to see you?"

"He has. Have you got your money out of him yet?"

"These things take time," she said confidently.

"Till the Nile freezes? He's spent it all on his lousy cannibals! He's brought light to the heathen by burning your five-pound notes!"

"I think it's just his very muddled accounting."

She shrugged and glanced at the watch on her slim wrist—his present for her twenty-first, bought with money saved out of Mr. Oldcastle's regular donations. "We'll see. Let's not waste time talking about the Black Death. Mrs. Peters has been a love, but I absolutely must catch the 3.40. Tell me what happened the weekend before Whitsun."

"Before Whitsun? By Jove, that was when I took the most gorgeous girl in the world out to the park and explained—"

"Not in London. At Fallow." Again she glanced warningly at the door, where the copper must be writing all this down. "I was tracked down at the hotel by your Ginger Jones. He gave me those books for you. He wants them back. I gather they're all racy French novels he didn't dare let you read when you were a pupil."

"They don't sound like my cup of tea."

She grinned momentarily—that intimate, secretive grin that had meant mischief in their childhood and now hinted at vastly more magnificent possibilities. Or at least he hoped it would, one day soon.

"You're a big boy now. You're going to be even taller if that leg stretches much, you know. Do you suppose the other one will reach the ground? The weekend before Whitsun you got an exeat and while you were gone there was a burglary at Tudor."

Why was this important, when they had only an hour to be together and the entire future threatened to crumble in ruins?—his personal future, the Empire, Europe. . . . Why talk about a nonsensical schoolboy prank? But her expression said it was important, and he would not argue with her.

"Ginger knows more about it than I do. He never really convinced anyone else that it was a burglary. The bobbies listened politely and yawned. The front door was still bolted on the inside. Some chaps in Big School were in on the wheeze, whatever it was, but their door was bolted, too. A couple of juniors claimed they saw a woman wandering through the dorms, but they couldn't have been very convinced at the time, because they just went back to sleep. It was dodgy, all right, but no one ever did work it out." He stared at her doubt and then said, "We are discussing a community of three hundred juvenile males. Do you expect sanity?"

Alice reached for the *Times* on the bed and began using it as a fan. "He said something about a spear."

"Oh?" Ginger had mentioned that, had he? "A Zulu assegai from the Matabele display in Big School was left in my room in Tudor. That seems to have been the whole point, if you'll pardon an obscure pun. Possibly there had been scandalous rumors about what I was doing in town that night. Prefects sometimes make enemies, if they wallop a little too hard or too often, although I had been remarkably self-controlled for weeks before that, in anticipation of seeing you. Apart from that, nothing was missing or . . . What's wrong?"

"Where exactly was this spear when you found it?"

"Ginger found it. He made a complete search. He has keys to all the rooms, of course."

"Thrust right through your mattress?"

"So he said. Why is he riding this hobbyhorse again?"

Alice glanced at the door, giving him a view of her profile.

She looked best in profile, rather like Good Queen Bess in her prime.

"Mr. Jones is wondering now if you were supposed to be present when the spear was rammed through your bed. Your name was on your door, right? Whoever it was broke into Big School and located your house in the files—someone had been rummaging there, too, he said. Then the intruder pulled two steel brackets off the wall to get the assegai, went across to Tudor and found your room. You were missing, and in a fit of frust—"

Edward started to laugh and jarred his leg. "Bolting and unbolting doors from the wrong side? A lock is one thing, but a bolt is another! The old coot's off his rocker!"

Alice did not seem to have noticed his wince. She smiled. "He did admit he reads the penny dreadfuls he confiscates." Then she sobered. "He now assumes that there has been a second attempt, and this time the wrong man . . . " She raised an eyebrow archly, waiting for Edward to complete the thought.

"Strewth! I always thought the old leek was one of the sanest men there. Why should anyone try to kill me, of all people? I have no money. Even if Holy Roly's left anything of the family fortune for me to inherit, it will be only a few hundred quid. I have no enemies that I can think of."

Once more into the breach, dear friends, once more; Or close the wall up with our English dead. . . . Why had he thought of those lines? Oh yes, that weird dream of a Dickensian apparition claiming to be Mr. Oldcastle. Two nights ago, and yet it still stuck in his memory. Dear friends?

"Anyone can have enemies," Alice said emphatically.

He thought of the letter, but he would not worry her with that until Mr. Oldcastle had commented on it.

"You refer to my brains, good looks, and personal magnetism, of course. Admittedly they arouse enormous envy wherever I go, but that's only to be expected. Rival suitors are the real threat. Seeing the burning love you bear me in every bashful glance, consumed with jealousy, some dastard seeks to clear me from the field. Who can it be, this wielder of spears who opens bolts from the wrong side of . . . "

Alice raised both eyebrows and he stopped, feeling stupid. She did not speak, but her eyes said a lot. Ginger must have his reasons. Explain one impossible intruder and you might be able to claim another? Did a bolted door in the Grange case make Edward Exeter the only possible suspect in the killing of Timothy Bodgley?

"It's an interesting problem," she said, toying with her gloves. "What about the woman the boys thought they'd seen? Did they mention her before or after the unbolted door was found?"

"I have no idea! I can't believe you'd swallow any of this. You are usually so levelheaded!"

"Reliable boys?"

"Good kids," he admitted.

"Mr. Jones said that perhaps you, as prefect, uncovered some hints that the masters didn't. Often happens, he said."

"Not in this case. Most of the chaps tried to blame the suffragettes. The Head was pretty steamed. He canceled a half holiday because no one would own up."

"Is that usual?"

"Communal punishment, or no one having the spunk to own up?"

"Both."

"Neither," he admitted. And even rarer was the absence of any retaliation on the culprits by those who had suffered unjustly, but there had been none of that at all, or he'd have heard of it.

Into his mind popped a sudden image of solemn little Codger Carlisle, nervousness making all his freckles show like sand, babbling of a woman with long dangling curls and a very white face. *He could have been describing that half memory from the Grange that still haunted Edward!* Codger would never be capable of telling a convincing lie if he lived to be a hundred. It must be coincidence! Or else in his drugged stupor in the hospital Edward had remembered that testimony and converted one fiction into another.

He returned Alice's stare for a moment before he realized that she was genuinely worried. "Forget the silly prank, darling! It was months ago. It has nothing whatsoever to do with what happened at the Grange, the thing we mustn't talk about. Let's talk about us!"

"What about us?"

"I love you."

She shook her head. "I love you dearly, but not that way. There is nothing to discuss, Edward. Please don't let's go through all that again! We're first cousins and I'm three years older—"

"That matters less and less as time goes by."

"Nonsense! In 1993 I shall be a hundred years old and you will only be ninety-seven and still pursuing wenches when I need you to wheel me around in my Bath chair. I hope we shall always remain the best of friends, Eddie, but never more than that."

He heaved himself into a more comfortable position, although he had tried them all and none of them was really comfortable now.

"My darling Alice! I am not asking you for a commitment—"

"But you are, Edward."

"Nothing final!" he said desperately. "We're both too young to go that far. All I'm asking is that you consider me as an eligible suitor like any other young man. I just want you to think of me as—"

"That was your final offer. You asked a lot more than that when you started!"

Her fanning had grown more vigorous. He ran a hand through his sweaty hair. Ladies' garments were even less suitable than gentlemen's for this unusually hot summer. In a way he was fortunate to be wearing only a cotton nightgown, but how could man woo maid when he was flat on his back with one leg in the air? "Then I'm sorry I was so precipitate. Put it down to transitory youthful impatience. You said you had no intention of making any final—"

"Edward, stop!" Alice slapped the newspaper noisily on her knee. "Listen carefully. Our ages don't matter very much, I'll agree with you on that. That is not the problem. First, I will never marry a cousin! Our family is odd enough already without starting to inbreed. Secondly, I do not think of you as a cousin."

"That's promising!"

"I think of you as a brother. We grew up together. I love you very much, but not in the way you want. Girls do not marry their brothers! They do not *want* to marry their brothers. And thirdly, you are not the sort of man I should ever want to marry."

He winced. "What's wrong with me?"

She smiled sadly. "I'm looking for an elderly rich industrialist with no children and a very dickey heart. You're a starry-eyed romantic idealist student and strong as a horse."

Edward sighed. "Then may I be your second husband and help you spend the loot?"

Eventually they found their way to happier ground, talking about their childhood in Africa. The whites they had known had all died in the massacre, of course, but their native friends had survived. They speculated on who would now be married to whom. They talked of all sorts of other things, but not what he wanted to talk about, which was their future together. He discovered several times that he was lying there like a dead sheep, smiling witlessly at her, just happy to be in her presence. And at last Alice glanced at her watch and gave a little shriek and jumped to her feet.

She clutched his hand. "I must run! Take care of yourself! Look out for Zulu spears."

He felt a heavenly touch of lips on his cheek and smelled roses. Then she was gone.

Later he looked through the books Ginger had sent and decided that they were definitely not the sort of thing he wanted to read in a hospital bed, and probably not ever. That came of being a romantic, starry-eyed idealist, he supposed. Most of them were suspiciously tatty, as if the old chap had read them many times, or they been passed around a lot. Then he chanced upon a flyleaf bearing an inscription in green ink:

Noël, 1897

Vous Inculper,
   Avant de savoir ce lui qui est arrivée,

Gardez-vous Bien.

Every book contained a similar inscription, each in a different ink and handwriting. It was a reasonable assumption that Constable Heyhoe knew no French. Arranging the volumes in alphabetical order by title and reading the fragments as a single message, Edward translated:

"The back door was bolted on the inside; the door from the kitchen premises to the house was locked, but the key is missing. They cannot charge you until they discover where it has gone. Beware of admitting anything that may be used against you."

Two men in a locked room, one dead, one injured—from which side had the door been locked? Yes, that was just mildly critical, wasn't it?

Three cheers for the devious Welsh!

26

ELEAL AWOKE SHIVERING, LYING ON HER PALLET IN darkness. She could not remember going to sleep. Cold and hunger had wakened her—distant sounds of evensong from the temple told her that the hour was not late. The troupe would be in Sussvale now, very likely still performing *The Fall of Trastos* for the kindly folk of Filoby. Curse Filoby and its cryptic testament!

Her fingers were sore from plucking chickens. She had left the casement open—never a wise move in Narshland. She scrambled up stiffly and limped across to close it.

Below her, lights showed in windows, here and there. In the crystal mountain air the skies were bright with a myriad of sparkling diamond stars, and two moons. Narshians bragged about their stars. Eltiana was a baleful red spot, high in the east, gloating over her prisoner, perhaps. Below her, just rising at the far end of the valley, Ysh's tiny half disk cast an eerie blue glow on the peaks of Narshwall. Of green Trumb there was no sign at all. Eleal leaned out and scanned the sky to make sure—*and Kirb'l appeared right before her eyes!*

She had never actually seen him do that before. Always she had just realized that the night had become brighter or darker, that she had just gained or lost a shadow, and looked up to see that Kirb'l had come or gone, as the case might be. This time she had been watching! One minute there had been only stars at the crest of the sky, and the next moment there was Kirb'l's brilliant golden point, putting them to shame. She even thought she could make out a disk. Usually Kirb'l, like Eltiana, was merely a starlike point, although no star was ever so bright, or such a clear gold.

All the moons went in and out of eclipse, but none so abruptly as he. Sometimes Kirb'l even went the wrong way, and a few minutes' watching were enough to show her now that his light was indeed moving against the stars, sinking in the east. He was also heading southward, to avoid Eltiana and Ysh. Kirb'l, the moon that did not behave like the others— wandering north and south, moving the wrong way, sometimes bright, sometimes faint—Kirb'l was also the Joker, Kirb'l the god, avatar of Tion in Narsh. Was that a sign to her that she must not give up hope? Or was the Joker laughing at her plight? Kirb'l the frog had given her a sign! Good sign or bad?

She decided to treat it as a good sign. She closed the casement, wrapped herself in her blanket, and knelt down to say some prayers. She prayed, of course, to Tion. She would not pray to the goddess of lust, nor to the god of death, not to the Maiden who withheld her justice. Chiol the Father had taken her coins and thrown a very cruel destiny upon her. But Tion was god of art and beauty and in Narsh he was Kirb'l and he had given her a sign.

27

"YOUR FULL NAME, IF YOU PLEASE."
Edward supplied his name and date of birth. He felt as he did when he faced an unfamiliar bowler. The opening balls would be simple and straightforward while the opponents summed each other up. Then the googlies would start.

It was Tuesday afternoon, a full day since Alice had departed. The most exciting thing that had happened in those twenty-four hours was the bandage around his head being replaced with a sticking plaster, half of which was on scalp and sure to hurt like Billy-o when it came off.

He was half-insane from boredom, and a battle of wits with the law was a most welcome prospect. Being not guilty, he had nothing to fear if the game was played fair; if the deck was stacked, then devil take him if he could not outwit this country bumpkin copper. Anything he said might be used in evidence. He had never expected to hear the dread words of the official caution directed at himself.

"You feel well enough to answer questions now, Mr. Exeter?"

"Yes, sir. I'll do anything I can to help you catch the killer."

"What do you recall of the events of Sunday last, August first? . . . "

Leatherdale looked weary. The man was suffering from his weight and the heat. His face was more florid than ever, gleaming with perspiration, his neck bulged over his collar, and the points of his waxed mustache were drooping instead of standing up proudly. Edward had considered inviting him to remove his jacket and even his waistcoat and had then decided that fair play could be carried too far. Leatherdale for his part was not being at all sporting—he had set chair back almost against the wall, so Edward must keep his head turned hard over on the pillow to see him. The uniformed sergeant was on the other side of the bed, evidenced only by an occasional scratch from his pen.

However absurd his apparel, Edward was much more comfortable than either of his visitors, except for the strain on his neck. His leg had stopped hurting much except when he moved it. Let the game begin!

Next question: "You are familiar with the kitchen premises at Greyfriars Grange?"

"Yes. I've stayed there before. Timothy and I always raided the larder after everyone else went to bed. It was a tradition we started when we were kids. We used to feel frightfully depraved, but I expect Mrs. Bodgley knew what we were up to and didn't care."

"Would she have cared on Sunday?"

"What?" Edward almost laughed. "Timothy could have treated me to the best Napoleon brandy and his parents wouldn't have minded. I expect we'd have felt a pair of real mugs if anyone had walked in on us sitting there by candlelight . . . "

"You would have been embarrassed if anyone had found the two of you in the kitchen at that hour of the night?"

"Mildly embarrassed," Edward conceded, realizing that the conversation was coming around to—

"Was that why you locked the door?"

"We didn't." He must not reveal what Ginger Jones had told him about missing keys. He must not show any interest in keys.

"You say your memories of the night's events are foggy, and yet you recall a detail like that? You would testify under oath that neither you nor your companion locked the kitchen door?"

"I would testify that I do not recall locking it or seeing Bagpipe lock it—neither that night nor any of the half dozen or so times we had been there under similar circumstances before. I do remember people beating on the door later, trying to get in, so somebody must have locked it." It was hard not to smile at that point.

"Or bolted it."

"There's no bolt on that door . . . is there?"

Leatherdale smiled placidly. "I'll ask the questions, if you don't mind."

He continued to send down simple balls and Edward continued to stonewall them. He had recalled quite a lot in the past two days, but it was patchy—Bagpipe showing him to his room, the talk of war over the port, Bagpipe coming to chat, Bagpipe raving about *The Lost World.*

The inspector reached out and took the book off the bed table and eyed the title. "Sir Arthur Conan Doyle? Good man. Liked what he wrote about the war and those Boers. Well, it would be his Mr. Sherlock Holmes we would be needing now, wouldn't you say, sir?" With his homely, West Country voice he might have been discussing the prospects for the harvest, but he was not fooling Edward.

"Run through the clues for me, Inspector, and I shall solve the case lying here in my bed."

"I hope you do." Leatherdale twirled his mustache and somehow made that commonplace gesture seem sinister.

Edward resolved to make no more jokes.

If what Ginger Jones had reported was correct, then there was no chance of Edward Exeter being kept under unofficial arrest much longer. At the end of this interview he would ask to be moved out of solitary. A ward full of other men would be infinitely preferable, even if they were all farmers and tradesmen. At least there would be the crisis to talk about. The order mobilizing the army was going to be signed today. Belgium had rejected the German ultimatum. If the Prussian jackboot came across that border, then Britain would be in the war. Meanwhile he must be nice to the rozzer. . . .

"Had the rest of the household retired to bed?"

"I don't remember, sir."

"What exactly did you do in the kitchen?"

"All I recall of the kitchen is what I already . . ."

The sensation was oddly like being called to walk the carpet, but he had not been in serious trouble at Fallow since his wild youth in the Upper Fourth, and he knew the stakes now were considerably higher than a breeching or a few hours' detention. His neck was growing devilish stiff. He addressed his next few answers to the ceiling, aware that the foe was still watching him and he could not see the foe.

Of course the most likely explanation of the tragedy was that the two of them had blundered into a gang of burglars and tried to be heroes. In the resulting fracas the intruders had stabbed Bagpipe, thrown Edward down the stairs, and departed. But if Ginger's information was correct, they had not escaped out the back door, which had been bolted, but had gone through into the main house, locking the door and taking the key. Although Ginger had not mentioned the front door and other means of escape, there must be a possibility that the killer or killers had not been intruders at all, but someone in General Bodgley's household. As Bodgley was practically lord of the manor around Greyfriars, this investigation must be much more than a routine for Inspector Leatherdale. He would be under terrific pressure; he would play every trick he knew. Even a romantic, starry-eyed idealist knew the googlies must start soon.

The voices droned, the constable's pen squeaked, and faint sounds of carts and motors drifted in through the open window. Visitors' voices wandered up and down the corridor, and Leatherdale continued to use up Edward's visiting hours. Quite possibly Ginger Jones or others might be cooling their heels outside there somewhere, waiting to be admitted.

"But you had never seen this woman before?"

"I'm not sure I even saw her then, Inspector. I have only a few very vague images. She may have been a delusion." Should he have admitted that?

"You threw something at your uncle yesterday?"

Googly!

Edward turned to look at Leatherdale quizzically, and then reached up to the bedside table.

"No. I did heave this dish, or one just like it."

"Why?"

He resisted the temptation to say, "I didn't know what else it was for." Instead he explained calmly, "I threw it at the book he was holding. Had I wanted to hit him instead, I would have hit him. I can hit a sixpence at the far end of a cricket pitch." He raised the dish. "Choose any flower in the room and I'll hit it for you, even lying flat like this."

"That won't be necessary. Why did you throw the dish at Dr. Exeter?"

"I didn't."

"Why did you throw the dish at the Bible, then?"

"Because my uncle is a religious fanatic. I'd say a religious maniac, but I'm not qualified to judge that. For years he has been trying to convert me to his beliefs, and he is absolutely unstoppable when he gets going. I could not leave, and the only way I could think of to get rid of his ranting was to make a scene. So I made a scene."

"You did not just ask him to leave?"

"I did try, sir."

"You could have rung for a nurse and asked her to show him out."

"He is my legal guardian and a well-known divine. He would have resisted and probably won."

"Trying to convert you from what?" Leatherdale changed topics like a juggler moved balls.

"From believing what my parents believed."

"And what is that?"

"My father told me, 'Don't talk about your faith, show it.' "

"You refuse to answer the question?"

"I did answer the question." What on earth did this have to do with Bagpipe's death? "I was taught that deeds count and words don't. The guv'nor was convinced that rabid, bigoted missionaries like my uncle Roland did incalculable harm to innumerable people by thrusting an alien set of beliefs and values on them. They finish up confused and adrift, with their tribal ways in a shambles and no real understanding of what they are expected to put in their place. He used to quote . . ."

May be used as evidence . . . Even if Leatherdale himself was broad-minded and tolerant—and there was no evidence of that—the average English jury would certainly contain some dogmatic, literal-minded Christians. Edward took a long breath, cursing his folly at letting his tongue run away with him. "He believed a man should advertise his beliefs by making his life an example to others and to himself and to whatever god or gods he believed in. You don't really want a sermon, do you, Inspector?"

"And this provoked you to throw the dish?"

Another curved one! "He insulted my father." As Leatherdale was about to speak, Edward decided to get the words on the record. "He accused him of worshiping Satan." Try putting that before twelve honest men and true!

"Those exact words, 'worshiping Satan'?"

"Close enough. How would you react if someone—"

"It is your reactions we are investigating, sir. Do you normally become violent when someone makes an insulting remark about your father?"

"I don't recall anyone else ever being such a boor."

As the interrogation continued, Leatherdale's West Country growl seemed to be growing broader and broader. Edward wondered if his own public school drawl was also becoming more marked. He ought to try and curb it, but he had no spare brain cells to put in charge of the attempt. He had also realized that the policeman disliked him for some reason, and was enjoying this.

"Why would your uncle have made such an accusation?"

Edward rubbed his stiffening neck. "Ask him. I do not understand my uncle's thinking."

"In his youth he was a missionary himself."

"I know that much."

"Where were you born, Mr. Exeter?"

What did this have to do with Bagpipe's murder? "In British East Africa. Kenya."

The questions jumped like frogs—Kenya, Fallow, the

Grange. Any time Edward questioned a question for relevancy, Leatherdale would change the subject and then work his way back again. The ceiling could do with a coat of paint.

"And how did your father treat missionaries in Nyagatha?"

"I have no idea. I was only twelve when I left there. I was only twelve when I last spoke to my father. Boys of that age barely regard their parents as mortals, let alone question them on such topics."

"That was not what you said earlier."

"That's true," Edward admitted, angry with himself. "I know what he said to me about missionaries, but I don't know what he did about them in practice. I remember missionaries visiting the station and being made welcome."

"Can you name any of them?"

"No. It was a long time—"

"And the Reverend Dr. Exeter is your father's brother?"

"Was my father's brother. My father died when I was sixteen."

Leatherdale twirled his mustache. "Your father's younger brother?"

"Hardly! Much older."

"Have you any evidence of that, Mr. Exeter?"

"I knew them both very well."

"Any documentary evidence?"

Edward stared. "Sir, what does this have to do with what happened at Greyfriars Grange?"

"Answer the question, please."

"I expect the guv'nor's age is recorded on my birth certificate. I don't remember. I don't read my birth certificate very often."

Manners! He was growing snippy. Was that a glint in Leatherdale's eye? He was against the light, so it was hard to tell.

"When a British subject is born in the colonies, who issues the birth certificate?"

"The nearest district officer, I expect."

"So your father made out your birth certificate?"

"Perhaps he did. I'll look and see when I get out of hospital."

"I was asking about your father's age. Have you any evidence handy at the moment—a photograph, for instance?"

Impudence! Unmitigated gall! The bounder had gone through Edward's wallet when he was unconscious! The urge to try and take him down was becoming dangerously close to irresistible.

"I have a photograph."

"Will you show me that photograph, please?"

Glowering, Edward opened the drawer and took out his wallet. "Be careful of it, please. It is fragile and it is the only picture of my parents I have."

Leatherdale hardly glanced at it.

"This shows you and your parents in Africa?"

"Yes. It was taken by a visitor who had a portable camera. He sent it to us just before I left."

"So it was taken around when?"

What the devil was all this leading to?

"In 1908. I would be eleven, almost twelve."

"And how old would you say the man in this picture is, sir?"

Without releasing it, Leatherdale held the photograph out for Edward to see.

"Around forty, I suppose. Not fifty. More than thirty." It was hard to tell. The image had always been blurred, and six years in his wallet had worn it almost blank, as if a heavy fog had settled on that little group on the veranda. His mother's face was in shadow. He was standing in front of his parents, his father's hand on his shoulder, and he was grinning shyly.

"Your father was Cameron Exeter, son of Horace Exeter and the former Marian Cameron, of Wold Hall, Wearthing, Surrey?"

Edward was completely at sea now. He had a strange sensation that the bed was rocking. This was worse than a geometry exam. *Prove that angle ADC equals angle DCK.* . . .

"I think so. I don't know where they lived, except it was somewhere in Surrey. I'm not even certain of their names."

Leatherdale nodded as if a trap had just clicked. "Their eldest child, Cameron, was born in 1841, Mr. Exeter. That would make him sixty-seven in 1908. How old did you say this man seems to you?''

Edward desperately wanted a drink of water, but he dared not reach for one in case his hands shook. "Forty?"

"His mother, your grandmother, died in 1855, almost sixty years ago."

"You've made a mistake somewhere. Tricky stuff, maths."

"Has your uncle seen this picture?"

"I have no idea. I may have shown it to him when I first came Home. I don't recall."

"Try."

"It was a long time ago. I really don't remember, sir. What are you suggesting?"

"I am suggesting that the man in the picture is either not your father or else your father was not who he said he was."

This conversation made no sense at all! It must be a ruse to rattle him. Bemused, Edward ran a hand through his hair and realized that it was soaked—he was soaked. He turned his head to ease his neck, and watched the sergeant finish writing a sentence, then look up, waiting for more.

He turned back to Leatherdale, who was impassively twirling his mustache again. That, apparently, was a bad sign. But the man could not possibly be as confident as he was pretending.

"You've been busy, Inspector!" He was ashamed to hear a quaver in his voice. "Unfortunately, you've been misinformed. Yesterday was Bank Holiday. I suppose you telegraphed to Somerset House first thing this morning, or the Colonial Office, perhaps? Whitehall must be in turmoil just now with war about to break out. Someone has blundered."

"I obtained the information from your uncle."

Oh, Lord! Edward reined in his tongue before it ran away with him. "I suggest you obtain confirmation of anything he says. Check with the Colonial Office."

"Ah, yes. Can you give me the name of someone to get in touch with there, sir?"

With a rush of relief, Edward said, "Yes! Mr. Oldcastle. I'm sorry I don't know his title. I always wrote to him at his home."

"His full name?"

"Jonathan Oldcastle, Esquire."

"And do you remember his address?"

"I should do! I've written to him every week or two for the last couple of years. The Oaks, Druids Close, Kent."

Leatherdale nodded and eased himself on the chair. "That was the address in the school records, Sergeant?"

Pages rustled. "Yes, sir," said the sergeant.

"And this Mr. Oldcastle replied to your letters, sir?"

"Religiously. He was very kind—and generous."

Again the thick fingers caressed that gray mustache. "Exeter, there is nowhere in Kent called Druids Close. There is nowhere in Great Britain by that name."

"That's impossible!"

"Sergeant, will you confirm what I just told the witness?"

"Yes, sir."

After a moment Edward said, "I think I need a glass of water."

From then on it got worse, much worse. Having succeeded in rattling him, Leatherdale gave him no chance to recover. Suddenly they were back in Greyfriars Grange—

"Did you stab Timothy Bodgley?"

"No!"

"You're sure of that? You remember?"

"No, sir, I don't remember, but—"

And back in Africa—

"Who is 'Jumbo'?"

"Who?" Edward said furiously. Bounder! The letter!

"Is there anyone in England now who knew your father?"

"I don't know."

And back in the Grange—

"Had you ever been down in the cellar before?"

"No, sir. Not that I remember."

"Would a schoolboy forget visiting a fourteenth century crypt?"

"Probably not. So I suppose I never—"

"You heard people banging on the door while the woman

was still screaming? How long did she scream at you? How long did you hold her off with the chair? . . . "

Eventually, inevitably, Edward blundered.

"Do you recognize this, Mr. Exeter?"

"Oh, you found it!" *Oh, you muggins!*

Leatherdale pounced like a cat. "You knew it was lost?"

"That's a key. I don't know what it's the key to, though . . . No, I don't recognize it. . . . Lots of keys look like that, big and rusty . . ." Avoid, evade, distract . . . "I assumed that since you asked earlier about the door . . ." It was hopeless. In ignominious defeat, the suspect told of the message Ginger had sent him. *Traitor! Snitch! Nark!*

Leatherdale followed up his victory, slashing questions like saber blows.

"Why did you kill him?" "Why did you argue with him?" "Why were you shouting?" "What were you shouting?" "What secret had he discovered about you?" "Describe the kitchen."

"Big. High. Very old. Why?"

"How high? How high is the ceiling?"

Edward wiped his wet forehead. "How should I know? Fifteen feet?"

"Twenty-one. Do you remember the shelves on the wall under the bells?"

"I remember shelves, and dressers, I think bells . . ." A long row of bells, one for every room in the house.

Leatherdale smiled grimly. "Yes, this is the key to the kitchen quarters at Greyfriars Grange. We found it, Mr. Exeter, in a pot on the topmost shelf."

"Oh."

"Twenty feet up in a poor light. There were no marks in the dust on the lower shelves, Mr. Exeter. What do you say about that?"

"What do you say about it, sir?"

"I say that the only way it could have been put in that pot was to throw it up there and bounce it off the wall just under the ceiling. Whoever managed to do that first try in a poor light must be a very expert thrower indeed. A bowler, perhaps?"

★   ★   ★

When at last the ordeal ended, Edward watched in misery as Ginger's books were impounded as evidence, along with his cherished photograph, the most precious thing he possessed in the world. The policemen departed.

He had not confessed. He had not been charged, either, but obviously that was only a matter of time now.

28

ELEAL HAD ENDURED A SECOND DAY IN HER LONELY prison, plucking chickens. Her fingers were worn raw. She had done the work conscientiously because anything else would have just brought her more hunger and perhaps a beating. She had been given boiled chicken and chicken soup to eat. She never wanted to see another chicken ever again.

Tomorrow the festival began and she would not be there. She would never see another festival, never sing for a real audience again, never be an actor. Worst of all was the certainty that she could not stand many more days of this torment without breaking. Soon she would kneel and kiss Ylla's shoe, just to beg for some company, someone to talk to.

She hadn't done so yet, though.

She had cried herself to sleep.

She awoke in darkness. It was not like the time the reaper had wakened her. She swam up from sleep slowly, reluctantly, annoyed by an exasperating noise. She tried to pull the skimpy blanket up over her ear and succeeded only in exposing her toes to the cold.

There it came again! Something tapping.

Angrily she lifted her head.

Tapping at the window! . . .

She scrambled to her knees. She could barely make out the squares of the casement. There was *something* out there, though! Tap, tap! Not just wind in a tree.

A momentary fear was followed by a rush of excitement. Still clutching her blanket around her, she stumbled to her feet and stepped over. The end of a rope was swinging against the glass: *tap! tap!*

She struggled with the hasp in frantic impatience and hauled the little casement open. She leaned over the sill and peered up, but she could see nothing. Clouds scudded over the sky, their edges tinted with blood by Eltiana's ominous red. No other moons were in sight, and that was ominous—only the Lady!

A wicked breeze blew through Eleal's hair and chilled her skin. The rope slithered up a few feet and then dropped down in her face. She grabbed it and pulled it inside the room with her. Fumbling in the dark, she established that there was a loop tied in the end of it. It was not a noose, but the association of ideas made her uneasy. She pulled in the slack while she tried to work out what she was supposed to do with it. Light faded as Eltiana vanished behind a cloud. Was that an omen?

Then the rope reversed direction as the unknown prankster on the roof hauled it in. She hung on, thinking, *Wait! Wait! I need some time!* She was dragged to the window. She hung tight, refusing to let this opportunity escape her. The rope slackened.

Obviously someone was signaling intentions. She pulled the noose over her shoulders and scrambled up on the sill. The gap was small, even for her, but she was agile. She twisted around and wriggled, until she was sitting on the hard ledge, with most of her outside and only her legs inside. She clung very tightly to the sides of the opening. The wind tugged at her robe, which was no warmer than a nightgown would have been and definitely not a garment she would have chosen for midnight acrobatics two stories above a very hard-looking courtyard. Better not to think about that! Her face was against the stone above the lintel. She waited for the pull, feeling all knotted up inside as she did on a mammoth, crossing Rilepass.

The noose tightened on her, and then stopped before it had taken her weight. Teeth chattering, she peered anxiously up at the dark clouds. The cornice was barely visible, but then a faint glimmer showed over it—a face? Checking that she was doing what he wanted? She dared not shout, and neither did he. She hoped he had big, strong hands and arms. She thought he waved. She assumed it was a man. No woman would be mad enough to try this. She waved back. He disappeared.

She was going to freeze to death if he didn't do something soon. The cold and the discomfort of her perch were making her eyes water. The rope tightened under her arms, cutting into her back. She pulled herself up on the line and pushed herself out with one foot, prepared to walk up to the roof. She did not look down. For a moment a pinkish glow heralded Eltiana's reappearance, but then it faded behind the clouds again. *Hurry!* she thought. *Before the goddess sees!*

The rope slackened. Taken by surprise, she tipped backward with a squeal of alarm. She swung free and banged her knees into the wall below the window. Now she realized she was expected to walk *down* the wall, not up. It was cold and rough against her bare toes. She tried to forget that awful drop below her.

Her rescuer must be immensely powerful, for he was letting the rope out very evenly and smoothly. She saw the next window coming and avoided it—lucky the openings were so small. Then there would be another window on the ground floor. There was, and it was larger, but at last she felt cold, cold cobbles under her feet. With a gasp of relief, she leaned against the wall and muttered a prayer of thanks to every deity she could think of. Except the Lady Eltiana in all her aspects, of course.

Several rooms away to the right, a single window at ground level showed light. The rest of the temple slept. If the goddess knew of this violation of her sacred precincts, she had not yet roused her guardians.

Eleal slipped free of the rope, which continued to descend

and collect at her feet. Shivering violently, she began to gather it up in coils. Good rope was expensive. She should have thought to bring her sandals. A scratching noise made her look up—and jump back in disbelief as small fragments of stone rattled down on her. A huge shape showed against the sky, dark against dark, and two eyes glowed faintly. The dragon began to descend the sheer face of the wall. The noises became dangerously loud as its claws struggled for purchase. She moved farther out of the way, having no desire to be struck by a falling dragon and no chance of being able to catch one effectively. She had always known that dragons were skilled climbers, but she had not known they could scale a sheer masonry wall.

A dark forked tail came into view, swinging vigorously from side to side. It felt the ground and then swung up out of harm's way as the hindquarters followed. A *very* dark tail! Of course this could only be Starlight, and her rescuer must be T'lin himself—what other dragon owners did she know? She resisted a desire to call out to him. Clawed feet reached the cobbles. Starlight balanced on them for a moment, his frills extended and flapping for balance like small wings. He tipped around and down and settled on all fours, puffing. His eyes glowed faintly green, and blinked.

Eleal ran to him and looked up. "T'lin Dragontrader!"

"No," said a whisper. "But his dragon. It won't hurt you." The rider had twisted around to untie the rope attached to the baggage plate at his back. It had been Starlight who had lowered her down the wall.

"Of course he won't. He's Starlight."

"Oh. Well, up with you!" He reached down.

She hesitated only a fraction of a second. Whoever he was, she had already trusted her life to him. She accepted the hand and waited for the heave. It came in the form of an ineffective tug. She realized that the hand she was holding was far too small and smooth to be T'lin's.

"Mmph!" said the whisperer angrily. "You're too heavy. *Choopoo!*" The dragon twisted its neck around and blinked at him. "*Choopoo!*" he repeated. "Oh, *Wosok!* I mean."

Starlight sighed and obediently folded his legs, sinking into a crouch.

"Now!" said the rider. "Step on my foot. Squeeze in here, in front."

He was hardly more than a boy, not nearly large enough to be T'lin Dragontrader, but Eleal was not about to look gift dragons in the mouth now. She scrambled into the saddle in front of him. It was a very uncomfortable position, for her robe pulled up to expose her legs and she was squeezed between the rider and the bony pommel plate. Two leather-clothed arms closed around her.

A light came on in the nearest window.

"Oops!" said that young voice in her ear. "Hang on for all you're worth! *Wondo! Zomph!*"

Telling Starlight to *zomph* turned out to be a miscalculation. *Varch* would have been more prudent. He was up and off across the courtyard like an arrow in flight. He sprang to the top of the wall and over, and an instant later was racing through shrubbery and trees. Branches cracked and whipped. Eleal choked down a scream and doubled over, clinging for her life to the pommel plate. Fortunately Starlight had folded his frills back tightly out of harm's way, and she managed to tuck her head underneath one. Leaning on her back, her companion cursed shrilly.

A tooth-jarring leap almost unseated her as the dragon bounded to the top of another wall. Coping stones fell loose and they all descended into the road beyond with a crash in the night. Having been given no further instructions, the dragon might well have crossed the road and proceeded to scramble up the house opposite, but fortunately he wheeled to the right and began to gather speed.

"Five gods!" yelled the youth. "What's the word for *slow down?*"

"*Varch!*" Eleal shouted, straightening up.

Starlight reluctantly slowed to a breathtaking run. The night streamed past in a rush of cold air and a clattering of claws. Luckily the street was deserted.

"Phew! Thanks. I'm Gim Sculptor."

"Eleal Singer."

"Glad to hear it. Would be bad manners to rescue the wrong damsel. Which is left and which is right? I've forgotten already."

"*Whilth* and *chaiz*. You mean you don't know how to do this?"

"*Chaiz!*" Gim ordered. "No. I've never been on a dragon in my life before. The god will preserve us! He sent me."

EDWARD SPENT THE HOURS AFTER INSPECTOR LEATHER-dale's departure stewing in misery, going over and over the ghastly interrogation and wishing he could call back a lot of his answers. His bragging about the accuracy of his bowling had been the worst sort of side—it might not justify a hanging, but it seemed likely to provoke one now. From what he recalled of the Grange kitchen, the feat the bobbies were suggesting was absolutely impossible. Far more likely, that key was an unneeded duplicate that had been lying in the pot for years, but if there was no other explanation for the locked room, then a jury would accept the police version. The only alternative was magic, and English juries were notoriously disinclined to believe in magic.

So was he.

The mystery of his father's age was maddening, although it seemed completely irrelevant to the murder. His knowledge of his family was the knowledge of a twelve-year-old, for he had never discussed such things with Holy Roly. He knew that the brothers had not met since Cameron had emigrated to New Zealand; he thought he could recall the guv'nor saying once that Roland had been in divinity college then. The old bigot had probably been ordained sometime in the late sixties, judging by his present age. Edward's parents had been married in New Zealand and had then returned to England, briefly, before going out to Africa. There had been no family reunion, because by then the Prescotts had been in India and Roland still in Fiji or Tonga or somewhere. That was as much as Edward knew.

On the face of it, though, Leatherdale had a case. If Cameron Exeter had been a clerk in government service in New Zealand in the sixties, how could he have been forty years old in Kenya, forty years later?

But if District Officer Exeter had been an impostor, then why had that fact not emerged at the board of inquiry? Edward had read the hateful report a hundred times and there was no hint of any such mystery in it. It did not mention his father's background at all. In his present state of dejection that curious omission suddenly seemed ominous, like a potential embarrassment swept under a rug.

Obviously Holy Roly must know more than he had ever revealed, and Edward might yet have to grovel to him for enlightenment. Had he shown his uncle that photograph when he arrived in England? He could not remember, but it would have been odd if he had not. Assume he had. The old bigot must have seen right away that the fortyish man in it could not be his brother. So why had he not said so at once? Why had he not said so four years later, after the massacre, when he was landed with custody of the impostor's son?

In order to lay his hands on the rest of the family money?

The Crown proposes that when Grandfather Exeter died and left the remains of the ill-gotten family fortune to his three children, the genuine Cameron Exeter was already dead and buried at the far side of the world. Somehow a much younger man assumed his identity, was accepted in his stead, pocketed the loot, and promptly left New Zealand, where he was known by his real name. Thereafter he could never be unmasked as long as he stayed away from the dead man's brother and sister. My Lud, the prosecution rests its case.

Learned counsel for the defense expresses disbelief. Why would such a rogue then go and bury himself in the African bush?

Because, counters the prosecution, the Reverend Roland Exeter had retired from active missionary service and was on his way Home. The impostor would be exposed.

But why Africa? Why not Paris, or Vienna, or even America?

Edward tried to consider the question as judge and ended as a hung jury. He could not deny the evidence of the photograph; he could not believe that the father whose memory he cherished had been such a villain. When Mildred Prescott died, the guv'-nor had become Alice's guardian and therefore custodian of her share of the dwindling family fortune. He had taken the child in and treated her as his own daughter; he had not rushed off to Europe to spend her money. He had remained to serve the people of Nyagatha until his death.

What if, four years before that death, Roland Exeter had seen the photograph? That made nonsense of the hypothesis! Holy Roly would have blown the gaff, denounced the impostor, reclaimed the money, and thrown Edward out in the gutter. Wouldn't he?

So Edward could not have shown the guv'nor's picture to Roland. He would certainly give odds that it was presently on its way to London so the reverend gentleman might view it now. The mystery could have nothing to do with the murder at Greyfriars Grange, but surely no copper would resist a chance to solve a twenty-year-old fraud case so easily.

Edward barely touched the leathery slab of haddock that came at teatime.

By nine o'clock the nurses were making their rounds—giving the patients back rubs, bedding them down for the night, removing the flowers because it was not healthy to sleep with flowers in the room. Germany had invaded Belgium, Britain had declared war. Men were enlisting by the thousands. Even that stirring news failed to penetrate Edward's black mood. He was out of it for at least three months, until his leg mended, and death on the gallows now seemed much more likely than glory in battle.

He noticed a change in the nurses' attitude. They passed on the latest news, but they did not seem to want to talk with him. Even when he roused himself to be cheerful and chatty, they failed to respond. Now they knew he was a murderer.

He tried to read the last chapter of *The Lost World,* and the words were a blur. All he could take in was the awful relevance of the title.

The lights were turned off. The hospital fell quiet and gradually the clamor of hooves and engines outside faded into night. Greyfriars would never be a riotous place in the evening, and tonight most men would be at home with family and friends, coming to grips with the catastrophe that had so suddenly befallen the world. If there was a patriotic rally in progress somewhere, it was being held out of earshot of Albert Memorial.

Completely unable to sleep, he squirmed and fretted in his sweat-soaked bed. Tomorrow he must ask to see the solicitor Mrs. Bodgley had mentioned. Or would that be an admission of guilt? Should he wait until Leatherdale arrived with the warrant? Who could possibly have killed old Bagpipe, and how, and why? Nothing made any sense anymore.

The only certainty was that he had no choice but to stay and face the music. Even if he were able to run, he had no one to run to—except Alice, and he would never impose on her like that. He could never impose on anyone like that. As it was, he could not walk, he had no money or clothes; he would not even be able to pull his trousers on over his splints. If he even had a proper cast on his leg . . .

Suppose he *had* shown the photograph to Holy Roly? Suppose Roly had recognized his brother, but his brother thirty years younger than he should be? That would explain his references to devil worship. He had been implying that Cameron, like Dr. Faustus, had sold his soul to the devil in return for eternal youth.

Oh, Lord! That was even madder than keys jumping into pots or murderers going out through locked doors.

He might have been asleep, he was not sure. Sudden light startled him as the door swung wider and a nurse entered, making her rounds. He saw her only as a dark shape. He raised a hand in greeting.

"Not sleeping?" she asked. "Pain?"

"No. Bad news."

"Oh, they'll hold the Germans off until you get there." She laid an appraising hand on his forehead.

"Not that. Personal bad news."

"I'm sorry. Anything I can do to help?"

"Find me a good solicitor."

She said, *"Oh!"* as if she had just remembered who he was. "Want me to ask the doctor for a sleeping draft for you?"

He thought about it.

He very nearly said yes.

"No. I'll manage."

"I'll look back later." She floated away and the room filled again with darkness, except for one thin strip of light along the doorjamb.

He went back to his worries. Eventually a new thought penetrated—the nurse's belated reaction suggested that Leatherdale had removed his watchdog. Perhaps he had been needed for more urgent duties tonight. Marvelous! Now the suspect could tiptoe out of the hospital and run off to Brazil or somewhere. When the nurse came back he'd ask her for a set of crutches.

Again a sudden flowering of light startled him out of semiconsciousness. He blinked at the same dark shape against the brightness. He wondered why she'd removed her cap at the same moment as he registered her long braids and realized that this was no nurse.

"Dvard Kisster?" The voice was husky and heavily accented. It jarred loose an avalanche of memory.

He flailed like a landed fish, half-trying to sit up, half-trying to reach for the bell rope, and the result was that he jolted his leg. It hurled a thunderbolt of pain at him. He yelled.

Then he saw a glint of metal in her hand and screamed at the top of his lungs.

She left the door, coming around on his right. *Danger!*

He began to yell for help, using the first words that came into his head. *"Once more into the breach, dear friends!"* Grabbing the nearest weapon, which happened to be the kidney-shaped dish, he continued to shout. *". . . once more; or close the wall up with our English dead. In peace . . ."*

He hurled the dish with all his strength. *". . . so becomes a man as modest stillness and humility . . ."* She had not expected his attack and the missile took her full in the face. She stumbled back with a cry; the dish clanged and clattered on the linoleum. *". . . imitate the action of the tiger; stiffen the sinews . . ."*

He started to reach for the bell again, but it meant extending himself and would leave him open. He needed that hand for throwing. *". . . hard-favored rage . . ."* She flashed toward him, cursing in some foreign tongue and raising her blade. *". . . then lend the eye a terrible aspect . . ."* He hurled the water carafe, she flailed it aside; glass crashed. Where was everybody? *". . . like the brass cannon; let the brow . . ."* He followed with the tumbler and scored a hit. *". . . galléd rock o'erhang . . ."* He was o'erhanging the side of the bed now, earthquakes of agony running through his leg.

She was holding back, watching him, a sinister dark shape. He continued to scream out his speech as loudly as he could: *"Now set the teeth and stretch the nostril wide . . ."* He had Bagpipe's book ready. Why, why, was no one coming? *". . . on, you noble English, whose blood . . ."* She lunged forward and he hurled Conan Doyle. He thought it hit her, but she laughed, and spoke again in her guttural accent. "What next, Dvard?"

She was right; he was running out of missiles. Why could no one hear him? He had never been louder in his life. *"Be copy now to men of grosser blood, And teach them how to war."* She came, fast as an adder. He swung farther to the right as she slashed down at him, flailing his pillow around with his left hand, parrying the blow. But he had almost fallen off the bed, and the jolt on his leg brought a howl to his throat. That was the worst ever—he thought he would faint, and thrust the possibility away. Feathers swirled like smoke. He scrabbled with his right hand and found the empty urinal bottle. *". . . none of you so mean and base . . ."* He swung it as a club against her arm as she struck again, wishing it had been weighted with contents. She cried out and dropped the knife on the floor. He tried to grab her dress with his left hand, thinking he might be able to strangle her if he could pull her close, but she slipped away. Oh—his leg again!

His throat was sore with shouting, *"I see you stand like greyhounds in the slips . . ."* She made a dive to snatch up the knife. He swung the bottle at her head and missed. She came at him again and this time he thought it was all over *". . . straining upon the start. THE GAME'S AFOOT!"*

"Desist!" said a new voice in the corner.

The woman spun around with a shriek.

Edward had not seen him come in, but without question this was the same Mr. Oldcastle he had imagined before. Even in his fur-collared overcoat, with his ancient beaver hat set square on his head, he was a small and unimpressive ally. Yet, with one hand pointing his cane at the armed madwoman and the other tucked in his pocket, he was certainly the calmest person present.

"Begone, strumpet! Go lick thy scurvy masters' boots in penance lest they feed thy carrion carcass to the hounds."

The woman hesitated, then fled out the door without a word. Her footsteps seemed to fade away almost instantly.

The crisis was over.

"Hey!" Edward gasped. "Stop her!"

"Nay, nay, bully lad, it were no profit to deed her to the watch." Mr. Oldcastle removed his hat and brushed it absently with his sleeve. "That wight has been accorded arts to rook their locks and manacles. Wouldst sooner close a cockatrice in a cockboat than jail yon jade."

"You mean," Edward said, easing himself back onto the bed,

"she can get out through a bolted door?" He was soaked and shaking, his heart seemed to be running the Grand National, jumps and all, but he was alive. He was almost sobbing with the pain, but he was alive.

"Aye, or in withal. Had they who seek thy soon demise invested her with deeper skills, thou hadst not fared so well." The little man chuckled. "The recitation was most gamely done! It wanted something in smoothness of phrasing, methinks, but 'twas furnished well in vehemence. Hal himself could not have seasoned the lines with greater spice."

He stepped over to the bed and peered down at Edward with an intent expression on his puckish, wrinkled face. He brought a strange odor of mothballs with him. "The pain in thy leg is not beyond thy strength to bear."

"Er. No, it's not too bad." Edward panted a few times. "Amazingly good, considering." It was not what he would describe as comfortable. He did not need a bullet to bite on, but he was making his teeth work hard.

"It needs suffice for the nonce. Compose thyself a moment. I shall return betimes."

With that Mr. Oldcastle laid his hat and cane carefully on the bed and bustled over to the door. Edward caught a brief glimpse of his tiny, stooped shape against the light, and he had gone.

"Angels and ministers of grace defend me!" he muttered, as this seemed to be Shakespeare night. "What in the name of glory is going on here?" His heartbeat was gradually returning to normal. He was definitely awake and not dreaming. Feathers and water and sparkles of glass on the lino—and splatters of blood also, so he must have scored a hit, perhaps with the tumbler.

And certainly an antique hat and stick lay on the bed, so Mr. Jonathan Oldcastle had really been present and did intend to return. Perhaps he had popped over to Druids Close, the town that received mail and did not exist? *Steady, old chap! We'll have no hysterics here.*

Strangest of all—why was the hospital not in chaotic uproar?

The racket should have wakened every patient on the floor and brought every nurse for miles. Edward thought about trying the bell and then decided to wait for his mysterious guardian to come back.

That did not take long. The little man minced in with a pale garment over his shoulder, carrying a pair of crutches almost as long as himself. His stoop and the forward thrust of his head made him seem to be hurrying even when he was not.

"Thy baggage waits without, Master Exeter." He uttered the little cackling chuckle that was now starting to sound very familiar. "And thy breakage must wait within! Do don this Oxford." He handed Edward a recognizable left shoe and threw down a dressing gown across his chest.

"Hold a minute, sir! I can't walk on this leg!"

"Indeed you will have to make like the wounded plover, dangling a limb to lure the plunderer from the nest. Be speedy, my brave, for worse monsters than the harlot may soon snuff thy scent, such as may overtop my wilted powers." Mr. Oldcastle proceeded to fumble with the tackle that held Edward's leg in traction.

"But running away is an admission of guilt!"

"Staying will be a demonstration of mortality."

Edward's response was stifled by a searing jolt of pain as the leg settled on the bed. He glared up at the old man until he had caught his breath and wiped the sweat out of his eyes.

The puckish face frowned. "Ah, my young butty, dost not know that dragons of war are now full awakened? Beacon fires shall become funeral pyres and flames will consume a generation. Horror soon bestrides the world."

"Yes, but what has that to do—"

"Master Edward, those same elements that spawned this evil dissonance can now turn satisfied from that labor and address their intent to destroying *thee*. Until now they minded more those weightier matters particular to their desires. Thee they gave but little thought, for you are a mere favor they perform for other parties—who shall shortly be discovered to you. Thus thy foes dispatched to your dispatch only that demented trollop who has thrice ineptly sought to undo thee. Now at greater leisure they will loose such grievous raptors to contrive thy demise that thou surely will not see another dawn unless you now take urgent flight."

In other words: *Beat it!*

Absurd as it sounded, his convoluted speech carried conviction. There was no arguing with his obvious sincerity—after all, he had undoubtedly saved Edward's life a few moments ago. Edward pulled up his left leg and struggled into the shoe.

The next few minutes were a stroll on the cobbles of Hell. He made the distance, but only because he chose to regard it as a test of manhood. He sat up and donned the dressing gown. His right foot was lowered to the floor with much help from Mr. Oldcastle, and he pushed himself up to stand on the left. Then he was on his crutches, heading across the litter of feathers to the door. To hold his right leg up was agony; to let it touch the ground was infinitely worse.

It wasn't going to work, of course. The nurses would see him and take him back. They would telephone the police. But he had no breath to argue, and he sweated every step in silence along the wide, dim corridor, wobbling on his crutches with Mr. Oldcastle at his side. The little man had recovered his hat and silver-topped walking stick, and seemed to be fighting back a case of fidgets at the cripple's tortoise pace.

The duty desk was deserted. His old battered suitcase stood beside it, his boater resting on top. Mr. Oldcastle placed this on his head for him at a jaunty angle and took charge of the case. Then he went ahead and opened the door to the stairs.

Edward tried to say, "There's a lift," but he had his teeth so tightly clenched that the words would not come out. Mr. Oldcastle might think that the rackety old cage would bring nurses and orderlies running, or perhaps he did not understand modern machinery. Edward went down three flights of stairs on one foot, one crutch, and a white hand gripping the rail. Mr. Oldcastle carried the other crutch. From the way he managed the suitcase, he must be much stronger than he looked.

There was no one about, no one even tending the admittance desk by the front door. Edward reeled out of the hospital into the cool night air, wondering if he had left a trail of sweat all the way from his bed.

<h1 style="text-align:center">ᖶ᷒᷈30᷈᷒ᖶ</h1>

"Wosok!" GIM COMMANDED FIRMLY, BUT NOTHING happened. Starlight had his head down, buried in T'lin Dragontrader's loving embrace, and was purring so hard he could not hear the order.

"Wosok!" T'lin murmured. The dragon sank down on his belly, still nuzzling his owner and purring loud enough to waken the neighborhood.

There could be few places in cramped Narsh where a dragon might be hidden, but a sculptor's yard was one of them. Even so, Starlight was squeezed in between blocks of stone and half-completed monuments, and the space was hardly enough. A man with a lantern had just closed the gates.

Eleal swung a leg hastily over the pommel plate and slid to the ground in an undignified rush, wincing as her bare feet struck gravel. She had barely rearranged her robe when Gim landed beside her, stumbled, and pitched over with a shrill oath. That was not a very dignified descent for a noble hero on what must surely be his first chivalrous exploit. He scrambled up, muttering and sucking an injured palm.

Eleal had taken two unsteady steps toward T'lin when a portly woman came rushing out of the house with another lantern.

"My dear! You must be frozen! Come inside quickly." She

propelled Eleal bodily over the sharp gravel and into a cozy, fragrant kitchen, brightened by no less than four candles. Swathed in llama wool blankets, Eleal was tucked into a chair close to the big iron range. The woman swung the door open and clattered a poker in among the glowing coals. Then she began stoking it with big lumps of coal from a shiny brass scuttle, using brass tongs. Shiny copper pans hung on one wall. There was a tasseled rug on the floor; painted china plates stood along a shelf so the pictures on them were visible. Gim's family might not live in a palace like the king of Jurg, but they were wealthy compared with a troupe of actors.

Eleal began to shiver uncontrollably. She could not tell whether that was from the change of temperature or from nervous reaction, but she felt in danger of falling apart.

"Hot soup!" the woman proclaimed as if invoking a major god. Granting the range fire a few moments' mercy, she knelt to bundle her visitor's feet in her own still-warm fleece coat.

Eleal forced her reply through chattering teeth. "That would be wonderful, thank you."

"Vegetable or chicken broth?"

"No chicken please!"

"I'm Gim's mother, Embiliina Sculptor, and you must be Eleal Singer."

"Yes, but how—"

"Explanations later!" Embiliina insisted. She was much less bulky without her coat and hood. In fact, she was slim and surprisingly youthful to be mother of a boy as old as Gim. Her features were fine-drawn, her complexion pale and speckled with millions of tiny fair freckles. Her hair was a spun red-gold, hanging in big loose curls to her shoulders. She wore a quality dress of the same blue shade as her eyes. She wore a smile.

T'lin Dragontrader strode in, filling the room, black turban almost touching the ceiling. His weather-beaten face and coppery beard seemed vulgar and barbaric alongside Embiliina's more delicate red-gold coloring. He began to peel off outer garments, scowling at nothing with a taut, grim expression.

When he stepped closer to warm his fingers at the range, he was still avoiding Eleal's eye.

And the door closed behind the man who must be Gim's father. He was of middle height and husky, although he looked small alongside the dragon trader. He clasped Eleal's icy hand in one twice as large and rough as a rasp, studying her with solemn coal black eyes. He was as swarthy as his wife was fair.

"I am Kollwin Sculptor."

"Eleal Singer."

He nodded. "You are younger than I imagined. If you did what I think you did, then you're a brave lass." He spoke with great deliberation, as if reading his words.

"I d-d-didn't have time to think! The honor is G-g-gim's."

The dark man shook his head. "The honor is the god's. Gim has gone to thank him for a safe return. When you are ready, you will wish to visit him also?"

"Of course! At once." Eleal stood up shakily.

"Later!" Embiliina said, clattering pots. "The child's half-froze to death and the soup—"

Eleal had almost resumed her seat when the sculptor said, "First things first." His voice was slow, but not to be argued with. "You will promise not to discuss or reveal the place I am about to take you?"

That settled Eleal's indecision—her curiosity reared like a startled dragon. "Of course! I swear I never shall," she said eagerly.

The sculptor nodded and turned to T'lin. "Dragontrader?"

But T'lin had found himself a chair and spread out his long legs. He was a startling, many-colored sight in variegated leggings and a doublet of embroidered quilting. He was also a figure of menace. His long sword in its green scabbard lay by his feet, he still wore his black turban. He shook his head. "Secrets make me nervous. They are more often evil than good."

Kollwin's ruddy face seemed to bunch up with shock at the refusal. "It is no great secret, a shrine to Tion. Just . . . private."

T'lin's green eyes stared back coldly. "Then why require oaths of secrecy?"

"Because there are valuables there and I do not want them talked around. Not everyone is above stealing from a god."

"Gods can afford the loss better than us poor workers. No, I shall give thanks in my own fashion later."

Kollwin scratched a dark-stubbled cheek in contemplation. "Has that ring in your ear some special significance, Dragontrader?"

T'lin drooped his red eyebrows menacingly. "If it has, then it did not deter your god when he needed my assistance."

The sculptor thought for a moment and seemed to accept the reasoning, although he was not pleased. "Come then, Eleal Singer."

"Just a moment!" Embiliina barred the way like an enraged deity. "You are not to drag that poor child outside again on a night like this in her bare feet."

There was a minor delay while Eleal donned her hostess's boots and fleece coat, all much too large for her. There was another minor delay when Kollwin tried to go out and came face-to-face with a dragon. Starlight, being as nosy as any of his kind, had wriggled forward to see what was going on and his head filled the doorway.

"Try opening the drape," T'lin said drily from his chair. "And close the door before he tries to come in."

That worked. The great head swung over to peer in the window, and then the sculptor was able to squeeze out past the scaly shoulder, followed by Eleal, stepping over claws like sickles.

Ysh's tiny disk shed her cold blue light through a gap in the clouds, sparkling like frost on the dragon's scales. Carrying a lantern, Kollwin Sculptor led Eleal all around the dragon to reach a small shed against the wall of the yard. The door was open, but she noticed that the timber was thick and it bore at least three locks. If that was merely "private," then what was "secret" like? The inside was cluttered with all the litter she might have expected: tools and balks of wood and oddly shaped scraps of stone or metal. More interesting than those was the trapdoor in the floor, and a staircase descending.

The sculptor went first, lighting the way. "This is very old."

His voice echoed up eerily. "There was probably a temple here, once upon a time."

And now there was a shrine. The room was small and low, more like an oddly shaped volume of shadow than a chamber, a bricked-off portion of an ancient cellar. Where the walls were visible, some parts were of very rough, crude masonry, others had been cut out of living rock. The only light came from a pair of braziers standing on a rug, thick and richly colored and oddly out of place. Those were the only furniture. The air was chill and yet headily scented with incense.

Beyond the rug was an alcove, and in the alcove stood the god.

Gim knelt on stone in the center of the chamber, but he must have concluded his devotions, because he scrambled to his feet and turned to smile a welcome as the newcomers approached. It was the first time Eleal had really seen him. He was still bulky as a bear in his coat, but he had removed his hat, revealing a floppy tangle of gold curls, and his eyes were as blue as his mother's. His lip bore a faint pink fuzz, which he probably thought of as a mustache. Politely disregarding that, she concluded that her rescuer could be considered a very handsome young man—how appropriate! She returned his smile. Only then did she look at the god.

The image had not been set in the alcove. Rather, the mottled yellow stone of the cave had been dug out to leave Tion in high relief, exquisitely carved. He was life-size, identifiable by a beardless face and by the pipes he held. The Youth was most often depicted nude, but here he wore a narrow scarf around his loins—an impractical garment that would rapidly fall off any mortal. He was striding forward out of the rock, one foot on the floor and the other still buried in the wall. He held his head slightly bent and turned, as if he were about to put the pipes to his lips or had just finished playing, while his eyes looked out at the visitors with a curiously enigmatic smile. As the creeping flames of the braziers danced, reflections moved on his limbs, his shadow fidgeted on the back of the hollow. He almost seemed to breathe.

"He's gorgeous!" Eleal whispered. "You made him yourself, Sculptor? Oh, he is beautiful!" Then she took a longer look at that perfect face and swung around to stare down at Gim, who bent his head quickly.

"I'm sorry," she muttered. "I didn't mean . . . Well, I did, but—"

"I did not bring you here to admire art, Singer," Kollwin growled, but he was fighting back a smile.

"Oh, but . . . Gim? Look at me."

Gim looked up, redder than a bloodfruit in the dim light. He smiled a little . . .

The likeness was exact! Or would be. He was not quite old enough, but the faces were already the same. Gim seemed taller only because he was wearing boots; otherwise he would be the same height as the god stepping out of the wall.

"An older brother, Kollwin Sculptor? Or did you imagine him as he will be in another couple of years?"

"My son was not the model. I never use models."

She could only stare from the god's inscrutable smile to Gim's scarlet embarrassment and back again.

"Tell her, Father. Please?"

"I carved the blessed likeness long ago," Kollwin said in his ponderous way. "The night I completed it I thanked the god and went up to the house and was told my wife was in labor."

She dared another glance at Gim, and he was redder yet, but wearing an idiotic grin now.

"Then the god? . . ." The god had fashioned the boy to the statue!

"The carving is the older," the sculptor said. "Gim takes after his mother and I was very much in love with her—and still am, of course. That may explain any resemblance you see, but we came here to give thanks, not to discuss art."

Eleal was about to kneel, then saw that Kollwin had more dissertations to intone.

"I think you are old enough to keep a secret, Eleal Singer. I will risk a word of explanation, if you will swear never to carry it outside this holy place."

She swore, anxious to learn the purpose of a covert shrine. This was almost as exciting as escaping down a wall in the middle of the night and much less nightmarish.

He rubbed his chin with a raspy noise. "I am not sure how much I may say, though."

Gim was staying very quiet.

"The Tion Fellowship?" she prompted.

Kollwin's eyes glinted; his swarthy face seemed to darken.

Error? "All I know," she said hastily, "is that Trong Impresario and his son came, er, *went* to a meeting two nights ago. A mutual friend said they belonged to some club he called the Tion Fellowship. They did not mention it themselves." But now she knew where they had come.

The sculptor sniffed grudgingly. "The Tion Mystery is not a club! But, yes, they asked their brethren of the Narsh Lodge for aid. Of course we offered prayer and sacrifice on their behalf, both here and in the Lady's temple. Our pleas seemed to be heard." He cleared his throat awkwardly, looking up at the god. "We know what happened, because we had one of our local brothers in the temple anyway."

Doing what, she wondered? But of course special dedication to one god would not reduce anyone's obligations to worship all the others also. The ceremony had been public.

Kollwin smiled—a slow process like sunshine moving on mountains. "We sent along someone who would understand the ancient speech, just to be on the safe side. The priests did not reveal everything the oracle had said, but they did not distort the holy words unduly. The goddess specifically directed that you were to be taken into her clergy. She insisted you be kept locked up and guarded for a fortnight. She said the rest of the troupe must contribute a hundred stars to her temple treasury, either by donation or service, and then should be run out of town as soon as possible.

"So it seemed that the Lady had turned aside her anger and all but one of the troupe was free to leave." The sculptor cleared his throat harshly. "Frankly, that one seemed of very little importance to us. The youngest, dispensable. . . . One cracked egg in a dozen is not a disaster. We thought the problem had been solved.

"But Holy Tion did not think so! He looks after those who serve him, as we should have remembered. It so happened—and this is what I ask you not to repeat—that my son had begun his initiation into the Tion Mystery." He hesitated, then shrugged. "The ceremony includes a period of prayer and fasting, which concludes when Kirb'l next appears. That night the skies were clear and Kirb'l appeared."

"I saw him." Eleal stole a glance at Gim. He smiled down at her shyly.

"At the conclusion of the ceremony," his father continued, "the initiate sleeps before the figure of the god. Here, on the floor, Gim was vouchsafed a remarkable dream, indeed a vision. Tell her, lad."

Gim rubbed his upper lip with a knuckle. His blue eyes sparkled in the candlelight. "I saw myself on a black dragon, riding to the temple." His voice rose in excitement. "Just as it happened! I knew which window, and exactly what to do with the rope. It all came true! And I knew it wasn't just an ordinary dream! I mean, I've never even touched a dragon before! So I told Father and—"

The older Sculptor chuckled. "He hauled my bedcovers off at dawn! Understand: Gim was not present when the actors came! He had not been told of the oracle, or of Eleal Singer. Yet here he was babbling about rescuing a girl held against her will in the Lady's temple! I knew then that the god had heard our prayers and issued instructions. We inquired and learned that there was a dragon trader in town, so we went to talk with him. And he did have a black dragon in his herd. And he knew you personally."

This was something out of one of Piol Poet's dramas! "And?" Eleal demanded.

Kollwin Sculptor chuckled. "And I think he should be in on the rest of the telling. Your soup must be ready. My wife will skin me. You know enough now to know who to thank."

"It was the god who rescued you, Eleal," Gim said modestly.

Yes. But why why why?

And which aspect of Tion had answered the prayers? Dropping to her knees, Eleal took a harder look at the image that so much resembled the young man now kneeling beside her. The enigma in the smile, she decided, came from the turn of the head and eyes—lips smiling in one direction, eyes in another. He held Tion's pipes, but a god who would steal a girl away from a goddess's temple by sending a dragon and a boy who had never ridden one before might well be the same god who was causing that boy to grow up as an exact replica of his father's masterpiece—Kirb'l, the Joker.

Kollwin had somehow contrived to put her in the center. It was his shrine, so she waited for him to begin. One of the nice things about the Youth was that he spurned written texts. There were red, green, white, and blue scriptures, but no yellow.

While she was preparing words in her head, Kollwin addressed the god. Even in conversation with mortals he sounded as if he were reading a text; his prayer was a monumental inscription. "Lord of art and youth and beauty, I thank you for the safe return of my son this night, for the trust you have shown in us, and for the chance to be of service. As always, I am grateful for the blessings of the day passed and the opportunities of the day ahead. Amen."

Gim said, "Amen," so Eleal did also. This intimate sharing of religion was unfamiliar to her, but obviously it was her turn now. She looked up at the god; his eyes smiled back with infinite patience and the same mysterious amusement as before.

"Thank you, Holy Tion, for rescuing me from the most disgusting, degr—"

The sculptor barked, *"Careful!* You must not blaspheme against the Lady!"

Eleal took a deep breath and began again. "Then I'll just say that I am very grateful for being rescued. . . . Thank you, Lord." She paused, the others waited. "And I promise to serve, er, the lord of art and beauty as well as I can." She thought of the festival, and tried to imagine Uthiam mounting the steps in the great temple to receive a scarlet rose from the hand of the god.

"And I ask you to look after my friends, because they have suffered because of me, and, well, I'd like them to do well in your festival. To your honor, of course. Amen."

Gim said, "Amen."

His father coughed. "I am no priest, Eleal Singer—but may I make a suggestion?"

"Please do."

"If your trouble was caused by some offense you committed against Holy Ois, or against Holy Eltiana herself, then you might perhaps ask Lord Tion to intercede for you."

"I didn't do anything. . . . I don't think it was anything I did," Eleal said. "But yes. Please, Holy One, keep me safe from the other gods' anger and whatever is prophesied. Amen."

That had not come out quite as she had intended. Again Gim echoed her amen, but there was a distinct pause before his father did—Kollwin had noted the cryptic reference in her prayer. Gim was still too stirred up by his adventure to be concerned with anything else.

"I already spoke my thanks to Holy Tion, Father, but I will do so again if you want to hear."

The sculptor chuckled. "You are not a child that I need supervise your prayers, but I can understand if your heart is still full, and anything I can understand must be very obvious to a god."

Gim needed no more encouragement than that. He raised his hands in supplication to the image. "Lord of art, I thank you again for the opportunity to serve you and for giving me such an adventure and bringing me back safely. All I ever want is to serve you, Lord, and I especially hope to serve you by bringing more beauty into the world in art or music, but I dedicate my whole life to pleasing you in any way I can. Amen."

"Amen," Eleal said.

The sculptor bowed his head to the floor and said, "Amen" loudly as he straightened again. Then he clambered to his feet to indicate that the ceremony was over.

Ambria Impresario had been known to complain more than once that the gods had given Eleal Singer exceptionally sharp ears. She knew that Kollwin Sculptor had whispered a few other words—quickly, softly—in that sudden genuflection. *"Lord, remember he is very young!"* She had heard. Gim almost certainly had not. Had the god?

ACT III

ROAD SHOW

31

"So I had visitors," T'lin Dragontrader said. "A very lovely lady named Uthiam Piper came to see me, with a distraught young man named Something Trumpeter. They both seemed to know my business better than I did. How was I ever going to get any work done in Narsh if people kept cornering me to pour out tragic sagas of young women adopted by a goddess?"

His tone was amused. His expression was not. There was tension in that cozy kitchen. Dragontrader had refused to visit the family shrine. That was a very unusual act, which might be taken as a serious insult. The fact that the sanctuary was more than that—was the center of a mystery—might help a little, or perhaps it made things even worse, for he had probably declined a very rare honor.

Eleal was no stranger to late hours and odd sleep patterns, but this was the middle of the night. The soup had been hot and delicious. Embiliina had insisted on tucking her into her chair with loads of blankets. She was feeling woozy.

"What did they think I could do against a goddess?" T'lin said, rolling his green eyes. "Did they think I was crazy?" He was very large. Although he sprawled at ease, legs and arms spread, his size and beard and black turban were daunting in that kitchen. His sword lay within reach. "They did not even know where missy was. I threw them out, and they went away on the mammoths."

Kollwin Sculptor had stripped down to a threadbare, well-washed yellow cotton smock and battered old leather leggings. He sat hunched forward on his chair, leaning meaty forearms on his knees, mostly scowling at the range but sometimes at the dragon trader. His arms and his feet were bare. Such informality was surprising and perhaps deliberate. Although he could not match T'lin for sheer bulk, he was a broad, thick man, and he was showing he was not intimidated by his visitor.

Two enormous green eyes kept watch through the window. Dragons looked ferocious, but they were pretty harmless usually.

Gim was still so jittery with excitement that he could barely sit still. His mother kept telling him to stop fidgeting. He, too, had stripped off his fleeces, losing half of himself in the process. In cotton smock and woolen leggings, he was all long limbs and grin. His resemblance to the god in the crypt was astonishing, but his bare arms showed that he needed to fill out yet; the divine artist needed a few more years to produce a perfect replica of the model.

Eleal wondered sleepily what his trade was. His hand had been smooth and he lacked his father's brawn, so he was probably not a sculptor, and yet he retained the family name. He was certainly old enough to be apprenticed to something, though.

"The next morning I had two more visitors," T'lin said, "and those two they told me a god wanted me to get involved! How, I asked them, is a man ever going to earn a living in this city?"

Gim grinned and ran a hand through his golden curls. Yes, he was even more handsome than Golfren Piper and he would make Klip Trumpeter look like a gargoyle. Eleal wondered sleepily if he had any talent for acting. Even now he would be a natural as the Youth in the tragedies! She must offer to give him lessons. That idea was amusing, except he seemed to have forgotten her altogether. He would be regarding her as a mere child, of course. She would have to demonstrate her maturity.

What more could she do to impress him than climb down a wall in the dark on a rope?

"Madness!" T'lin grumbled. "They wanted to borrow my favorite dragon for a kid who didn't know *Whilth* from *Chaiz!*"

"What persuaded you?" Embiliina Sculptor asked quietly. She was the only one of the group who seemed at ease, playing the role of hostess beautifully, passing around homemade biscuits. There was no hint of worry in her eyes.

Had Eleal's mother been as pretty as she? She had never had a chance to be motherly.

T'lin grunted. "I needed peace and quiet to earn a living. Besides, I was sure the brat would break his neck and I could trust Starlight to come home to me."

Gim grinned again.

"Why didn't you ride him yourself?" Eleal asked.

T'lin's green eyes registered horror. "Me? I'm much too heavy for escapades like that. Obviously Holy Tion had chosen a racing jockey for the task. To be honest," he admitted ruefully, "and you know I am always honest, Jewel of the Arts, I did not expect such success. I thought it was suicide."

Gim chuckled with delight.

"What if the temple guards had caught him, though?"

T'lin stroked his copper beard complacently. "Then I would have denounced him as a thief to get my dragon back."

Gim's jaw dropped.

A sour smile crossed his father's face. "You hadn't thought of that? You'd have been hanged!"

"But it worked," T'lin said in disgust. He fixed his cold green gaze on Eleal, and she started at his frown. "I came here to trade dragons and I have earned the enmity of the senior divinity of the city! I must leave quickly and never return." He gripped the arms of his chair with his big hands. "The priests and guards will be scouring the streets already. Well, you have her, Sculptor. I have done my part. I must go!"

For a moment Eleal toyed with the idea of staying in this cozy family kitchen forever—forsaking drama and travel . . . becoming one of this kindly family. . . . It did have a certain appeal in her present condition, but she knew that it was not going to happen.

"Not so fast," Kollwin growled, eyeing her. "Now we need to know why! Why did Eltiana want this girl so badly? Why has Kirb'l Tion snatched her away? And what on earth are we supposed to do with her now she is here? Explain, Singer!"

"My part is done," T'lin repeated, but he settled back in his chair to listen.

Four sets of eyes were waiting, five counting the dragon's, although he was having trouble because he kept steaming up the window. Two sets of blue, two green, one black . . .

Eleal swallowed a yawn. She decided she must tell the tale with the majesty it deserved, although it needed Piol Poet to do it justice. She would have to stick to prose. She threw off the blankets and sat up like the Mother on the Rainbow Throne in *The Judgment of Apharos*.

"Are you feeling all right, dear?" Embiliina asked anxiously.

"Quite all right, thank you. Dost any of you mort . . . do any of you know what the *Filoby Testament* is?"

T'lin and Kollwin said, "Yes," as Gim shook his head.

"Book of prophecies," his father explained. "About eighty years ago some priestess over in Suss went out of her mind and began spouting prophecies. The others wrote them down. Her family had it printed up as memorial. What about it?"

T'lin uttered his dragon snort. Eleal knew she could never guess what he was thinking, and yet somehow she felt sure that he was surprised by this mention of the *Testament*. He seemed displeased, and certainly wary.

"Most prophecy is so thin you could drink it," he growled. "Quite a lot of the Filoby stuff turned out to be hard fact—so I've heard. What about it?"

"It is prophesied therein," Eleal declared mysteriously, "that should I happenstance attend the festival of Tion in Suss this year, then the world may be changed."

There was a thoughtful silence. The range crackled. Starlight's green eyes blinked at the window.

"Does she often behave like this?" Gim asked.

"No," T'lin said, staring hard. "She's putting on airs, but she's telling the truth as she knows it. Carry on, Avatar of Astina."

"The oracle proclaimed me a child of Ken'th."

"Yecch!" T'lin's red beard twisted in an expression of disgust.

"It's not my fault!" Eleal protested,

"No. Nor your mother's either. Can you confirm that, Koll-win Sculptor?"

"I was told that the oracle implied it. The Lady is always enraged when her lord philanders with mortals."

Embiliina said, "Oh dear!" and patted Eleal's hand. "It doesn't matter, dear."

Eleal recalled Ambria in *The Judgment of Apharos* again. "Per-adventure, it may. Both the Lady and the Man decreed that I must not be allowed to fulfill the prophecy."

"Eltiana yes," T'lin said. "How do you know about Karzon?"

Eleal drew a deep breath.

"A reaper told me."

Gim sniggered. He looked at his father . . . at the dragon trader . . . at his mother. His eyes widened.

"Go on," T'lin said, his eyes cold marble.

Eleal told the story carefully, leaving out Dolm's name. She described him only as "a man I know."

It was a very satisfying performance. When she had finished, Embiliina seemed ready to weep, Gim's eyes were as big as Starlight's, and the two men were staring hard at each other. Dragontrader chewed at his copper mustache. Sculptor had clasped his great hands and was cracking knuckles.

"By the four moons!" T'lin growled. "Your god is the Joker!"

"He is," Kollwin said stubbornly, "but he is my god. We are supposed to get her to the festival, I think."

"That would be my interpretation."

Eleal protested. "I'm not sure I want—"

"You have no choice, girl!"

"Apparently not," the dragon trader agreed.

"Is it possible?"

T'lin did not answer that. He clawed at his beard with one hand, staring morosely at the range. "We seem to have been sucked into a serious squabble in the Pentatheon! I did not tell you of my first visitor—a doddering old crone trailing an un-sheathed sword."

The others waited in silence. Embiliina moved her lips in prayer.

"A blue nun, of course," T'lin continued. "Of all the lunatic regiments of fanatics that harass honest workingmen . . . It was barely dawn and I had a hangover. I listened with a patience and politeness that will assuredly let my soul twinkle in the heavens for all Eternity. Then I sent her away!" He clenched a red-hairy fist. "I thought she was senile. I should have known better, I suppose."

Kollwin raised heavy black brows, pondering in his deliberate fashion. "She came *before* the oracle spoke?"

"Before the holy hag could have scampered down there from the temple, at any rate. She babbled about Eleal Singer being in trouble. I pretended I did not know who she was talking about. She smiled as if I was an idiot child, then tottered away, saying she would return. I told my men I would flatten every one of them if she ever got near me again."

"Who are these blue nuns?" Gim asked, worried.

"Followers of the goddess of repentance," said his father. "A strange order, rarely seen in these parts. Harmless pests."

T'lin shook his head. "But the stories . . . When Padsdon Dictator ruled in Lappin—him they called the Cruel—one day he was haranguing the citizens from a balcony and a sister in the crowd pointed her sword up at him and began calling on him to repent. Padsdon's guards could not reach her, and he either could not or would not depart. Before she had finished, he leaped from the balcony and died!"

Kollwin shrugged dismissively. "You believe that?"

"I do," T'lin said with a scowl. "My father was there."

In the ensuing silence, the range uttered a few thoughtful clicking sounds.

"So the Maiden is on Eleal's side—the Youth's side," Embiliina Sculptor said softly, blue eyes filled with concern now. "What of the Source? Have we any word of the All-Knowing?"

Her husband shook his head. "If the Light has judged, the others would not be still at odds."

"That is obvious!" Eleal declared. "Tragedies always end with the Parent deciding the issue. It's not time for Visek yet."

Gim grinned, but no one argued.

"You must take the girl to Sussland, T'lin Dragontrader," the sculptor said heavily.

The big man groaned. "Why me?"

"Who else? The priests will be scouring the city already. The Lady . . ." Kollwin shrugged, looking thoughtfully at his son. "It is possible?"

"Normally I would say it was," T'lin growled. "Normally I would say I could run over to Filoby and be back before dark. But Susswall is treacherous at the best of times. How will it be now, with the Lady of Snows enraged and bent to stop us? May colic rot my guts! And when I arrive I may find armies of reapers waiting for me!"

Eleal had already thought of that complication—how could she return to the troupe when Dolm was there?

Gim was wilting under his father's stare.

The sculptor cracked his knuckles again. "I shouldn't ask this. Don't answer if you don't want—"

Gim relaxed and smirked. "No I didn't."

"Didn't do what?" his mother demanded.

Kollwin laughed and clapped his son's knee. "When he took his vows last night . . . the night before last I suppose it is now . . . When he prayed to Tion, he was going to ask to go to the festival. Right, lad?"

Gim nodded wistfully, looking much more like a child than a romantic hero of damsel-rescuing prowess. "I thought about it, but you asked me not to. So I didn't."

Now approval shone in his father's smile. "I noticed you didn't actually promise! I was sure you wouldn't be able to resist the opportunity. I'm proud that you did. But the holy one knew how much you want to go. He has overruled us."

Gim's grin returned instantly. "You mean I get to go?"

"You have to go, son! You were the one who profaned the Lady's temple. Her priests will blunt their knives on your hide if they catch you. It is your reward, I suppose. You will do this for us, Dragontrader?"

"It won't take much more avalanche to bury three of us than two," T'lin agreed morosely.

Kollwin uttered a snort that would not have shamed the dragon trader. "Four! You think the blue sister has gone back to her nunnery?"

T'lin threw back his head and howled, but whether from rage or merriment Eleal could not tell. Starlight's answering belch rattled the casement.

"Oh that does it!" the big man said, heaving to his feet. "That'll waken half the city. That'll fetch every priest in the Lady's temple!"

Eleal stood up, but he frowned at her.

"I can't take you! Every lizard in the streets is going to be stopped and questioned. Can you dress this troublesome wench to look like a boy, Embiliina Sculptor?"

Gim's mother looked Eleal over and pursed her lips. "I think we have some old castoffs that will fit."

"Excellent!" T'lin turned a thoughtful gaze on Gim. "Never knew a city without a lovers' gate."

"I know a way over the wall, sir," the boy said.

T'lin nodded. "Have you a trade yet, stripling?"

Gim smiled nervously. "I am apprenticed to my uncle, Golthog Painter. I play the lyre, but . . ."

"As of now you're Gim Wrangler!" Dragontrader pulled a face. "Remember I hired you in Lappin last Neckday and I pay you one crescent a fortnight." He grinned. "But I may make it two. I don't usually pay that for greenies, understand, but you made a good start on impressing me tonight. Bring the girl down to my outfit as soon as she's ready. You'll impress me a lot more if you make it."

"Very generous of you, sir!" Gim straightened his shoulders. "The god will guard us."

"He'll have to." T'lin on his feet could not have dominated the kitchen more effectively had he been one of his dragons. He swung around to the sculptor. "What of you and your lovely wife? The priests will be after you also."

Husband and wife exchanged glances. "Us and our other

fledglings?" Kollwin said. "What sort of a family picnic are you planning to conduct over Narshwall, T'lin Dragontrader?" He shook his head. "We have friends who will help us offer penance to assuage the Lady's wrath."

T'lin did not argue—he had scowled at the mention of children. "Probably cost you a whole new temple." He stooped to cup Eleal's chin in his raspy hand. He tilted her face up and frowned at her menacingly. "Most women wait until they have tits. You have set the world on its ears already, minx!"

Eleal had been thinking the same, but she knew Ambria would not tolerate such vulgarity. She assumed her most disapproving expression. "Wait 'till you see what I'm going to do in Suss, Dragontrader," she said.

32

A DOGCART STOOD UNDER THE GASLIGHTS. THE DRIVER jumped down and came trotting up the steps. He wore a sporty suit and a bowler hat, but no overcoat. He was scowling under a bristly hedge of eyebrows. He had a clipped, military-style mustache, and a clipped, military-style bark: "You brought him!"

"Aye!" Mr. Oldcastle chortled. All Edward could see of him was the crown of his hat and his Astrakhan collar. "I bring thee a doughty cockerel for thy flock—truly a recruit of sinew."

"The devil you do! But I'm not at all sure I want him, don't you know?"

"Well, thou hast him now. Present thyself by whatever name thou deemest most fitting."

The man eyed Edward disapprovingly. "Name's Creighton. I knew your father." He began to offer a hand, then realized that both of Edward's were engaged. He was obviously an army man, very likely Army of India, for there was a faint lilt to his speech that such men sometimes picked up after years of commanding native troops.

"Pleased to meet you, sir," Edward said. Balanced precariously on one foot and his crutches, he was shaking so violently that he was frightened he might fall, and the thought was terrifying.

"By Jove!" Creighton said. "The man looks all in. Couldn't you have made things easier for him, sir?"

Mr. Oldcastle thumped the ferrule of his walking stick on the granite step with a sharp crack. "I have already expended resources I would fain husband!"

Creighton's reaction was surprising. As a class, Anglo-Indian officers were self-assured in the extreme, yet he recoiled from the little old civilian's testiness. "Of course, sir! I meant no criticism. You know we are extremely grateful for your assistance."

"I know it not, sirrah, when you presume so." Then came the familiar dry chuckle. "Besides, I let him demonstrate his mettle. He tests an admirable temper in the forge."

"I expect he does," Creighton said offhandedly. "But he cannot cross over with that leg."

"It shall be attended to, Colonel."

"Ah!" Creighton brightened. "Very generous of you, sir. Well, lean on me, lad. We'd best get you out of here, since you obviously can't go back."

Edward could tell he was not welcome, but that was hardly surprising. War or not, there was going to be a hue and cry after him very shortly. "I have no desire to cause trouble, sir."

"You already have. Not your fault. And my esteemed friend here has made a good point. I know spunk when I see it. Just what I would expect of your father's son. Come."

After that remark, Edward had no choice but to descend the steps and install himself in the dogcart without screaming even once.

★   ★   ★

Creighton took the reins, with Mr. Oldcastle sitting beside him. Edward sprawled along the backward-facing bench behind them. The pony's hooves clattered along the deserted road. Soon the gaslights of Greyfriars were left behind, and they were clopping along a country lane under a bright moon. He had been rescued from both the law and the knife-wielding woman, but he was now a fugitive from justice, utterly dependent on Mr. Oldcastle and this Colonel Creighton. He did not know who they were or what their interest in him was.

He was wearing a shift and a dressing gown, one shoe and a straw hat—hardly the sort of inconspicuous garb he would have chosen for a jailbreak, and certainly not enough for small hours travel in England, even in August. He shivered as the cool air dried his sweat. His leg throbbed maliciously with every bounce and lurch. He suspected it was swelling inside the bandages; he wondered what more damage he had done to the shattered bones. He felt utterly beat.

"Gentlemen?" he said after a while. "Can you tell me what's going on?"

Creighton snorted. "Not easily. Ask."

"I didn't kill Timothy Bodgley—did I?"

"No. The objective was to kill you. He got in the way, I presume. Damned shame, but lucky for you."

"Why, sir? Why should anyone want to kill me?"

"That I am not prepared to reveal at this time," Creighton said brusquely. "But the culprits are the same people who killed your parents."

After a moment, Edward said, "With all due respect, sir, that is not possible. The Nyagatha killers were all caught and hanged."

Creighton did not turn his head, concentrating on the dark road ahead. His rapid-fire speech was quite loud enough to be heard, though.

"I don't mean that bunch of blood-crazed nigs. They were dupes. I mean the ones who incited them to go berserk."

"The missionaries who threw down their idols? But they were the first—"

"The Chamber was behind that Nyagatha incident, and even then the purpose was to kill you."

"Me?" Edward said incredulously. "What chamber?"

"You. Or prevent you from being born, actually. There was a misunderstanding. It's a very long story and you couldn't possibly believe it if I told you now. Wait a while."

That ended the conversation. He was right—Edward could not even believe what he had already seen and heard. To be suspected of killing Bagpipe was bad enough. To be held responsible for his parents' death and the whole Nyagatha bloodbath would be infinitely worse.

And yet that cryptic Jumbo letter had hinted at unknown dangers and secrets his parents had not lived to tell him. Whoever Jumbo was, he had never received that letter.

Damnation! He had forgotten to bring the Jumbo letter! It was back at the hospital.

Obviously there was not going to be any logical, mundane explanation. Mr. Oldcastle had said that those behind this whole horrible mystery were involved in the outbreak of a worldwide war, and he had claimed that the ringlets woman had occult abilities to bypass locks—implying that she had both entered Fallow and exited Greyfriars Abbey through bolted doors. The little man himself had sent her away without any visible use or threat of force. One or the other of them had most certainly arranged for the patients and staff of the hospital to be smitten with inexplicable deafness, at the very least. Where had all the nurses gone? Had they met the same fate as Bagpipe? How had Mr. Oldcastle himself arrived in answer to Edward's Shakespearean summons?

None of it made real-world sense, nor ever would. You could not expect Sherlock Holmes if you already had Merlin.

The only brightness in the murky affair was the thought of Inspector Leatherdale's face when he learned of his suspect's disappearance.

★   ★   ★

A halt and sudden stillness jerked Edward out of a shivery daze. Creighton jumped down at the same moment. He went to open a gate and lead the pony through it. After it was shut again, he scrambled back to the bench and the dogcart went lurching slowly across a meadow, climbing gently. The sky was starting to brighten in the east, and the moon was just setting.

Edward was not sure how long they had been traveling—an hour, perhaps—and he had no idea where he was, but then his familiarity with the country around Fallow did not extend as far as Greyfriars. Lately Mr. Oldcastle had been giving directions, so Colonel Creighton did not know either.

He was stiff and cold. His leg throbbed abominably. But he was alive, and at the moment he was free. Both conditions might be transitory.

Beyond another gate the track was thickly overgrown, winding into the patch of woodland that crowned the little hill. The pony picked its way cautiously, brush crackled under the wheels, and overhead the sky was almost hidden by foliage. The air smelled heavily of wet leaves. After about ten minutes of that, the trail ended completely, ferns and high grass giving way to bracken and broom. No farmer's cattle grazed here. A faint predawn light was evident, but not enough to show colors, only shades of gray.

Creighton reined in. "We get out here, Exeter. I'll give you a hand down."

Getting out of the dogcart was even worse than getting in. The accursed leg felt ready to burst the bandages and the splints as well. The grass was cold and wet.

"Leave one crutch and lean on me," Creighton said. "Just a few steps. And leave your hat, too."

In that undergrowth, a few steps were plenty. Eventually Edward reeled and almost fell.

"Two more yards'll do it," Creighton said. "Other side of this stone. Good man. Now, you'd best sit down. No—on the grass. I expect it'll be chilly on your you-know-what, but this shouldn't take long."

Edward was already aware that the long grass was soaked with dew, and he did not see why he should not try to make himself comfortable on the wall instead, but he was hugely relieved just to sit, leaning back with his hands in the dewy leaves, his legs stretched out before him. He took a moment to catch his breath and then looked around. Creighton was kneeling at his side, bareheaded. It was highly unusual to see an Englishman out of doors without a hat.

"Where's Mr. Oldcastle?"

"He's around somewhere," Creighton said softly. "He can undoubtedly hear what you say. Any guesses as to what this place is?"

Puzzled, Edward took another look. The trees were mostly oaks, but very thickly grown together, mixed with a few high beeches. The stillness was absolute—not a bird, nothing. Eerie! He was tempted to start cracking jokes, and knew that was merely a sign of funk. Funk would also explain his teeth's strong desire to chatter, however much he might prefer to blame the cold.

The low wall at his side was not a wall at all, but a long boulder, mossy and buried in the undergrowth. Eventually he made out a tall shape within the bracken at the far side of the glade. Then another, and he realized that he was within a circle of standing stones. Scores of them dotted the countryside of southwestern England, relics of a long-forgotten past. Sometimes the stones were still upright, sometimes they had fallen or been pushed down by followers of newer gods. The great boulder beside him had been part of the circle.

Feeling very uneasy, he said, "It makes me think of The Oaks, Druids Close, Kent."

"You're on the right track. It's very old. And what we are about to do is very old, also—there's a price to pay. You're going to have to trust me in this."

Creighton had produced a large clasp knife. He unfastened his right cuff and pulled back his sleeve to uncover his wrist. He drew the blade across the back of it, holding it to the side, well clear of his pants. He stretched out his arm and let the blood dribble on the mossy boulder. In the gloom it seemed black.

He passed the knife to Edward.

It was exam time.

Edward wondered what Uncle Roland would say if he were present, and thought he could guess the exact words.

The cutting hurt more than he expected, like cold fire, and his first attempt was a craven scratch that hardly bled at all. He gritted his teeth and slashed harder. Blood poured out, and he adorned the stone with it—like a dog peeing on a post, he thought.

"Good man," Creighton muttered. He accepted the knife back, closed it one-handed, and dropped it in his pocket.

"Now what, sir?"

The reply was a whisper. "Wait until it stops dripping. Don't speak—and it may be best if you keep your eyes down and don't look too directly at, er, anything you may notice."

Edward himself could refrain from speech, but his teeth were going to chatter. His fingers and toes were icy. Even his leg seemed to have gone numb; it hardly throbbed at all now.

Something moved at the far side of the circle, a shadow in the undergrowth. He tried not to stare, but that was not easy. Whatever or whoever was moving might have been very hard to see clearly in any case.

The shape flitted from stone to stone, peering around this one, over that one, darting to and fro, pausing to study the visitors like a squirrel or a bird inspecting a tempting crust. A man? A boy, perhaps? He made no sound. He was a darkness in the shrubbery, as if shadow went with him, or was deeper where he was. He would grow brave and approach with a mincing, dancing step, then suddenly scamper back as if he had taken fright or had decided that the other way around the circle would be a safer approach.

Gradually Edward built a picture in his mind: no clothes, thin, terribly thin, and no larger than a child. His head seemed clouded with silver hair, but without taking a direct look, Edward could not decide if it was a juvenile ash-blond or white with age. He was too small and much too young to be Mr. Oldcastle, and yet there was something familiar about him—the way he held his head forward, perhaps? Or perhaps he was much too *old* to be Mr. Oldcastle. He was not an illusion.

He was not human, either, and the grove was silent as a grave.

Advance, retreat, advance . . . At last the numen was only ten or twelve feet away, behind the closest of the standing pillars. He peeked round one side, then the other. There was a pause. Then he repeated the process. Suddenly the decision was made. With a silent rush, he scampered through the undergrowth and took refuge on the far side of the fallen boulder, out of sight but more or less within reach.

Edward discovered that he was growing faint from holding his breath too long. *What* was now on the other side of this rock? Out of the corner of his eye he watched the streaks of blood, half-expecting them to disappear, but they didn't.

The voice when it came was very soft, like a single stirring of wind in the grass. "Take off the splints, Edward."

There was no doubt about the words, though, nor the meaning, and no Shakespearean mumbo jumbo either. Exam time. Finals.

Edward looked down at the white cocoon of bandage that extended from his toes to the top of his thigh. Then he looked at Creighton, who was staring back at him expectantly.

A cripple on the run could hardly be any worse off. Edward began to fumble with pins and bandages. In a moment, Creighton handed him the knife again. Then it went faster. No use wondering how he was going to wrap the whole thing up again.

He wasn't. He knew that. He ripped and tugged until his leg was uncovered—damned good leg, not a thing wrong with it.

Creighton doubled forward until his face was on his knees, and stayed there, arms outstretched.

Oh, Uncle Roland, what do you say now?

Edward pulled his legs in under him—no trace of stiffness, even—and adopted the same position, kneeling with head down and arms extended.

God or devil, it was only right to thank the numen for mercy received, wasn't it?

A few moments later, the pony jingled harness and began to

munch grass. A bird chirruped, then others joined in, and soon the glade exploded into song. The sky was light, leaves rustled in a breeze that had not been there a minute before. The world had awakened from an ancient dream.

Creighton straightened up. Edward copied him. Then they scrambled to their feet, not looking at each other. There was no one else present, of course.

Edward closed the knife and offered it.

"Leave it," Creighton said gruffly. "And the bandages also." He strode over to turn the pony.

Feeling very thoughtful, Edward gathered up the bandages, the splints, the crutch. He laid them tidily alongside the blood-stains. He limped after Creighton in one shoe and one bare foot, but when he reached the dogcart, Creighton silently handed him the second crutch.

He hobbled all the way back to the circle again. The grass was trampled where he and Creighton had knelt. On the other side of the stone, where the numen had been, there was no sign that it had ever been disturbed. What else would you expect?

He stooped to lay his burden with the other offerings. Then he changed his mind and deliberately knelt down first. He bowed his head again and softly said, "Thank you, sir!"

He thought he heard a faint chuckle and an even softer voice saying, "Give my love to Ruat."

It was only the wind, of course.

⟨⟩ 33 ⟨⟩

WHEN PLAYING CHILLY NARSH, THE TROUPE WAS
forced to compromise on classical costuming. In her herald role,
Eleal had worn long Joalian stockings under her tunic and still
shivered; she had never experimented with real Narshian mens-
wear. It was even more fiendishly uncomfortable than she had
suspected—and difficult! In warmer lands the deception would
not have been possible at all, for although she had not matured
in the way T'lin had so crudely mentioned, she had progressed
to the point where she would not be mistaken for a boy if she
paraded around in just a loincloth. So there were advantages to
the Narshland climate after all, but she would never have managed to dress without Embiliina's motherly assistance.

The breechclout was a band with a tuck-over flap. Then
came well-darned wool socks and the diabolical fleece leggings,
cross-gartered all the way up, the tops held by a web strap that
looped around the back of her neck. How fortunate that she
had little bosom yet to worry about! On top went a wool shirt
for the mountains, so often washed that it was thick as felt, and
a smock that reached halfway down her thighs; then boots. She
pinned up her hair under a pointed hat that tickled her ears. She
eyed herself disapprovingly in the looking glass. As she had been
warned, the garments were all shabby castoffs. One of her leggings had a hole in the knee and the other was patched.

"How does it feel?" Embiliina Sculptor said, smiling.

"Drafty!"

"Mmm." Gim's mother chuckled mischievously. "Men seem

to like the freedom. If you need to, er . . . well, pick a good thick bush to go behind, won't you, dear?"

Her smile was so inviting that for a moment Eleal wanted to throw herself into this so-kindly lady's arms. Her eyes prickled and she turned away quickly. She was no longer a mere waif supported by a troupe of actors and given odd jobs to make her feel useful. In some way she did not understand in the slightest she was important—a Personage of Historic Significance! She must behave appropriately. Perhaps in a hundred years poets like Piol would be writing great plays about her.

She headed for the bedroom door. Without her specially made boot, her walk was very awkward. Not just *Clip, clop,* but rather *Step, lurch* . . . "Fortunately," she said brightly, "my dramatic training has taught me how to portray boys."

"Er . . . yes. This way, dear."

Gim was waiting in the kitchen, bareheaded, but otherwise already wrapped in outdoor wear. He had a lyre case slung on his shoulder. He smirked bravely when he saw Eleal, but the smirk faded quickly. His eyelids were pink, as if he was fighting back tears. It was all very well to trust a god, but she wished Tion had provided a more convincing, experienced champion to escort her.

His father looked even more worried, trying to act proud.

"Oh, dear!" Embiliina said. "Have you said good-bye to your sisters?"

"They're asleep, Mother!"

"Yes, but did you go in and see them so I can tell them you did?"

"Yes, Mother," Gim said with exaggerated patience. He turned to his father. "I don't suppose I can go and say good-bye to Inka, can I?"

Kollwin shook his head. "I don't think Dilthin Builder would be very happy to have you hammering on his door at this hour. Your mother will tell Inka in the morning and give her your love."

"And tell her I'll write?"

"And tell her that you'll write. Now you must hurry. The

entire watch must be searching for Eleal Singer by now. The priests will have half the city roused. Keep your eyes open. Hurry, but don't be rash. And especially look out for pickets around the trader's camp—they must know she escaped on a dragon."

Gim's fair face seemed to turn even paler. "What'll I do then?"

"You're the hero, son. I think you leave the girl by the wall and go on alone to investigate—but you'll have to make your own judgment."

Gim nodded unhappily. "The guards may just arrest Dragontrader and seize his stock!"

"No. That'd need a hearing before the magistrates—but I suppose they may even drag them out of bed for something this big. Off with you, my boy, and trust in the god."

The ensuing farewells became openly tearful. Eleal turned her back and tried not to listen. She could not help but think that no one had ever said good-bye to her like that.

She had no baggage except a few odd clothes Embiliina had insisted on giving her, and they were easily tucked into the top of Gim's pack. He was already burdened with the lyre, but he made indignant noises when Eleal offered to carry either. He strode off along the dark, windy street, long legs going like swallows' wings. Suddenly he slowed down and peered at her.

"Why're you limping?"

"I'm not. It's just your imagination."

"Good!" Gim said, and speeded up again. He seemed to have forgotten that she was the heroine and he only her guardian, but she would never ask him to go more slowly, not ever! Soon she was panting in the heavy fleece coat that had been added to all her other ridiculous garments. She grew hot, except where the night wind reached. Perhaps men would be better behaved if they dressed more comfortably.

At the first corner Gim stopped and peered around cautiously. Then he strode off again into the wind.

"Who's Inka?" she asked.

"My girlfriend, of course."

"Pretty?"

"Gorgeous!"

"You love her?"

"Course!"

"Does she love you?"

"Very much! You scared?"

"Yes. You?"

"Horribly."

He was supposed to be a strong, comforting supporter! He had not studied his role very well. "You weren't scared on the dragon, were you?"

Gim turned into a narrow alley. "Yes I was—and Holy Tion had shown me that bit! He didn't show me this at all. Along here. Besides, all I had to do was shout *Choopoo!* and close my eyes and hang on. I'm a painter, not a hero!"

Of course he was brave! Of course he must be a hero if the god had chosen him. She decided Gim Sculptor's modesty was more admirable than Klip Trumpeter's pretenses.

"And I'm an actor, not a Historic Personage."

He chuckled. "I wouldn't believe you were either if the gods didn't keep saying so. What you need instead of me, Eleal Singer, is someone like Darthon Warrior."

"You came?" she exclaimed.

"Dad took me. Just the *Varilian.* Couldn't follow half of it. Wish you'd done a masque."

"So do I. I get to sing three songs in the masque."

He did not ask for details, so she prompted, "Was I a convincing herald?"

"You were all right," Gim conceded, "if heralds were ever girls."

Eleal did not say another word to him for quite some time.

He led her along narrow lanes, down smelly alleys, across cramped, sinister courtyards. Soon she was hopelessly lost, but he insisted this was a shortcut. She kept thinking of Kollwin Sculptor's warnings about the guard, but the streets seemed to hold no people, only windy darkness. Bats flittered overhead, and a couple of times she noted small eyes glinting in garbage-strewn corners.

Ysh shone bright blue in the east and that should be a good omen if the Maiden was supporting Tion's rescue efforts. But Eltiana dominated the sky, glaring red, and that was bad. There was no sign of Trumb, who must be due to eclipse one night soon. That was always a bad omen, and it would be especially scary now.

> When the green moon turns to black,
> Then the reaper fills his sack.

"What's a lovers' gate?" Eleal asked.

"A way over a city wall. You'll understand when you're older." Gim stopped at a dark archway.

"I understand now."

He hissed. "Sh! Watch your step in here."

"Here" was a black tunnel. He felt his way, leading her by the hand.

They emerged into a well enclosed by sheer walls stretching up to a tiny patch of sky where two bright stars were visible. There was no visible exit except the tunnel arch and one stout wooden door that looked very determinedly shut. The smell was nauseating.

"Made a mistake?" Eleal inquired in a whisper.

"Not if you can climb like my sisters. Hold this a moment. And be careful with it." He handed her his lyre case while he removed his pack. Then he showed her the handholds and foot-holds in the walls, leading up to a patch of not-quite-so-dark darkness. She had missed it because it was higher than even his head and a long way above hers.

"I'll pass the pack up," he said, taking his lyre back for safer keeping.

"What's on the other side?"

"Kitchen yard. Private house. Don't expect they're hanging out washing at this time of night."

"Can you fit through there?"

"Could last fortnight. Up with you."

Leggings did have some advantages over long skirts when it came to climbing. Eleal scrambled up, feeling the stones icy cold in her hands, but it was an easy climb, as he had said. The opening had once been a barred window, although which side had been "inside" and which "outside" she could not tell. Now it was a gap between two yards, only one bar remained, and there was room for a child or a slim adult to squeeze through— the sort of illegal shortcut every child in the city would know about and love to use. She wriggled her head and shoulders through and then stopped.

The yard was small, not large enough to hang very much washing, just house on one side and sheds on the other. No lights showed, but moonlight revealed that the way was definitely not clear. She looked back down at Gim, his face a barely visible blur.

"There's a small problem," she whispered.

Gim said, "What?" impatiently.

"A dragon."

"*What?*" He sounded as if he did not trust her to know a dragon from a woodpile. She was blocking the preferred route, but he stepped on his pack, leaped up with long arms and legs and a scrabbling of boots on stone, catching a grip on the bar and hauling himself up beside her, dangling by one hand and one elbow.

"I'm so sorry," Eleal said in his ear. "I see it's only a watchcat after all."

It was Starlight. He was crouched directly below her, and he knew she was there, for he was snuffling inquiringly. With his neck almost straight up, the soft glow of his eyes seemed close enough to touch. Any minute now he might decide to recognize her and issue an earsplitting belch of welcome. He would probably dislike having people drop packs and lyres and themselves on him.

Gim grunted. "Better take the long way round." He let go and dropped. He had forgotten his pack. The sounds of body parts thumping stone seemed to go on rather a long time.

Eleal clambered down cautiously. By then he had stopped using bad words and was sitting up, trying to rub his head and an elbow at the same time.

"You didn't dirty your coat, I hope?" she inquired solicitously.

"Shuddup!"

"Whose house is that?"

Gim clambered painfully to his feet, rubbing his hip. "Gaspak Ironmonger's."

"Do you suppose he has a private shrine, too? Do you think T'lin Dragontrader belongs to another mystery?"

"Probably. Most men do."

Interesting! She'd suspected that. "Not Tion's, though? Then whose?"

"Why do girls talk so much? Keep quiet." Gim hoisted his pack again, but he made no objection when Eleal slung the lyre strap over her shoulder.

They crept back to the tunnel. This time the way was easier, for Ysh's eerie beams shone in from the street entrance.

Now Eleal had a whole new problem to consider. T'lin had said he would give thanks to the gods in his own way. That suggested that he had gone to seek out the Narshian lodge of whatever god bore his particular allegiance.

Would he be giving thanks or seeking instructions? And what god would he favor? Obviously not Tion, or he would have prayed at Sculptor's shrine, nor Eltiana, or he would not have aided in Eleal's rescue. She could not imagine T'lin dedicating himself to the Maiden. Astina was the patron goddess of warriors, true, and athletes, oddly enough, but her attributes included justice and duty and purity. None of those sounded like T'lin Dragontrader's preference. Visek was the All-knowing, of course, but he was rather an aloof god, and not easily swayed, god of destiny and the eternal sun. T'lin ought to be more concerned with commerce and domesticated animals, and the gods for those were avatars of Karzon, the Man.

Who was also Zath, who had told his reaper not to let her reach Sussland alive.

Who was also Ken'th.

Daddy.

Gim grabbed Eleal's arm and pulled her back into a doorway. She waited, but he did not explain what he had seen, or thought he had seen. Of course the guard would not necessarily parade around on dragonback with bands playing. It might be skulking in alleyways just as she and Gim were.

Gim did not move for some time. Shivering at his side, Eleal realized that T'lin might have more mundane concerns than gods. She had told him about the Thargians, and she had specifically mentioned the Narshian she had recognized in their company—Gaspak Ironmonger. The dragon trader had laughed then, and made a joke about farmers buying leopards to guard chickens.

Perhaps T'lin Dragontrader was a Thargian spy himself.

The lyre was becoming unpleasantly heavy on her shoulders when Gim reached his objective.

"We scramble up this trunk," he said, "along that branch, and across the roof to the wall. Think you can manage that?"

"No. You'll have to carry me."

"Stay here then." He reached for the first branch. "There's quite a drop on the other side, so don't break any ankles."

A couple of minutes later, they were outside the city. Neither of them had broken an ankle, although Eleal's hip was hurting now, missing her special boot. Gim yanked her back into shadow while he scanned the moonlit meadow. Light shone on a bend of Narshwater in the distance, and the mammoth steps stood like a monument to a forgotten battle. The pen was invisible. Although this was spring, the grass seemed covered with a shimmer of silver frost. Perhaps it was only dew. T'lin's camp was an isolated patch of darkness, from which the wind brought faint belching noises.

"See anyone?" Gim asked nervously.

"No."

"This is ridiculous! There's *gotta* be soldiers out there waiting for us! Dad said so. T'lin did too, more or less."

Eleal yawned. She knew she ought to be excited and keyed-up, and she very definitely did not want to be captured and dragged back to Mother Ylla, but . . . she yawned again. The night had gone on too long.

She understood what was worrying Gim, though. There were few dragons in Narsh and those mostly belonging to the watch. Ranchers owned dragons, but the guard would very soon have accounted for all the dragons in the city itself and learned that none of them had been involved in her escape. The next move would have been to investigate the trader's camp outside the wall. It was absolutely certain that there would be soldiers there still.

Furthermore, the camp was visible from the city gate, which was closed and guarded until dawn. Two people walking away from the wall would be as visible as a bear in a bed.

"Why're they making all that noise?" Gim muttered.

"Dragons always make that noise. If there were strangers around, they'd be making a lot more."

"Really?"

"Really," Eleal said with a confidence she did not feel at all. She yawned again.

"Come on, then!" Gim said. "It's trust the god or freeze to death!" He marched off across the meadow, leaning into the wind. Eleal followed by the light of the moons.

As they reached the huddle of sleeping dragons, a tall shape stepped forward to meet them.

"Name?" The voice was low, and not T'lin's.

"Gim, er, Wrangler and, ah—my cousin, Kollburt Painter."

"Goober Dragonherder. Follow me, Wrangler." He led them to a tent, dark and heavily scented by the leather it was made of. It thumped rhythmically in the wind, but the inside seemed almost warm after the meadow. "Sit," said the man.

There was a pause while he laced up the flap, and another while he flashed sparks from a flint. Eventually a very small lantern glowed dimly, showing a few packs and a rumpled bed-roll, no furniture, three people kneeling on the blankets, and beyond them the dark walls and roof swallowed the light, so that there was nothing more in the world.

Goober was a thin-faced man with a dark beard, solemn as if he never smiled. Gold glinted faintly in the lobe of his left ear. He was garbed in the inevitable llama skin garments, plus a black turban. He pointed to it. "Can you tie one of these?"

"No," said the fugitives together.

He produced two strips of black cloth and wrapped their heads up. Then he made them practice. To Eleal's fury, Gim caught the knack much faster than she did. She was too sleepy.

"You'll do, Wrangler," Dragonherder said. "You keep try-ing, Small'un. You look like a boiled pudding. Don't uncover the lantern until you've laced up the door again. Wrangler, you come with me."

"To do what?"

"To learn how to saddle a dragon and stop asking questions. I'm told you know the commands."

By the look on Gim's face, he had already forgotten them, but he did not say so. The two departed. Left on her own, Eleal struggled with the infernal turban until it felt as if she had it right. Then she had nothing else left to do except wait.

She inspected the mysterious packs—not opening them, in case she was interrupted, but feeling them carefully. She decided they contained little else but spare clothes.

Sudden weariness fell on her like . . . like an avalanche. Why did she keep thinking about avalanches? She leaned back against a pack. There had been no guards around the dragons, so the god was still helping her, right? Right.

Goober Dragonherder had known she was coming, so T'lin had returned here from Kollwin Sculptor's and then gone back into the city again to visit Gaspak Ironmonger. Right?

That must be right, too, but it seemed very odd. What had that meeting been about, and what had T'lin learned that eve-ning that had made it necessary?

~~~34~~~

EDWARD JUMPED DOWN TO OPEN THE FIRST GATE. HE DE-liberately closed it from the wrong side so he could vault over it, dressing gown and all. He felt a whirling sense of wonder as he swung back up to the bench, agile as a child. Being a cripple had been a pretty stinky experience. The dogcart set off across the meadow.

"Is his name really Oldcastle, sir?"

Creighton shot him a frown, as if warning that they were not out of earshot yet.

"No it isn't. There is no Mr. Oldcastle. Oldcastle is a sort of committee, or a nom de plume. Our friend back there is . . . He's just that, a friend. He's been there a long, long time. I don't know his name. Probably nobody does anymore."

The dogcart rattled down the slope toward the next gate. In daylight the land was bright with goldenrod and purple thistles.

"Robin Goodfellow?"

"That was the name of the firm. He would have been the local representative."

No wonder his face had seemed *Puckish.* "Why blood? I thought a bowl of milk and a cake was his offering?"

Creighton's tone had not encouraged further questions, but he must appreciate a chap's normal curiosity when he had just received a miracle.

He cleared his throat with a *Hrrnph!* noise. "Depends what you're asking him to do, of course—or not to do, in his case. The value of a sacrifice is in what it costs. Blood's pretty high on the list." He stared ahead in silence for a while, then said, "He would have lost on the exchange, though. You heard him say he husbands his resources. The *mana* he used to cure your leg he has probably been hoarding for centuries, and he can't replace it now—I don't suppose he gets any worshipers at all these days. We wouldn't have given him much, even with the blood. He's one of the Old Ones, but he does not belong to any of the parties involved in this. My associates here were desperately shorthanded and asked him to help, as he lives in the neighborhood. He agreed, much to everyone's surprise. For that you should be very, very grateful."

Edward licked the cut on the back of his wrist. "I am, of course. Anything else I can do, sir?"

"Yes. As soon as you've opened this gate, you go behind the hedge and get dressed. You look like a bloody whirling dervish in that rig-out."

As he stripped, Edward discovered that his assorted scrapes and bruises had not been cured, only his leg. The flannel bags and blazer he wanted were badly crumpled, but he found a presentable shirt. His cuff links seemed to have disappeared altogether, his collars were all limp. He detested tying a tie without a looking glass, so he left that to be attended to on the road. In record time, he tossed his case into the dogcart and scrambled up beside Colonel Creighton, once more a presentable young gentleman.

Except that he had only one shoe.

As the pony ambled forward, he adjusted his boater at a debonair angle to cover the sticking plaster, and began fighting with his tie. Beautiful morning. Health and freedom! Breakfast now?

In the light of day, Creighton was revealed as a man of middle years, spare and trim and indelibly tanned by a tropic sun. His close-cropped mustache was ginger, his eyebrows were red-brown and thick as hedges. His nose was an arrogant ax blade. He was staring straight ahead as he drove the pony, with his face shadowed by the brim of his bowler. As he seemed in no hurry to make conversation, Edward remained silent also, content to wait and see what the day would offer to top the night's marvels.

Pony and cart clattered along the hedge-walled lanes, already growing warm. As they passed a farm gate, a dog barked. The damp patches on Creighton's trouser legs were drying. Somewhere a lie-abed cock was still crowing.

Suddenly the colonel cleared his throat and then spoke, addressing his remarks to the pony's back.

"You have seen a wonder, you have been granted a miracle cure. I trust that you will now be receptive to explanations that you might have rejected earlier?"

"I think I can believe anything after that, sir."

"*Hrrmph!*" Creighton shot him a glance, hazel eyes glinting under the hedge of red-brown eyebrow. "Did you *feel* anything unusual up there, by the way, even before our friend appeared?"

Edward hesitated, reluctant to admit to romantic fancies. "It did seem a 'spooky' sort of place."

Creighton did not scoff as a hard-bitten army man might be expected to. "Ever felt that sort of 'spookiness' before?"

"Yes, sir."

"For example?"

"Well, Tinkers' Wood, near the school. Or Winchester Cathedral on a school outing. I didn't tell anyone, though!"

"Wise of you, I'm sure. Probably several of your classmates would have felt the same and kept equally quiet about it, but there's really nothing to be ashamed of. Sensitivity's usually a sign of artistic talent of one sort or another. Celtic blood helps, for some reason. It doesn't matter either way. When you get to . . . Well, never mind that yet. There are certain places that are peculiarly suited to supernatural activities. We call them 'nodes.' They have what we call 'virtuality.' Some people can sense it, others can't. They seem to be distributed at random, some more marked than others, but here in England you'll almost always find evidence that they've been used, or are still being used, for worship of one kind or another—standing stones, old ruins, churches, graveyards."

"That was why Mr. Old . . . er, Mr. Goodfellow . . . why he

didn't cure my leg in the hospital?" Edward had wondered why he had been made to endure that journey.

"Of course. It would have been much harder for him to do it there than at home in his grove, on his node. Perhaps even impossible for him nowadays."

Creighton turned out of one lane into another, apparently confident that he knew where he was heading. For a while he said no more. Edward began to consider his options. To go to any local enlistment center might be dangerous. Of course the police would be much more inclined to look for him in a nursing home than at a recruiting office, but near Greyfriars he might be recognized by someone. His best plan was probably to head up to town and join all the thousands enlisting at Great Scotland Yard.

Then the colonel began addressing the pony's arse again. "Officially I am Home on leave. Unofficially, I intended to observe the developments in Europe, do a bit of recruiting, and keep an eye on you."

Edward said, "Yes, sir," respectfully.

"Things went—*Hrmph!*—a little askew. The European thing sort of ran away with us. You see, the nature of prophecy is that it usually comes in a frightful muddle, with most incidents undated. Nevertheless, it describes a single future, so it must relate to a unitary stream of events, right?"

"Er. I suppose so." What had prophecy to do with anything?

"Some foretellings you'd think you can do nothing about— storms or earthquakes. Others you obviously can. If a man is prophesied to die in battle and you poison him first at his dinner table, then you have invalidated the entire prophecy, you see? Prophecy is by nature a chain, so that breaking one link breaks the whole thing. If any one statement is clearly discredited, then the future described is no longer valid and none of the rest of the prophecy applies anymore. If the prophecy foretelling a man dying in battle also foretells a city being wrecked by an earthquake, then by poisoning the man, you can prevent the earthquake."

Edward muttered, "Good Lord!" and nothing more. He

seemed to have stumbled into a mystical world that was definitely going to take some getting used to.

"It's all or nothing," Creighton said. "Like a balloon. Poke one hole in it and the entire thing fails. And you were mentioned in a prophecy."

"I see." The Jumbo letter had mentioned a chain! Why had Edward been such a fool as to leave it behind?

"About twenty years ago," Creighton continued, "someone tried to kill your father, Cameron Exeter. The attempt did not succeed, but an investigation revealed that he was mentioned in a certain well-substantiated prophecy, the *Vurogty Migafilo*. *Vurogty* is a formal, legal statement. *Miga* means a village, like the English *ham* or *by,* in the genitive case. So in English *Vurogty Migafilo* would be something like *Filoby Testament*. It has been around for many years, and many events foretold in it have already come to pass. Many more remain. You see that to be mentioned in such a document is virtually a death sentence?"

He paused, as if to let Edward make an intelligent comment, which seemed an unlikely possibility.

"Because anyone who does not like anything else in the prophecy will try to block its fulfillment?" That felt reasonably intelligent, considering the hour.

"Right on! Good man! In this case, the specific prophecy about your father was particularly unwelcome to the Chamber, and of course that increased his danger considerably."

The trap jingled and joggled along the lane. A thrush sang in the hedgerow. The dawn clouds glowed in decorous pinks. It was all very normal—no genies going by on magic carpets, no knights in armor tilting at dragons.

"What was that specific prophecy, sir?"

"It was foretold that he would sire a son."

"*Sir!*" This was starting to sound suspiciously like a leg-pull in very poor taste.

"Furthermore, the date was specified very clearly."

"June first, 1896, I presume?"

"No. Sometime in the next two weeks."

Edward said, "Oh." He studied the thick hedges passing by.

Life had been much simpler a few days ago. "Well, that's impossible, so this *Testament* has now failed?"

Hrrnph! "No again. The date was a misinterpretation. The seeress may not have understood correctly herself, and she expressed herself poorly—the ordeal drove her insane and she died soon after. Prophecy requires an enormous amount of mana, which is why it's so rare. The person who had given her the talent miscalculated. He was utterly drained by her outburst. Almost died himself, or so it's said. That's beside the point. Anyway, the Service decided that your father had better go into hiding until the danger was past. And so he did."

"He left New Zealand?"

"He went back to New Zealand! Ultimately he went on to Africa. A year or so later he was blessed with a son, namely you." Creighton spoke in sharp, authoritative phrases, as if he were instructing recruits in the mysteries of the Gatling gun. If he had been, then at least one recruit would have been totally at sea.

Edward was tempted to ask if the prophecy had saved him from being a girl, but that would sound lippy.

Creighton was still talking. "The Service has rather mixed feelings about the *Filoby Testament,* but all in all we tend to favor the future it describes. So he fulfilled that element of the prophecy and stayed where he was, at Nyagatha, killing time until the—"

"Killing time? Sir, he was—"

"I know what he was!" Creighton barked. "I dropped in there in '02 and met you. Cute little fellow you were, lugging a leopard cub around under your arm everywhere. Nevertheless, take my word for it, as far as your father was concerned, Africa was merely an extended working holiday."

"A twenty-year holiday, sir?"

"Why not? Exeter, when I say that your father belonged to the Service, I am not referring to His Majesty's Colonial Office. The Service to which I belong and your father belonged is something else entirely, and probably a great deal more important."

Edward muttered "Yes, sir," wondering how to bring up the question of his father's true age.

Creighton did not give him the opportunity. "Now you understand why I waited until you saw your leg healed before I tried to tell you any of this."

"It will take a little time to adjust, sir."

Creighton might be crazy, but he seemed to know exactly where he was heading. The dogcart was entering a fair-sized village. A baker's wagon was making its rounds, but otherwise the streets were still deserted.

"Time is something we don't have," he said testily. "The opposition have tried three times to nobble you, Exeter. Five times, if you count the first attempt on your father and the Nyagatha massacre. They probably assumed they'd got you that time, by the way. That would explain why they left you alone for so long afterward. But this spring a certain building was buried by a landslide, and then everybody knew that the *Filoby Testament* was still operative. Your parents were definitely dead, so you must be alive. They set the hounds on you again. You can't expect your luck to hold indefinitely."

"How can they find me now, sir? If I can hide from the law, then I can hide from . . . Who exactly are the opposition? I mean, if someone's out to kill me, I'd like to know who."

Creighton directed the pony down a side road. He made his *Hrrmph!* noise. "Ultimately the people who are so eager to put your head over their fireplace are the group we refer to as the Chamber. It has no official name and its membership varies from time to time. This is a little hard to . . . Look at it this way. You know that His Majesty's Colonial Office doesn't operate in England. The Home Office doesn't operate overseas. But the two would cooperate if—oh, say a dangerous criminal wanted by one of them escaped into the other's territory. They'd pass the word. With me so far?"

"Yes, sir."

"Well the Chamber doesn't operate here—its members have no power at all in this, er, environment. The Service that I belong to doesn't operate here either, but we're allied with a sort of local branch that we usually refer to as Head Office, although the relationship is informal. We help each other out from time to time—in matters like this, in recruiting, and so on. They were the ones who got your father appointed D.O. at Nyagatha, of course, as a favor to us. He, in turn, did certain favors for them while he was there. The two organizations have similar aims and goals, so we cooperate with them and they with us, but you understand that here I am only a private citizen, with no authority."

Hrmph! "Now, the opposition here is as variable and poorly defined as the Chamber—knock one down and two more spring up—but at the moment Head Office is tangled with a really hard bunch they're calling 'the Blighters.' It's a very apt description! Blighters here and Chamber there both oppose the aims that the Service and Head Office aspire to, so they're natural allies. It's the Blighters who killed your father and who are after your hide, as a favor to the Chamber."

Which was all very clear, Edward thought, but it had told him nothing except meaningless names. "Would you mind defining a couple of terms, sir? Where exactly do you mean by 'here'? If the Service you refer to is not the Colonial Office, then what is it? What sort of people make up the Chamber, and the Blighters?"

"That's a deuce of a lot of defining. As for what sort of people, well Mr. Goodfellow is one example, although he has always remained neutral until now."

This was definitely too much to swallow on an empty stomach. "Sir, are you telling me these groups are made up of *gods?*"

Creighton sighed. "No, they're not gods, not in the sense you mean. They may act like gods, and they do have supernatural powers. The one you met is a faint shadow of what he would have been in Saxon or Celtic times, and he cured your leg out of kindness, because he'd taken a fancy to you. Snap of the fingers, you might say."

"If he's not a god, then he's some sort of numen, or woodland spirit, or a demon, or—"

"He's a man, like us. Born of woman. He's a *stranger*, that's all."

"Well certainly! But—"

"And I won't define 'stranger' either. Not yet. He has a store of mana and I'm sure that a long time ago he was much more powerful than he is now. Yet he was probably always a pygmy in his class, whereas some of the Blighters are giants—look what they've achieved in the last month. This bloody war in Europe was provoked by them. Head Office have been struggling to prevent it for years. The Blighters outmaneuvered them. Now it's happened, utter disaster. But on that level the battle is over, and the big bad wallahs can sit back and savor their rewards. They can also turn their attention to other things. Like you."

Mr. Goodfellow had said very much the same thing about the war, Edward recalled, and whoever or whatever Mr. Goodfellow was, he was no ordinary mortal.

The dogcart had left the village and was bumping across a common on the far side, heading for some trees by the river.

"You see," Creighton added in a terse tone, as if he was tired of explaining things to a very thick child, "part of the trouble has been that both Head Office and the Blighters have been so occupied with political conniving these last few months, that they had no real assets to spare for peripheral matters such as doing favors for friends. That's why they just sent a crazy woman against you. They say she truly is crazy, by the way. She's a Balkan anarchist with a bad case of bloodlust. In other circumstances, they could have disposed of you without any trouble. On the other hand, had things been normal, Head Office could have defended you better."

"So it canceled out?"

"Perhaps it did. But now Head Office are in disarray. They have lost badly and will need time to lick their wounds. The Blighters are about to reap an enormous harvest of mana. This is definitely a good time to do a bunk!"

"But I don't have any choice—" Edward said, and then stopped in astonishment. The dogcart had rounded the trees and was almost into an encampment of Gypsies—half a dozen wagons and a couple of tents. Smoke trickled up from a central fire. Small children were running for cover and several dark-garbed men had turned to inspect the visitors. *Gypsies?*

"Any choice of what?" Creighton demanded, reining in the pony.

"I mean I'm going to enlist, of course. There's a war on!"

Creighton turned to him with an air of exasperation. "Yes," he said. "So there is. I've been trying to tell you."

35

"YOU SHOULD HAVE TURNED OUT THE LAMP BEFORE YOU went to sleep," T'lin grumbled. "Waste of oil. Come on."

Rubbing her eyes, Eleal stumbled out of the tent behind the big man and hobbled after him as he strode in among the sleeping dragons. There was no sign of Gim or Goober. She was stiff and cold. She must have slept a couple of hours, because the sky was bright, and she could see the mountains. The stars had almost gone, but Ysh's tiny blue half disk and Eltiana's fiery point still shone. It was going to be a fine day.

"This is Lightning," T'lin said, stopping so suddenly Eleal almost bumped into him. The dragon twisted his long neck around to inspect her. She rubbed the big browridges automatically, and he snorted warm hay scent at her, perhaps approving of her size.

T'lin inspected the girths. "He's not as young as he used to be, but he's wise, and he won't even notice your weight." He lifted Eleal effortlessly to the saddle and began adjusting the stirrup leathers.

"Hill straps?" she said apprehensively. Lightning was large, making her feel very far from the ground already. She had never ridden except on the flat. Truth be told, her riding experience could be described as *extremely limited.*

"Just buckle them loose for now, so they don't flap. I'll tell you when to tighten them. There. Now let's see how far you can make him go. That way." He pointed west, upstream.

"That's not the way to Rilepass."

T'lin's big hand closed fiercely on her knee. His face in the twilight was hard as rock. "I know that, Little Missy. And understand one thing: You don't argue or talk back on this journey, all right? This isn't a joyride to amuse a usefully nosy little child anymore. This is serious, and I didn't ask for the job of rescuing you."

"I'm sorry."

"Good." He snorted. "Your business is costing me a lot of money. It may cost me my life, or even my soul. And when I say 'Do this!' you do it. Don't waste a moment. Clear?"

If he was trying to frighten her, he was succeeding. She had never heard him speak so sternly. "Yes, Dragontrader." She gripped the pommel plate with chilled fingers. "Lightning, *Wondo!*"

Lightning turned his head around again and stared at her with big eyes, their glow still just visible in the fast-brightening dawn.

"Wondo!" Eleal shouted.

Lightning lifted his head high and looked over the rest of the herd. Then he faced Eleal and yawned insolently, showing teeth as big as her hand.

"Shouting doesn't help," T'lin sighed. "Kick him."

Eleal kicked in her heels. *"Wondo! Zaib!"*

Uttering a muffled belch of disgust, Lightning lurched to his feet and Eleal found herself staring down at the top of T'lin Dragontrader's turban. The dragon strolled insolently forward, picking his way between his sleeping mates, but in a moment he began to curve around. He did not want to leave the herd.

With much kicking and directions of *Whilth!* and *Chaiz!* she directed him to the open meadow and tried *Varch!* He eased

into a feeble pretence at a run, but in a moment he looked
behind him and slowed down again. Then he began to curve
to the left. Eleal drummed her heels on his scales and scolded.
He straightened momentarily but soon started edging around to
the right. In a few minutes she admitted defeat, afraid she was
about to be taken ignominiously all the way back. *"Wosok!"*
she said, and was relieved when her stubborn mount accepted
the compromise. He lay down, still disgustingly close to the herd
and facing toward it.

Another dragon had risen from the mass and was approaching
at a slow run. It came willingly as far as Lightning, and then
balked. Gim shouted angrily; Eleal was secretly pleased that he
did no better than she had done. His mount settled on the grass,
nose-to-nose with Lightning as if to compare notes on this disgraceful waste of valuable sleeping time.

"Stupid lizards!" Gim muttered. His pack and lyre were
strapped alongside the baggage plate at his back. His face was
pale and unweathered under the black turban, unconvincing as
the face of a wrangler. "Why all this *wosok* and *varch* stuff anyway? Why not teach them to understand good, honest Joalian?"

Eleal restrained a snigger—what Gim Wrangler spoke was a
long way from true Joalian. "Because common words like 'run'
may differ between the dialects. The dragon commands are the
same all over the Vales, and they're very old. So T'lin says," she
added to forestall argument.

Gim grunted.

"You'll like Sussland," she said cheerfully. "It's much warmer
and more fertile than Narshland."

"And the people riot all the time."

"Sussia's a democracy." She hoped that was the right word.
"They meet every year to elect the magistrates."

"So do we. The adult men, anyway."

"But in Narsh the elections are a foregone conclusion. In Suss
it's always a free-for-all. So T'lin says."

Gim mumbled something sadistic about the dragon trader,
ending the conversation. The two of them sat in shivering silence, not even looking at each other.

The east was growing brilliant and color had returned to the world. Lightning was revealed as a nondescript dun, Gim's mount was a glacier white. Eleal realized that the city gate was clearly visible now, so she must be visible to the guards on the parapet. Eventually she could stand the quiet no longer. "He's not bringing the whole herd?"

"Evidently not." Gim twisted around in his saddle to see what was happening. Nothing was. "Maybe they're going to head off in the opposite direction after we leave," he added, sounding as if he'd just thought of that. "Lay a false trail."

Then a third dragon emerged from the herd and came racing toward them. It was dark-colored and soon recognizable as Starlight, but he seemed to have no rider. He slowed as he reached the watchers. Someone cried, *"Zomph!"* shrilly, and he continued on at a smooth run.

"Gods preserve me!" Gim said, kicking angrily. *"Wondo,* Beauty, you scaly horror! *Zomph!"*

Beauty and Lightning rose as one, taking off after the newcomer. The meadow rushed past so fast that the wind seemed to fade away. Dragons were a smooth ride.

"Zomph!" Gim yelled again, but Beauty and Lightning were already going flat out. Gradually Beauty fell behind, despite Gim's curses. Starlight was still pulling ahead, making a race of it.

Then he veered to avoid a clump of bushes and Eleal caught sight of a small figure cowering over in the saddle, almost hidden by a bulky pack strapped to the baggage plate. Garments streamed in the wind, stirrup leathers and hill straps were flapping free. The light flashed on a strip of steel, but she had already guessed that the rider must be Sister Ahn.

Apparently Gim had not realized that T'lin was missing. He could do nothing about it even if he did. Eleal twisted around and stared back at the dawn. Already the camp was invisible and the city was receding into the distance, with the spires of the temple dominating its skyline. Another dragon was coming in pursuit.

The old woman must certainly be crazy. She would be killed

if she fell off. *"Zomph!"* Eleal yelled, kicking madly. Lightning could go no faster, though. He was breathing hard, while white steam poured from his nostrils. Starlight was younger.

The river had disappeared. The bizarre little caravan was racing along an obvious track now, with scattered cottages and dry stone walls. The hills of Narshslope marched alongside to the north, drawing no closer. The sun rose suddenly and in minutes the dragons were chasing their own long shadows over dry wheel ruts and scraggly grass.

So Eleal Singer had escaped from Narsh, if not yet from Narshvale. As far as she could remember, the western end was closed. Rilepass led north to Sussland and Fandorpass east to Lappinland. There were other passes to the south that she did not know, leading to Tholand and Randorland, but she recalled none to the west. Soon she thought she could see brightness in the distance, probably morning sun sparkling on the dew-wet thatch roofs of a village. That must be where this road went, and probably where it ended.

Then a largish stream blocked the way. The trail dipped to a ford and Starlight balked, because dragons disliked water. He wheeled around, apparently with no objection from his rider. Lightning made gasping sounds of approval, and slowed. The three dragons came together, uttering joyous roars, nuzzling each other in greeting.

Gim's jaw dropped when he saw the old woman crumpled in the saddle. He leaped down, shouting *"Wosok, Starlight! Wosok!"*

Eleal made Lightning crouch before she dared dismount, and then she went to help Gim. The old woman seemed unconscious, but her twisted hands still held a fierce grip on her staff and the pommel plate. Carefully avoiding the sharp-looking sword, the youngsters dragged her from the saddle and lowered her to the grass like a heap of washing.

She blinked up at them, her eyes watering. When she spoke, though, her creaky voice sounded amazingly calm. "The Maiden be with you, child. Introduce your friend."

"Gim Wrangler, Sister."

"He is not mentioned," Sister Ahn proclaimed, as if dismissing Gim from consideration. She struggled up to a sitting position and began tucking white strands of hair back under her wimple.

"He rescued me from the temple."

"The god rescued her!" Gim said.

Sister Ahn nodded. "Praise to the Youth. But the Maiden is worthy of thanks also. I did not injure the dragon with my sword, did I?"

Gim bent and inspected Starlight's flank. Starlight turned round and puffed grass-scented steam at him.

"A couple of faint scratches on his scales. Nothing serious."

"How did you make him leave the herd?" Eleal demanded.

"I gave him some nice hay and told him how beautiful he was. It is always best to pay in advance, whenever possible."

"The dragon trader didn't know, did he?" Eleal said.

Sister Ahn frowned at her, and then suddenly smiled. Probably her smile was well intentioned, but it seemed just as gruesome as it had two days ago, involving much crunching of wrinkles and a display of lonely yellow teeth. "Sometimes action must come before explanation," she explained wryly. "I always wanted to try a ride on a dragon!"

She took a firm grip on her staff and held out an arm. Gim helped her rise, studying her with rank disbelief.

"You've never done it before?"

"I implied that, did I not? Had I not overheard you, young man, I would not have known the correct command. Now, what place is that?" Apparently her watery eyes were not as useless as they seemed.

"Morby, sister. Just a little place."

"Never heard of it." Her tone implied that it was therefore of no consequence.

"It has a wonderful bakery," Gim said wistfully.

The fourth dragon arrived in a scramble of claws, being greeted by belches from the others. T'lin Dragontrader seemed to hit the ground running before it had even stopped. His face was flushed with fury and he towered over the nun.

Sister Ahn attempted to straighten, but the move merely emphasized her hump. Her long nose was about level with the middle of his chest.

"You *stole* my dragon!" His fists were clenched.

"Borrowed it, merely. Time was short and you would have argued."

"By the moons, I would have argued! And now I suppose you expect to accompany us to Sussland?"

He was speaking much louder than usual. The dragons were all watching curiously. Eleal caught Gim's eye. He did not seem to know whether to be amused or concerned. Neither did she.

"Accompany you? I don't know anything about you," the old woman proclaimed. "You are not mentioned. It is written, *Before the festival, Eleal will come into Sussvale with the Daughter of Irepit.* This is Thighday. The festival begins tonight, does it not? You don't expect to negate holy prophecy when the goddess Ois failed, do you?"

T'lin shook his fists futilely and then grabbed his beard with both hands as if to keep them from doing violence to the maddening old woman. Starlight was Dragontrader's personal mount. They had been together as long as Eleal could remember. She had never seen rage portrayed so clearly, not even when Trong Impresario played Kaputeez in *The Vengeance of Hiloma.*

"Is that so? Really so? As I understand your discipline, sisters of the sword always offer value in return for service."

Sister Ahn nodded complacently. "Always."

"Today the price for passage to Sussland is one million stars, payable in advance!" T'lin pushed his bristling red beard almost into her face. "Well?"

She raised hairless brows. "Or something greater?"

"Greater? Name it!"

"Your life, my son. Without me you would presently be chained in the city cells."

T'lin made a choking noise.

"Why do you think the guard did not come after you?" she asked pityingly. "Do you believe they are all so stupid, or that the priests of Our Lady are?"

T'lin wavered. "What did you do?"

"I told them I had seen a black dragon with two people aboard climbing over the wall and heading in the direction of Nimpass. A mounted patrol left immediately and all the rest went back to—"

"You *lied?*"

"Certainly *not!*" Again Sister Ahn tried to look down her long nose at him, but he was still much too tall. "I was vouchsafed a vision of this, in a dream. It was very clear."

T'lin Dragontrader moaned and covered his face with his hands. Eleal bit her lip to restrain a snigger. There was silence, until Gim said hesitantly, "It was odd that the guard did not come after us, sir."

"Not odd at all!" the nun sniffed. "I gave them my oath that I had seen what I said. Sisters of my order are impeccable witnesses. Courts have accepted the sworn word of a Daughter over the testimony of phalanxes of magistrates. You owe me your life, Dragontrader. Or if not, at the very least they would have impounded all your worldly goods. I have paid fairly."

36

CREIGHTON SEEMED TO HAVE AN INFINITE CAPACITY TO astonish. First he had produced ancient woodland gods out of pagan legend, and now Gypsies. Gypsies were thieves, poachers, charlatan fortune-tellers, and altogether not the sort of people whose company any self-respecting gentleman would cultivate. Nor was this encounter a sudden impulse, for he had obviously been recognized. A man was approaching. There was no smile of welcome on his face, but he was not scowling either.

"Get your bag," Creighton said, "and then wait here." He jumped down.

Edward followed and retrieved his suitcase. Without a word, the Gypsy took charge of the dogcart and pony. He was nattily dressed, although his clothes had more elaborate pleats and stitching than those of any ordinary Englishman. His waistcoat was too fancy, his hat brim too wide, and he had a colorful kerchief around his neck. He returned Edward's smile with a sullen glance and led the pony away. Only now did Edward register that the dogcart was an outlandishly gaudy affair of shiny brass fittings and bright-hued paints. So were three or four of the wagons, in varying degrees. Others were plainer, scruffy by comparison.

Creighton was already in conversation with an elderly woman sitting by the fire. She was so muffled up in bright-colored clothes that she resembled nothing more than a heap of rainbows. She said something, nodding, then looked up to stare across at Edward. Even at that distance he sensed the piercing dark eyes of the true Gypsy. He tried not to squirm.

Waving to him to follow, Creighton headed for one of the gaudiest of the wagons. When Edward arrived, he was regarding it with distaste.

"I don't suppose the police can put the bite on you in here, old man," he said, "but I can't answer for fleas." With that, he trotted up the ladder. Edward followed. By the time he was inside, Creighton had stripped off his hat and jacket.

There was barely room for the two of them to stand between the chairs and table and stove and shelves and various bundles and boxes. The air was heavy with an unfamiliar scent, and everywhere there was color—reds and greens and blues rioting on walls, furniture, garments, and bedding. The ceiling had not been designed for a six-footer. At the far end were two bunks, one above the other. From the assortment of clothes littered everywhere, this was home to a large family, and the lower bunk had pillows at both ends. In the middle of it lay a notably new and clean pigskin suitcase. Edward assumed it had been stolen, but when Creighton had stripped to his undervest, he began stowing his shirt and waistcoat in it.

"Close the door, man! They said we could help ourselves to anything we find. I don't suppose there's much here that will fit you. Have to do the best you can."

Edward began to undress. "Sir, you said the guv'nor was killing time in Africa. My uncle Roland accused him of engaging in devil worship because—"

"Terminology depends on whose side you're on. One man's god is another man's devil. I'll explain about your father later." Creighton was rummaging through heaps of garments.

"And where does Christianity fit into this?"

"Anywhere you want. Good King George and his cousin the Kaiser worship the same god, don't they?" Creighton held up a pair of pleated black trousers and frowned at them. "Britain and Germany pray to the same god. So do the French and the Russians and the Austrians. They all trust him to grant victory to the righteous, meaning themselves. Here—these look like the longest." He handed them over. Then he selected a pink-and-blue shirt and wrinkled his nose.

"Something wrong, sir?" Edward inquired, discovering that the pants did not reach his ankles.

Hrmph! "Just wondering about, you know, cleanliness."

"I don't think you need worry. They will. You must be paying them handsomely? Or Head Office must be?"

Creighton shot him a glare that would have softened horseshoes. "Just what're you implying?"

"Well, anything that's been worn by a *gorgio* will be *mokadi,* and will be burned as soon as we leave."

"What?"

"*Mokadi*—ritually unclean. In fact I suspect they'll burn the whole wagon."

"Burn the? . . ." The hazel eyes scowled out from under hedges of eyebrow in the sort of glare Edward had not faced since he was one of the crazy imps of the Fourth Form. "What the devil do you know about Gypsies?"

"They quite often camp at Tinkers' Wood, sir, near the

school," Edward said blandly. "A family named Fletcher." He reached for a rainbow-embroidered shirt.

"Out of bounds, I hope?"

"Er, yes, sir."

"They're swindlers and horse thieves!"

"Oh, of course!" Fascinating people—even as a prefect, Edward had sneaked out at night to visit them. "They'll steal and lie and cheat any *gorgio* who comes within miles. That's just their way. But isn't it also true, sir, that they've been known for centuries as the finest spies in Europe?"

A reluctant smile twitched the corner of Creighton's mouth. "I daresay."

"The true Rom are about the most fastidious people in the world." Edward was enjoying this. "They make high-caste Brahmins look like slobs."

Hrmph! "I suppose their fleas are frightfully *pukka*, too?"

"I doubt if they're as fussy, sir."

Creighton laughed approvingly, and proceeded to dress. Edward wondered if he'd just been tested in some way. . . .

"You feel spooky at all?"

"No, sir. Should I?"

"This is a node, I think."

"It is?"

"Well, of course here I'm no more certain than you are. I can always detect virtuality on Nextdoor, but here's trickier. The Rom prefer nodes for campsites, for obvious reasons. The headman's name is Boswell, by the way, but the real power is his mother. You look awfully sweet in that shirt. Old Mrs. Boswell's a *chovihani*—a witch, and a good one. Be respectful."

"Oh gosh, sir! I grant you I saw a miracle this morning. I met Puck himself, an Old One. I know I would not have believed this yesterday and it was the experience of a lifetime—but please! Do I have to believe in Gypsy witches now?"

Creighton flashed him another menacing, hazel glance. "Caesar, Alexander, Napoleon, Bismarck, Jenghis Khan. . . . You ever study any of those men in your fancy school, Exeter?"

"Some of them."

"They all had a lot of what's called *charisma*. Know what I mean by that?"

"Er, leadership?"

"More than that, much more. It's a faculty to absorb their followers' admiration and focus it. A charismatic leader can persuade men to believe what he tells them to believe, to die for his smile, to follow him anywhere he goes; the more he demands of them, the more they are willing to give. He grows by their loyalty and induces more loyalty because of it. Generals, politicians, prophets—sometimes actors have charisma."

Creighton paused in his dressing, and sighed. "I once saw Irving play Hamlet! Incredible! Half the audience was weeping, and I don't just mean the ladies. You must believe in faith healing? Well, in extreme cases, a charismatic leader can literally inspire miracles. And a *chovihani* has charisma. You'll see."

Hunger and lack of sleep had made Edward short-tempered. Argument burst out of him before he could stop it. "Come, sir! Charisma is one thing. Magic's something else!"

"Is it? Sometimes it's hard to tell where one ends and the other begins. So you plan to enlist, do you?"

Thrown off-balance, Edward said, "Of course!" His country was at war—what else could he do? Let the beastly Prussians take over Europe? If they won, they'd attack the British Empire right afterwards anyway. They had to be stopped now.

Creighton sighed, and bent to scrabble through a pile of socks. "Well, I suppose I might have felt the same at your age. Do you know Germany has invaded Belgium? The British and French are going to try and stop them, and sheer hell is going to stalk the plains of Flanders. The oracular reports are terrifying. The last few days have darkened the entire century. But I suppose at your age you feel immortal."

"It is my duty!"

The colonel straightened up and scowled. "I think you have a greater duty, although you don't know it yet. I think I have a duty to your father to save his only son from being hanged for a crime he did not commit. But I'll make a bargain with you. My friends and I saved you from an assassin. We've rescued you from a murder charge that would undoubtedly have sent you to the gallows. We've cured your leg. I think you owe us a little something, don't you?"

Put like that, the question had only one answer.

"I owe you a lot, sir, a devil of a lot."

"Too bloody Irish you do! I'm calling in my debt, Exeter. Pay now."

"Pay what?" Edward asked grumpily.

"Parole. I want you to—I demand that you—put yourself under my orders. You will obey without question!"

"For how long?"

"One day. Until dawn tomorrow."

"That's all? Then we're quits?"

"That's all."

"You're asking for a blank check!"

"How much did you have in your account last night?"

Creighton was not without charisma himself. Edward could not meet those eyes glittering under the hedgerow brows.

"Thruppence! Very well, sir, I agree."

"Right. Word of honor, of course?"

Strewth! What did the cocky little bastard expect? Edward stared cold fury at him and said, "I beg your pardon?"

Creighton nodded placidly. "Good. Then make yourself respectable and come on out. Rabbit stew for breakfast, I expect. Or pheasant, if we're lucky." He pushed rudely past Edward and headed for the door.

"Sir? What did you mean—"

"Without question!" Creighton snapped, and disappeared down the steps.

There was indeed stew for breakfast, and it might have contained rabbit. It certainly contained many other things, and it tasted delicious to a hungry man. Edward tried not to think about hedgehogs and succeeded so well that he emptied his tin plate in record time.

He sat on the ground in an irregular circle of Gypsies, mostly men. Woman flitted around in attendance, never walking in front of a man. The women's garb was brighter, but even the men seemed dressed more for a barn dance than for country labor. There were about a score of adults in the band, and at least as many children, most of whom were hiding behind their elders and peering out warily at the strangers. The campsite was an untidy clutter of wagons and tents and basket chairs in various stages of assembly. Heaps of pots and clothespins indicated other trades. A dozen or so horses grazed nearby, and the skulking dogs seemed to belong.

Creighton sat at the far side, deep in conversation with the ancient *chovihani*. Edward could hear nothing of what was being said, although there seemed to be some hard bargaining in progress. The few words he overheard near him were in Romany. He could not but wonder what the masters at Fallow would say if they could see him now in his grotesque garb. His wrists and ankles stuck out six inches in all directions. He was barefoot because he had been unable to find any shoes to fit him. The only part of his apparel not too small for him was his hat, and that kept falling over his eyes.

A slender hand reached down to his plate. "More?" asked a soft voice.

"Yes, please! It's very good."

He watched as she carried the plate over to the communal pot and heaped it again with a ladle. Her dress made him think of Spanish dancers, and she was very pretty, with her head bound in a bright-colored scarf and her dangling earrings flashing in the sun. Her ankles . . . Some ancient instinct caused him to glance around then. He saw that he was the object of suspicious glowers from at least half a dozen of the younger men. Good Lord! Did they think? . . . Well, maybe they were right. Not that he had been considering anything dishonorable, but he had certainly been admiring, and that was forbidden to a *gorgio*. Nevertheless, he smiled at her when she gave him back the plate. She smiled back shyly.

Eating at a nomad's campfire, he could not help feeling he was slumming, yet he knew that these were a proud people, and to them he was probably as out of place as a naked Hottentot at a dons' high table in Oxford. There was a lesson there and he ought to be learning from it. The guv'nor would have been able to put it into words.

The second helping he ate more slowly, feeling sleepiness creeping over him—he hadn't really slept at all in the night. There were so many things to think about! Could he trust Creighton, in spite of what the man had done for him? He was certainly being evasive. He claimed to have visited the guv'nor at Nyagatha, and he had known about Spots. He had pointedly avoided saying where he had come from, except for cryptic references to somewhere called "Nextdoor." He had contrasted it with "Here," without stipulating whether "Here" meant England or all Europe. The Service he talked about—what government did it serve? Some semiautonomous Indian potentate? The Ottoman Empire? China? China was in disarray, wasn't it?

Everywhere was in disarray now, and yet Creighton had never once hinted at the possibility of the war interfering with whatever his precious Service served. And what could the Chamber be? He had certainly implied that it was in some sense supernatural; if it was, then the Service must be also.

So what on Earth did that make *Nextdoor?*

Replete, Edward returned his plate to the owner of the ankles and wiped his mouth on the back of his hand. He wanted a wash and a shave, but sleep would do for starters.

Creighton called his name and beckoned.

He walked around the fire, being careful not to step on anything sharp. Creighton was paying court to the old woman. Perhaps she really was a *phuri dai,* a wisewoman, but Edward knew enough about Gypsies to know that their leaders were invariably male. Furthermore, the man beside her was sitting on a wooden chair, while everyone else was on the ground. That made him unusually important. Edward went to the man.

Boswell was probably in his sixties, thick and prosperous looking, with a patriarchal silver mustache. His face was the face of a successful horse trader, unreadable.

Edward doffed his hat respectfully and said, *"Latcho dives."*

The man's mustache twitched in a smile. *"Latcho dives!* You speak *romanī?"*

"Not much more than that, sir."

Still, Edward had scored a point. Boswell said something very fast in Romany—probably addressed to his mother, although he was watching Edward to see if he understood, which he did not.

Edward bowed and squatted down before her, alongside Creighton. She looked him over with the most extraordinary eyes he had ever seen. Her gaze seemed to go right through him and out the other side and back again. He barely noticed anything else about her, except that she was obviously very old. Only her lustrous Gypsy eyes.

"Give me your hand," she said. "No, the left one."

He held out his hand. She clutched it in gnarled fingers and pulled it close to her face to study. He was able to glance away, then. He raised a quizzical eyebrow at Creighton, who frowned. Then the old woman sighed and closed his fingers into a fist. Here it came, he thought—you will go on a long journey, you will lose a close friend, your dearest love will be true to you although you may be troubled by doubts, *et* blooming *cetera.* She was going to be disappointed when she told him to cross her palm with silver.

She was looking at him again, darn it!

"You 'ave been unjustly blamed for a terrible crime." Her voice amused him. It was straight off the back streets of London, almost Cockney.

"That is true!" He tore his eyes away and reproachfully glanced at Creighton.

"I told Mrs. Boswell nothing about you, Exeter."

Oh, really? Edward would have bet a five-bob note—if he had one—that Creighton had told the old crone a lot more than he thought he had.

"You will go on a long journey," she said.

Well, Belgium was a good guess, and quite a long journey.

"You will have to make a very hard choice."

That could mean anything—pie or sausage for supper, for instance. "Can you be more specific, ma'am?"

Creighton and Boswell were listening and watching intently. So was everyone else within earshot.

Mrs. Boswell twisted her incredibly wrinkled face angrily, as if recognizing Edward's disbelief. Or perhaps she was in pain. "You must choose between honor and friendship," she said hoarsely. "You must desert a friend to whom you owe your life, or betray everything you hold sacred."

Edward winced. That sounded *too* specific!

"If you make the right choice, you will live, but then you will have to choose between honor and duty."

"I beg your pardon, ma'am. How can honor and duty ever come in conflict?"

She turned her head away suddenly in dismissal, and he thought she would not answer, but then she added: "Only by dishonor will you find honor."

Bunk! Edward thought, more nettled than he wanted to admit, even to himself. "Honor or friendship, then honor or duty . . . Do I get a third wish?"

She did not reply for a long moment. Just when he had concluded that she would not, she whispered, "Yes. Honor or your life." Then she waved him away without looking around.

Soon the Gypsy caravan was ambling along the lanes of summer England, heading Edward knew not where. Creighton, having snared his victim with an oath of obedience, now refused to answer questions, or even hear them. Time for forty winks, he said.

"How are you at dancing?" he inquired brusquely while they were undressing.

Edward admitted he could probably manage a slow waltz.

"And how are your teeth? Any fillings?"

"Two."

"Pity." Creighton stretched out on the lower bunk in his underwear.

"Are those necessary qualifications in recruits to the Service?"

Edward clambered into the upper berth, banging his head in the process. Even with the windows open, the wagon was stuffily hot.

"Very much so," said a smug voice from below him. "A knack for languages helps. How many can you speak?"

"Usual school set: French, Latin, Greek. A bit of German."

"You took the medal in German. How about African?"

"Bantu."

"Which Bantu?"

"Embu, of course, and Kikuyu. A smattering of Meru and Swahili." That sounded like bragging, so he added, "Once you've got a couple of them, the others come easily. Anyone can read Italian or Spanish if he knows French and Latin."

Creighton chuckled at something. "A faculty for language helps, but you're far too young. If it wasn't for the *Filoby Testament*, I'd throw you back. I was looking for men in their fifties or sixties. Women even better. Didn't find any."

In five minutes the man was snoring.

ᘡᘡ 37 ᘡᘡ

DRAGONS HAD A NOTORIOUS DISLIKE OF WATER, BUT when Dragontrader had coaxed Starlight to cross Narshwater, the others had followed. He had relegated Sister Ahn to the fourth mount, named Blaze, and insisted that her sword be bound to its pack. There had been another fight over that, but she had yielded when he pointed out that the hilt would still be within her reach.

"What pass is this?" Eleal asked wonderingly as the procession raced northward over the grassy hills of Narshslope.

"No pass," he growled. He was still mad. "Dragons don't need passes. Your hill straps all right?"

She nodded. In fact the belt was uncomfortably tight, but having seen Starlight scramble down a temple wall, she had a strong suspicion she was going to need it.

The sun was climbing higher, shedding real heat. Soon a valley enclosed them, providing shelter from the wind, and she began to feel warm—a rare sensation in Narshvale. A few hours' sleep would be nice, and she remembered Gim's remark about the bread shop in Morby with regret, but obviously the fugitives must hurry on their way. The Narsh guard would discover Sister Ahn's deception soon enough.

Dragons in motion spread out and she had no one to talk with. The saddle had begun to chafe already. Yesterday at this time she had just begun plucking chickens—she cocked a mental snoot at the temple. *Pluck your own fowls, Mother Ylla!* The day before, the oracle had spoken, and the day before that she had unmasked Dolm. On Ankleday she had been an aspiring actor looking forward to a ride on a mammoth. Life had been very simple back then.

For half an hour or so the fugitives raced up a brush-filled valley, climbing steeply alongside rapids and waterfalls. Trees were rare in Narshvale, and no other obstacle was a hindrance to dragons. Eventually the valley curved off T'lin Dragontrader's preferred path; he put Starlight at the slope. At the top, he called a halt to let the mounts catch their breath, and they automatically closed up near one another.

Eleal was astonished how high they were already—perched on a windy, grassy ridge with all of Narshland spread out before them, cupped within the icy peaks of Narshwall and dappled by shadows of clouds. Even in summer it was more tawny than green; hard country good only for grazing. Here and there she saw the scars of mines. Gim was staring at it all openmouthed.

"Never seen it like this before?" she asked.

He shook his turbaned head. "I'm not like you. I've never been anywhere! Well, I've been everywhere down there." He waved at the valley. "We go on picnics sometimes, Mom and Dad and the girls and me. Thunder Falls, up there. Daisy Meadow over there. You know, you can walk across the whole land and back in a day, if you own some good boots. You can walk from one end to the other in two days—Dad did, once."

Eleal would not want to try that, but a strong man probably could. "There are smaller vales," she said helpfully. "And some larger. In Joalvale there are places there where you can hardly see mountains at all!"

Gim looked suitably impressed. "Sussland is much bigger, isn't it?"

"It's broader," she said. "Not much longer, maybe. Lower, hotter."

"Tell me about the festival," Gim said, but mention of their destination had reminded Eleal that she had prophecies to fulfill.

Sister Ahn was sitting as erect as she could on Blaze, one gnarled hand behind her, clutching her precious sword. Her haggard face seemed relatively content and unthreatening. Before Eleal could question her, though, T'lin Dragontrader intervened.

"Sister, I don't suppose your prophecies tell you which is the best way through this?" He waved irritably at the jagged rock and ice filling the northward sky—gray and white, with hardly a speck of green in view anywhere.

"No."

"Or whether Ois will contest our passage?"

"She may." The nun sniffed. "She wishes to stop Eleal and myself, but you and the boy may die also. I cannot say."

T'lin uttered his inevitable snort. "Religion is such a comfort in times of need!"

"Holy Tion will shield us," Gim said devoutly. "We are pilgrims to his festival."

"Indeed?" For the first time, Ahn showed some interest in him. "You plan to play your lyre for the god?"

"I'll enter if Dragontrader will permit me to."

T'lin snorted again. "Think you can win a rose, do you?"

"Oh, no!" Gim looked down at his boots and mumbled, "I'd be honored just to try."

The red beard parted in a toothy smile. "You might win the gold one."

The idea had occurred to Eleal a moment before T'lin spoke. Gim turned his face away quickly and said nothing.

The dragon trader shrugged, apparently regretting his ridicule. "Oh, never mind. I think we'll try for that gap there. Looks like a good place to be eaten by snow tigers."

Eleal saw her chance. "Sister, will you tell me now what is going to happen in Sussland?"

The old woman frowned, and then nodded. "Certainly! In fact I should probably give you some instructions as soon as possible, because the holy testament does not specify exactly which day the wonderful event will occur."

"Instructions?"

"Yes. There may not be time after we arrive, you see? Unless you are already experienced, of course."

"Experienced in what?"

At that moment T'lin shouted, *"Zomph!"* and Eleal was thrown back against the baggage plate as the dragons flashed into high speed. Whatever Sister Ahn said was lost in the wind.

The ridge curved as the valley had done; T'lin led his troupe down a steep slope and straight up the other side. Dragons were in their element in mountain terrain. Roaring with excitement, they raced one another up hills and slid down long scree slopes in showers of gravel. Eleal understood then why they stayed so far apart, and she also realized this crossing might take much less time than the plodding mammoths needed for their long trek over Rilepass. Soon the air grew cold, although the wind was not as fierce as she would have expected. Even grass became rare and gray stone stretched out everywhere.

Starlight was chief dragon, but he labored under T'lin's substantial weight. With his much lighter burden, Lightning took to challenging him for the lead position, and then the pace became fierce indeed. As T'lin had said, the old dun was wily, with a good eye for the easiest routes. The two females, Blaze and Beauty, scorned to play such foolish games and were soon left far behind.

Eventually they vanished altogether, and T'lin called a halt. Eleal rode up beside him. Starlight and Lightning belched weakly at each other, puffing clouds of steam into the wind. The dragon trader himself was flushed and grinning.

"You know what that is, Jewel of the Mountains?" He gestured at a wall of dirty white blocking the valley ahead from side to side. It was bleeding a torrent of frothy green water.

"It remarkably resembles snow, but I am sure you would not have asked if the answer was so obvious."

He nodded, uncorking his canteen. "It's an old avalanche."

Eleal looked around uneasily. On either side the valley walls rose in cliffs and scarps and impossible slopes, mostly still mantled with winter snow. At the top sunlight glinted on parapets of ice, a white frame around deep blue sky.

"Meaning this place is dangerous?"

He took a long drink. He nodded as he wiped his mouth. "If Ois wants it to be. Listen!"

She listened. There was only the dragons' puffing and the chatter of the stream and . . . a distant rumble of thunder?

"There goes another!" T'lin said with an unconvincing smirk.

They peered around, but the wall of snow prevented a proper view of the valley ahead.

"We should ride along the top," she said. "Then nothing can fall on us."

"It might fall on us as we went up. It might fall when we were on top of it. Praise the goddess." T'lin sighed, staring back the way they had come. "What does holy scripture tell us about squabbles between the gods?"

"Scripture I leave to the priests. I can tell you what happens in drama, though."

"So what happens in drama, Embodiment of Ember'l?"

"They usually appeal to the Parent."

"And what happens then, Wisdom?" His green eyes fixed on

her with a quizzical expression she could not read.

"He sends them away. That's in Act One. In Act Three he renders judgment. Then we all come out and bow and pass the plate again."

Dragontrader busied himself replacing his canteen in his pack.

"You think that's what's happening?" she asked. "You think the Lady has gone to appeal to Visek?"

He shrugged and smiled. "I am only a humble dragon trader. You are the fountain of the arts, the Avatar of Astina. If you don't know, then what mortal can understand the gods?"

She thought over all the tragedies she could remember. "Prophecy's one of Visek's attributes. Being god of destiny, he will not allow the others to block the fulfillment!"

"Truly your insight is comforting. Have you discovered yet what the prophecy prophesies for you?"

"No. Sister Ahn was about to tell me at the last stop, and you interrupted." And he had done so deliberately.

"It says that during the seven hundredth Festival of Tion— that's now, starting tonight—that the Liberator will be born." T'lin raised a coppery eyebrow to ask what Eleal thought about that.

"Who's the Liberator?"

"His name is not given. He is the son of Kameron Kisster."

"Who's he, and what's a Kisster?"

The dragon trader shrugged his bulky shoulders. "I do not know these things! Perhaps it is all his given name—Kameron-kisster?"

Eleal searched his face for signs that he was making all this up, in some stupid, stupid game. T'lin might, but Sister Ahn had displayed no signs of a sense of humor, and reapers had to be taken seriously.

"Who or what does the Liberator liberate?"

"And from whom? Or from what? That is not so clear at all. The *Testament* implies he will be very, very important, but it sort of takes that for granted and does not say how, except for one sort of hint."

"What sort of hint?" she snapped.

"It implies he will kill Death."

"I think I would class that as an important act."

"It probably doesn't mean what it seems to mean, though. What it does say is that he will be born sometime in the next few days, in Sussvale."

T'lin had not known this in Embiliina Sculptor's kitchen, or at least had not admitted knowing it. His obvious amusement was very irritating.

"And what does it say about me?" she demanded crossly.

"Ah. Here come the others now."

"You are being deliberately aggravating!" Eleal said in Ambria's most disapproving tone.

He stroked his red beard. "I think I would wager that you do not have the right sort of experience. You had best take those lessons from the old hag at the earliest possible opportunity."

"Lesson in what?" Eleal demanded through clenched teeth.

"Delivering babies."

"*What!?*"

"That is correct, Beloved of the Gods. *Naked and crying he shall come into the world and Eleal shall wash him. She shall clothe him and nurse him and comfort him.* That's what it says about you." T'lin shook with silent mirth, so that Starlight turned his head around and peered at him curiously. "I don't suppose 'nursing' means 'suckling,' unless there are some miracles mentioned I missed."

Personage of Historic Importance?

"That's all? There isn't any more? I don't believe you! Why would I be threatened by a reaper and imprisoned for life by a goddess if all I'm going to do is help some woman have a baby?" Let Kameronkisster go hire a midwife!

"But a very important baby! Even I was small and helpless when I was born. Beautiful, of course, because of my beard. All the witnesses agreed that they had never seen so—"

"So that's where you went last night? That's why you weren't at the camp when Gim and I arrived. You went to visit someone who has a copy of the *Testament?*"

Seeing a glint of suspicion in Dragontrader's eye, Eleal hastily added, "Some rancher friend, I suppose—outside the city?"

"A very shrewd guess, Goddess of Curiosity."

"There isn't any more about me, or you didn't have time to read any more?"

The other two dragons were closing in, puffing.

T'lin chuckled. "All right! No, I didn't have time to read the whole thing, or anything like the whole thing. It's a terrible jumble. There may be more about you in there—I don't know." He turned Starlight to face the newcomers.

That, she decided, was better.

Delivering babies? Yuu-uck!

A little later, walking their heated mounts up the valley, they saw an avalanche descend in white smoke and, later, thunder. It did not come close. Just a warning, Eleal thought, a sign that the Lady was still angry. She made the sign of Tion, and probably Gim did also. Sister Ahn clasped her hands in a prayer to Astina. T'lin made a gesture Eleal did not quite see.

The ascent out of the gorge was almost vertical, it ended in a scramble up a face of sheer ice. Nothing but a dragon could have gone that way, except birds. The surface of the glacier was a jagged nightmare, blindingly bright and swept by a cruel wind. It formed a saddle between two jagged peaks, and the mountains ahead were lower.

Soon it dipped. It dipped more steeply. Then Lightning launched himself like a toboggan and went sweeping off with Eleal screaming, "Zappan!" on his back and T'lin shouts of warning fading in the distance. She was too scared even to close her eyes. Cold wind rushed past, peppering her face with gritty snowflakes. Faster and faster, and she had heart-stopping visions of hurtling out over a precipice.

She did not. The crafty old dragon seemed to know what he was doing. He came to rest in a flat snowfield far below, belching contentedly to himself and twisting his long neck to watch the others follow the trail he had laid out.

"When we get to Sussland, lizard," Eleal said grimly, "I shall take off these accursed leggings and strangle you with them."

★   ★   ★

Going down was usually faster than going up, but Eleal—as an *experienced* traveler—knew that this descent would take longer than the climb, because Sussland lay so much lower than Narshland. Yet soon the snow had been left behind and what had seemed to be more snow ahead turned out to be the tops of clouds. Mist crept in on every hand, transforming the sun to a glowing silver disk and the world itself to a circle of rock no larger than the amphitheater at Suss. Always the dragons headed downward; the air grew steadily warmer and damper. The dragons had a discerning eye for the easiest path, although several times Eleal found herself leaning on the pommel plate and staring straight down while Lightning negotiated a near-vertical face. Once he turned around and descended backward, as Starlight had at the temple.

Grass appeared and eventually straggly shrubs, silvery with dew. It was still not yet noon when the first blighted trees emerged from the fog and T'lin called Starlight to a halt. The other dragons closed in, scales shining wetly, breath cloudy.

"Looks like a good spot for lunch," he said. "Strip off the tack and let them graze, Wrangler. Food's in that pack. *Wosok!*"

T'lin was in a good mood. He helped Sister Ahn dismount. She was probably too stiff to have managed by herself, although she did not utter as much as a wince. He retrieved her sword and attached it to her belt; then he escorted her over to the little stream where Eleal was already gulping ice-cold water.

With both men thus occupied, Eleal slipped off into the rocks to make some necessary adjustments. Already she was far too hot, and in Sussland itself the heat would be stifling. She removed her wool sweater, replaced the smock and coat, and headed back to see what Gim was unpacking.

With the suddenness of a cock crow, the sun's disk brightened. The sky turned from white to blue as if the gods had drawn back curtains. The mist dispersed and Sussland was laid out far below like a painting, framed between two massive cliffs. Gim was kneeling with a loaf of bread forgotten in his hands, staring openmouthed.

"There it is," Eleal said cheerfully. "Green, isn't it? Suss itself is over there. I don't suppose you can make out the city, but that bright spot is sunlight on the roof of the temple. It's gold, you know. The gap in the mountains beyond is Monpass, to Joalvale. I've been over that one lots of times. The place in the middle with all the trees is Ruatvil, but that's mostly ruins. I know—I've been there. The Thargians still call this Ruatland, did you know that? The gorge is Susswater. It's a *much* bigger river than Narshwater, and it flows west, not east. There's only two places you can cross it. Filoby is over there." She pointed to the right, although she suspected that Filoby itself might be behind the mountain.

Gim nodded, then sprang back into motion as T'lin came striding over. Eleal turned to him.

"We're coming down right on top of Thogwalby, Dragon-trader."

"Or will do, if we can find a way through the forest." He flopped down on the grass and produced his knife. As he reached for the bread, Eleal sat down also.

"Aren't you going to say grace?"

T'lin shot a penetrating green glare at her. "No. I earned this. You can thank the gods or thank me, as you prefer."

Even Eleal was surprised by that, and Gim looked truly shocked, but he said nothing. Sister Ahn was hobbling over to them, leaning on her staff and weighted down with her ridiculous sword.

"What's at Thogwalby?" Gim asked. He was apparently waiting for the nun to arrive before starting to eat.

Eleal bit into a peach. "A monastery."

"Not much else," T'lin said with his mouth full. "Green brothers. Don't allow women near the place."

"Not even these two?" Gim grinned shyly.

Dragontrader shook his head.

"Garward Karzon, god of strength," Eleal explained. "Men go there to train for the festival." She had never been to Thogwalby and was annoyed to hear that she might miss it this time. "Some of them stay there year after year!"

"And never see a woman," T'lin agreed. "Lot of sacrifice for a miserable flower in their hair, if you ask me."

Gim bristled. "The principle is that all mortal achievement is transitory, sir, and the roses fade after—"

"I know the principle, lad. It's the practice that would bother me."

Gim clenched his lips and did not reply.

Sister Ahn settled awkwardly to the ground, clasped her hands in prayer, then helped herself to a slice of bread and a piece of cheese. Apparently she considered the cost of food to be included in the fare, because she did not offer additional payment. Her face was gray with fatigue.

T'lin chewed for a while, studying her. Finally he said, "Sister? We're going to come down somewhere near Thogwalby. Where do we deliver our Maiden of Destiny?"

The nun blinked her faded, filmy eyes at him. "I am not familiar with the geography, T'lin Dragontrader. The prophecies do not specify a location. I am sure the gods will provide."

"One way or the other? According to our little Toast of the World, there are at least two reapers skulking around Sussia now, and at least one of them knows her and will kill her on sight."

"*Two* reapers?" Sister Ahn turned her head stiffly to look at Eleal. "Tell me, child."

All the taste had gone out of the food. Eleal recounted the tale of Dolm Actor again.

The nun frowned as if worried, but did not comment. There was a long silence while everyone waited for her to finish chewing, but she just kept on and on. Dragons crunched grass in the background.

"Why don't you mention his name?" Gim asked. "You didn't last night, either."

"Because if you know a reaper, he will know you know him! I am trying to spare your life, that's all."

Gim gulped, and looked at the other two for confirmation. The nun was still chewing, staring at the ground. T'lin was frowning. After a while he said, "The convent at Filoby will take you in, Sister."

The old woman nodded, not looking up.

"And the girl also."

"*Zappan* to that!" Eleal said. "I did not escape from the red just to be trapped by the blue. To be a priestess is not my ambition, T'lin Dragontrader!"

"No self-respecting goddess would have you anyway, minx. You want to go to Suss and join your friends?"

"Er, no." One of those "friends" was a reaper, and from the glint in T'lin's eye he had guessed as much.

"The sisters will grant you shelter while the festival is on, I'm sure." T'lin popped a last fragment of cheese in his mouth. "What happens after depends on what happens during. Maybe nothing."

Life, Eleal decided, had become very much like that journey in the mist—straight down with no clear future in sight. What happened after she had delivered that unthinkable baby? Would Tion reward her when she had fulfilled the prophecy? Would the Lady bear a grudge, so she would have to wander the world forever like Hoinyok in *The Monk's Curse?*

"Eleal?" Gim said, "tell me about the festival." He was smiling wistfully. Sister Ahn had drifted off to sleep where she sat, head down, a small huddle of threadbare blue cloth. T'lin had stretched out on the grass, soaking up sunshine.

"Well!" Eleal pondered. "It would take me all day to tell you everything. It always begins on Thighday evening, with a service in the temple. That's not in the city, it's outside. The next day there's the dedication. Then all the athletes go off on the circuit and the artistic events begin."

"Circuit of what?"

"Sussvale. It takes four days. They stay at Thogwalby, and Filoby, and Jogby. Every day the last few are disqualified and lots just drop out."

Gim's blue eyes widened. "Why?"

"Exhaustion, of course! Sussland's always hot as an oven. At Thogwalby they honor Garward. At Filoby they have another dedication, to Iilah. She's goddess of athletes. They spend the night in the sacred grove there." She sniggered. "One year there was a thunderstorm and they all caught colds! Next day they march to Jogby."

"What do they do there?"

"Lick their blisters."

"I mean what god do they worship?" Gim said crossly.

Eleal could not recall ever hearing of a temple at Jogby. "None! You don't *have* to go round by Jogby to get to Suss, so I've never been there. I suspect it's just a ploy to keep them out of the way. By the time the brawn gets back to Suss, we artists've usually got most of the individual performances out of the way, and a lot of the plays, too. The end is on Headday, of course. The roses are awarded and the winners parade into the temple to thank Tion, and all the cripples and invalids are brought in and the god performs a miracle . . . What are you grinning about?"

Gim scrambled to his feet and went sauntering off as if to admire the view. Eleal went after him.

"What's the matter?"

He grinned sheepishly. "Nothing."

"Tell me! I told you about the festival!"

He was turning pink. "Oh, I was just wondering if Holy Tion looks anything like . . . like Dad's statue of Kirb'l."

"He doesn't look at all! Don't you even know that? There's no image of Tion in the temple. No mortal artist could do justice to the lord of beauty."

"Oh. Dad's carving . . ." Gim squirmed.

"I'm sure it comes very close!"

His milky complexion reddened perceptibly. "Little monster!"

"That's what T'lin meant by the gold rose. There's one yellow rose given out, and the winner of that stands before the altar and represents Tion. He hands out the red roses."

Gim glowered. "I know that!"

"I am sure you will win the gold rose!"

She had thought that his face was red, but it had been barely pink compared with what it now turned. Scarlet spread from the roots of his hair to the collar of his smock. His misty mustache became fairer in contrast. She was fascinated. She couldn't recall ever managing to provoke such an all-encompassing blush, like a stormy sunset all over the sky.

"Go jump off a mountain!" Gim spun on his heel.

She hobbled after him. "But it's a very great honor to portray a god, and in your case you would be entering as a likeness of your father's carving. Perhaps the god is telling us that he wants your father brought here to make——"

Gim spun around furiously. "Go away and stop pestering me, little girl!"

Oo! "But I am drawn to your beauty as stenchbugs to honey——"

"Stenchbugs get stamped on!"

"But beauty should be recognized and all women——"

"What's the argument?" asked T'lin Dragontrader, strolling over to them. He had stripped down to a smock and baggy Joalian breeches, both colored like a flock of rainbow birds. His sword dangled at his belt. The little gold ring glinted in his earlobe.

"Nothing!" Gim barked.

"I was just explaining about the gold rose."

"Ah." T'lin shrugged. "Myself, I don't think good looks are anything to brag about. But they're nothing to be ashamed of, either, and you'll grow out of them soon enough. Don't let this little queen bee get under your skin, lad. How well can you play that lyre of yours?"

"I'll show you!" Gim said, eager for a distraction.

"I'm no judge."

"I am," Eleal said.

T'lin folded red-hairy arms. "You keep out of this, pest. Can you twang a note or two well enough to enter? Not win, necessarily, just reasonably enter?"

"Think so."

"Good. Then you'll do that. You can be our scout at the festival."

Gim frowned. "The festival is to honor the—"

"Then why are there reapers there? Your god told you to rescue this half-size bellyache, didn't he?"

Both men looked down at Eleal while she tried to think of a witty alternative to kicking Dragontrader's shins.

"I'm suggesting your responsibilities aren't over yet," T'lin said. "We've got her here, you and me, and we've got to try to keep her alive. Or do you put your trust in Sister Ahn's swordsmanship?"

Gim smiled. "No, sir."

"Ah, the old bag's awake, we can be on our way. Let's see you saddle up, Wrangler. Come, Jewel of the. . . . "

Eleal spun around to see why T'lin was staring. She saw smoke. Something big was burning in Sussland.

38

"PIOL POET WAS PLANNING TO WRITE A DRAMA CALLED the *Zoruatiad,* about the siege of Ruat," Eleal explained, "so of course that year we went there to let him look over the place. He never did write it, though. Once this was all Ruatland, and Ruat was a fair and mighty city. There was a bridge there in those days. Then came the Lemodland War. Ruatia fought for the Thargians, but the Joalians won, at least hereabouts, and Trathor Battlemaster razed the city and threw down the bridge. They made Sussby into the new capital, on their side of the river, but there's still only the two bridges, at Rotby and Lameby. So Sussby grew up to became Suss, Ruatwater became Susswat—"

"Do you *ever* stop talking?" Gim asked.

"Not when faced with such an abundance of ignorance in need of instruction." That was a quote from last year's comedy, and quite witty under the circumstance, Eleal decided. She would forgive him, then. Besides, he had smiled enough to take the sting out of his words and Gim Wrangler's smile would melt a statue of the Maiden. His face was scorched by the sun already and so coated with road dust that his eyebrows and mustache had vanished altogether. The latter looked much better when it wasn't visible.

T'lin was in the lead. Behind him Sister Ahn lolled in Blaze's saddle like a bag of cordroot. Even if she was as unconscious as she looked, she was well strapped on. The youngsters were bringing up the rear. They had gained enough control over their mounts now that they could ride side by side and converse.

The descent of Susslope had been easier than Eleal had expected, following the steepest route to avoid trees and then down avalanche cuts. Those in turn had led to a sizable river, which had soon entered a cultivated valley, and since then it had been all dirt road and dust and sweat. She had forgotten just how hot Sussvale was, or else the quick descent had given her no time to adjust. She had stripped down to breechclout and smock. Her legs were getting burned. So were Gim's, because he was wearing no more than she was.

Dragons did poorly in heat, and T'lin was holding them to a gentle *zaib*. On either hand sun blazed on lurid green paddy fields, where brown-chested men in wide straw hats would straighten from their work to inspect the travelers, and sometimes return their waves. Eleal suspected the water round their legs would be as warm as a hot bath. Some crop she should recognize and didn't was flowering in acres of pale pink, scenting the air like custard. Once in a while the road passed through orchards of the great dark bellfruit trees, and the black shade was a blessing. Sometimes, too, watchcats would yowl from the little farms as the four dragons ran by.

In Suss itself, and in the villages, men and women dressed in smocks that were no more than tubes of cotton with shoulder straps. Here the field hands wore only loincloths. For everyone, though, the brutal sun of Sussvale made the wheel-sized straw hats essential wear. Turbans were just not adequate. T'lin outfitted himself and his companions by buying hats right off the heads of children who ran out to see the dragons. Four copper mites bought four serviceable hats, which the original owners could replace with a few minutes' work. Even Sister Ahn made no complaint when T'lin leaned over and placed one on her head.

"We're still heading northeast," Eleal said. "So we're not going to come out near Thogwalby at all. Probably nearer Filoby. And I wish I knew what that smoke was!"

The black pillar had not dispersed; indeed it still seemed to be thickening. It stood almost dead ahead, towering over the hills like a menacing giant. The top spread out in a sooty layer, drifting gently westward, but for most of its height it was a vertical scar upon the hot, still afternoon.

"I expect we'll find out soon enough," she added. The side valley was about to enter Sussvale proper.

"How big is Filoby?"

To avoid saying she had no idea, Eleal risked a guess. "About a hundred homes, more or less."

Gim nodded. "Built of what?"

"Er. White stuff. Like those." She pointed to a cluster of farm buildings.

"Adobe. That doesn't burn very well. What else is there at Filoby?"

"A waterfall."

Gim rolled his eyes and joined in her laugh.

"The Convent of Iilah," she said.

"Describe it."

"I'm not sure," she admitted. "I've only passed by. The buildings are mostly hidden in the trees. There's this sacred grove, you see. It's a little round hill covered with mighty oaks. The temple is quite small. All you can see is the dome and some red tile roofs."

"Tiles need beams. Anything else?"

"No," she admitted, worried.

"Then there's your answer," Gim said with a frown. He nodded at the smoke. "The late sacred grove."

Almost imperceptibly, the valley widened into Sussflat. The peaks of Susswall came into sight to the north, shimmering behind veils of heat haze. The rich plain was familiar to Eleal—a mosaic of orchards, bright green crops, tiny white hamlets—but she knew it must seem strange to Gim, native of a bleaker land. At times a star flashed in the distance; she pointed it out to him, explaining that it was sunlight reflecting from the temple roof in Suss itself. To the east, the ominous smoke still crawled into the sky.

Red dirt tracks between the fields led eventually to the main Filoby–Thogwalby highway, which was no more than a wider version of the same rutted trail. In this hottest part of the day traffic was light: scrawny herds being driven to fresh pasture, a few ox wagons. Once Gim cried out in astonishment and pointed to a party of men riding long-legged moas in the distance. Eleal suspected they were soldiers and was relieved to have missed them.

Eventually T'lin halted Starlight and waited for the others to gather around. "We must take a break," he said, scowling at the mounts. "They can't take this heat." He nodded at a hillock ahead, capped by tall trees. "Head over there; I'll catch up with you." He rode off toward a cluster of farmhands, who were gaping at the dragons.

Normally the others would have tried to follow Starlight, but now they were too dispirited to argue. Gim persuaded Beauty to move. Lightning and Blaze followed. The trees were smooth pillars, erupting into green canopies very high from the ground. Their shade seemed dark as a cave, and nothing else grew in it.

Gim said, *"Wosok!"* and beamed when all three dragons obeyed him. He looked around approvingly at the grove. "Cool!"

Eleal slithered down from Lightning's saddle, feeling as old and stiff as Sister Ahn. "It isn't really. It just seems cool after the heat outside."

"You have to argue, don't you? What are these trees called?"

"Parasol trees."

"Do you know that, or are you guessing?"

"I know that, of course." After all, she had just called them parasol trees, so they were called parasol trees by her, even if other people had other names for them. She sat down on the sand and leaned back against one of the great leathery trunks. The air did feel sort of cool. Filoby could not be much more than five or six miles away; even the flames were visible now.

Gim had helped the nun dismount. The old woman seemed barely conscious. She did not ask for her sword, which was a bad sign.

Ahn had never said that she was Eleal Singer's protector. Although the sword seemed to imply that, the nun had firmly denied that it was a weapon. Nor had she ever claimed that the Maiden had sent her, only that she was fulfilling the prophecy. The Youth had designated Gim to rescue Eleal from the temple, but had sent him no further orders, no vision of later events. T'lin Dragontrader was Eleal's guardian and keeper now. Her secret friend had turned out to be the most important person in her life. He was big and gruff, and she knew he had secrets she did not share, but she had no one else to trust. She wished she knew which god had sent him.

T'lin joined them in a few minutes. He sat down, wiping his forehead with a brawny arm. His face was as red as his beard, and he was glaring. "Well, that's the sacred grove, as we thought. Last night a large group of men went by here, heading for Filoby. Fifty or sixty of them. They joked that they were going to call on the goddess."

"What?" Eleal shouted. "You mean it was deliberate?"

"Typical Sussian atrocity."

Defile the abode of a goddess? "Who were these savages?"

Gim was frowning. Sister Ahn was slumped over, apparently barely conscious.

T'lin's green eyes were cold as ice. "The trainees from Garward's monastery, led by some of the monks. At dawn they roused the people of Filoby to join them, and they sacked the convent. Anyone who refused to help was beaten and his house destroyed."

"Why would they do such a thing, sir?" Gim asked softly.

"What happened to the nuns?" Eleal demanded.

T'lin shrugged, apparently in answer to both queries.

Despite the heat, Eleal now felt thoroughly chilled. "Last night you said there was a serious squabble in the Pentatheon, didn't you?"

"Seems I was right, then."

She was a token in a game being played by the gods. Garward was another avatar of Karzon and apparently just as much involved in this affair as Zath. The Man and the Lady were against her in all their aspects. The Youth was helping her, and now it seemed that the Maiden was on her side also—or at least on the opposite side from the Man, which must mean the same thing . . . mustn't it? And the stake in this whole evil game was the Liberator, a baby.

Sister Ahn stirred and tried to sit up straight. She still wore her woolen habit, which must now be intolerably hot. Somehow her face was both flushed and haggard. After a moment she spoke in a surprisingly firm voice: *"Woe to the Maiden, for the Man shall ply his strength against her. Woe to her holy place. Virgins are profaned. See blood and ashes paint the face of sanctity. The sacred place yields to the strength of the Man and only lamentation remains."*

"I suppose that's part of your precious prophecy?" T'lin sneered.

She nodded, blinking tears. "It is so written in the *Testament,* but there is no date given. I weep to see it."

"Me too. Doesn't make any sense until it's too late, does it?" He scowled contemptuously. "We need a change of plan. The thugs are probably on their way to Suss and the festival now, but there's no point in us going to Filoby. We certainly can't risk Thogwalby after this." He eyed Eleal shrewdly. "And we can't take you to Suss, either, can we?" He had guessed about Dolm Actor.

"Wouldn't I be safe if I took refuge in Tion's temple?"

"Would you? Would the priests let you? Besides, we must stop soon—the dragons can't take this heat." He was looking at Sister Ahn, though, who had slumped over again in abject exhaustion.

"That only leaves one choice, sir, doesn't it?" Gim said calmly. "We go to Ruatvil."

"There's nothing there!" Eleal protested, and then realized that *no*-thing might be a very *good* thing under the circumstances.

T'lin cocked a coppery eyebrow. "Know it, do you?"

"Oh, yes!"

"Nowhere to stay?"

"Well, yes. There's a hostelry."

"And do you know the Sacrarium?"

"Of course," she said, relieved that he had asked something easy.

"Good. Then let's *zaib!*"

The big man rose to his feet and headed for the dragons before Eleal had a chance to find out why T'lin Dragontrader should want to go sightseeing. It seemed out of character.

It was not true that there was nothing at Ruatvil. There were ruins, and trees, and hummocky pasture. As Eleal explained to Gim while they were riding in—repeating what Piol Poet had told her two years before—much of mighty Ruat had been built of clay bricks, and those parts had collapsed to mud once their roofs had gone. The stone buildings stood as isolated walls, broken towers, and stark, useless arches. Some families dwelt in shanties within these relics, in constant risk of death from storm or earth tremor. Other cottages had been constructed from fallen masonry and then roofed with turf, so that goats grazed on them. The result was a strangely widespread settlement, a village scattered like seed corn over the grave of a metropolis.

"I think I could have worked all that out for myself," Gim said, looking around disparagingly.

"If you win the gold rose, the priests will make you shave off your mustache."

"What has that to do with anything?"

"I've been meaning to ask you the same question."

They were all weary. None of them had slept much in the previous night, and the journey had been hard.

Ruatvil was not completely abandoned. The main street was still wide, although its paving lay buried in grass and heaved by tree roots. A few inhabitants were going about their business—herding goats, bearing loads of food and charcoal. They all paused to stare at the dragons.

Eleal directed T'lin to the hostelry, which he would doubtless have found quite easily by himself. It brought back memories for her, yet it was smaller than she remembered. Once the building must have been some rich man's mansion or a public edifice, and the walls still stood three stories high. Now only the ground floor was in use, and sky showed through the empty arches of the windows, for the roof had long since vanished. The entrance was an imposing portico, but the doors themselves had cooked meals for persons long dead, and only their rusty hinges remained.

Piit'dor Hosteler was a large, ruddy-faced man with a gray-streaked beard and a prominent wart on his nose. Playing his role in traditional fashion, he rubbed his hands gleefully when T'lin flashed gold, gabbling at length how he anticipated an invasion of refugees from Filoby, and how the civic authorities of Ruatvil would require him to provide them with shelter, but if the noble guests were already in residence, of course, then they would not be disturbed, and fortunately his very best accommodation was still available . . . and so on.

Gim was already unbuckling the straps that held Sister Ahn in her saddle. T'lin eased him out of the way. "Civic authorities!" he muttered under his breath. "Ten to one they're his brother."

He lifted the old woman bodily in his arms, her sword dangling. Piit'dor Hosteler flinched with astonishment. His joviality vanished, and he backed away until he stood squarely before the steps to his front door, all the while staring hard at that sword.

"Something wrong?" T'lin demanded.

The hosteler began to mutter about evil omens.

"All of us or none! Which is it?" T'lin was still holding the old woman as if she weighed nothing. He rolled forward menacingly.

"She is ill?"

"Merely fatigued."

Obviously unhappy, Piit'dor faltered. Daughters of Irepit must be rare in Ruatvil, but visitors with real money would not be common either. He forced an ingratiating simper. "Oh, my lord is most welcome, and all his companions. The reverend lady shall be fittingly attended." He scurried up the steps muttering, "My wife . . ."

"I'll bet the ceilings leak," Gim said.

"Yes, they do." Suddenly Eleal began to yawn. She was too weary to relate how much it had rained on her previous visit. It had not seemed funny at the time. She thought that even a cloudburst as bad as that one would not waken her tonight, once she found somewhere to lie down.

Hayana Hosteler was even larger than her husband, boisterous and motherly, with a matching mole on her nose. She knew all the traditional business of her role—the smear of flour on the forehead, the fast shuffle on flat feet, the wiping of hands on apron—and she arrived with an entourage of several adolescent assistants. Displaying no superstitious dread of a Daughter of Irepit, she bemoaned the poor sister's distress, saw her laid on a mattress, and then chased the men away.

Furnished with a bucket of water of her own in a corner of the big room, Eleal set to work to remove the sediment of her journey. Although her inclination was just to fall over and sleep, she could not do so until Hayana and her brood stopped fussing around Sister Ahn. They were to share the same bedchamber. That mattered little; there would have been ample room for a couple of the dragons as well.

Sunlight poured in two huge empty window arches, so there was no privacy—and no security either, for anyone could approach through the woodland outside. The roof was partly composed of the original beams and upstairs flooring, now sagging badly. Where it had collapsed, the holes had been patched with tree trunks. The beds were oddly placed, obviously in the driest locations, for much of the mosaic floor was grimed by dry watercourses, relics of rain.

She had no garment other than the smock Embiliina Sculptor had given her, and it was red with dust. With her hair still damp and her feet still bare, she found herself hustled off to eat. Gim was already doing so, sitting in lordly solitude in a vast room furnished with rough-hewn tables and benches. Faded fragments of frescoes clung to the walls. His hair was as damp as hers, but he did have a clean smock. There was no sign of T'lin, who was probably fussing over his precious dragons.

Lunch—or perhaps dinner, or maybe supper—comprised heaps of fruit and hot bread and goats' milk cheese. Gim, his new cleanliness emphasizing his sunburn, tried each sort of fruit in turn, demanding to know its name. Eleal told him, making up suitable noises when she wasn't sure. Apart from that, neither spoke much.

Eventually she could keep her eyes open no longer, although she knew the sun would not set for a couple of hours yet. "I am going to bed!" she announced firmly.

Gim donned a superior, tough-male expression. "I am going to practice my lyre, unless Dragontrader needs me."

"You can practice drums and you won't keep me awake," Eleal said, and headed off to her room.

A mattress in one corner was invitingly empty. Another near the center bore a snoring Sister Ahn. No matter! Eleal would sleep if—*Eek!*

A man was peering in the window. It took her a moment to realize that it was T'lin Dragontrader in a straw hat and a drab-colored local smock. She had never seen him without his turban, and there was something odd about his beard.

"Only me!" He dropped a bundle over the sill. "Brought you something to wear. Up all night—expect you want to sleep now?"

"Oh, yes!"

"Just tell me how to find the Sacrarium."

Fogged by fatigue, Eleal regarded him blankly for a moment. He had apparently smeared his beard with charcoal, dulling its normal copper red. Why did Dragontrader want to be incon-spicuous?

And why did he not just ask one of the locals to give him directions?

"You can't miss it," she said. "Follow the main road north to the old bridge. It's east of the road, 'bout half a mile. There's a sign, and a path."

"Oh. Good. Er . . . anything you need before you kip?"

Eleal yawned and stretched divinely. "Can't keep my eyes open."

"Right." T'lin eyed her with bright green suspicion. "If you do wake up when I'm not around . . . Well, this isn't Narsh or Suss, remember. You stay here!"

Eleal walked over to her mattress and sat down, promising faithfully that she would go no farther from the hostelry than the dragons, which she could hear belching faintly.

"Just remember what happened at Filoby this morning," T'lin said thoughtfully. "They catch bigfangs hereabouts sometimes, too."

She went on the offensive. "Are you trying to keep me away from something, T'lin Dragontrader?"

"No, no! You sleep well." He disappeared.

Perhaps food had revived her. Perhaps it was only curiosity. Either way, she knew she could not sleep now. She rushed over to the bundle he had tossed in, discovering a smock and a pair of sandals. He would almost certainly hang around for a while and watch the window in case she tried to follow him. She changed quickly into the clean smock, grabbed up the sandals, and ran out the door. *Slop slap slop slap . . .*

❧❧ 39 ❧❧

EDWARD HAD NOT EXPECTED TO SLEEP, BUT HE DID. THE wagon was hot and noisy. From time to time he would become aware of snores, wheels rumbling, axles squeaking, and the clopping of hooves. Very rarely a lorry would go by or children would shout abuse at the hated Gypsies. Dogs barked hysterically. At such times his worries would surge in on him again and for a while he would stare at the painted slats above his nose while plot and counterplot raced around in his mind. What proof of age or identity would he need to enlist? He would not dare use his own name. His OTC Certificate would be useless and was unobtainable now anyway, back in Kensington, so he could not hope for early routing into officer training. Well, he would not mind the ranks. But how long could he conceal his identity? How long until word filtered back to Fallow and Greyfriars?

Sometime during the morning the caravan halted for a while. He did not bother to investigate the reason for the stoppage. He did not think it would be a police roadblock looking for him, but if it were, the Gypsies could handle it. They had centuries of practice at dealing with rozzers. Creighton continued to snore.

By now Alice must have heard of his disappearance. She

would be worried crazy. On the other hand, he thought with much satisfaction of his uncle's reaction, wishing he could somehow take him to that hilltop grove and introduce him to Puck. He wondered how Head Office had contrived the Old-castle sham for the last two years. A committee, Creighton had said, and yet all his letters had been answered in the same hand-writing.

The wagon rolled again. He slept again.

He dreamed of his parents and awoke shaking.

In the dream they had been sitting on the veranda at Nyaga-tha, writing a letter together like a committee of two, and in the way of dreams he had known they were writing to him.

That Jumbo letter was what was bothering him. It tied in so well with what Creighton had told him! Without it, he probably would dismiss all of the colonel's story as rubbish—mended leg or no mended leg.

"I see you're awake at last." Creighton was stripped to his undervest, shaving with a straight razor. "Was that the sleep of the just, or just sleep?"

"Yes, sir," Edward said, with what he thought was admirable self-control. He felt limp and sweaty in the noon heat. There was no room for him to climb down. The wagon was still mov-ing and he might jostle Creighton and make him cut his throat. The man was infuriatingly tight-lipped, but that would be going a bit far.

The wagon lurched as Creighton stooped to see in the look-ing glass, preparing a stroke. He cursed under his breath.

"Will you tell me where we are, sir?"

"Halfway to where we're going. We'll be there tonight."

"And where is that?"

"Stonehenge."

Edward sensed a leg-pull and then realized. "A node, of course?"

"The most powerful in Britain, so I'm told."

"And who do we meet there? Druids?"

"Druids? I suppose they would have used it, but I suspect it was ancient even in their time." Creighton aimed another stroke at his neck. Apparently he was in a more informative mood now, for he carried on talking as he wiped the razor. "It has no resident genius now, so far as I know—so far as my friends in Head Office know. Nodes have another purpose, many of them. They can be used as portals."

He had just confirmed something Edward had been afraid of.

"Portals to where?"

"Various places. Most of the European ones connect with a territory known as the Vales, but that may just be a peculiarity of the keys we know—something to do with the languages or the cultural trends in rhythm. Try this." He laid down his razor and beat a rapid tattoo on the table. "Can you do that?"

Edward reached up to the roof in front of his nose and repeated the beat.

Creighton whistled. "First time? That was perfect, I think. Do it again."

Edward did it again, wondering what the catch was.

"Let's see if you can do the whole thing then!" This time Creighton repeated the refrain and continued drumming. The whole thing was long and extremely complex, but obviously just a series of variations and syncopation. Edward played it back to him exactly.

"Exeter, you're a wonder! How the deuce did you manage that? I thought it would take you all afternoon to get it."

"I was raised in Africa. The natives have far more complicated beats than that. Try this one." His fingers were rusty, and it really needed two drummers, but he managed a fair imitation of one of the simpler Embu rhythms.

Creighton listened in silence, and then suddenly laughed. It was the first real laugh Edward had heard him utter, a raucous bray. "I could never come close! Well, that takes care of one problem. How are you at learning stuff off by heart?"

"Average, I suppose."

"Modesty? You played the king in *Henry V*. That's a tough part."

"How did . . . You read my letters to Mr. Oldcastle?"

"A summary of what you've been up to." Creighton seemed to have forgotten that half his face was coated with soap. "Repeat this:

"*Affalino kaspik, fialybo tharpio,*
Noga nogi theyo fan
Affaliki suspino."

"What's it mean?"

"Lord knows. It's in no known language. Probably older than the pyramids. Try it."

That was tougher. It took him several tries and repeats.

"They go together, don't they?" he said. "What's the melody?" He began to sing the words to the beat.

"Stop!" Creighton barked. "Do not mix the ingredients until I say so!"

"Sir?" Edward wondered yet again if the man was crazy.

"Beat, words, melody, and dance. You must learn them separately. Together they're a key."

"A key to what?"

"A key to a portal, of course. I hope it's one of the keys to Stonehenge. Let's try the next verse."

"A key to a portal to where?" Edward said angrily.

"Obedience without question! Second verse—"

"Sir!

They glared at each other, but Edward was so riled now that it was Creighton who looked away. He smirked into the looking glass and picked up his razor again.

"The keys are all very ancient," he remarked cheerfully. "Shamanistic, most of 'em. Been used for thousands of years. We've got a chappie at Olympus who's made quite a study of them, trying to figure out how they work. Not all keys work at all nodes. In fact we know how to work very few of them as portals, and not all of those lead to Nextdoor, although most of them do—that's why it's called Nextdoor, I suppose. The European ones are definitely biased in favor of the Vales and *vice versa,* he says, but there are exceptions. There's one in Joalland itself that connects to one in New Zealand. Does that surprise you?"

"No," Edward admitted. "And another in the Valley of the Kings?"

Creighton cut his cheek and barked out an oath that would have had any boy at Fallow sacked on the spot.

"What do you know about *that?*"

Apparently Edward had poked a very sensitive tooth, which he found highly satisfying. "It's sometimes called the Valley of the Tombs of Kings. Near Luxor. A bunch of pharaohs were buried there."

Creighton glared, blood streaming down his neck. "Answer my question, boy!"

"Will you first answer some of mine?"

"No, I will not! I am not playing games!" He was, though. "This is a matter of life and death, Exeter—your death, certainly. Possibly mine too. Now tell me how you learned of the Valley!"

Reluctantly, Edward conceded. "A letter my father wrote just before his death, sir."

"Where did you see this letter? Where is it now?"

"Back at the hospital."

With another oath, the colonel took up a perfectly good shirt and dabbed at his cut. "Who was he writing to? Not you."

"No, sir. A chappie called Jumbo. The letter was never sent, obviously. I found it in his papers last week."

Creighton grunted. "Well, you're right. Jumbo is one of us. There is a portal in Egypt. Now the opposition may learn of it! Damn it to hell! I wonder if I can send a telegram from one of these villages?" He glared wordlessly at the shirt.

"I expect the police will impound my belongings, sir."

"You think that will stop the Blighters? Well, you didn't know; it's not your fault. The Luxor portal is handy because it leads directly to Olympus. Some others do, but they're better known. This key I'm teaching you usually leads to somewhere in the Vales. What else was in that letter?"

"I think," Edward said icily, "that you cheated."

"Absolutely unthinkable," Creighton told his reflection blandly.

"I think that when my parole ends, you will have made it impossible for me to enlist!"

"Did I ever say I wouldn't?"

"That," Edward snarled, "is hairsplitting! Bloody lawyer talk!"

Creighton made his *Hrrnph!* noise and glared again. "And that is insubordination!"

"You extracted my word of honor. Where's your honor?"

"Insolence! Impudent puppy!"

They were both shouting now.

Edward swung his legs around, dropped to the floor, and straightened up to confront the colonel. He cracked his head resoundingly against the roof, seeing blue flames.

Creighton snorted mockingly. "See? You can't even stand on your own two feet. You're a dead man without me around to save you, Exeter. You'd never get into uniform. The Blighters will track you down, and this time they won't beat around the bush. They'll snuff you like a candle."

Edward sank down on a suitcase to massage his scalp. Trouble was, he had every reason to believe the maniac. "One of the first things I heard you say, at the hospital, was, 'He cannot cross over with that leg.' Cross over to where?"

Not getting an answer, he looked up. Creighton was regarding him sourly. Then he shrugged. "Nextdoor, I hope. Nobody's ever tried Stonehenge before, that I know of, but we'll have to risk it. If it doesn't work, we'll head over to the big circles at Avebury and try there. All our usual portals in England will be under surveillance. According to the *Filoby Testament,* my lad, you arrive at one of the nodes in Sussland, which is in the Vales, on Nextdoor. We must trust the prophecy."

"*On* Nextdoor? Not *in* Nextdoor? Nextdoor's an island?"

Creighton turned back to the looking glass. "No," he said. "Not an island. Nextdoor is a lot more than an island."

"And that's where the guv'nor was living before he *came back* to New Zealand? The missing thirty years when he did not grow old?"

"You're a sharp little nipper, you are!" Creighton said. "Give me that first verse again."

SUSSWATER WAS SAID TO BE THE LEAST NAVIGABLE RIVER in the Vales. Muddy yellow, it roared along the bottom of a canyon whose sides were hundreds of feet high and usually sheer. In only three places was it narrow enough to bridge, and the bridge at Ruat had been the first and most splendid. When Trathor Battlemaster had laid siege to the city he had begun by throwing down the stone arch on the north bank. The south arch still stood, a notable landmark dangling vestiges of its ancient chains and straddling a paved road now trod by none. From its base the towers of Suss were clearly visible to the north, the sun glinting on the roof of Tion's temple. They seemed but an hour's stroll away, yet it would take a strong walker all day to reach them. The citizens of Suss had blocked any effort to rebuild the bridge, lest Ruatvil rise again as a rival.

So Piol Poet had said.

The Sacrarium must once have been a noble and imposing monument, standing by itself near the edge of the cliffs. It was revered as the oldest holy building in the Vales, its builders long forgotten. Even Trathor had not dared violate a temple so sacred, but time, storm, and earthquake had done it for him. All that could now be seen was a pentagonal platform of giant blocks bearing remains of a circle of pillars. Many were represented only by their bases, less than a dozen still retained their full height. What sort of roof or lintels they might once have supported was unknown, and theologians could not explain why they had originally numbered thirty-one. Pilgrims still came, although rarely, and devout persons had kept the inside of the circle clear of rubble. The surrounding land had been too holy to plow; it had grown a forest instead, and now the lonely ruin was buried in jungle.

Eleal was confident she could find a shortcut. Rather than follow the old highway and the pilgrim path, she would head directly northeast until she reached the edge of the gorge and then approach the Sacrarium from the other side. Holding her hat on with one hand and her sandals in the other, she ran barefoot through the grassy woodland of Ruatvil, skirting its stony ruins. A few young goatherds watched her, but no one challenged her or jeered at her awkward lope. Puffing and sweating in the heat, she came to the woods and realized her error. She had forgotten how dense the jungle was.

Thorns and brambles became so thick that she was slowed to a stumbling walk. Masses of stone lay hidden everywhere. She found the way hard going in sandals, but she forced her way through, being as quiet as she could. Her hat kept catching in branches; she took it off and carried it in front of her to shield her face from twigs. The grove was utterly silent in the heat of the afternoon. Not a bird sang. Even insects seemed to be sleeping.

Then she discovered a stream by almost falling into it. Where had that come from? It crossed her path in a deep gully, whose sides were muddy and crumbly. She slid and floundered down to the water, and was infuriated to discover that it was flowing from right to left. As far as she could remember, the pilgrim path never crossed a creek, so she must be on the correct side already. She struggled back up again, and set off to follow the gully—it could only flow to the river, and the cliff.

It certainly did not flow *directly* to the river. It wound and twisted until she lost all sense of direction and began to think that the sun was setting in the east. Her legs shook with weariness; her hip ached fiercely. Soon she was tempted to turn back and forget stupid T'lin Dragontrader and his idiotic interest in ruins. Trouble was, she would have to follow the stream all the way.

In the distance, someone began whistling a solemn refrain. She halted and listened. It was not a tune she knew. It stopped suddenly. She started to move again, heading in that direction. Soon she saw steps rising out of the undergrowth, the edge of the plinth. Directly above her stood a stub of stone pillar as thick as a man's outstretched arms and furred with dense ivy.

She heard a murmur of someone speaking.

Step by step she approached. When she reached the base of the mossy, crumbling stair, the voice was clearer, and apparently coming from just behind that same pillar. Barefoot again, she tiptoed up until she stood beside its ivy-coated bulk, and then she could make out the words.

". . . the boy to bring her to my camp. I went and told my men to expect them. Then I went back into town and reported to Narsh Prime."

T'lin himself!

That was better. Eleal eased around the curve of the stone like growing moss.

A man chuckled. "And what did he make of all that?"

A Thargian! He was speaking Joalian, but the guttural accent was unmistakable.

T'lin again: "He thought the Service would be interested."

"He was right, of course."

T'lin sighed. "Glad to hear that! Well, we thumbed through the *Testament*—as much as we had time for—and found her name, as she had said. Funny, that! I've known the brat for years and never guessed she was anyone of consequence. She's an incredible little busybody. I always thought she might make a good recruit when she's older."

"Sounds like she might."

"Well, Prime agreed I ought to bring her if I could. When I got back to my camp, I found the kids had arrived safely—much to my surprise. So I loaded them up on mounts. What I hadn't realized was that the old nun was skulking in the herd. I geared up my own dragon and turned my back for a moment. Before I knew it, she'd scrambled into the saddle and taken off." He paused, then added diffidently, "In the end I had to bring her also."

The other man chuckled. He sounded quite young. Peering with one eye around the pillar, Eleal made him out. He was seated on a fallen block of stone, his back to her. T'lin must be at his side. They were facing into the empty paved space within the Sacrarium.

"I'm not surprised! The *Filoby Testament* has turned out to be astonishingly accurate. It said the girl would come with a blue nun, so she came with a blue nun. Only a miracle could have prevented it."

"It's a miracle I didn't strangle the old witch!"

The Thargian chortled loudly, as if that were a good joke. "Violence is not advisable with her kind!"

Eleal eased herself a few more inches around the ivy so she could watch with both eyes. The two men were sitting in shade, and had removed their hats. The Thargian was as tall as T'lin, but he was leaning back on his arms, and they were sinewy, youthful arms, well burned by the sun. He was a much younger man. His hair was black and when he turned his head she saw that he was clean-shaven.

He wore a small gold circle in his left ear!

"She's back at the hostelry now, sir," T'lin said. "So what do I do with her?"

Sir? T'lin Dragontrader addressed this stripling as *Sir?*

"Good question!" The Thargian straightened up and ran his fingers through his hair. "What do you get when you cross a wallaby and a jaguar?"

T'lin said, "Huh? Oh! 'Fraid I don't know, sir."

"That's all right. Just means there are some things I'm not supposed to tell you. Don't feel slighted, now! I'm sure you have secrets in the political branch that I don't know. This is a religious matter, that's all."

T'lin uttered his familiar snort. "I had gathered that! Subversion and infiltration I can understand. I'm totally out of my depth with something like this."

"You're not the only one, believe me! How much have you put together?"

"Very little. There's supposed to be some child born in Sussland during the festival. The girl delivers it. The Karzon and Eltiana faction is trying to prevent this. Tion and Astina seem to be in favor. I gather the Service is in favor also?"

The younger man grunted. "We are. Zath and Ois are opposed, certainly. Karzon and Eltiana, probably. But don't ever trust Tion! He plays his own dirty games."

Eleal gasped. *Blasphemy!*

"Tion sent the boy to rescue the girl," T'lin demurred.

"Kirb'l did, you mean! I shudder to think what his reasons may be. Kirb'l is an outright maniac. Astina herself is staying out of things at the moment."

"That was her grove got burned this morning."

The Thargian sighed. "No! That was Iilah's grove. Iilah is more or less on our side—or she was. She may be dead now. Listen, I'll tell you some things I'm not supposed to, so be discreet, all right? The priests' theology is totally muddled, understandably. Their idea of five great gods, the Pentatheon, is a useful simplification, but it has definite limits. Yes, the five are all very powerful—Visek, Karzon, Eltiana, Astina, Tion. But some of the others carry a lot more weight than you'd expect, and their loyalties are not always what you'd expect either. All the aspect-avatar business is stable washings. Iilah is not Astina; Kirb'l is not Tion; Garward is not Karzon! Ois is not Eltiana, either. She's an utter bitch, that one, with her ritual prostitution—and immensely powerful because of it, of course. She probably can cause avalanches as she claims. For all his patronage of art and sport, Tion is just about as depraved as she is."

This was foul, foul heresy! Why was T'lin Dragontrader listening to such blasphemy?

"Fortunately," the stranger added, "they don't all support the Chamber. There's some decent types, and a lot of fence-sitters."

After a moment, T'lin laughed ruefully. "And I thought politics was complicated! Thargdom's going to annex Narshia, you know. Any day now."

"Doesn't surprise me," the Thargian said. "And the Joalians won't stand for it. Idiots! But that doesn't matter much compared to this. Wars come and wars go. The Liberator may turn out to be far more important than any war. You arrived in Sussland after dawn?"

"Well after. After noon."

"Ah! Garward's mob sacked the Filoby grove before that. So he didn't succeed."

Silence followed. Eleal resisted a temptation to scream. She was relieved when T'lin said, "Succeed in what?"

There was another pause then. The Thargian bent over and produced a bottle from near his feet. He drank and passed it to T'lin. "I'll have to explain a few things. First of all, the birth thing is a misinterpretation. We're not expecting a baby. This Liberator the *Testament* mentions will be a grown man."

T'lin chuckled. "My young friend will be relieved. She did not enjoy hearing she was going to be a midwife."

"Don't tell her any of this!" the Thargian said sharply.

"Of course not, sir. I won't tell anyone."

"Right. She has to act on her own volition. If she knows what's expected of her, she may do the wrong thing altogether. Not that I know what is expected of her either, so it probably doesn't matter, but we mustn't risk upsetting the prophecies now. The Chamber's been trying to do that for years, and whatever they want we don't want, if you follow me." He paused again. "That's why Garward sacked Iilah's grove this morning—he wanted to break the chain of prophecy. I think he just strengthened it. He's a headstrong bully and none too bright."

This was a god he was insulting!

"Nevertheless," the blasphemer continued, "the Chamber has much greater resources in this than the Service does, Seventy-seven. Zath is deeply involved, for one."

"Death!"

"The person who claims to be Death. The Liberator sounds like a personal threat to him."

"He's got a couple of his reapers here, apparently."

"More than just a couple. We're pretty sure he's done a fore-seeing of his own—he's plenty strong enough to risk it. He probably knows exactly where the Liberator is going to arrive, and we don't." The young man laughed ruefully. "At least we didn't until you came. I thought I had an easy watch here, and now you've thrown me right in the thick of things."

"Bringing the girl, you mean?"

The Thargian made an affirmative sound as he tipped the bottle again.

"I should have left her at some handy farmhouse and come on alone!" T'lin said, sounding annoyed.

The other passed him the bottle. "Maybe. Maybe that would have fouled up everything—who knows? Why did Narsh Prime send you here, to Ruatvil?"

T'lin wiped his lips. "Didn't. He suggested I go to Filoby and report to Thirty-nine. He mentioned this place as a backup. Said there was sure to be someone from religious branch here."

He tried to pass back the bottle and the Thargian said, "Finish it. See, as far as we know, there's only six places in Sussland where the Liberator can realistically be expected to appear. Tion's temple is one, the Thogwalby monastery's another. If he picks either of those, the Chamber's got him and he's dead meat. We were banking on Iilah's grove at Filoby, because she'd have sheltered him. Probably she would. Garward's taken care of that possibility! You can bet your favorite organ that he's left some henchmen there to look after matters if the Liberator does arrive. There's a roadside campground just outside Filoby that has loads of virtuality . . ."

"Loads of what?"

"Forget that. I just mean it's another possible choice. That leaves this place, the Sacrarium, and another node . . . place, I mean . . . up in the hills near Jogby. That was our second choice, after Filoby, because it's unoccupied."

"You've lost me, sir."

"Nothing there, I mean. No temple or shrine. Too obvious, perhaps? Well, never mind. Question is what to do now. The festival starts tonight."

He thought for a moment. "First, you've got to dump the boy. If he really is a Tion Cultist, then Kirb'l may have marked him in some way. So give him some money and send him off to the festival. That's easiest. After that, he can fend for himself. He'll never be any good to us. There's still a couple of hours of light. Take your dragons over to Filoby and see if you can help ferry survivors to Rotby. Go back and forth several times. You've drawn attention to this place with the dragons, so you'll have to try and muddy the waters."

T'lin seemed to swell. "They're tired, sir!"

"Kill 'em if you have to and put it on your expense account!"

The dragon trader subsided again. "Yes, sir."

"Sorry, but the stakes in this are higher than you can imagine. Leave the girl at the hostelry."

"I'd best keep her away from this place, you think, sir?"

The young man laughed. "You can try, but I'll put my bets on the prophecy."

Eleal liked him a little better for that remark. She was fighting an urge to walk out and ask T'lin if he'd had any trouble finding the Sacrarium, just so she could see his face.

The Thargian stretched his ropy arms and yawned. "We've got a courier coming round tomorrow on a fast moa, so I'll pass word to the others and hope they can spare me some reinforcements. It's not likely. Got all that?"

And again the strangely humble T'lin said, "Yes, sir."

"It's a pity the Chamber identified the mysterious Eleal before we did, but perhaps our turn is coming. I suppose there couldn't be *two* Eleals, could there? She sounds too young."

"She's twelve, I'm sure."

"Mmph! Mostly she just appears in the bit that sounds like delivering a baby, but another passage says she will be the first temptation. Little hard to relate temptation to a twelve-year-old, isn't it?"

T'lin uttered a dragon snort. "There's many a time I've been tempted to thump her ear, sir!"

I will get even with you for that remark, Dragontrader!

The Thargian chuckled. "How about cavemen, then? You haven't run into any cavemen in your adventures, have you?"

"Cavemen, sir?"

"One of my favorite verses: *Many mighty shall go humbly, even as Eleal took him to the caveman for succor, then they are going mightily again.* That's about average for clarity."

"It doesn't mention the Liberator."

"No, it may have nothing to do with him at all. Or it may refer to events years from now, because there's lots of unrelated stuff about him: The-Liberator-comes-into-Joal-crying-Repent! sort of thing. But Eleal is only mentioned four times and that sounds like she is still helping the Liberator, so it may be relevant to what's about to happen this fortnight. Just wondered."

"No cavemen," T'lin growled. "I wouldn't like anything to happen to the kid, sir."

"Nor I," the Thargian said, rising. He was very tall and skinny. "But you could put the whole Joalian army around her and it couldn't protect her from the Chamber. Until the Liberator himself arrives, she's the obvious weak link in the chain. If Zath's reapers find her, she's dead. Nobody in the world could do anything for her then."

T'lin rose also. "The saints, sir?"

The younger man cleared his throat harshly. "Ah, yes. Well, of course we must pray to the saints to intercede with the Undivided. Come over to the tent and . . ."

The two men strolled away across the bare stone floor of the ruined temple. Eleal heard no more.

41

Eleal stumbled down the steps and pushed off into the bush.

The enormity of what she had overheard stunned her. She had trusted T'lin Dragontrader! Gim was only a boy, Sister Ahn a senile maniac, but she had thought that T'lin was a strong man and reliable and a friend. Now she knew that he bore no loyalty to her at all, except some vague idea of one day enlisting her to work for his diabolical "Service," whatever that was. Her last protector had failed her.

T'lin had taken orders from the Thargian. He had not spoken out against the blasphemy. He was probably a Thargian spy himself! Eleal had never pondered her own political convictions very deeply. Had she been forced to declare her loyalties, she would probably have claimed to be a Jurgian, because she spent more time in Jurg than anywhere else and she liked the king, who clapped when she sang for him. She approved of the Joalians' artistic principles and the concept of Joaldom, which gave peace to the lands she knew, and she had always heard bad things about the Thargians and their harsh military ways. Spying for them seemed like betrayal.

Her religious loyalties were in no doubt at all. Tion was lord of art and beauty. Ember'l, the goddess of drama, was an avatar of Tion. So was Yaela, the goddess of singing.

The Thargian had done one good thing, though—he had unwittingly told Eleal a lot about the *Filoby Testament*. She would not be required to deliver any messy baby. A grown man was going to arrive—young and handsome, undoubtedly—either here or somewhere . . . how? Nobody had said *how* he would arrive, she decided. And when the Liberator arrived, Eleal Singer was going to help him. Wash him and clothe him, T'lin had said that morning. She could do with a good wash again herself, to get rid of all the mud and perspiration. The flies had reappeared. Her smock was ripped and filthy. Her legs were so weary they would hardly hold her up.

She staggered and lurched through the thickets, stumbling over hidden blocks of stone. If she kept the sun on her right, she would come to the city.

What she would do when she arrived was another problem altogether. To return to the hostelry would be to put herself back in the hands of the despicable dragon trader and his Thargian overlord, but she had no money and no other friends. Gim would jump at the chance of going to the festival and would probably be gone before she returned anyway.

She must seek out some sympathetic peasant family to take her in and let her stay a while. She could wash dishes or something for them in return for her keep. Sew, maybe—she was handy with a needle. She would pretend to be a refugee from Filoby! *My name is Antheala Battlemaster. My father is chief of the Jurgian army and loves me dearly. He plans to betroth me to one of the king's sons when I am a little older. Fearing that his enemies would strike at him by kidnapping me, he sent me to Iilah's convent for safekeeping.* That had been two fortnights ago, she decided, so she had not had time to learn very much about the convent, in case she was asked. The green monks had arrived at dawn and there had been terrible shouting and raping and she had fled out into the dark and had walked all day until . . .

She stepped where there was no ground. Her short leg betrayed her, and she pitched forward through the shrubbery—smashed her shoulder into something—twisted her ankle—screamed—landed hard on her side—rolled—fell again—banged her head—slithered down a steep hill—pitched into a torrent of icy-cold water—was twirled around, thumped against a rock or two, and then wrapped around a submerged tree trunk.

She flailed wildly, struggled against the deadly press of the current, and finally managed to get her head up. Spluttering and gasping, she could breathe again. She would freeze to death. How could water be so cold in this hot land? She shook her ears dry and was horrified by the roar of the stream. She must be very close to the edge of the canyon, and might even have been swept into a waterfall had she not caught on the tree.

Struggling back to the bank was fairly easy. Clambering up the long, steep slope was not. Near the precipice, the little brook had dug a canyon of its own, narrow and dark. Eventually she hauled herself up into the bushes and just lay there, sore and cold and shaking.

Tion! she thought, *Tion, lord of art and youth, hear my prayer. I do not believe what those men said about you. I do not believe in that heretical Undivided god of T'lin's. Tion, save me!*

After a while she concluded that her sufferings were not going to elicit a miracle. Perhaps Tion could not hear her prayer over the racket of the stream. Bigfangs had sharp hearing. The sun was close to setting. She tried to imagine climbing a tree to sleep in. She would surely fall out, and a tree would be a very uncomfortable bed anyway. Scrambling wearily to her feet, she set off along the edge of the little gorge again, limping through the prickles. The stream had stolen her sandals, but it would guide her back to Ruatvil. Thorns tugged at her smock and scraped her limbs.

In just a few moments there were no more trees ahead, only shrubs, with the sky above them. She had reached the town already! She could see the peaks of Susswall glowing pink, and off to the right, just rising clear of them, the green disk of Trumb. When Trumb rose shortly before sunset, he was due to eclipse. Reapers . . .

As she pushed her way out of the last of the bushes, her foot came down on nothing. Everything happened in a flash and yet seemed to take hours. She yelled in terror; she grabbed at a shrub; the ground crumbled away beneath her heel. She realized where she was—gazing at the sky, she had not been watching where she was going. She had climbed out of the stream on the far side, and followed it the wrong way. Her seat hit the ground and seemed to bounce her out into space. Her right hand had hold of something. The left joined it.

Her shoulders struck rock, skidded, and stopped. The one green cane she clutched so tight had bent double, like a rope, but not broken—yet. She dangled from it, a sharp edge digging into her back, her arms above her head, and her legs flailing in empty air. Hundreds of feet below her, muddy Susswater roiled in its canyon.

"Help!" she screamed. Then she just screamed. Off to her left, the stream emerged from its narrow gorge and sprayed out in a shiny cataract that faded away to the river below. It was much louder than she was.

There was no one around to hear her, anyway.

Her feet could find no purchase; nothing at all. The cane was liable to come out by the roots any minute, and her hands were crushed between it and the rock, so she could not even free them to try and pull herself back up.

Her hands were slipping on the sappy twig.

She tried to swing a leg up to the rock, but it wouldn't reach, and the bush made ominous cracking noises. She tried to turn over, and couldn't.

"Help! Oh, help! Tion!" Her cries were a croak: she could not breathe against the pressure on her back and her arms were about to pull out of their sockets.

I don't want to die! I don't want to fulfill any stupid prophecies! I am only twelve years old! I don't want to deliver babies or wash grown men or do any of those things! I don't want to be a holy whore for Ois. I don't want to be a Historic Personage. I don't want to be killed by a reaper! I just want to be Eleal Singer and a great actor and faithful to Tion and beautiful! I didn't ask for all this and I don't want it and it isn't fair! And I don't want to die!

Then strong fingers gripped her wrist and hauled her upward.

ᔓᔕ42ᔖᔗ

THE THARGIAN HAD MENTIONED A CAVEMAN.

Eleal had found him.

Where the stream neared the great canyon of Susswater, it had undercut its bank on one side, to make a hollow roofed with rock and paved with sand and fine gravel. Ferns masked the entrance, so no one would ever find it. Someone had planted those ferns. Someone had made the shelter deeper and fitted it out with a little hearth, a bed of boughs covered with a fur robe, a store of firewood, a few misshapen jars and baskets. Someone was living there.

He was sitting there now with his skinny legs crossed and a crazy leer on his face. His hair and beard were white, flowing out in all directions. He wore only a loincloth of dirty fur. His skin was dried leather. In the flickering light of the tiny fire, he looked more like a bird's nest than a man.

Eleal sat on the bed, bundled inside another robe, and gradually managing to stop shaking. She was even nibbling some of the roots and berries the hermit had brought her, just to please him. She just couldn't stop talking, though. She was telling him the whole story for at least the third time.

He was not speaking. He couldn't speak.

He did not look as scary now as he had when she first saw him, but perhaps she had just grown used to him. He had explained with signs, and by writing on sand, that his name was Porith Molecatcher. He had lived here for many years—he did not seem to know how many. She was the first visitor who had ever come to his cave. He was originally from Niolland, which was many vales away. He had been a priest of Visek until he had been convicted of blasphemy and his tongue had been cut out. At that point Eleal concluded he was fantasizing. Visek's temple at Niol was supposed to be the greatest in all the Vales and hence the greatest in the world. On the other hand, she could not recall any other crime for which tongues were punished.

He was not totally without human contact. He traded skins with someone in Ruatvil for the few essentials he needed—salt and needles and perhaps others. A comb would be an excellent innovation, Eleal thought, regarding the undergrowth in his beard.

He listened to her story with mad grimaces. He frowned when she mentioned reapers, leered when she talked about crazy old Sister Ahn, and pulled faces of fierce disapproval when she described the harlots in the temple, but he might be just reacting to her tone or facial expressions.

She wondered what T'lin and Sister Ahn had made of her disappearance. They would expect her to come staggering out of the forest all repentant. Well, she wasn't going to! She could stay here, with Porith. Tion had sent the caveman to help her.

Night had fallen. The festival would be starting about now, with the service in the temple. Funny—the temple was only a few miles from Ruatvil. She might even be able to see the lights of the procession if she went out to the cliff edge. She wasn't going to, though. Of course it was on the other side of the river and to reach it on foot would be a very long day's walk.

To break the chain of prophecy—that was how the Thargian had described Garward Karzon's attack on Iilah's sacred grove. *The world may be changed,* Dolm Actor had said. Dolm must still believe she was safely locked up in Ois's temple in Narsh, plucking chickens—unless Zath had informed him otherwise. Who could hide from the god of death?

Well, another god could, because gods were immortal. She must not forget that Tion had rescued her from prison and sent

Porith to pull her up the cliff. Tion was on her side! He would protect her still.

"Trumb will eclipse tonight, won't he?" she said, and Porith nodded, pulling faces.

Why was she so apprehensive about an eclipse of the big moon? It happened just about every fortnight, if the weather was good. Sometimes Trumb eclipsed twice in a fortnight, and then the temples were filled as the priests sought to avert misfortune. There were even stories of *three* eclipses in one fortnight, which meant someone very important was about to die.

She was worried over that silly rhyme about reapers filling sacks, that was all. In a couple of days, very likely, Wyseth would eclipse too, and day turn to night. That ought to be a lot more hair-raising, but somehow it never was.

She chewed another root. She must not expect first-class fare while she stayed with a caveman. Seven days would do it. If her host would let her stay with him until the end of the festival, then she would feel safe to return to civilization, because the prophecy would no longer apply.

Tion had provided the aid she had prayed for. He had brought her to this sanctuary.

What did the god want in return, though? The prophecy fulfilled? If she had been saved by a miracle, then surely it must have been so that she could fulfill her destiny. She was a Historic Personage. She was to help the Liberator—*Eleal shall wash him* and so on. The Liberator would bring death to Death.

Death was Zath, Dolm's god, the god who had sent the reapers after her. If Eleal Singer wanted anything, surely she ought to want to get her own back on Zath?

Trumb would eclipse tonight. The festival had begun. The Liberator might come tonight. Maybe tomorrow or any other time in the next half fortnight—by night, she thought, not by day. And Trumb would eclipse tonight.

She looked across the glowing embers and their tiny flickering flames to mad old Porith, who was hugging his knees with arms like brown ropes, and watching her through the crazy glitter of his eyes.

"I have to go to the Sacrarium, don't I?" she whispered.

He nodded.

"Holy Tion brought me here to Sussland so that the prophecy can be fulfilled," she said, working it out. *Nod.* "If I am ever to succeed in my chosen career as an actor, I must do as my god commands." *Nod.* "He guided my steps today so I could overhear those two blasphemers, because I learned a lot from them."

For some reason Eleal Singer had to wash and clothe a grown man and then the world would be changed.

The Liberator was coming. If she did not go and watch, she would never forgive herself. Just watch—she need not *do* anything.

"That horrible Ois wants me kept away, so that means I should go!" *Nod.* "And afterward I'll be safe, too, because I'll have played my part in the prophecy!" *Nod.* "The Thargian said something about, 'until the Liberator arrives!' He meant that as soon as that happens, then the reapers will go for him and not me!" *Nod, leer.* "Then I won't matter to anyone anymore. So I'd better do what I have to do and get it over!"

Nod.

"Will you come with me?"

Porith shook his head violently.

She felt disappointed by that, but of course he was not protected by any god specially and not mentioned . . . yes he was! "But I'll bring the Liberator back here?"

Another violent shake—so violent that the old man's white hair and beard seemed to lash to and fro.

"It is prophesied! I told you!"

Porith cringed down as if he were sinking into the ground. He made little whimpering noises. Probably he hid in his burrow if anyone came near—it was only her youth and distress that had persuaded him to reveal his existence to her. He was a crazy old recluse.

"The *Testament* doesn't say I bring the Liberator to the *cave!*" Eleal said sharply. "It says I bring him to the *caveman!* That's you! For succor. So you stay here and be prepared to give succor!"

The sky was darkening, Trumb glowing brighter. She felt sick with fear, but she had known that feeling before. It was only stage fright. That thought cheered her up. This was her greatest role! Tonight she played for history and the gods themselves were in the audience! All the same, she had better get on with it or she might lose her resolve. She might even faint.

"Now, what's the quickest way to the Sacrarium? Can I walk around the cliff edge?"

Nod.

She frowned at her bare feet, already sore and blistered. She eyed the pile of furs—moleskins, she assumed. "Could you make a pair of slippers? Just furs with sort of laces, maybe, to keep them on?"

Porith leered and nodded again, but made no move.

"Well, get started, then!" she said.

ACT IV

DUET

43

THE CLIFF EDGE WAS EASIER WALKING THAN THE JUNGLE, because there was a lot of bare rock there. At times she had to choose between undergrowth and hair-raising acrobatics, but she made good progress. Soon she saw a distant twinkle of lights and guessed they were the bonfires at the temple.

I do your bidding, Holy Tion. Watch over me!

She began to worry that she might go right past the Sacrarium without seeing it. She should have asked the mad old hermit to give her directions. Well, if she arrived at the ruined bridge, she would know she had gone too far. And in the end there was no doubt. The forest thinned and she saw bare pillars standing over the trees, palely shining in Trumb's uncanny light.

Then she became very cautious. The distance was not great, but she moved one step at a time, feeling for her footing so she would not crack twigs or stumble on rocks. Her fur slippers were very good for that. She lifted branches out of the way; she stooped and at times even crawled on hands and knees. She clambered carefully over the fragments of masonry strewn around. There was no hurry—she had all night. She assumed that the forest was full of reapers, and that helped her to concentrate.

When she came to the steps, she sat down and took a breather. Then she wriggled up on her tummy through the litter of leaves and twigs until she could see into the court, staying close to a pillar. The ruin was empty and apparently deserted, haunted in the bright moonlight.

Well, if anyone else was around, he would be keeping quiet as she was. He would be flat on his belly as she was. He would be breathing very quietly as she was.

The mossy stone was cold. She should have brought one of Porith Molecatcher's fur blankets. But then she might have gone to sleep. She might have snored!

The Sacrarium seemed completely deserted. Not even the owls were making noises tonight. From the looks of the place, no one had come here in a hundred years. She had a deep conviction, though, that she was not the only one watching that circle of paving. The Thargian would be around somewhere, and perhaps the reinforcements he hoped for. Zath would have a reaper or two. T'lin Dragontrader? Sister Ahn?

Tion? Garward? Eltiana?

Even the gods would be watching.

But no one coughed. No one cracked a twig.

Why was the jungle so quiet?

Trumb climbed slowly up the sky.

The shadows played strange tricks. Eventually Eleal became convinced that there was a reaper standing on the far side of the Sacrarium, alongside one of the unbroken pillars. She told herself firmly that she was imagining things. No man would stand when he might have to wait for hours—he would sprawl on the ground as she did. Nevertheless, her eyes insisted on telling her that there was a dark figure standing beside that pillar, a man in a black gown with a hood. She thought she could even make out the paler glimmer of his face. Of course it had to be a delusion, a trick of the light.

She was too cold and uncomfortable to sleep, too frightened now to go away. No reaper would find her unless he stepped on her. Aware that she might have to wait until dawn, she stayed where she was, and the forest made no sounds at all.

44

An hour or so after midnight, the dogcart clattered through Amesbury and began the gentle climb westward to Stonehenge. The moon was barely past the full, playing hide-and-seek in the clouds. A chill wind was blowing—the weather had turned nasty.

Creighton was on the rear-facing seat, idly tapping on one of the little drums the Gypsies had made for him. Edward was talking with the driver, Billy Boswell. Billy was about Edward's age, short and swarthy and naturally reticent. Under the *gorgio*'s blandishments he had gradually been persuaded to talk about his life and himself. Now he was telling his worries that he might have to go and fight a war. That was exactly what Edward did want, but he was having trouble transferring his viewpoint to the Gypsy. He did not know how the Rom fared in Germany, and the greater benefits of English civilization were somewhat irrelevant to a man who spent most of his year on the road selling clothespins.

"Now, I was born in Africa—"

"Never 'eard of it."

Mm! Edward tapped his feet in counterpoint to the drum.

"By the way," Creighton said suddenly at their backs, "where did you get the fancy shoes, Exeter?"

"Billy gave them to me after we passed through Andover this afternoon. Very kind of him, I thought." They were a size too small, but a man must not look a gift shoe in the tongue. . . .

"Didn't cost nuffin'," Billy said in his Cheapside accent.

Mm! again.

Creighton stiffened, and pointed. "See lights over there?"

"Yes," said the front bench unanimously.

"Where's that?" Edward added.

"It must be the Royal Artillery Barracks at Larkhill. Means we're getting close."

Salisbury Plain, apparently, was not a plain. The road dipped into another hollow.

Edward felt scruples. This sneaking around in the small hours of the morning with a Gypsy and a highly suspect character like Creighton was probably going to involve him in trespassing at the very least, and Lord knew what else. "Does anyone live at Stonehenge, sir? Who owns it?"

"It's owned by Sir Edmund Antrobus. There's a policeman lives in a cottage about quarter of a mile to the west. Let us trust that the worthy constable does not suffer from insomnia." After a moment Creighton added, "The aerodrome's even closer, but I don't suppose there will be anyone there in the middle of the night."

Edward looked up as a patch of cloud began to glow fiercely silver. He shivered.

"Ah!" Creighton said. "You feel it too? How about you, Boswell?"

The Gypsy muttered something in Romany.

"Incredibly strong, if we can feel it here. There it is!"

The moon sailed out from behind its veils. Glimmering on the skyline a short way ahead stood the ghostly circle of trilithons—ruined, sinister, inexplicable. At first it seemed very small, surrounded by so much emptiness. As the cart grew closer, the height of the stones began to register. Who would have erected such a thing in so desolate a spot, and above all *why?* It was archaic insanity in stone, alone in the wind and time. The pony continued to trot along the dusty track, unaffected by such morbid wonderings.

Edward's scalp prickled. "Are you sure we couldn't try somewhere a little less spooky first, sir? Not so much 'virtuality'?"

"We could, but I have my reasons for wanting to start here.

The Chamber knows the prophecy too, remember. There are only five or six nodes in Sussland, so it would not be an impossible task to interdict them against you."

"I don't think I quite follow that. In fact I'm sure I don't."

"Think of a magic spell: 'No one named Edward Exeter may come this way.' "

"Magic is that specific?"

"Call it mana, not magic. If it's strong enough, it can be. I'm hoping that a portal this powerful will overcome that sort of blockage, if it's been tried." *Hrrmph!* "It's a great mistake to assume that your enemy is infallible, you know. They may have forgotten that you have a middle name."

Edward wished Creighton's words would justify the confidence in his tone. "What about guards at the other end? I mean, if the Blighters are hunting me here, why won't the Chamber be waiting for me there?"

"I'm sure they will be," Creighton said breezily. "I hope some of our chaps will be on hand to make a fight of it. I'll be on my own turf, too, in a manner of speaking."

Affalino kaspik . . . The nonsense words were going around and around in Edward's head. He could feel the complex stirrings of the rhythm, too. Was that some sort of response to the occult power of the node? Sheer funk, more like.

"There's a fence!" He hoped that the fence would be the end of the matter and they could go home now, but he didn't really expect that. It was a confident-looking barbed wire fence strung on steel posts.

"Yes, and the attendant is not on hand to accept our sixpences or whatever they charge."

"We can climb that."

"We could, but Mr. Boswell can deal with the fence for us, can't you, Mr. Boswell?"

Billy said nothing while the cart dipped where the track crossed a wide hollow and a bank. Then he reined in the dogcart alongside the fence. "Didn't tell me t'bring me tools. Can just 'eave it dahn fo' ya."

"Why not?" Creighton said, jumping out of the gig. "Devil

take it! Beastly bad form to disfigure a national treasure that way." His obnoxious heartiness was probably concealing the same sort of eerie nervousness as Edward was feeling. "Now, Exeter, I have bad news."

Edward sighed. "Yes, sir."

"You can take nothing with you when you cross over. Nothing can translate except a human being, not even the fillings in his teeth. You needn't worry about those, but clothes are an impediment."

"We have to go through with this rigmarole in the nude?"

"Starkers." Creighton tossed his hat into the dogcart and began unbuttoning. "Quick, while there's moonlight."

Groaning, Edward began to strip also. He removed his shoes with relief. Dawn would appear in about two hours, he thought. The moment the sun's edge showed above the horizon he would be free of his oath, and then he was going to shed his lunatic companion, even if the only way to do it was to walk into a police station and give himself up.

Billy led the pony forward a few feet. A section of fence tried to follow with a long squeal of agony, the posts pulling free from the chalk. "'At aw'a do ya," the Gypsy remarked, and backed up the cart so he could recover his rope.

Edward looked nervously at the lights of Larkhill to the north; he stared across the dark plain to the vague shapes that might be the aerodrome buildings, but no lights had come on in their windows. He tossed his socks into the wagon.

"Splendid fellow!" Creighton said patronizingly. "Now, Boswell, you'll wait here for twenty minutes or so, won't you? Just in case. Hate to have to walk to Salisbury in my birthday suit."

He reached into the dogcart for the drums. He hung one around his own neck and looped the other over Edward's.

"Come, Exeter!" he barked cheerfully, stepping carefully over the fallen wire. He set off across the turf, a ghostly white shape in the moonlight.

Still fumbling with the buttons of his fly, Edward suddenly said, "No!"

Creighton stopped and wheeled around. "Word of honor!" he barked.

"Sir, you extracted that by unfair means. I have a duty to King and Country."

"You have a duty to your father's memory and his life's work, also."

"Sir, I have only your word for that. You have not been fair with me."

Creighton growled. "You have no concept of what is going to happen in this war. Millions of men are going to die! The mud of Europe will be soaked with blood!"

"I have a duty!"

"Idiot! Even if you managed to get to the front—which I doubt very much—you would be nothing there but more cannon fodder. Your destiny lies on Nextdoor. Shut up and listen to me! You don't know what the prophecy calls you—the Liberator!"

"Me?"

"You! Why do you think the Chamber fears you? These are the people who killed your parents, Exeter! If you refuse to come with me now, then your mother and father died in vain!"

Edward shivered in silence for a moment, the night air icy cold on his bare chest. "I have your word on that, sir?"

"I swear it as your father's friend."

With a sigh, Edward unfastened his trousers.

Naked, he followed Creighton through the gap in the fence, shivering with both cold and a bitter apprehension. Nudity seemed only fitting, somehow. The last few days had progressively stripped him of everything—his good name, his prospects for a career, his chance to fight in a war, his future inheritance, his most precious possessions, like his parents' picture and that last letter to Jumbo, even Fallow, which had been in fact his home. Alice. He might never even know how *The Lost World* turned out at the end, he thought bitterly. All gone.

"Might as well go right to the center," Creighton remarked. "We'll be less conspicuous there if anyone should happen to come along the road."

What would Billy Boswell do in that case? Better not to think about it. Better not to think about anything. Edward followed his leader between the towering stones, into moonlit mystery. At close range, Stonehenge was not just a clutter of standing stones, it was a building—a ruined building, but an awe-inspiring one.

Creighton's teeth gleamed at him in a smile. "One last warning!"

"Tell me."

"Passing over is quite a shock to the system, especially the first time. You'll be badly disoriented. I should react better, although it's a bit like seasickness—you can never predict. It may last some time. I hope we'll have some friends there to help. They won't speak any English, of course."

"How can I tell if they're friends or enemies?"

"Well, look out for johnnies in black gowns like monks. They're called 'reapers' and they're deadly. They can slay a chap with a touch. Otherwise—friends will help you. If they try to kill you, assume they're enemies."

"Why didn't I think of that?" Edward muttered under his breath. "Lay on, Macduff!"

Creighton turned his back, and began to pat out the rhythm on the drum with his hands. In a moment he said, "One—two—three!" and began the chant.

Jumping, jiggling, gesturing, singing, they pranced around, following each other in a small circle. *Inso athir ielee . . . paral inal fon. . . .* The moonlight faded, then brightened.

There were a lot of beastly sharp stones in the grass.

Edward decided he was not cut out to be a witch doctor. This was the most ridiculous thing he had ever done in his life. He would freeze to death. And it was wrong! Those great pillars looming over him in the darkness were an ancient mystery, sanctified in ways he could not imagine. He was profaning something mighty, consecrated by the hands of time itself. . . .

He cried out and stumbled to a halt, shivering and sweating simultaneously, shaken to the core by a sense of revulsion and awe. "No, no!"

Silence returned to the night.

"Aha!" Creighton said triumphantly. "You felt that?"

"No. Nothing. I felt nothing!"

"Hrrnph! Well I did! It was starting. So it works. It's going to take us somewhere, even if not where we want to go. Sure you felt nothing?"

"Quite sure," Edward said, jaw chattering. "Quite certain."

"Mm? Clench your teeth." Creighton reached out and prized up a corner of the sticking plaster on Edward's forehead. "Now!"

Yank!

"Ouch! You scalped me!"

"Let's see if that helps. All right, we'll start from the beginning again. Now, concentrate! Be sure and get the movements right. Ready? . . ."

"No!" Edward shouted, backing away. "Oh, no!" He was naked and cold and he had been duped into behaving like a lunatic. "You're just trying to fulfill the prophecy, aren't you? That's what all this is about!"

"I'm trying to save your life! If what we do fulfills the prophecy, then so be it. You'd prefer to die? Take it from the beginning—"

"I won't! I'm not coming."

"Boy!" the colonel thundered. "You gave me your word!"

Edward backed away farther. "You cheated. You lied to me!"

"I did not!"

"You said the Service supports the prophecy! You said my father was one of them—you said he did, too! But the guv'nor didn't, did he? He wanted to break the chain! He said so in that letter!"

After a long moment, Creighton sighed. "All right, old man. You're right. I never lied to you, but you're absolutely right. Cameron Exeter did not approve of all the things prophesied about the Liberator. Some, yes, certainly, but not all. He split with the majority on this. He did not want any son of his to be the Liberator."

Edward backed up another step and cannoned into a monolith. It was hard and cold and jagged. He recoiled. "The guv'nor did not approve of turning worlds upside down! That's what he said."

"That was partly it—what you will do to the world. But it was more what the world will do to you."

"What do you mean: 'What the world will do to me'?"

"He didn't think you could possibly be man enough to . . ." Creighton shivered. "Look, you haven't any alternative now, have you? Trust me! When you get to Olympus we'll give you the whole story from beginning to—"

The silence of the night exploded in noise. Something enormous roared nearby, the sound merging into the pony's scream of terror. Billy howled curses as the dogcart rattled and jangled away into the distance, taking him with it and leaving the two men stranded, naked, on Salisbury Plain.

"What in the name of Jehoshaphat was *that?*" Creighton demanded, staring into the darkness.

The hair on Edward's neck was rising. "That was a lion!"

"No!"

"Oh yes it was! That's the grunt they use to scare their prey when they're hunting. How do lions get to Stonehenge, Colonel?"

"Ask rather what they eat at Stonehenge. Let's try the key again, shall we? And this time it had better work."

Edward thought he agreed with that. He had heard lions often enough, but never so horribly close. That fence would never stop a hungry lion, and there was a gap in it now anyway.

"Ready?" said Creighton. "One—Two—Three . . ."

Affalino kaspik . . . The drumbeats throbbed. Arms and legs waved—even head movements were supposedly important, and he kept wanting to watch the wall of trilithons, to see what might be coming through. To look for green eyes in the night.

The moon sailed into a cloud and died.

Half the beat stopped as if cut off by a guillotine, and so did Creighton's voice. His drum bounced and rolled away on the grass. Edward stumbled to a halt. He was alone.

45

IT BEGAN AS A FAINT SIGH IN THE DISTANCE. IT CAME closer. It was a rushing of wind through the trees and soon seemed all around, everywhere but where Eleal lay in the darkness. At last it arrived and the leaves stirred. Boughs creaked, thrashed. Gradually it faded, traveling on, and the night stilled. Trumb shone unchallenged in a cloudless sky, drowning out the stars with his baleful splendor.

She shivered, wondering what god had sent that wind sign. She was cramped and cold. She flexed herself, one limb at a time, frightened of making any noise among the trash of leaves and branches that covered the steps. She had no idea how long she had been lying there, too tense even to doze. Her neck was appallingly stiff.

Her eyes were still insisting that there was a reaper on the far side of the court. It could not be just a trick of the light, for the big moon had moved a long way since she arrived, and was very bright. It must be a tree stump, perhaps a dead sapling coated in ivy. No man could stand for so many hours like that.

Trumb *must* eclipse soon! There had been a hint of shadow on one side of his disk when he rose, but now it was a perfect circle and that meant . . .

A scream rent the silence of the night and a man rolled to the paving only a few yards from her. His limbs flailed and he cried out again. Her hair rose. *Where had he come from?*

Naked, a grown man—this must be the Liberator! He sounded as he was in terrible pain. She started to rise and then stopped, hearing feet slap on stone. Another man came running out of the darkness on her right, and then a second from the left.

The first was T'lin—big, and heavily bearded, and wearing a black turban that barely showed in the moonlight, so that the top half of his head seemed to be missing. He carried a bundle. And the other was the lanky Thargian, drawing a sword and looking around as he ran.

Huh! Well if those two were here, they could attend to all the washing and nursing required. Eleal's services were not needed, not wanted. She could have enjoyed a good night's rest instead.

The Liberator's cries of pain had faded to grunts and moans. He retched and vomited, then groaned again.

"*You,* sir!" the Thargian exclaimed. "We expected someone else." He knelt, and helped the man sit up.

T'lin stayed standing, peering around warily at the darkness with his hand on the hilt of his sword.

"Gover?" The Liberator retched again, and doubled up as if cramped—except that the Thargian had implied that this was not the Liberator. "Good to see you."

"We should leave!" T'lin growled.

"Calm down, Seventy-seven!" the Thargian snapped. "If there was anyone out there, they'd be all over us by now."

"Yes, but—"

"Just wait a minute! Can't you see the man's in pain? Bad crossing, sir?"

The reply was a suppressed bubbling shriek from the new-comer, as another spasm took him. The Thargian put an arm around his shoulders and cradled his head like a child's.

"All right, Kriiton," he muttered. "You're among friends. It'll pass."

The comforting seemed to help. In a moment Kriiton muttered, "Thanks!" and pushed himself free. "Where's Kisster?" He looked around. "God Almighty! He . . . He didn't make it?"

"No sign of anyone else, sir."

The reply was lost in another groan, another spasm of cramps.

Again the Thargian cuddled the sufferer, and again the physical comforting seemed to ease the pain.

The men were fading! Eleal tore her eyes away and looked up in sudden terror. Trumb was well into eclipse already. Darkness raced over the great disk.

"Gotta go back 'n get'm!" Kriiton mumbled.

"You're in no state for another crossing, sir! It would kill you! We've got no key for it anyway, not that I know of."

"Where is this?"

"The Sacrarium at Ruatvil."

Kriiton sighed. The others were almost invisible now; his bare skin showed up better. "In Sussland! So it should have worked! Let's hope he keeps trying!"

"First time is hardest sometimes, isn't it?" the Thargian said.

The Kriiton man suppressed a groan, as if he was being racked by more cramps. "Can be. Maiden voyage. Trouble is, the opposition was moving in on us."

Trumb had dwindled to a thin line, a sword cut in the sky. The darkened disk was faintly visible, black against the reborn stars.

"Opposition may move in here, too, sir," the Thargian said. "Seventy-seven's right. We ought to go, soon as you're ready. Damned moon'll be back in a minute. We've brought some clothes so let's get you up now and——"

T'lin uttered a yell of warning. Another figure had entered the darkened courtyard, gliding swiftly over the ancient stones, black and infinitely menacing. Eleal thought of flight, her limbs twitched uncertainly, and then she just froze, like a small animal facing a large predator. Dolm had been able to see in the dark!

"Up!" Kriiton yelled. "Get me up!"

The other two grabbed his arms and hauled him to his feet. Trumb's final crescent had gone. Starlight flashed as the Thargian brandished his sword in the reaper's face.

The reaper stopped just out of reach and chuckled. "You expect to block me with that, Gover Envoy?" That was not Dolm Actor's voice! Eleal was too terrified to move an eyelid, barely even to think, but she knew that was not Dolm's voice she was hearing.

The Thargian cried out and his sword clanged to the ground.

"Don't fandangle with me, Reaper!" Kriiton croaked. He was leaning hard on T'lin's shoulder, as if unable to straighten properly. "Go now and I'll spare you."

"But I will not spare you! Prepare to meet the Last Victor."

The men were half-seen shapes in the faint gleam of stars. Trumb's disk was a round black hole in the stars, the moon of Zath. The reaper stretched forth his hand and took a step forward.

Flash! Thunder!

Ruins and jungle jumped out of the night and then vanished again.

Eleal cried aloud and jerked back, her ears ringing from the crash. Her eyes burned with a dazzling afterimage, as if she had been blinded. *Lightning out of a clear sky?* She wiped away tears with shaking hands.

"By the moons, sir!" Gover Envoy was shouting, but his voice sounded muffled through the hum in her ears. "You answered his arguments!" He laughed shrilly.

T'lin was muttering. Forcing her eyes to work, Eleal saw that he had fallen on his knees in prayer. The reaper was stretched out flat on his back, motionless. Envoy was supporting Kriiton. There was a strange, tingling scent in the air.

"Crude!" Kriiton muttered. "Lost control."

"It worked!" said the Thargian. "That one filled no sacks."

"Worked too well. Drained me. Far too much!" He made an effort to stand by himself. "I wanted to stun him, not fry him. All right, where are those clothes?"

Eleal's eyes were recovering. Her ears still buzzed. In the heavy darkness, tiny red fireflies shone on the body of the reaper, and she did not understand those. She heard, more than saw, that T'lin had scrambled to his feet and unrolled his bundle.

So where was the Liberator? And what was this Kriiton, who appeared out of empty air and called down thunderbolts? Was he man or god? His paleness faded away as he hauled a smock over his head, and then he was just a dark shape like the others. He staggered, and Envoy reached out an arm to steady him, but obviously he was recovering.

"Right," he grunted. "Shoes? Fornication! I had D'ward right with me. Damned good kid, too, from what I saw."

A razor cut of light in the sky in the background heralded the return of Trumb. The pillars glimmered back into view and the stars faded. Puzzled, Eleal strained to make out what the men were doing. There seemed to be four of them. There *were* four of them! She opened her mouth to yell a warning, but her dry throat made no sound. Another reaper had joined the group.

Two men went down in fast succession, without a sound. They thrashed on the ground and then she heard some muffled choking, but that was all.

The third one yelled, and leaped back. Then he turned and fled. His feet slapped noisily over the stones.

The reaper laughed, a deep and horribly familiar sound. "Come back! I want you!" It was Dolm Actor! He also ran, but in total silence, a black cloud flowing swiftly across the court. His quarry vanished between the pillars, and shrubbery crashed as he plowed into it. The reaper followed him out without a rustle. The two dying men lay still.

Gone!

The sounds of the fugitive's flight had stopped, but that might be either because he had reached the path or because the reaper had caught him—and would then return, perhaps.

Eleal felt sick. Her heart was hammering its way out of her chest and there was a bitter swirling sensation in her head. Swift, unwelcome brightness was flooding the Sacrarium as if a door was opening, revealing the carnage. She wanted to cry *Stop!* She preferred the dark. Three bodies, three men dead, and probably one more corpse out in the woods now. Dolm Reaper might come back at any moment, to gather more souls for Zath. Hers.

She couldn't leave dying men, however little she expected to be able to help.

And she had to know which ones they were.

Quick, then! She staggered to her feet and tried to run forward. It was only a few yards, but she was so stiff and unsteady from lying still that she nearly fell. She stumbled to her knees beside the Thargian, almost on top of his fallen sword. Gover Envoy lay on his side because his back was bent like a bow, his limbs twisted behind him. His mouth was still dribbling blood, black in the green light, and his dead eyes bulged as if he had perished in terrible agony. He had not made a sound, but obviously a reaper death was not an easy one.

The first reaper lay on his back, spread-eagled. He had a gaping black hole in his chest, and there was a nasty scent of scorched cloth and charred meat around him, but at least his ending had been quick. His cowl had fallen back to expose his face. She had never seen him before, a bearded man of middle years. His eyes were rolled up, the whites shining green in the light of his god.

The third corpse lay in the same contorted arch as Envoy, but he was on his belly, head and limbs bent up grotesquely. His face was distorted by the same rictus of agony—teeth exposed, dead eyes bulging, and a puddle of blood congealing under his mouth. He was not T'lin, and therefore had to be the strange Kriiton, whose powers had been able to slay one reaper but not defend against another. His nose was prominent, his eyebrows heavy, and he had a stubbly mustache. Man or demon, he was very obviously as dead as the other two.

So T'lin Dragontrader had escaped, if he had managed to run fast enough. *Run, T'lin, run!* Very faintly, she heard a dragon burp in the distance.

Nothing Eleal could do here.

She scrambled to her feet and glanced around to make sure no reapers were approaching. Right before her eyes, a man rolled to the paving out of empty air. He thrashed a whirl of bare limbs, and screamed.

∾⌇46⌇∾

WHEN EDWARD SAW CREIGHTON'S DRUM ROLLING ON the grass, he felt as if time itself had stopped. He knew his heart had. He was conscious of the darkness, the wind on his heated skin, and utter disaster. Billy and the dogcart had gone and would not return.

To be arrested stark naked on Salisbury Plain would certainly reinforce a plea of insanity, but he did not want to spend the rest of his life locked up in Broadmoor. That might be the better choice, though, if his only alternative was to be eaten by lions. He did not for one moment believe that some escaped circus animal had chanced to wander past Stonehenge. There might or might not be a flesh–and–blood carnivore out there, but without doubt there was an enemy.

Time had not stopped, and he had none of it to waste. For a brief moment he considered trying some of the African chants and dances he knew, but he saw at once that those might take him to the wrong place. He must believe what Creighton had told him. He must follow Creighton; without Creighton he would be hopelessly lost. As he was about to start tapping, he heard laughter in the darkness, human laughter. He did not look. He began the ritual again, concentrating on the beat, trying not to think about the interdiction Creighton had mentioned.

Laugh away, friends! We'll try this again.

He let the rhythm grow in his mind, shutting out everything else. *De-de-de-DAH-de, DAH-de* . . . He began the beat.

Creighton had been taking it too slowly. He began the dance. *Affalino kaspik . . .* He ignored the laughter. *DAH de-de-DAH Affaliki suspino ayakairo . . .*

Faster, faster! He let the rhythm flower, seeking its subtleties, its complex cross-beats, three against four, left against right, four against five, tasting it in his mind, living it. The words rolled and jigged. The movements flowed. He absorbed the ritual soaking through him, bearing him back to childhood and farther yet, to atavistic tribal memories. *My fathers danced here in the Dreamtime!* He felt the response, the surge of power, the thrill, rising like a life force, a thrill permeating his whole body.

Now the aura of awe and sanctity swelled in wonder.

Here it comes! DAH-de, DAH-de-de . . . The power grew up around him. Waves of excitement surging—he could feel them in his blood and along his bones. His heart moved in time. He felt awe, sanctity, power. The laughter had stopped. Legs, head, elbows—hands beating the intricate rhythm, primitive, primal. *Kalafano Nokte! Finothoanam . . .* Stronger, harder. He was one with the world and the pulse of worlds. The power roared. Something tried to block it and he overrode it, wielding strength and will. A voice howled in sudden fury. The cosmos opened for him and he plunged through.

He had a momentary sensation of flying. He felt himself as infinitely tiny, swept past shapes infinitely large. Dark and cold. Speed.

Impact!

Were it possible to be smashed flat and live, then that was the sensation. Not physical pain—emotional. He had never guessed at anything approaching such shame, such sorrow and despair. All his muscles knotted up in horror, and then it was physical also. He heard himself screaming and he wanted to die.

Someone was hugging him, soothing him. In his wrenching abyss of misery, he sensed a spark of human compassion. He clung, clung desperately. Agonies of cramps, waves of nausea—but someone cared, and that was salvation. The spark was there, life amid the measureless void of death.

There was a hand over his mouth, but he could not stop screaming. Every muscle strained, every tendon was pulling free of his bones. His gut was a fire pit and his heart was tearing itself to ribbons. *Die, die, oh please die!*

A voice shouted his name, over and over.

He opened his eyes and saw the moon. *Godfathers!* What had happened to the moon? The screaming had started again. Was that him?

Who was this he was crushing to him?

He was rolling around on cold stone, hugging someone. In the dark. The air was hot and scented. Moonlight, *green* moonlight.

Nextdoor was much more than just an island.

47

THE MAN FELL STILL, HIS MUSCLES TOO EXHAUSTED TO DO more than quiver like leaves in a wind. His arms had been holding Eleal in iron bands, and now they dropped away limply. His eyes were open, staring, but they did not seem to be looking at anything. His breath came in frightening, irregular gasps.

She backed off a few feet on hands and knees. "Liberator?"

"Yes," said Dolm's resonant voice. "I fancy that is the Liberator this time."

Eleal opened her mouth to scream and nothing happened. She stared up in paralyzed silence at the reaper looming over her, immensely tall and dark against the sky. He shook his cowled head sadly. His face was in shadow, but she could not mistake the voice.

"I have no option, Eleal. You do understand that?"

She wriggled farther away.

"Running will not save you," Dolm said. "You belong to my master now. First the Liberator, then you."

"No!" she whimpered.

"You are young and your soul is worth much."

"All souls are worth much," said another voice.

The reaper turned in a swirl of black cloth to regard the newcomer as she hobbled across the courtyard, pounding her staff with one hand, trailing her sword in the other. Its point scraped across the stone with a bloodcurdling scratching.

Dolm laughed. "Yours is not, old woman. Depart and cherish the days that are left to you. If you are gone when I have taken these two, then I shall not pursue you."

Eleal leaped to her feet and raced around the litter of corpses to Sister Ahn's side. The bent old crone dropped her stick and rested her gnarled hand on Eleal's shoulder instead. She kept her eyes on the reaper, though. "Repent, Minion of Zath!"

He paced toward them. "I have nothing to repent, hag."

"Not the deeds you commit in his name, no." Her harsh, corroded voice was surprisingly powerful. "But there is another, or he would not have enlisted you to his dread band. Repent, I say, and be free!"

"Never!"

"Here, my dear," Sister Ahn said. "Lift this sword with me. Both hands. We must fulfill a prophecy."

It did not occur to Eleal to refuse. Trembling, she took hold of the hilt around the nun's frail grasp, and between them they raised the long blade until it pointed unsteadily at the man in black.

Dolm laughed again, a grotesque parody of that jovial laugh Eleal knew so well. "You know that weapons are useless against a reaper! Come then, to my master!"

He strode forward. In a creaky chant, Sister Ahn gabbled something so fast that Eleal made out few words. "Holy-Irepithear . . . transferthesin . . . thathemaysee . . . pay here not elsewhere . . ." The sword seemed to swing of its own accord. The reaper screamed and fell. Sister Ahn crumpled. The sword dropped clanging to the stone.

Eleal staggered away with a shriek of fright. For a moment the temple swayed about her and she stuffed knuckles in her mouth. Her knees wobbled. Then she saw that the danger was gone. Dolm Actor was a shapeless, motionless heap of black. The old woman was sitting on the ground, doubled over, her head between her knees.

Eleal knelt down to hug Sister Ahn's thin shoulders.

"Sister! Sister!"

The nun fell sideways and rolled on her back. Dark blood was already soaking through the front of her habit.

Eleal uttered a shrill sob that was almost a scream. "What happened?" The blade had never touched the nun, she was certain.

Eyes flickered open. The emaciated face twisted into a smile. The pallid lips moved, but Eleal heard nothing.

"What?" she leaned closer on hands and knees, frightened now even to touch the old woman's garments. So much blood!

"My part is over, child," Sister Ahn said, soft but clear. "Yours begins. Eleal has the stage now—for a little while."

A moment later, her eyes rolled up, lifeless. As Eleal watched in horror, death and moonlight smoothed out the wrinkles like melting wax, leaving only a hint of a smile. The sword had never touched her, but it had obviously slain her. One dead woman and four dead men and . . .

The Liberator was trying to sit up.

Eleal ran across to him. He would explain what was happening. He could defend her against whatever other horrors the night might bring. He was a much younger man than she had expected, only a very tall boy—unless he shaved off his whiskers, of course, in which case she supposed he might count as a grown man. His hair was dark, yet his wide-stretched eyes were light. Blood from a gash on his head had painted one side of his face and dribbled down his neck and chest, black in the greenish moonlight.

"Liberator?"

He stared blankly at her for a moment, then seemed to realize that he had no clothes on. He moved his hands to cover himself. The movement brought on a spasm of cramp; he gurgled and doubled over.

Eleal found a garment, one that T'lin had dropped. She took it to the Liberator; he tried to take it from her and again went into convulsions. Eleal put it over his hands, one at a time, and then lifted his arms to let it drop around his neck. With difficulty, frequently twisting and writhing with cramps, he managed to pull it down and tuck the hem over his thighs. Then he looked up and again tried to speak, but what he said was still gibberish. It ended in a sob of pain and despair.

Naked and crying he shall come into the world and Eleal shall wash him. She shall clothe him and nurse him and comfort him.

She would have to do something about that blood.

"Are you the Liberator?" she shouted.

More gibberish. Partly he had trouble even speaking, for the least movement seemed to start all his muscles into cramps. Partly he was using some language she had never heard. It was not Thargian, or even Niolian.

"Eleal," she said, tapping her chest. "Liberator?" She pointed at him.

He said something that sounded like, "*Ed*ward."

She sniggered at that. "D'ward?"

He nodded faintly.

"Good! Come, we must go! There must be some sandals you can have."

More gibberish—"Kriiton?" He had his back to the corpses.

She pointed. The youth turned carefully to see and gave a cry. He tried to rise, only to collapse in a whimpering tangle. Then he began dragging himself over the ground, moving one limb at a time. Obviously the effort was agony for him, but he persevered. Her efforts to help merely hindered him, so she stood aside and let him crawl. She tried to warn him about more reapers coming, but he paid no heed. He hauled himself all the way to Kriiton's body and peered at the face.

He shuddered, then gently reached out and closed the eyes,

muttering something Eleal could not understand. She brought him sandals and Sister Ahn's staff and pointed urgently to the north. He nodded, and began the ordeal of rising to his feet.

Leaning heavily on the walking stick and the child's shoulder, Edward moved his feet one at a time in the direction she had suggested.

The night was a blur of nightmare for him. He knew he was in deep shock and should not try to make sense of anything until he had recovered. Creighton had warned him, but he had not expected so much pain, so much confusion and weakness. Half his muscles were useless and he did not know how much he could trust his senses. Was that really Creighton lying there? Who were the others? Reapers, Creighton had said, but all the clothes had seemed black. The moon was pure hallucination— three or four times the size a moon ought to be and a lurid green. The markings on it looked like a hammer. Its light drowned out the stars.

The building was a vague echo of some ruined Greek temple, with remains of a circle of pillars on a paved plinth. Beyond that lay jungle. It had a humid, tropical smell. There were mosquitoes, although any attempt to swat them—any sudden movement at all—brought on the terrible muscle cramps. Even resting, his whole body ached from them.

His tongue had found two gaping holes in his teeth. They felt enormously larger than they would look, of course, but again Creighton's prediction had been correct. The fillings were back on Earth, in the grass of Wiltshire. So were his stitches and sticking plaster; his face was caked with blood from the reopened wound on his temple. It drew insects.

Bodies all over the place, five of them. Expect friends or enemies, Creighton had said, but obviously both had been waiting. There had been an ambush and a battle. Had Edward crossed over at the same time as Creighton, would he also now be stiffening in that charnel house? He might as well be—for what did a man do in a strange world when he could not speak the language, had no friends, no money, nor even any concept

of who his friends and enemies were? Why had Bloody Idiot
Creighton been so secretive about what Edward was to expect?

And the girl—who had brought her here and why? Was one
of these dead men her father, perhaps? She was understandably
terrified, of course, shaking almost as much as he was. Every
few minutes she would jump at some shadow, but for her age
she was doing amazingly well. She had a pronounced limp,
which made her an unsteady support. Every lurch, every effort
to lift the staff, threatened to make his muscles cramp up in
knots.

She seemed pathetically eager to help and please. And since
she showed no signs of wanting to add Edward's corpse to the
collection, he must assume that she was a friend. Her impatience
suggested that she had some associates waiting, or a safe refuge.
Transportation, perhaps. At the very least she would know how
to get word to the Service that Cameron Exeter's son had arrived on Nextdoor.

48

THINKING *MONEY*, ELEAL AWOKE AT FIRST LIGHT, HAVING
slept very little, and poorly. The bed she had chosen was grav-
elly, but the only reasonably flat area near the shelter. D'ward
had suffered even in his sleep. His moans and cries had disturbed
her often and she had gone to inspect him several times.

She threw off her rug and went to take another look. He was
sleeping peacefully. She had washed the blood from his face,
but the pad of moss she had bound to his head was caked. She
had also bathed as many of his scrapes as she could without being

indecent, although by the time she and Porith had brought him in, he had been more or less unconscious.

She glanced around the shadowy gully. Where was the mad old hermit? Very likely he was curled up under a bush somewhere nearby, but she did not know where. With any luck he was already out hunting breakfast, three breakfasts. Well, she would enlist his aid later. Right now she had some pillage to attend to.

She clambered up the bank and set off back to the Sacrarium. The bodies would have to be buried, or disposed of in some other way if Porith had no spade, and she had seen no signs of one. T'lin's friends or more of Zath's reapers might investigate the ruin soon, and there was always the chance of a stray pilgrim. Whoever found those five corpses would surely raise a hue and cry. She did not want that, so she would have Porith remove them. First they should be looted. Almost certainly there would be money on some of those dead men and she did not see why she should share it with Porith Molecatcher. He had no use for silver and she did.

She would also collect Sister Ahn's magic sword and present it to the Liberator. Anyone with so many enemies should be armed, and tall, lean men like D'ward always looked good with swords dangling at their belts. It would certainly look better on him than it had on Sister Ahn.

The walk seemed much shorter than it had the night before, especially when she had been half-carrying D'ward. Grown men were heavy, even young, skinny ones. From that point of view, a baby would have been much easier to manage.

The sun rose while she was working her way along the cliff top. It warmed her and revived her. Birds sang cheerfully. She saw the pillars and turned away from the cliff, moving with more care amid the trees. Soon she passed the spot where D'ward had collapsed. She had left him there while she went and fetched Porith. He had been very unwilling—she had almost had to punch him to make him come back and help her. Stupid, crazy old man!

She reached the Sacrarium steps . . .

The bodies had gone.

She stood like a tree, staring in disbelief. Nothing stirred. Eventually she crept forward and took a closer look. There were dried bloodstains on the stone, nothing more.

She soon discovered a trampled trail through the woods, leading to the cliff. Someone had dragged the corpses along there—probably just one man, she thought, or the weeds would not be so crushed. She found a fragment of black cloth snagged on a thorn.

At the edge she lay on her tummy and peered over. Far below her, Susswater was a slowly roiling yellow snake. She could guess that it would be a deafening torrent if she were down there, but from up here its motion was barely detectable, just a hint of life, like muscle moving below skin. Specks of birds were circling about halfway up the cliff, so some of the bodies might have caught on rocks.

Who could have done this? Certainly no stray pilgrim would have chanced by in the middle of the night. Old Porith Molecatcher was too frightened of the reapers. There might be more reapers about, and she reminded herself that she could not recognize a reaper unless he was wearing his work clothes. T'lin Dragontrader might have escaped and returned. Or the Service he had mentioned might have sent more agents. The reapers she did not want. The Service blasphemed, so she thought she probably did not want that either. In any case, she had no idea who the Service was, or where it could be found. D'ward must know, and he could decide.

She found Porith drinking at a pool some distance upstream from his shelter. She knelt down on the edge of the gully and remarked cheerfully, "Good morning!"

He jumped like a frog and then scowled up at her.

"Did you move the dead bodies from the Sacrarium?" she demanded.

He shook his head, mad eyes wide.

"What's for breakfast?"

He scowled even more at that, and shook his head. Then he

pointed in the general direction of the cave and made a "Git!" motion.

"You wish my friend and myself to depart?"

Emphatic nod.

"I'm sure we will withdraw as soon as he is rested. But right now he's still very weak and must be fattened up and strengthened for the journey. Red meat and lots of it!"

She tried a winning smile and it was poorly received.

"Don't you make obscene gestures at me, Porith Molecatcher! You're a priest, you said. Well, this is gods' work. You're mentioned in the prophecy, the *Filoby Testament,* and Holy Visek is god of prophecy. So the gods know you and what you're doing, and they expect you to give succor to the Liberator. The seeress said so!"

Glare.

"Breakfast, if you please?"

Eleal rose and walked away with as much dignity as her limp allowed. Ambria Impresario would have been proud of her.

She found D'ward sitting outside the cave. He smiled weakly at her and said, "Eleal!"

"Godsbless, D'ward! Have you remembered how to speak yet?"

He looked at her blankly. His eyes were intensely blue, although his hair was as black as any she had ever seen. She would not call him handsome, she decided. He was plain. He was bony. On the other hand he was certainly not ugly.

It was hardly fair to judge him now. His features were pale and drawn, his arms and legs a mess of scrapes and bruises. Caked blood disfigured his bandage and his mouth was swollen where he had bitten his lips. All in all, though, he was alert and probably on the mend. He seemed older than he had in the night. Lots of men shaved their faces, especially Thargians. Golfren and K'linpor did because they played juvenile roles sometimes and could add a false beard when they needed one. Boys like Klip Trumpeter did, because their whiskers were still patchy.

"Drink?" she said. She mimed drinking and pointed to the stream. "Water?"

He nodded. "Drink."

She took a gourd down and brought it back full. She taught him *I drink* and *you drink*.

"I drink," he said, and drank. His hands trembled. Smile, gibberish.

"Thank you."

"Thank you?"

She nodded.

He tapped his bandage and said, "Thank you," again. He had a very winning smile.

Eleal made herself comfortable and began lessons: man, woman, boy, girl, tree, sky, fingers, happy, sad, angry . . .

Edward was one big ache. Every muscle was bruised from the cramps, and he had battered all his bones repeatedly against stone paving. The spasms had stopped, though, and his head was clearing. He felt giddy if he tried to stand, but he would be all right in a day or so.

Nextdoor was surprisingly Earthlike—gravity and temperature, sky and clouds and sun all much the same. The plants looked like vegetation he had seen in the south of France, and the day was going to be hot accordingly. Nevertheless, this was not Earth. The moon had been very wrong. The beetles had eight legs.

Ridiculous! His mind rejected the evidence. He would wake up soon and find himself back in Albert Memorial. And when he did, he would refuse any more drugs!

He could recall seeing metal swords in the night, but not firearms. That put the culture somewhere between the Stone Age and the Renaissance, quite a gap. Both Eleal and he were dressed in very simple garments like overgrown undervests, leaving arms and shoulders and lower legs exposed. Natives in Kenya could get by in such costumes, or even less, but he would be arrested if he tried to walk along an English beach like this. The homespun material had never seen the looms of Manchester. That did not mean that there was no advanced civilization around somewhere. Earth had its Nyagathas as well as its Londons. A world was a big place and he must not judge this one by a hole in the woods.

The accommodation left a lot to be desired. He did not remember arriving at the cave. The girl could not have carried him by herself, so she had friends around somewhere. And probably enemies also, else why was she hiding him here? Her obvious intent to teach him the language suggested that she was not expecting any English-speaking collaborators to arrive in the near future. He'd learned German by spending a summer in Heidelberg with the Schweitzes, but Frau Schweitz had been proficient in English. It would be tougher without an interpreter to clear up misunderstandings, even if he did have a knack for languages.

Eleal was a pretty thing, with curly hair and a snub nose. He guessed she was eleven or twelve, no more. She had a deformed leg. She was certainly Caucasian, and could even have been English as far as looks went. And she was a sharp little dolly. Once they had gone through everything she could point to, she fetched a fur rug and spread it out on a flat rock. It was full of fine brown sand and she used this as a drawing board. Then the conversation began to grow interesting.

Four moons? Trumb, Ysh, Eltiana, Kirb'l. Two men, two women—meaning gods and goddesses, of course. The sun was Wyseth and both, which seemed odd. Well, now he was starting to get a feel for the genders. All languages except English had gender problems, and even in English ships and whales were feminine.

Eleal, Ysh, Eltiana. That was why the girl laughed when he tried to correct her pronunciation of his name—it must sound feminine to her. She was as fussy as a Frenchman about pronunciation. He tried his surname, Exeter, and she grinned again. "Kisster?"

He decided he would rather be D'ward than Kisster.

He sketched the ruined temple, and learned its name, or the word for temple. Or the word for ruin? She began to tell him the story with gestures and illustrations. She had gone there by herself, apparently—he wondered why. Creighton had appeared and her word, "Foop!" sounded much like the "Plop!" he might have used. She knew Creighton's name! Then two men had run in, separately, T'lin and Gover. She looked inquiringly; he shook his head to show that the names meant nothing to him.

He tried "Service" and "Chamber," but those meant as little to her. Nor did "Olympus," which Creighton had mentioned as if it were the Service's headquarters. But all those words were obviously codes, club talk that members of the Service used among themselves. The inhabitants of this world would not call it Nextdoor, nor yet the equivalent of that expression. They would just call it the World. Olympus might be a private house in some city as far from here as London was from Stonehenge.

A whole world to explore? Even Columbus had not blundered into anything quite so unthinkable.

Columbus had not wanted to rush home and enlist in the army, either, but Edward did. The only way he could do that was to locate the Service, and that meant he must learn to talk. He hauled his mind back to work.

Then he recalled two words he already knew in this unnamed language.

"Vurogty Migafilo?"

The girl started and clapped her hands in delight. She pointed southeast. "Magafilo!"

Migo, Creighton had said, meant a village in the genitive case, so *maga* must be nominative or dative. The language was inflected, like Latin.

At that moment a third person joined the group. Edward had not heard the apparition approach and his start of surprise gave him a shocking spasm of cramp in his back.

Robinson Crusoe, or the Wild Man of the Woods? No it was Ben Gunn, straight out of *Treasure Island.* Emaciated and weather-beaten, with untamed white hair and beard, this near-naked scarecrow could pass as an Indian fakir. Obviously he was the owner of the cave and Edward had slept in his bed. The glint in his crazy eyes was distinctly unfriendly, implying that hermits did not appreciate uninvited guests. He had brought a bag of berries and some dirty tubers. He dropped them and spun on his leathery heel to leave.

Edward said the words that seemed to mean, "Thank you."

The girl spouted a long, angry speech. The hermit turned back and fixed his glittery, Ancient Mariner gaze on Edward. He could not possibly be as deranged as he looked, could he?

Edward pointed to the cave and said, "Thank you," again.

The hermit showed his teeth in a sneer and stalked away without a word. Unfriendly chappie!

"Porith," Eleal said, pointing at the scrawny back vanishing upstream. She stuck her tongue out and cut it off with a finger.

Edward thought *Good God!* and confirmed his understanding with more gestures. Why would anyone cut out a man's tongue? Perjury? Sedition? Blasphemy, perhaps?

He tried to convey the question but either did not succeed or did not understand the answer.

One look at Porith's offering made him nauseous. He explained that with more gestures and pushed it all to the girl. She ate while continuing her story of the night's events. Eleal was quite a storyteller. Even understanding less than a tenth of her words, Edward could appreciate her dramatic performance. She rolled her eyes and waved her hands until he was hard put to keep a straight face.

She began using berries and roots to denote the characters on stage. The roots were the baddies. She explained them by cutting imaginary corn with a sickle. He nodded, recalling Creighton's warning of *reapers*. Soon, though, his head ached with the effort of trying to memorize so many words at one sitting. He would forget most of them. It was like playing charades with no one to tell you if you had guessed right. What did she mean by reapers, the sun, a crescent, and kneeling?

The reapers sounded very much like the dreaded thugs of India, the murderous worshipers of Kali. The British had struggled for years to wipe out thuggee.

They went back to the temple story and Eleal dropped a hint

of advanced technology. Possibly she was fantasizing or had made a mistake, but it sounded as if Creighton had killed one of the reapers with a loud noise—a gun, obviously!

The picture was becoming clearer. Eleal had gone to spy, by herself. Creighton had crossed over, arriving dazed and shocked. The next two arrivals, T'lin and Gover . . . how did Eleal know their names? Those words might not be names at all but visible categories like "policeman" or "Chinaman." Whoever or whatever they were, the "t'lin" and the "gover" had welcomed Creighton, so they were almost certainly Service. They must have brought a gun for him, because then the first reaper had attacked and Creighton had shot him dead.

The girl's observations might be more reliable than her beliefs. She thought the reapers came from the god of death. Of course! Earthquakes came from Poseidon and thunder from Thor, yes? The reapers belonged to, or were agents of, the Chamber. But who were the Chamber? Who were the Service?

The T'lin man had escaped. He was Edward's road to sanity and assistance. He was the lead to the Service and Home and duty.

"T'lin! Er, *want?* T'lin!" he said.

Eleal scowled and said something about T'lin and gods and bad.

Nextdoor certainly seemed to have gods in both abundance and variety.

"No religion is wholly bad," the guv'nor had told him often enough. "Without gods of some sort, life seems to have no meaning, so mortals need gods. But no religion is wholly good, either. Every religion at some time or another has persecuted strangers, stoned prophets, burned heretics, or extorted wealth from the poor."

Edward did not believe in gods. He believed in progress and love and tolerance and ethics. He did not think Nextdoor was going to change his mind.

Eleal tired of the word game. Teaching D'ward to speak good Joalian was going to take much longer than she had expected.

His accent was worse than a Niolian's and he kept forgetting things she had told him. Just when she thought she was making progress, he would come out with absolute nonsense like, "Onions sings bluer gentle?"

The day was hot and still. All her nights seemed to be full of wild adventures now, and her days needed for sleep. He was yawning too. She sent him off to the cave to rest, and he went without argument, moving as stiffly as a very old man. It would be cooler in there for him. She climbed up the bank and stretched out on a mattress of ferns under a tree.

For a while her mind kept racing. Obviously Porith Molecatcher wanted her to leave and take her Liberator with her, and he could probably starve her into obedience. Somewhere farther from the Sacrarium would be much safer. Perhaps tomorrow D'ward would be strong enough to go.

Go where?

Go to Tion, of course! Her god was a just and benevolent god. He had saved her from Eltiana's jail and Zath's reapers. The Maiden had helped by sending Sister Ahn to kill Dolm Actor, but Irepit's convent was many vales away, in Nosokland, wherever that was. Here in Sussland the Maiden's grove had been destroyed. So that left Tion, and now it was safe for Eleal to rejoin the troupe, because Dolm was dead. So she would deliver the Liberator safely to Tion's temple in Suss, and Tion would reward her.

Reward her how?

Paa, the god of healing, was another avatar of Tion. Tion, therefore, was god of healing as well as god of art and beauty. Tion could cure sicknesses—and deformities! Eleal drifted off to sleep, thinking about the reward she would like best of all.

Porith shook her awake. The crazy old man was so excited he was hooting like a goose and drooling all over his beard. He made beckoning gestures, he tugged her hand. Grumpily she rubbed her eyes and stood up.

Come! he said in sign language. *Come quickly!*

She followed on dragging feet. The afternoon was half-gone,

the air as hot as fresh milk. Porith kept running ahead and having to wait for her.

Soon she realized that he was following a faint trail. Many branches hung across it, so it was never visible for more than a few feet, but it was an easier way through the forest than any she had found. It must be a path of his own making, for no one else would come here. It led past the Sacrarium on the side away from the cliff. Just beyond there, Molecatcher plunged through some bushes and made more wild whooping sounds.

She followed, and found him capering alongside a tent. It was a small tent, of good linen, colored a very inconspicuous green, and well concealed in the undergrowth.

"Oh, wonderful!" she cried, suddenly as excited as he. "I heard Gover Envoy invite T'lin to his tent! So whoever stole the bodies didn't know about this! And the man who owned it is dead, so we can have it!"

Apparently that was all the reassurance the old man needed. He knelt to fumble with the ties. Then he plunged inside on hands and knees with Eleal at his heels. The interior was a cavern of riches, straight out of *The Fall of Tarkor*. There were six or seven bales and packs there, leaving barely room for a man to lie down. Some spare clothes and a couple of straw hats lay on top of them, and a pair of good-looking boots, also. Eleal's fingers itched to start exploring this wealth, but she knew she must wait until it had been transported back to Molecatcher's cave. Gover Envoy just might have friends who knew where his camp was. He had mentioned a courier on a fast moa.

They needed two trips to transfer all their treasure, and by the time they brought in the last of it, D'ward was awake and sitting beside the first load. Eleal was relieved to see he had not opened anything, because she thought she deserved that pleasure. It would be like a birthday feast, with presents. He seemed strangely interested in the packs themselves, studying the fastenings and the stitching. In some ways D'ward Liberator was very odd!

She began with the lumpiest pack, because that seemed likely to be the most interesting. Most of the others smelled like food—bacon and onions and dried fish. Right at the top she found a bronze mirror and a razor. The Thargian had been clean-shaven, so these confirmed that the tent had belonged to him and not a reaper who might come in search of it. D'ward's blue eyes had lit up at the sight of them, so she gave them to him as a gift. The soap she kept, but she would let him share.

Next came two iron cooking pots. She gave those to Porith, because she would not be able to carry them away and he was host, and cook. He gibbered over them. And then—wonder of wonders! A leather-bound book—the *Filoby Testament* itself!

She beamed in joy and held it up for the others to see.

D'ward snatched it out of her hand.

A printed book, by George! A hide-bound, gold-embossed beautiful book! Nightmares of the Stone Age vanished, the Renaissance dawned in certainty, and even the Industrial Revolution began to seem possible.

Then the title jumped off the cover at him:

βυρογιε μιγαφιλο

Vurogty Migafilo! He flicked the pages. The language was jabber, but the letters were unmistakable. There were a few unfamiliar accent marks and obviously some of the pronunciations had changed—β was V, as in modern Greek—but overall the alphabet used was too close to classical Greek to be coincidence.

He barely noticed as Eleal grabbed the book back from him. Creighton had said that the keys to the portals were very ancient. Edward had not understood the significance of that at the time. While the Earth had been inventing steam engines and hot air balloons and now aeroplanes, it had been forgetting the antique wisdom of the shamans and witch doctors. People must have been crossing between worlds for thousands of years. Not many of them, but enough to found races and influence culture. They could have brought nothing with them, no tools or domestic animals, nor even fillings in their teeth, but their memories had come.

Someone had brought the art of writing from Earth to Next-door, or someone had taken the art of writing from Nextdoor to Earth. The Greeks were supposed to have copied the alphabet from the Phoenicians and improved it, but perhaps both had come from outside. The Greek alphabet had spawned the Latin and the Cyrillic and many others. This language of Eleal's was written in yet another variant of the Greek alphabet.

What else, who else, had crossed between worlds? For example, Edward thought—wishing he had someone to argue this with—Prometheus, who had stolen fire from the gods, might be an ancient memory of some interworld traveler. Perhaps many myths would make sense as muddled records of people vanishing mysteriously or appearing even more mysteriously. Suppose a man, or woman, popped out of nowhere into the middle of a druid ceremony at Stonehenge—would not the newcomer be hailed as a god?

With a squeal of delight, Eleal found her name where some-one had marked a passage. She showed it to Edward. He nodded and smiled, but his mind was busily chipping out a whole new view of human history.

ᖇᖇᖇ49ᖇᖇᖇ

By EVENING, HE WAS FEELING MUCH STRONGER. WITH Porith's fumbling help, Eleal had pitched the tent in thick shrubbery on the east side of the stream. She probably hoped that any reapers who came snooping around would not venture to cross the gully. The old hermit was so delighted to have his own house back that he had become almost jovial; at sundown the three of them ate a celebratory feast outside his cave.

Edward's appetite had come back with a rush. He suffered a stabbing toothache in consequence, but did not inquire about local dentists. His muscles and joints were recovering from their bruising, so he no longer moved like a centenarian. Later he managed to scramble up the bank for the first time, and then Eleal led him to the edge of the cliff.

The sun had just set. The view was superb—not merely the breathtaking canyon and the waterfall plunging into it, but also the many little white farmhouses standing out clearly on the far bank as if arranged there by an artist. Each had its own cluster of heavy shade trees and lighter, feathery things like palms or frozen green fountains. A background of fertile countryside faded off into distant foothills and a jagged frame of mountains. The land was prosperous, and obviously either tropical or subtropical, because the sun had been overhead at noon. It was better watered than his Kenya birthplace, he decided, and probably at a lower elevation—judging by terrestrial standards, which might not fit the case at all. Westward the ranges were a dark saw-edge against the last glow of evening. To the east the icy summits burned in gold and pink, and some of those peaks could match anything the Alps had to offer. Another range loomed over the forest behind him. The basin itself was about the width of the Mittelland at Lausanne, but closed off to east and west. The river was much bigger than the Rhine, the largest he had ever seen.

Waving an all-encompassing arm, Eleal explained that this was *Something*-Suss, which he assumed was what Creighton had translated as Sussland. When Edward asked the names of the ranges to north and south, they were both *Something-else*-Suss. The river was *Yet-Another*-Suss, and so was the little town he could see in the distance. He had a lot to learn.

Still, the town was promising. A gleam of reflected light there was somehow related to another god, Tion—a good god, apparently. Nice to hear that some of them were not horrors! Having discovered that Eleal had strong religious convictions, Edward had resolved to be very cautious on the subject of gods.

She indicated that tomorrow she was going to take him to that Town-Suss. He could manage that, he thought, five miles or so. Then he asked with gestures about crossing the canyon and learned that there would have to be a detour to the east, to Maganot. Still thinking in English, he translated that to Village-Not . . . Notham? Notting? Notby?

"Magathogwal," she explained, pointing the other way, and then, "Magalame, Magajot."

He pointed straight down. "Query name."

"Ratharuat."

Ratha must be yet another geographical prefix, perhaps meaning "forest" or "place smaller than a village" or "old ruins, nobody lives there now." *Ruat?* That name sounded familiar, but his memory was reeling from overwork and he could not place it.

The two of them sat in contented silence as the stars came out. Birds or something were making a strange racket in the trees and once in a while his stomach would rumble loudly, provoking Eleal to giggles. Then she began to sing. He could not follow the words, but the melody was pleasant. She was a competent little songstress.

She was a pretty girl, too, although she would never be a classical beauty; her nose tipped up and her hair was more frizzy than curled. She had a quick smile and a remarkable self-confidence. He suspected she was short for her age, but of course he was only guessing, for the local population might be stunted by twentieth century European standards. He wondered what had happened to her leg. It could not be rickets in this climate.

The song ended. The singer glanced up to see what her audience thought of it. Edward clapped, not sure if that was the local sign of applause. Apparently it was, because she beamed. On impulse he smiled, took her hand, and squeezed it. She blushed. He released it quickly, recalling Miss Eleal's dramatic tendencies. She was probably old enough to start having romantic notions also. He had no wish to provoke an embarrassing juvenile crush. *Call me in five or six years, perhaps.*

Five or six *years?* Five or six *days* ago, he had been on the boat train from Paris. Now he seemed to be stranded for the rest of his life on a world unknown, more exotic than anywhere Haggard ever Rode or Rudyard ever Kipled.

The giant green moon, Trumb, seemed to have disappeared. A small blue light just above the sunset was Ysh, Eleal said, and then she became excited and pointed to a brighter, yellow star. That was Kirb'l, and apparently seeing Kirb'l was an honor, or a good omen, or something. Kirb'l Tion, she said, and gestured toward Suss town.

Gods again! To change the subject Edward asked about her home and parents. She evaded the question and asked about his. They still conversed in baby talk and gestures, and that could become a bad habit. He decided to give himself one more day of that and then insist on using proper grammar.

The stars were lighting up with tropical swiftness. He could see the Great Bear low over the mountains to the northeast and Arcturus above that. He asked Eleal about their names, and again she became evasive. She would never admit ignorance. He wondered what other planets might circle this sun, but did not embarrass her by asking, and he probably could not have made himself understood anyway. He located Vega and the Summer Triangle. Then he turned around and peered up the stream gorge, which gave him a south view through the trees. There was the Centaur, which the guv'nor had pointed out to him when he was only—

He uttered a grunt of astonishment that made Eleal jump. Impossible! These were the stars of Earth.

Even before he went to sleep, he knew he was in for trouble. In the middle of the night it arrived. He crawled out of the tent without waking the girl.

Don't drink the water—but if he was going to be stranded on Nextdoor for the rest of his life, he must drink the water, and his insides would just have to learn to deal with the local germs. He'd suffered from the traveler's curse in France and in Germany and lived through it, but he was not familiar with the interplanetary variety. What he needed now was a good dose of codeine, Dover Pills. Without that he might be in for a severe case of Delhi Belly.

By morning he had a corker.

There was no question of leaving that day. He could barely crawl in and out of the tent, and eventually he stayed outside. He tried to reassure Eleal, but lacked the strength to explain the cause of the problem. She fussed and worried and prayed. She brought him water to drink, and made some thin soup, which he sometimes managed to keep down. Her concern was very touching, and she demonstrated remarkable patience at just fanning flies off him, although she was annoyed that he would not continue the language lessons. Another day ought to do it, he thought.

The next day he was running a high fever and things were looking dicey. His first term at Fallow he had caught every disease known to childhood, although he must have had as much inbred immunity as any native-born English boy. Those mumps and measles and whooping cough would have killed his

Embu friends at Nyagatha. He had inherited some resistance to English diseases, and he was better fitted to survive as an adult in Africa than any homebred white man, but he was not equipped for Nextdoor.

He began to wander in and out of delirium, never recognizing it until it was past. He did not want to die here, so far from home and everyone he knew. Where was *home?* Not Fallow. Nor Nyagatha. Certainly not Uncle Roly's house in Kensington. How ironic to escape the hangman's noose only to succumb to fever on another world! Oh, Alice, Alice! Perhaps he would have fallen to a German bullet had things turned out otherwise, but that would at least have had a certain dignity. Interplanetary disease had killed H. G. Wells's Martians.

Little Eleal was distraught, not knowing what to do. He tried to tell her that she was doing everything possible, but he could remember nothing of the language except her name. Alexander the Great had sighed for new worlds to conquer. They would have killed you, Alec.

O, brave new world! Lost world.

He did not want to die.

The next day he was weakening fast. The girl brought him drinks and washed away his sweat and held his hand. He was immeasurably grateful and could not tell her so. She was a gritty little thing. He heard her berating the old hermit. He tried to say that she should leave and go home to her parents. She didn't understand the King's English, poor child.

A whole new world and he was going to die without ever seeing more than a few square feet of it. He had so much wanted to find Olympus and talk to people who had known his father.

Creighton came to see him, fading in and out of illusion, talking of strangers.

Mr. Goodfellow came, sorrowfully. "I can do nothing, Edward," he said, clutching his beaver hat. "I have no authority here."

Why was the girl still hanging around? What was her interest in Edward? The way she bullied old Ben Gunn was really very funny. What day was this?

That night—whatever night it was—a monstrous thunderstorm lashed the jungle, while Edward raved in delirious arguments with Inspector Leatherdale, trying to convince him that miracles still happened and could open bolted doors. Poor Bagpipe Bodgley came by and talked of the *Lost World,* asking how the story had ended.

Then he found himself in jail, explaining to the doctor that his broken leg had been cured by a minor god left over from Saxon prehistory.

Eleal was praying again.

"That won't do any good!" he said crossly, aware that she could not understand.

"Well, you never know, old man," Creighton said. "Let's just hope nobody hears, that's all. I told you that they're not gods, but may behave like gods. But even if somebody does hear, well they're not all horrors."

"Did you give my love to Ruat?" Mr. Goodfellow asked.

His fever broke that night, and he lived. By morning he was lucid, but as weak as a newborn babe. He watched the dawn steal in through the leaves and smelled the new, wet scent of a cleansed world; he was infinitely grateful just to be alive.

He hoped he could stay that way, but obviously it would not be easy. Daylight had brought enlightenment. Sometime in his madness he had worked out who the opposition was, and why the Service referred to it as the Chamber.

The Chamber of Horrors, of course.

He was young and superbly fit, and he recovered quickly. One day he was a raving maniac and the next he was sitting up and very shakily trying to shave himself. The looking glass showed him the narrowness of his escape. That afternoon he began the language lessons again. The next day he was managing small walks.

Porith had hidden most of the food. Eleal screamed and

threatened until he produced it. She wanted it for D'ward, to build up his strength.

With much glee she showed him the passages in the *Filoby Testament* that mentioned her, and the others that mentioned him—Δϖαρδ. He was also sometimes identified by a title that Eleal did not even try to translate but which must be the "Liberator" Creighton had mentioned, and once he was called the son of Καμερον Κιστρ. That was a fair attempt to transliterate a name that must surely have been unique on Nextdoor. The reference had worked well enough to bring death to his parents and might yet do the same to him.

Edward knew that Eleal was keeping secrets from him. She could follow his pidgin and gestures perfectly well when she wanted to. When he asked some question she preferred not to answer, he became completely incomprehensible and remained so until she could change the subject.

She was very impatient to leave. He suggested that she go on ahead and he would follow or wait for her to return, but she refused, and for that he felt very grateful. He owed her his life, but to embark on a walk of perhaps several days' duration before he recovered his strength would be real folly, risking a complete relapse. He tried to explain that.

She managed to explain the need for haste—she had friends who would be leaving soon. He made her a promise: He must stay one more day, and he would do some walking to build up his strength, but they would leave the day after.

ᘒ 50 ᘓ

THE NEXT MORNING ELEAL TOOK D'WARD EASTWARD along the cliff edge. He leaned heavily on Sister Ahn's staff and persevered until they reached cultivated fields. He needed a rest before he could walk back. In all they had covered no more than a couple of miles, yet he was exhausted and slept through the whole afternoon.

In the heat of the day she lay on the grass and swatted flies and wondered how Uthiam had made out with *Ironfaib's Polemic*, and the others in their individual pieces. She even wondered if young Gim had done well with his harp or won the gold rose for his beauty. How that would embarrass him!

She also thumbed through the *Filoby Testament*. It was a terrible muddle. She had found the four references to her that Gover Envoy had mentioned. That had not been difficult, as he had marked them all in the book. The order did not seem to matter.

Verse 386 was the important one, about clothing and washing. In Verse 401, she brought "him" to the caveman for succor, and "him" had been D'ward of course.

Verse 475: *Before the festival, Eleal will come into Sussvale with the Daughter of Irepit. The minion of Zath seeketh out the Liberator, but he will be called to repentance.* Well, they had done all that! What use was a prophecy after you'd done it?

The only Eleal prophecy she had not yet fulfilled came right at the end of the book. Out of 1102 verses altogether, there she was again in number 1098: *Terrible is the justice of the Liberator;*

his might lays low the unworthy. He is gentle and hard to anger. Gifts
he sets aside and honor he spurns. Eleal shall be the first temptation
and the prince shall be the second, but the dead shall rouse him.

What prince? Tempting to do what? A lot of the prophecies
were like that—they almost meant something but not quite.
Like Verse 114: *Men plot evil upon the holy mountain. The servants*
of the one do the work of the many. They send unto D'ward, mouthing
oaths like nectar. Their voices are sweet as roses, yea sweeter than the
syrup that snares the diamond-fly. He is lured to destruction by
the word of a friend, by the song of a friend he is hurled down among
the legions of death.

The book spoke of D'ward and the Liberator separately and
never said they were the same man—perhaps she was in there
under other names too. Nor did it ever say who or what he was
supposed to liberate.

Sussians were very fond of liberators. This year's tragedy was
called *The Tragedy of Trastos,* and it was about Daltos Liberator,
one of their ancient heroes, who had slain Trastos Tyrant, his
own father, and brought democracy to Sussland. It was a very
good tragedy, with lots of gods and goddesses. Suss would love
it. At the festival it would have won the rose for the best play
easily . . . maybe! Dolm Actor had played major roles in both
the tragedy and the comedy. Dolm had been slain by Sister
Ahn's sword. K'linpor was his understudy, but Golfren was
K'linpor's, and Golfren acted like a rock.

This was Neckday and the festival would end tomorrow.
Eleal did not want to think about that. Usually the troupe stayed
on in Suss, because the winning group was allowed free use of
the temple amphitheater and many citizens would come to see
the winning play. Those performances often brought them
more money than any others in their year. But without Dolm
they could not stage either the *Varilian* or *Trastos,* only the
masque, and unless they had won the rose, they would not have
a free theater available.

In other words, there was a very good chance that the Trong
Troupe would leave the following day, Toeday, and there was
no hope of D'ward reaching Suss before then. Once the troupe

had crossed Monpass, it might wander almost anywhere in Joal-land.

Eleal might never manage to get him to Suss at all, because she had no money to pay the toll over the bridge at Notby.

There! She backed up a page in the *Testament* and yes, there was D'ward's name again.

D'ward shall become Tion. He shall give heart to the king and win the hearts of the people. D'ward shall become Courage.

What in the world did that mean? There was nothing to say that it referred to the Liberator. What a terrible muddle! Well, at the least it proved that she would be right to take D'ward to Tion's temple.

51

THEY PLANNED TO LEAVE AT DAWN THE NEXT MORNING, to make progress before the day grew hot. Edward had no idea what dangers lurked out there in the world: slavers, press-gangs, or knights in armor challenging passersby to joustings? He would have to rely on Eleal to lead him safely to wherever she thought he ought to be—for his benefit or hers. Clearly, she had plans, and they had involved careful preparation and much discussion with old Porith.

Whatever those plans were, he would have to go along with them. He could not spend the rest of his life in a jungle tent, certainly not while there was a war on that he must fight in.

Judging by garments looted from the dead Gover's baggage, standard dress in Sussland was a smock of drab gray material with a touch of bright-colored embroidery on hem or shoulder

strap. Eleal had been improving on one of these costumes. Below the neckband she had stitched a jagged sunburst of white
cloth, cut from a flour bag. Below that again, out to either side,
she had attached a green hammer and a red Ø, and underneath
them, but closer together, a yellow triangle and a blue star. The
colors were vital—having nothing else green to hand, she had
cut a piece out of the tent to use for the hammer. This armorial
creation was to be Edward's wear. He concluded that anything
so lacking in sense must obviously be very holy.

That evening she repeated her instructions solemnly and emphatically, a ragged urchin sitting cross-legged in the dirt, literally wagging a finger at him. He was to be a *gods' man,* walking
to gods' houses—a pilgrim, in other words—and he was not to
speak to anyone. She would do the talking. He was not sure if
she was to be his guide, pupil, or assistant, but the role seemed
to be formal and well-defined. He would play the lama, she the
chela. His only communication was to be a gesture of blessing,
and she made him practice that.

The idea was ingenious and might save him considerable
trouble if he attracted the attention of the authorities. Nextdoor
had no British consuls to stand bail or threaten to send gunboats.
On the other hand, all cultures he knew of imposed certain
obligations on their able-bodied young men—honest labor and
military service being two that came to mind at once. This
handy cop-out as a pilgrim might work for the elderly, but he
worried that his ingenious young accomplice was overlooking
some snag. He certainly put no faith in the addled wits of old

Porith, the ex-priest. Nevertheless, having no better plan of his own to propose, Edward agreed that he would be a holy man. He just hoped he would not be called upon to perform some sacred ritual. Public flagellation, for example.

Before the sun rose, the travelers left their tent for the last time and ate a hurried breakfast. They scrambled down the bank and called at Porith's cave to say farewell. Eleal gave him a kiss, which flustered him. The crazy old man was much richer than he had been before she arrived, because he had inherited all the valuables from the tent. He had resented Edward when they first met. The last couple of days he had become quite friendly.

Edward was not sure of the proprieties of handshaking and was certainly not inclined to kiss the shaggy old gargoyle, so he used his pilgrim-blessing gesture instead, a raised palm with fingers spread. The hermit stared at him for a moment, and then sank to his knees and bowed his head.

Eleal and Edward exchanged startled glances and took to their heels before they began to laugh. They looked back from the top of the bank, and the old man was still on his knees, as if in prayer.

Edward trudged along the jungle path with Eleal hobbling eagerly ahead. Besides his pilgrim's smock, he wore sandals and an absurd Chinese coolie straw hat like a wheel, all looted from the dead Gover. He leaned on his walking stick, which had belonged to some woman called Ahn, who had slain the second reaper. He was still not sure who she had been or how she had died.

He thought he might manage five miles if he were lucky. If he were unlucky, then he would discover that beggars were set to work picking oakum or mending roads. He had already identified the first snag in Eleal's pilgrim deception—by the rules of the game, neither of them could carry any baggage, not even a packed lunch, although he had slipped the razor and a lump of soap into his pocket when she wasn't looking.

When he neared the ruined temple, his skin rose in goose-flesh. The eerie sensation he had known in Winchester Cathedral and at Stonehenge was enormously magnified, into a dread sense of cold and dark and sanctity. He remembered Creighton saying he could always recognize virtuality on Nextdoor. Apparently the talent was amplified in strangers and Edward was a stranger here.

Did portals work in both directions? He still knew the key; he could easily make himself a primitive drum. But would that key take him back to Stonehenge, or on to some other world? Even if he dared take the risk and did reach Stonehenge, he would arrive there penniless and stark naked. By now Inspector Leatherdale would have a warrant out for his arrest. There was no easy way out of this mess.

He was glad to leave the temple behind. Beyond it the path was much clearer and in half a mile or so it emerged from the forest close to another ruin, a monumental arch. Despite Eleal's protests, Edward went to inspect it. Once it had anchored the end of a suspension bridge. Corroded remains of chains still hung from it, and the base of a matching arch was discernible on the far side of the gorge. Had he seen its like on Earth, he would have guessed that it dated from Roman times. Here it might be more recent, but no traveler had crossed Susswater at this point for several centuries.

The ancient road it had served was still evident, leading southward through a curiously diffuse settlement, a hodgepodge of farmland, trees, ruins, and cottages. No one else was about yet, so he was free to chat with Eleal. He soon established that this was Ruatvil. He learned how the language distinguished between small, medium, and large places—villages like Notby, towns like Ruatvil, cities like Suss. He suspected that even a city would seem very small by his standards. London or Paris would fill the whole valley.

"Hello, Ruat!" he said in English. "Mr. Goodfellow sends his love."

Eleal looked up quickly to frown at him. Her hat fell off and they laughed.

★　★　★

He felt very strange, walking under a tropic sun again, disguised as a peasant, but he had been seven days in this new world now and was eager to see more of it.

Beyond the remains of Ruatvil, he noticed real peasants toiling in the fields under coolie hats like his. People could pass through the portals, animals could not. The concept of agriculture could; the domesticated species would have to be local. He saw beasts of burden and herds of others that might be edible. They had a rough similarity to oxen and goats, and he thought he recognized geese until he observed that they had fur instead of feathers. The vegetation was unfamiliar, but none of it would have seemed out of place in a terrestrial land he had not visited before.

The biggest surprise of the morning was a man racing past on the back of something shaped like an ostrich. It was gone before Edward had time to see it properly. Soon two more riders approached from the south, and then he had time to observe that their mounts had hair and hooves. They moved very fast. Eleal told him they were *mothaa,* so he classified them in his mind as moas, although they must be more mammal than bird. He was trying hard to think in the local language, but he had not succeeded yet.

The road now was merely a red dirt trail, rutted and pocked with weeds. Hedges defined the fields and he saw no barbed wire, no eyeglasses or steam engines. He no longer believed in Creighton's gun—he had another theory now to explain the reaper's death—but he still hoped that the culture of Ruatvil did not represent the limits of Nextdoor's technology. An interplanetary traveler arriving at some isolated Chinese or African village would not find motorcars or telegraph wires.

No policeman asked to see the travelers' papers, no highwayman demanded their money or their lives. By and large the population just ignored them—field workers, herders, men driving oxcarts. The only exceptions were a few pedestrians coming along the trail in the opposite direction. They mostly regarded the holy man with surprise or disapproval, and in some cases with open amusement. Edward tried giving his sign of blessing, but that met with outright laughter and ribald comments. Thereafter he maintained a dignified impassivity, but obviously an eighteen-year-old prophet was no more convincing on Nextdoor than he would have been on Earth. He needed old Porith's white beard.

To his shame, he soon found himself hard put to keep up with the crippled child at his side. Eleal might have less than two complete legs, but she made good use of what she had. He wondered why she did not wear a built-up shoe to make her stride more even.

The road continued to wander south. As their destination lay to the north, he concluded that the detour was going to be sizable, probably dictated by the availability of bridges. After five or six miles he had reached his limit. Happily, just there the road crossed a small knoll, capped by a grove of tall trees like gigantic umbrellas, casting black velvet shadow. Eleal pulled faces, but agreed to let him rest.

An hour or so later, they set off again and soon came to a junction. Eleal turned to the east. A short distance on this new road brought them to a fast-flowing river, whose milky water told of its glacial origin, like streams Edward had seen in the Alps. He was staggering now, his legs trembling. He had a nagging toothache and blisters from the unfamiliar footwear.

"Rest!" he said as he staggered down the incline to the ford. Such weakness was humiliating, but his illness had drained him of strength.

Clutching her hat, Eleal looked up at him with a worried frown. "Not speak!"

"Not speak," he agreed. The last thing he needed now was the strain of trying to make conversation.

She led the way over a long line of stepping stones, into a small grove on the far bank. Several groups of travelers were taking a noontime break in a wayside campground. Two oxcarts stood by the road; a few of the strange moa bipeds grazed on tethers under trees resembling beeches. Watchdogs that looked more like oversized shaggy cats guarded a herd of goatlike creatures. Flower-bedecked shrubs brightened the grove. Almost all the blossoms were some shade of red, and he had noted the same thing at Ruatvil. It reminded him of Kenya, where blue and yellow flowers were similarly rare. Delicious odors of cooking came wafting from the fires.

Eleal pointed to a log near an unoccupied hearth, seeming to imply that Edward should sit on it, so he did. He thought he heard his knees utter sighs of relief. He felt like one big ache. He had a sunburn, and he was trembling with fatigue.

Was it *all* fatigue? He looked around uneasily at the pillared tree trunks. Something creepy . . . Then he realized that it was virtuality again. This campground was a node—not on the scale of the Ruat temple or Stonehenge, but awesome enough to make his skin prickle. He could see no shrine or ruins; he could only hope that it had no resident numen.

Eleal had gone hobbling over to the largest group of wayfarers, eight or nine men busily eating and arguing. They broke off their conversation to inspect her. Then they scowled across at her pilgrim companion.

Undeterred, she began to make a speech. Edward could not understand any of it. One of the men shouted angrily, waving her away. They were a nondescript gang, rough and weather-beaten. A couple of the youngest wore only loincloths, the rest were clad in the customary drab smocks, their straw hats lying on the grass beside them. Every man had a knife at his belt and they all sported beards. Most were stocky and dark-complexioned. Apart from their clothes, they could have been rural Italians.

Eleal was never easily discouraged. She continued her harangue, gesturing dramatically in Edward's direction—no doubt explaining how holy and worthy he was. He did not feel holy and worthy, but he did feel hungry, and unbearably weary. The throb in his tooth hurt almost as much as his feet.

One of the younger men said something witty and all the others laughed. The oldest, a graybeard, shouted at her again. They were not speaking the language Eleal had been teaching Edward, and neither was she. It had a more guttural sound to it, but he caught a word or two and decided it might be only a dialect variation. She grew shriller and more insistent. Graybeard stood up and advanced on her menacingly. Evidently her plan to elicit charity for her pilgrim was not going to work. Nice try.

Abandoning hopes of lunch, Edward rose also. He limped forward and laid a hand on Eleal's shoulder. She jumped, and fell silent. He had intended to draw her away, but she did not move and that turned his gesture into one of protection and support. Suddenly there was confrontation. Graybeard was no longer threatening a child, but a man both younger and taller than himself. He could not possibly back down now.

From the looks of him, Graybeard was a seasoned old rover. His face was burned by the sun, with lines of red road dust marking its wrinkles. His shoulders were impressively hairy and beefy, his dark eyes bloodshot and menacing. He said something contemptuous; the words could have been Chinese for all Edward knew, but the tone was an unmistakable warning that certain young scroungers should go and find themselves honest work before they had the living daylights knocked out of them. His companions jeered their agreement.

Oh, is that so? Before he realized it, Edward had raised his eyebrows in challenge. He was not going to take that remark, whatever it meant, from a gang of vagrant peddlers. *Never let them see you're afraid of them. . . .*

Too late he registered that his Fallow training might have betrayed him. He was not dressed to play the role of the young gentleman; these were not insubordinate English navvies. He was not His Majesty's District Officer, backed by the invincible might of the British Empire. He was not even Bwana's son at Nyagatha. He was exactly what these men thought he was, a beggar. Public school airs were inappropriate under the circumstances.

Too bad! To back down now would only make things worse.

He returned the man's stare with contempt, holding the eye contact: *Do your worst!*

Graybeard shouted again.

Really? You don't say?

Doubt flickered over the other man's craggy features. Had he never seen blue eyes before? He asked a question.

Still Edward said nothing. Eleal said nothing. The doubt curdled into worry. The old man turned away; he strode quickly back to the fire and returned bearing a stick with a sizzling lump of charred meat on it. Eleal snatched it from him and peremptorily demanded another, holding out her hand. Another man hurried over with a second.

Edward nodded in acceptance, and offered his spread-hand blessing. Both men laid palms on their hearts and bowed low, apparently relieved.

The holy man returned to his log, trying not to limp on his blisters. He did not sit immediately, but took a careful look around to make sure the trouble was over. He had won the attention of the whole campground. Eleal came to stand beside him. Her face was paler than usual, but she flicked him a wink. He kept his features impassive, deciding it would be safe to eat.

But then one of the younger men followed and knelt to offer Eleal a bowl of cereal mush. Edward gravely blessed him as she accepted it. Another came with a gourd of water. One by one, men hurried over to kneel and buy the holy man's blessing. Other men from other groups joined in, bringing food from their own meals. Soon there was a feast spread out around the venerable pilgrim's feet.

Eleal's eyes grew wider and wider every time she looked up at him. Edward remained inscrutable, as if this sort of tribute was no more than his due. Eventually he realized what was expected of him—he sat down to show that he was satisfied. Then the offerings stopped coming. He hoped the two of them could do justice to such a banquet. He had collected half the food in the campground, enough to feed a monasteryful of starving monks.

His mouth was watering. He bit into the meat, feeling delicious hot fat run down his chin. His tooth had stopped aching.

Graybeard's oxcart was piled high with what seemed to be small blue carrots. They did not make a very comfortable throne, but

Edward sat cross-legged on the top under the shade of his hat and made the best of the ride into Filoby. He clutched his staff, trying to look holy and ineffable, dribbling unholy sweat in the heat of the afternoon. Eleal sat beside the old man and chattered imperiously. God knew what sort of tale she was spinning, although Edward heard his name being mentioned. Her religious scruples were starting to seem surprisingly flexible. Every now and again she would twist around and address some remark to him, but he rarely caught more than a couple of words. *Migafilo* was one.

Eventually they came to another river. A ford and a steep hill out of the valley brought them into a village of whitewashed cottages with roofs of red tiles. This must be Filoby, the Magafilo of the prophecy. It was an unimpressive clutter of narrow clay lanes and perhaps fifty homes, but a rank odor of charred wood hung in the air. Several cottages had been burned—recently, for repairs were under way. There were more people around than might have been expected at that time of day. They looked up with interest at the pilgrim on his chariot.

Then worse destruction came in sight. Beyond the village rose a small conical hill, spiky with black tree trunks. As the oxcart approached, Edward began to feel the now-familiar sense of virtuality. He shivered despite the heat. That hill was a node and a sacred place. It must be the birthplace of the *Filoby Testament,* and it had been ravaged by fire. Gutted ruins of many buildings stood stark amid the ashes of the grove. From what Creighton had told him about prophecy, he could only assume that this destruction was more work of the Chamber, striving to block fulfillment of the *Testament.* The people who had devastated Nyagatha had struck here also, the killers of his parents, the enemies who would still be seeking his death.

Here Graybeard's road parted from his. The holy pilgrim descended from the carrots with as much dignity as he could contrive in his skimpy frock.

Mumbling apologetically, the old man knelt in the dirt and removed his hat to receive the pilgrim's final blessing. Feeling mischievous, Edward went so far as to lay his outspread hand on the man's head. That must be a signal honor, for when the old rascal rose to his feet, tears were cleaning small tram lines down the dust on his weather-beaten cheeks. He gabbled thanks, fumbling with his hat.

Edward turned and walked briskly in the direction his small disciple indicated. He could not see her face under her hat and he wondered what she was thinking. It was not like Eleal to remain silent.

The street was narrow. He was constantly passing close to people. Almost without exception, they bowed to him. One or two women knelt as he went by. He responded with his sign of blessing and saw faces light up.

This was all very creepy! Not everyone was dark-eyed and swarthy—he saw auburn hair, some mousy brown. He saw hazel eyes and gray eyes. His own blue eyes might be rare, but they could not be unique in the world, so they were not what was provoking superstitious respect. He was tall by local standards, but again not uniquely so. His was not the single white face among a thousand black. Above all, he was only a youth. Why should his pilgrim garb merit this sudden veneration? Were the inhabitants of Filoby so much more devout than those of Ruatvil, who had laughed at him that morning?

No, something had changed when he faced down Graybeard in the campground. That confrontation had given him confidence, of course, which might be part of it, but his wildest theories were starting to seem believable.

He could not ask Eleal to comment, for now the road was busy and a pilgrim must not speak. Even when he had left the village behind, there was no lack of travelers. As soon as one party had passed, another was in sight. They all seemed to be heading south, and he did not understand that. He was going the wrong way.

Nor were they all peasants. Well-dressed folk rode past on swift moas or in gigs drawn by animals resembling pony-sized greyhounds. Many of the pedestrians wore colored robes, and he guessed that those were priests and priestesses. Even they greeted him with respectful gestures—clasped hands, touches to breast or forehead. He responded with his five-finger blessing, and no one accused him of irreverence.

The travelers were more varied than the locals. He saw fairer skins, even some blond hair and eyes as blue as his own. One or two could have been Saxons or Scandinavians. Others might have been Indians or Arabs. Clothes showed more diversity, also—tunics and baggy pants like Turkish pajamas, gowns, simple loincloths. Men were bearded or clean-shaven or mustachioed, their limbs smooth or hairy. Noses were hooked or straight, broad or narrow. The population of Nextdoor was a cross section of European types, but of course that was to be expected. Creighton had said that most of the European portals connected with a territory he had called the Vales. Of course the racial types would be similar if people had been crossing to and fro for thousands of years, keeping the bloodlines mingled.

Fascinated, Edward strode along the dusty track. Heat and sweat and insects were minor inconveniences. He eyed the sprouting crops in the fields, the hedges, the livestock, the farmhouses. Many trees stood on carpets of fallen blossom—in England it was August, but in the Vales it was spring.

A troop of six armed men approached, streaking along on moas. As they came near, their leader drew his sword. For a moment Edward's muscles all tightened up in alarm, but the man merely raised the blade in salute and kept on going.

Suddenly Eleal took a grip on her hat and tilted her head to look up at him. Her face was flushed and worried. "Rest?" she pleaded. She was panting, her smock soaked with sweat.

He was so surprised and ashamed that he almost broke his presumed vow of silence. Nodding, he slowed down—blessing a passing pair of monks at the same time. Eleal limped to the shade of a hedge and flopped down on the grass. Edward joined her, lowering himself with more dignity. He had forgotten that his legs were so much longer than hers. He had run the poor cripple off her feet. How could he have been so thoughtless! And why had she not said something sooner? Obviously it was not only his teeth that were feeling better—he had recovered his physical strength, too.

Two well-dressed men stopped and offered canteens of water, inquiring solicitously after the holy man's health. Eleal replied in the same clipped dialect, obviously explaining that it was she who was weary. They nodded understandingly. Grateful for the drink, Edward sent them on their way with a blessing.

Whatever his magic was, it worked on Eleal also. She was regarding him with awe and delight and adoration.

He waited for a gap in the stream of passersby and risked a question. "Query many men going."

She replied with a long dissertation about the god Tion and the city of Suss, but he did not understand and had no chance to question her further. She seemed to know the reason for this migration and she was obviously not worried by it, so he could forget theories of plague or marauding Goths coming out of the hills. He would just have to wait and see. He hoped she would revive soon, so they might continue on their way.

Another half hour or so brought them to Rotby, which was much like Filoby, or slightly larger. The natives were just as respectful to the young pilgrim, just as pleased to receive his blessing, so the effect was showing no signs of wearing off. If anything, it seemed to be growing stronger.

The bridge beyond Rotby was marked by a great megalithic arch, a twin of the relic at Ruatvil. Another stood on the far bank of the gorge, several hundred feet away. The green-bronze chains looped between them supported a wooden roadbed barely wide enough for a single oxcart. Despite the steady flow of travelers approaching, few were heading north—Edward still wished he understood that imbalance—so there was no great press of people ahead of him at the massive timber gates. There were enough for him to work out the procedure, though, and to see that the men in metal helmets and leather armor were collecting a toll.

Eleal took his hand and squeezed it warningly.

He thought *Phooey!* Obviously a holy pilgrim who had taken an oath of silence and a vow of poverty could not be expected to have money.

He might be required to find some rich layman to pay his way for him, of course.

He laid a comforting hand on Eleal's shoulder as they approached the gate. Two guards were taking the cash, checking it carefully, and then dropping it in a bag—one doing the actual work, the other mostly keeping a careful eye on him, although sometimes they would both have to bite a coin before reaching a decision. Three other guards lounged on a bench in the shade behind, chatting in bored fashion. All five wore swords.

A peasant and his wife passed through. Edward and Eleal were next. The guard held out a horny hand.

Edward gave him his respect-compelling stare.

The soldier demanded money in unmistakable, no-nonsense terms.

Edward said nothing.

The soldier scowled, hesitated, and glanced at his companion. He, in turn, swung around and said something to the three on the bench. The man on the left and the one in the middle both looked to the one on the right. Obviously military procedures did not vary much from one world to another.

The one on the right was a grizzled bull of a man, and his expression as he sized up the juvenile prophet suggested that he would like nothing better in the whole world than a chance to have that stripling under his command for a few hours. Edward waited. For a long, unhappy moment there was challenge and confrontation, as there had been in the campground.

Then the leader rose to his feet, his two companions an instant behind him. He marched forward four steps as if to take a closer look at Edward's blue eyes. He stamped his feet, barked an order, and the whole squad came to attention. He saluted. Edward gave him a blessing and led Eleal through the gate, onto the bridge.

When I grow up, he thought, *I am going to be Pope.*

The gorge was especially narrow there. The walls fell sheer to the spray—in fact the north side looked undercut, which suggested that one day soon the Rotby bridge might be taken out of service by the river itself. Even upstream and downstream from this notch the canyon was much deeper than it was wide, the river barely visible in the shadowy depths. Its voice was a constant, threatening mumble, sensed more through the soles of the feet than the ears. The chains creaked softly. Many road-bed timbers were in need of repairs and the road itself had a worrying dip to the center. Edward decided he would be evermore content to remain on the far side when he reached it.

Other travelers stepped aside for him and bowed. The driver of an oxcart brought it to a halt—no easy task, for the roadbed sloped steeply at that point. The guard at the north gateway saluted as the pilgrim passed through.

A few cottages stood to the right; a grove of trees to the left was clearly another of the wayfarers' campsites. Several early bird groups were setting up tents and at least one hearth trickled smoke already. After the banquet he had eaten at noon, Edward did not expect to be hungry for several days, and his legs had found some sort of second wind—he could cheerfully have carried on walking—but the girl was flagging again and would appreciate a break. She must have come to that conclusion herself, because she turned off into the campground without hesitation.

He sensed no virtuality this time. This was not a node, but it was an attractive enough spot, well shaded and cool. Between the trees, massive flowering bushes shaped like giant puffballs displayed innumerable shades of red, from orange through almost to violet. Some of them were bigger than armchairs. Taking a second look, he wondered if each bush might be a single enormous blossom. Half a dozen moas were grazing off to the side, and he decided to go and take a look at those interesting . . .

A man shouted, "Eleal!" and came running forward.

Eleal screamed. She grabbed Edward's hand and hauled at him.

"*Reaper!*" she shrieked. "*Reaper!*"

Edward stayed where he was, ignoring her frantic tugging while he summed up the man who had provoked her terror.

Seeing the effect he had produced, the stranger had halted, so he was no immediate danger. He was standing about twenty feet away, staring. There was nothing threatening about his appearance—he was taller than most and in his late twenties or early thirties, but he bore no visible weapon. There was a rawboned awkwardness even to the way he was standing. He wore a yellow tunic and loose pants down to his knees.

Eleal was babbling, *"Reaper!"* and trying to pull Edward away.

He could see no danger in the man. His expression was one of extreme distress—pain, perhaps, or fear, or any one of several things, but more suffering than any desire to cause suffering. Both ignorance of the language and the role he was playing prevented Edward from arguing with the girl, but he was much stronger than she was. Effortlessly towing her along beside him, he strode forward to take a closer look.

ACT V

ENSEMBLE

52

"It is the way of the Daughters," Dolm Actor said sadly. "Irepit is goddess of repentance."

The three of them were sitting on the ground around an empty hearth of blackened pebbles. It was a private corner of the campground, almost surrounded by cloud blossoms. Eleal was cuddling very close to D'ward, for she did not trust the former reaper.

Yet Dolm had obviously changed. His face was haggard, and he seemed much thinner than she remembered. There were gray streaks in his hair she did not recall either. His eyes were bloodshot and underlined with darkness.

"I thought you had died," she muttered. "The sword moved by itself. I had both hands on it and Sister Ahn had one and yet it felt as if it moved by itself."

Dolm groaned and covered his face. "It did not touch me."

"I did not feel it touch you," she admitted.

D'ward was listening intently, but she could not tell how much he understood. They were speaking Joalian, which was what she had been teaching him, and his bright blue eyes flickered back and forth as she and Dolm spoke, but he could not be catching very much of this, surely. He was still playing his pilgrim role, being very relaxed and confident. Whenever she looked at him he smiled at her reassuringly.

"Did you not hear what she said?" Dolm asked. "She took my sin upon herself and then I saw what . . ."

"Saw what?"

"Saw what I had become, what I had been doing."

"You really aren't a reaper anymore?"

He shook his head, not looking at her.

She glanced at D'ward. He nodded to show he understood.

"What happened at the festival?" she asked.

Dolm straightened, wiping his eyes with the back of his hand. "Disaster! Well, Uthiam won a rose for her solo."

"Praise to Tion!" Eleal clapped her hands.

"But she was the only one. I didn't get there in time, you see." Dolm shook his head sorrowfully. "I had orders to go to Ruatvil."

"Orders?"

"Orders from Zath. When we arrived at Filoby, I left the group without telling anyone. Zath's orders override anything. I had been instructed to meet up with another . . . with a colleague."

"That was the one the Kriiton man killed?"

He nodded, staring at the stones of the hearth. "I don't know his name. The next night I was at the Sacrarium. You know."

"But if you weren't killed," she said, working it out, "then it must have been you who removed the bodies!"

Again he nodded. "I buried the nun—dug her grave with her sword and my bare hands. That seemed the least I could do. The others I dropped over the cliff. I looked for you, couldn't find you, and decided you had gone off somewhere with the Liberator." He looked across at D'ward, who was frowning in exasperation.

"So then what happened?" Eleal demanded impatiently.

"I went to Suss," Dolm said reluctantly. "I was too late. They presented the *Varilian*, because it's easier. K'linpor took my part and Golfren took his."

"Oh no!"

"Oh yes."

How awful! A yak could act better than Golfren, fine musician though he was. "So what are they doing now?"

Dolm picked up a thin twig and poked idly at the cold ashes. "Starving."

"Starving?"

"Almost. The priests in Narsh took all their money. They don't even have enough to get out of Sussvale, Eleal. And it's all my fault!"

This did not make any sense! "But you were back. Even if they didn't compete, or win, they can stage performances, surely? They're well-known in Suss! Surely people would—"

"I can't act anymore!" Dolm shouted. He put his face down on his knees, huddled in misery. "Trong fired me yesterday."

"Can't act?"

"No. I'm terrible! I forget my lines, I fall over my feet. It's all gone."

Again Eleal glanced at D'ward. He shrugged, obviously at a loss.

"So what are they doing?"

"Trying to hire a replacement for me," Dolm said, speaking to the ground. "As soon as he's learned his lines, they'll stage the *Varilian.*"

Eleal sighed. This was awful! "What does Yama—"

The immediate expression of agony on Dolm's face told her she was an unkind, blundering idiot.

"Do you really think I would tell her?" he said bitterly. "Or any of them?"

How strange!—she felt sorry for him now. This was a very different Dolm.

"What *did* you tell them?"

"That I went on a binge, drinking." He laughed, a very hollow sound. "It's better to be thought a lush than a mass murderer."

"Oh. I won't tell them, Dolm. I know I'm nosy, but I can keep secrets if I want to."

"I know you can, Eleal. Thank you. Thank you very much. It doesn't really matter, because they won't see me again, but I'd feel happier . . . Somehow."

The evening must be cooling, for she felt little goose bumps on her skin.

"Who won the gold rose?"

He shrugged. "Some pretty boy, of course."

"You didn't hear his name?"

"No. A musician, I think . . . There was some story that the judges told him to throw his lyre in the river and report to the chief priest. No one else had a look-in, they said. Why?"

"I met a boy named Gim."

"Yes, maybe that was his name, now you mention it."

"And how many miracles?"

Dolm's eyes flickered to her leg and then away again quickly. He smiled his stage smile. "One or two—the priests couldn't decide which. When the time came for the boy to call out a name, he called two names. They were sisters, identical twins, and all their lives they'd had a terrible skin disease. Even from where I was standing, they looked just horrible."

"And Tion healed them!"

"Oh yes! He laid his hands—laid your friend's hands—on their heads and they were cured."

That was beautiful! "Were they pretty? How old are they? What are their names?"

Dolm had lost interest in telling her about the festival. He was studying D'ward with a puzzled expression. "Why is the Liberator still here, in Sussland? Doesn't he know that Zath has reapers out looking for him? Doesn't he know he's in terrible danger?"

She sniggered. "He doesn't seem to know anything. He doesn't know the language, or the gods, or anything!"

Dolm's cavernous eyes widened. "The seeress described him as a baby! Why on earth is he going around dressed as a pilgrim?"

"I decided he would be safest that way, since he can't talk. And, Dolm, he's a wonderful actor! He's being making everyone think he really is a holy man!"

A pained smile twisted the actor's gaunt face. "Oh, Eleal, little idiot! Of course he can act a holy man! Don't you see what you've done?"

She bristled. "I've been ingenious and, er, resourceful under trying conditions! He's been terribly sick!" She looked to D'ward for support and he smiled encouragingly. How odd!

Except for the red wound on his forehead, he looked as if he'd never been sick in his life. "And he doesn't know anything about the world at all, but I thought he ought to get to Suss and appeal to Tion, and this seemed—"

"You are a small chump!" Dolm said. "Zath has I-don't-know-how-many reapers out looking for him, and you dress him like a pilgrim? Don't you understand? He's the Liberator! Of course he could make people think he was a holy man! He *is* a holy man! You disguised him as what he really is, you frog-brain!"

Eleal said, "Oh! . . . Oh?" Well, that might help explain a few of the surprising things that had been happening today.

"And I'm not at all sure about taking him to Tion," Dolm said uncertainly. "Some of the passages in the *Testament* suggest that the Liberator . . . All of Sussia's been talking about the birth of the Liberator. Well, never mind. I wish I'd thought of the pilgrim idea for myself, though. That's what I need to do! I shall don the holy pentacle and see if I can cleanse my soul." Another painful smile flickered over his haggard features. "I wonder if he'd—"

He turned to his pack and began unlacing it. Eleal recalled how she'd rummaged through that pack less than a fortnight ago and found a reaper's gown.

Dolm pulled out a tunic and pants. He held them out to D'ward. D'ward's blue eyes lit up and he looked to Eleal for her approval.

"Just what are you suggesting, Dolm Actor?" she demanded.

"I'll trade with him. I'll have to come back with you to Suss and start at Tion's temple, of course."

Eleal shivered. The Holy Circuit of the five great temples took at least a year—a year of begging and poverty, of penance and complete silence.

"But he really can't talk! What if someone asks him questions?"

Dolm shrugged. "You're planning to rejoin the troupe and take him with you, aren't you? It's only a few hours' walk. I'll come with you to the city. He can have my pack, too."

Eleal nodded uncertainly—she had nowhere to go except back to the troupe. D'ward grabbed the garments and jumped up. He strode off into the cloud blossoms. A moment later he came marching out again in his new clothes, grinning shyly. He and Dolm were about the same height and the garments were intended to be loose—but not so loose. If he let go of the pants, they would fall down. Chuckling, Dolm dug in his pack again and produced a length of cord.

"Better!" D'ward said, laughing. "Not women frighten. Talk now?"

"Talk now," Eleal agreed.

He sat down and smiled at Dolm. "D'ward!" He held out a hand.

"Dolm Actor." They shook hands. Dolm stuffed the pilgrim smock in his pack. "I tried to kill you!"

D'ward nodded. "Remember. Saw your voice under the night."

"He doesn't speak very well, does he?" Dolm said wonderingly.

"He's learning very fast!"

"Was reaper?" D'ward asked.

Dolm nodded solemnly.

"Better now?"

"Better."

"Good!" Again D'ward offered a hand to shake.

Dolm looked startled, and then accepted. He stared at D'ward afterward as if hunting something he could not identify.

"We can stay here tonight, can't we?" Eleal said. The sun must have slipped behind Susswall, for the grove was growing dark.

"I have a little food," Dolm said. "But only one blanket."

"We should have left D'ward a holy man. He just has to look at people and they throw charity at him."

Dolm scratched his scanty hair. "Where do you want to go, sir?"

Eleal turned away to hide a smile. She did not think Dolm had even realized that he had called a boy, "sir."

D'ward took a moment to work out the question. "Olympus."

"Who's she?"

"I don't know," Eleal sighed. "He raved about her when he was delirious."

D'ward said, "Query town. Query village."

"That's a woman's name!" she protested. "He must mean *Limpus.*"

Edward shrugged.

"Limpusvil?" Dolm said thoughtfully. "Limpusby? I never heard of either. Your first problem will be to escape from Sussvale. Zath set watches on the nodes and you slipped by us. Now he has all the passes guarded. Only four passes." At Edward's frown he explained more slowly, with gestures, scratching a map in the dirt.

"We need T'lin Dragontrader again!" Eleal said. Then she remembered and said, "Oh!"

Dolm's clouded face brightened momentarily. "He escaped me, if that's what you're wondering. The way he took off on that dragon, I don't suppose he stopped this side of Nosokland." He turned again to study D'ward. "Taking him to Tion is probably the best idea, I suppose, since none of us has any money."

"Tion god?" D'ward said, frowning. "No gods!"

Dolm raised his eyebrows. "Like that, is it? *The gods shall flee before him; they shall bow . . .*" He pondered. "Perhaps you weren't so foolish after all, Eleal Singer—disguising him as a holy man, I mean. The reapers wouldn't be looking for him in that role. And taking him to Suss but not going to the temple may be the same sort of thing. The best place to hide a man is in a crowd of men. Unless they're keeping an eye out for you also, of course."

"What do you mean?" Eleal demanded, feeling a cold shiver.

"They know you're involved, so they may be watching the troupe, in case you try to return. They're probably hunting me, too," he said sadly. "I don't think ex-reapers live very long."

She switched into Sussian, which D'ward would not understand. "Tion!" she said firmly. "We must go and seek the aid of our god!"

"I suppose you're right," Dolm agreed, shooting a worried glance at the Liberator.

ᒐ᷈ᴦ 53 ᴖᴐ

AT SUSS THE CANYON WAS MUCH WIDER THAN AT RUAT-vil. The land descended in steps and cliffs, a red and green land-scape fretted by intricate wadis. Tion's temple stood on an isolated mesa, a sprawling palace on a giant plinth, its gilded dome blazing under the tropic sun. It was a giant's cake of white marble, decorated and ornamented in pillars and cornices of bright color, in form like nothing Edward had ever seen, although unquestionably fair. If it resembled anything on Earth, perhaps "out of the Taj Mahal by the Kremlin," would sum it up best. Innumerable lesser buildings spread out over the steps of the valley wall, all set in gardens and park, lush vegetation contrasting with the ruddy soil. The whole complex was larger than the little walled town beyond it. Yes, it was beautiful. And so it should be, for Tion was god of art and beauty. It was vastly impressive—and so it should be, for Tion was one of the five paramount deities of the Vales.

It would be a node, of course, but it stood too far from the road for Edward to sense virtuality. Unlike Stonehenge and the Sacrarium, this node was *occupied*. He did not know whether the numen who dwelt there belonged to the Chamber or the Service. Eleal insisted that Tion was a benevolent god, but the teams in this game did not wear colored jerseys. Edward was not about to walk into any den until he had learned more about the lion. So far his only instructors had been a child and a confessed mass murderer.

Dolm Actor was the first adult he had been able to talk with since he arrived on Nextdoor. However willing and precocious, Eleal had a child's limitations. Dolm spoke clearly and slowly, repeating himself in ingenious variations to convey his meaning. He had a quick wit for untangling Edward's efforts to reply, the patience to correct his grammar, plus an actor's ear for pronunciation. He was a very good coach, but he explained that any wandering entertainer in the Vales must soon become a language expert. Every valley had its own dialect. The farther from home, the greater the difference.

How many valleys? How many peoples?

Dolm could not give an answer, barely even a guess. There were three main languages, Joalian, Thargian, and Niolian, and at least half a dozen variants of each. A score was the absolute minimum.

How many gods? That question produced a lecture on theology, the five great gods—Parent, Lady, Man, Maiden, Youth—and the many minor gods who were the five also. Edward recalled his father saying that people could believe anything they wanted to believe.

By the time noon rolled around and the weary travelers were approaching the turnoff to Tion's spectacular temple, he was often able to understand what was said at the first attempt. Speaking was harder, of course. Nevertheless, he had never picked up a language so quickly. There were uncanny things going on, and he was becoming more and more uneasy about them. He was a stranger here. Mr. Goodfellow . . . Oh, stuff it! That way led madness. *Here be dragons.*

The roads were almost deserted. Yesterday's traffic had been heavy because people had been heading home from Tion's Festival, which sounded like a sort of annual Olympic Games. That train of thought shunted Edward off onto a siding. He spent several minutes asking if there was any great home for all the gods—a sacred mountain, perhaps. Neither Dolm nor Eleal could recall hearing of such a place. Every god and goddess had a temple and important deities might have outlying shrines and chapels as well, but there was no central clubhouse where they were known to assemble. If they threw parties for one another, they did so at home. Scratch that thought. "Olympus" was only a nickname.

Eleal had been feeling ignored all morning and was being obnoxious in consequence. Dolm started asking her about her arrival in Sussland and her replies confirmed Edward's suspicions that she was keeping secrets from him. Having learned of her theatrical background, he could understand her affected airs and dramatics. She claimed that she had been kidnapped by a goddess and rescued by a god. Doubting most of this, Edward still moved Eleal to the head of his list of things to investigate as soon as he had mastered the language. He would like to hear much more about the T'lin man who had brought her to Sussland and had been Creighton's friend also—and especially so when Dolm confirmed that the man had managed to escape. He was an itinerant horse trader, although Edward had seen no horses so far.

But why was the Service so much less conspicuous than the Chamber? Why were enemies so much easier to find than friends? The goddess who had imprisoned Eleal in Narsh was an obvious Horror. Her ritual prostitution sounded exactly like Herodotus's tales of the temple of Aphrodite in Babylon that always so intrigued the Greek scholars of Fifth Form. Zath was another, with his reapers. Was Tion with them or against them? Was he with the Service or against it?

Tion was too much of a risk. The T'lin man had been a friend of Creighton's and was a much safer bet. He must find T'lin. Only if that proved impossible would he risk Tion.

The entrance to the temple precincts was a resplendent arch, ornamented with much gold and many symbols of the god: roses and triangles and animals that looked like frogs. A few worshipers were coming and going, ignored by half a dozen pike-bearing guards, who caught Edward's attention more than anything else did. A squad of fifty or so was being drilled in the distance. Their armor looked like solid gold but obviously couldn't be, or the poor beggars would collapse in heaps. Why should a god need such a force? To stop tourists writing on the pillars? Or just because they looked good standing there? As far as he could judge without going close, they were all at least as tall as he was and very well turned out—the Coldstream Guards of Nextdoor. Were they only for show, or were they an elite force? Smart troops were effective troops. None showed that better than the British Army.

Dolm hesitated, but it was not the guards that deterred him. This was where his pilgrimage must begin. "I'll walk a little farther with you," he muttered. "I think I can find the troupe for you." It was a reasonable excuse to put off the awful moment. The three of them carried on toward the city.

Suss occupied a salient of high ground protected on three sides by cliffs. It was no more than a small town by Edward's standards, and the sight of its walls was a shock, a reminder that he was living in a primitive world. He might have to acquire a sword! He had fenced during his stay in Heidelberg, but not enough to qualify as a swordsman.

As it neared the city gates, the road crossed a series of arched bridges spanning small tributary canyons. On one of these Dolm stopped and peered over the rail. He unslung his pack.

"Yes," he said. "Right first time. Down there. Rehearsing."

The valley below was wooded, but there was a clearing below the bridge; there two men and a woman were apparently having an argument. Other people lounged around in the shade, watching. Voices drifted up unintelligibly. The grouping was staged and unnatural.

Dolm groaned. "By the moons! They've taken on that idiot Tothroom Player!" He mumbled something about women and fighting.

Eleal was jumping up and down and clapping her hands. "Come on!" she said urgently.

"You go," Dolm said. "I will go back now."

"Come, D'ward!" she commanded.

"You'd better not tell them who he is," Dolm said.

That was hardly fair play! "Tell!" Edward said. He tapped his chest. "Danger to them? Tell them."

Eleal hesitated, looking from one to the other.

"Yes, perhaps you had better warn them," Dolm said, giving Edward an odd look.

Then he sighed and went down on his knees to her. "Eleal Singer, I want you to know that I am deeply sorry for what happened. I frightened you terribly and I intended to kill you. I do not ask you to forgive me, because I can never forgive myself, but if you could give me your blessing for the future, it would make me very happy, and very grateful."

Eleal was momentarily at a loss. Then she raised her chin. "Of course I forgive you, Dolm Actor!" she proclaimed magnanimously. "I pray that Holy Tion will protect you and that you will find peace." She hugged Dolm and kissed his cheek. Then she glanced sidelong at Edward to see if he had appreciated her performance.

"Thank you!" Dolm said, and his gratitude seemed genuine.

"Come, D'ward!" she repeated.

"You go," Edward said. "Warn them. I am following."

She pouted at him suspiciously.

"I must change into that pilgrim robe you made, which will always remind me of you," Dolm said. "Then I will give D'ward my pack. He will come."

Edward nodded his agreement. Reassured, Eleal went skipping off to the end of the bridge, and disappeared down a steep path.

The two men looked at each other.

"Tell me," Edward said.

Dolm shuddered and shook his head. "Never!" He unfastened his pack and pulled out the smock with the pentacle on it. Then he stood up and looked apprehensively at Edward.

"Tell me!" Edward repeated. "Tell of Zath. I need to know."

"Need?"

"Need! Am the Liberator."

Frowning, the actor leaned his lanky frame on the rail and stared down at his former friends far below.

"I did a terrible thing," he said quietly. "I hurt a woman, hurt her badly. I was an animal. I was drunk." He mimed drinking and touched his groin. "Understand? Next day I learned that she was likely to die. I went to the temple of Zath and prayed that he would take my life and spare the woman—that I would die, she would not die." He acted it out, pausing frequently to be sure that the stranger understood. "A priest said I must go to her and touch her, lay my hand on her, like this. It was dark, nighttime. Doors opened for me. Bolts slid. No one saw me. She was asleep, or unconscious. I touched her."

He shivered, staring out over the rail.

"She died at once. I felt great pleasure, a rush of joy. Perhaps you don't know yet what it is like to lie with a woman, or perhaps you do, but it was like that, only much more. Much more! I went back to the temple and was initiated. I became a reaper. At night the lust would come upon me. Not every night, but often. I would go out and walk the streets or enter into houses, and I would gather souls for Zath. They died in silence, but in fearful agony. They knew. They died terribly and I felt rapture."

He was weeping, his gaunt cheeks shining wet.

"Always I would feel that joy," he said, his voice breaking. "Especially if they were young and strong. Many, many of them."

Blood was pretty high on the list, Creighton had said. What could be higher than human sacrifice?

"Not you doing this," Edward said awkwardly. How could anyone console a man who bore such a burden? "The god was doing it, not you."

"But it was my crime that led me to him."

"Sister Ahn kill your, er . . ."

"Guilt? Sister Ahn took away my guilt?"

"Thank you. Sister Ahn took away your guilt."

"Yes. And gave me repentance instead. I was happy in my evil. Now I can never be happy again. I think I will kill myself."

"No. Sister Ahn died. You die also, her dying is no thing."

Dolm turned his head to stare at Edward with red-rimmed eyes. "She died for me!"

"You die also, then Zath wins!" How, Edward wondered, had he ever gotten himself into this? He was not qualified to be a spiritual advisor. He was a sanctimonious school prefect lecturing a mass murderer. Holy Roly would be proud of him. He barely knew enough of the language to ask for a drink of water, let alone argue ethics. But he could not stop now.

"Sister Ahn gave you back your life. You must take it. You must use it. Do good!"

"Maybe when I have been a pilgrim and made the Holy Circuit."

Edward thought about that. "No. Pilgrim is running away."

"What else can I do?" Dolm said angrily. "I can't act anymore!"

Their eyes locked.

This was Graybeard again, and the soldier at the bridge. This was Dusty Miller of the Lower Fourth, who'd broken an ankle playing rugby and been terrified to put on his studs after that. This was the First Eleven after they'd lost three in a row and were going up against the top of the league. But Edward did not have the words he had used on those occasions. All he had was baby talk. "Yes you *can*, Dolm. You *can* act. You *can* remember lines. You *can* move without tripping. Acting not changed. Nothing has changed."

He saw the resistance. He felt himself failing. He reached out and gripped Dolm's shoulders with both hands.

"You *can!*" he said. "I say you can!"

Dolm's eyes widened. Edward saw doubt rooting and pressed harder, using every scrap of conviction he could muster. "You can! *I* say you can. Trust me. I am D'ward Liberator! *Trust me!*"

Without warning, the actor screamed. He pushed Edward away and turned, doubling over the rail, racked by sobs. Edward staggered back, appalled at what he had done. The bridge seemed to sway under his feet. A terrible weariness came crashing down on him.

Dolm was weeping helplessly, hysterically, like a child,

pounding his fists on the balustrade. He sounded as if he were choking to death.

Edward could find no more words. *I had no right to torture the poor man, so! I should have left him to do what he wanted to do and suffer as he wanted to suffer.*

Angrily he limped away. He did not try to take the pack, because he did not think he could lift it. He was only two days off his sickbed and he must have walked fifty miles. He was crushed by exhaustion. He had blisters all over his feet and his teeth hurt.

There were too many people. He reeled down the path on jellied legs, stumbling with weakness and hanging on to trees, and when at last he had descended to the valley floor and found the clearing, there were just too many people. A dozen or more of them were clustered around Eleal's tiny form. They were enjoying collective hysterics.

They had not known. Dolm had not been able to tell them that Eleal had escaped from Narsh, because he dared not reveal how he knew. Now, suddenly, she had come skipping out of the bushes to join them. She was the center of attention and loving it—hugging and kissing and telling her adventures all at the same time. They must know of the *Testament* with its mention of Eleal and the Liberator, because all Suss had been talking of it. Their god had worked a miracle for them. Their baby was back. Everyone was talking at once, men swearing oaths, women weeping. High drama!

Were actors as superstitious on Nextdoor as they were reputed to be on Earth? She was their mascot, Edward thought, watching the reunion. They must see that! Their little crippled mascot had returned to them and now their luck would change. Or would it? The Tion presence in the temple must know of him, or would surely learn shortly. Zath's reapers might be watching the troupe. The Liberator could bring only trouble to these humble players. He must leave now, at once, before they saw him. Too many people!

Perhaps Dolm would have left the backpack on the bridge.

With that, and the smattering of language he had attained, Edward could survive on his own somehow—couldn't he? It was the thought of trying to climb that hill again so soon that delayed him. Then someone saw him.

Screaming with excitement, Eleal came skipping choppily over the grass to him, the whole troupe running in pursuit. Too many people. He staggered back a few paces and leaned against a tree for support.

He soon identified the leaders. The figurehead was the middle-aged giant with the silvery mane, Trong Impresario. He declaimed in a voice like distant gunfire. He rumbled platitudes and struck dramatic poses. The real power was his wife, Ambria, a woman taller than Edward, with steel in her eyes and a tongue like a lash. She was all bone and angles, and yet strangely reminiscent of the irrepressible Mrs. Bodgley of Greyfriars Abbey. The brains of the group might well be that little man with the stubbly white beard. Names, names, and more names . . . Good-looking men, handsome women, all putting on airs. Handshakes and thumps on the back and effusive gratitude for restoring their darling . . .

And then came reaction and withdrawal as they realized that this youth meant more trouble in their lives, not less. He was involved with the gods in ways they did not understand and were not likely to approve if they did. He could not give a straight answer or frame a grammatical sentence. He would be one more mouth to feed and could give nothing in return.

Excitement faded into a murk of uneasiness. The group began to break up and drift away in twos and threes to whisper.

The big Ambria woman said something to her husband. At once he began shouting orders for the rehearsal to continue. Edward sank down on a tussock and put his head in his hands. He should curl up and have a sleep—perhaps they would just take the chance to creep away and leave him.

"Hungry? Thirsty?" asked a voice. A woman was kneeling at his side. She was offering a clay flask and a slab of bread and cheese.

She was the sort of girl that turned a boy's thoughts to desert islands built for two, and her smock would have barely made one good dish towel. Edward was not accustomed to seeing so much beautiful skin—he felt daring when he caught a glimpse of Alice's calves. He knew his face was turning redder than that wilted blossom in her hair. He nodded dumbly several times before he found his voice.

"Thank you. Yes. Um, query name."

She smiled in vision of pearls. "Uthiam. Thanks to you for bringing Eleal back to us."

"Er, Eleal me brought! I fear I bring trouble."

She laughed joyfully. "Eleal is always trouble!"

And he laughed also, and thought that maybe things might be going to turn out not quite so bad as he had feared.

Possibly the food revived him. He sat by himself, staying out of sight and mind, and he watched the troupe's activities with growing interest. Some of the younger folk were engaged in juggling and acrobatics, but they seemed more interested in exercise and enjoyment than in polishing their skills. The main event was a rehearsal of a drama, and everyone was intent on that.

Trong portrayed Grastag King, a tragic, aging figure facing a young challenger. The gallant hero, Darthon Warrior, was being played by Tothroom, replacement for the failed Dolm. The newcomer clutched a script, to which he had to make frequent reference. This might be his first attempt at the role. Even allowing for such handicaps, his performance was insipid. Grastag had stolen his wife, but Tothroom was playing the role as though he had lost a hairbrush.

At first the ornate, high-flown poetry was quite beyond Edward's comprehension. By the fifth or sixth repetition it began to fit together. Like Shakespeare's, the words had a music that soared beyond literary sense, so that meanings missed here and there were of no importance. At times Trong's delivery soared close to opera, where meaning did not matter at all, only emotion. Tothroom mumbled and stuttered and barely seemed to understand his lines himself. Over and over the two men performed the same scene until Trong would roar, "Cut!" and begin bawling instructions. Then he would take it all from the beginning again.

The problem was mostly Tothroom. He was a sallow, pinch-faced man, sadly lacking in stage presence. The plot required him to accost Grastag at his prayers. At first Grastag would respond with contempt and indignation, but then Darthon was supposed to take over the scene, to overwhelm the older man with vituperation and a catalogue of his crimes, to achieve dominance, to grind him into repentance and despair. It was not happening that way, because Tothroom was simply no match for Trong. He was a sheep trying to cow a lion. Trong was at fault also, for he did not seem able to bridle his own flamboyance. He would not lie down unless he was bludgeoned into submission.

And whenever the action was broken off, he would scream more insults than instructions. Instead of encouraging his new recruit, he was browbeating him and threatening. Some team captain he was!

Thinking of the Sixth Form's *Henry V,* Edward began to reflect that even he might have more dramatic talent than this inept Tothroom—and at least he would understand that Trong's ranting should be ignored. He glanced around the clearing. The melancholy expressions on all the other faces suggested that Tothroom was not going to survive the day as a member of the troupe. It was quite clear why Dolm Actor, in his guilt and anguish, had been unable to portray the arrogant swashbuckling Darthon Warrior. Given Hamlet to play in his present mood, he would have dampened every eye in Sussland.

"You foulness clad in kingly," Darthon said mildly. "Raiment. Earth's bowels have never issued forth," he remarked, "more loathsome leech to suck"—he fumbled with the script and then found the place—"to suck the merit. From the people and," he continued apologetically, "warp their aspirations like, er, your own, too. Baseness?"

Trong bellowed, "Cut!" and loosed another torrent of abuse that Edward was glad not to understand.

Eleal bounced down to sit beside him. She was still flushed with excitement at being reunited with her family.

Trong, she said proudly, was her something.

"Query," Edward sighed.

"Father of mother."

"Ah. I see the likeness."

She giggled with delight, then frowned severely. "Darthon Warrior is not good!"

"No."

"Sh! They're starting again!"

"Insolent spawn of lowborn vermin!" Trong declaimed, giving the cue.

"You foulness clad in kingly raiment!" roared a new voice from the trees. Tothroom jumped and dropped his script. *"Earth's bowels,"* Dolm bellowed, striding out, brandishing a stick with such menace that it seemed to reflect the sun, *"have never issued forth more loathsome leech to suck the merit from the people and warp their aspirations, like your own, to baseness."*

The troupe was on its feet. Tothroom's jaw hung slackly.

"Say you so?" Trong fell back a pace, hands raised to ward off this attack. "Easier 'tis for whippersnapper to crack the air with words and slight his betters than man to balance judgment and uphold the laws with deeds."

"Uphold the laws?" Dolm stormed, advancing on him and leaving his unfortunate replacement completely out of the scene. A barrage of words exploded from the newcomer, an avalanche of scorn fell on Trong. Carillons of poetry soared far beyond Edward's comprehension, but the sense was obvious. Grastag King defied, argued, pleaded, and finally cringed, while Darthon Warrior thundered over him like a volcano.

The scene ended when Trong fled howling into the bushes. For a moment the grove was silent.

"Oh, that was much better!" Eleal remarked judiciously as the riot of welcome converged on Dolm. She turned to Edward with a puzzled frown. "He was never that good before. What did you do to him?"

"I just—"

No! No! No! Everything clicked into place and Edward could only stare at Eleal in horror.

⧫ 54 ⧫

NOW THERE WAS NO QUESTION OF THE TROUPE REJECT-ing Edward, for Dolm was restored to form and favor, and he was a strong Edward supporter. In fact no one gave a thought to the newcomer for the rest of the day except Eleal, who kept him advised of what was happening.

The incompetent Tothroom having been sent packing, performances could begin as soon as arrangements were made. The big amphitheater at the temple was still being used by the Golden Book Players, who had won that year's rose—a very inferior troupe, Eleal insisted—but the town had a smaller one just outside the walls. By nightfall, she was coaching Edward in the art of coloring placards, lettered in the strange Greek-style script. He shared his new friends' meager meal; he slept in a borrowed blanket in the shed they had rented. It was normally used to store some sort of root crop and had a strong smell of ginger. As a dorm for fourteen people it was embarrassingly intimate, but he had been accepted as one of the band, at least for the time being.

The next day he walked the streets of Suss carrying sandwich boards. He was still shaky and footsore, but the job was within his capabilities; Dr. Gibbs had stoutly maintained that the chief benefits of a classical education were versatility and adaptability. Edward found himself in trouble only once, when a visiting merchant asked him for directions to Boogiil Wheelwright's.

Suss was tightly cramped within its walls, yet prosperous. The walls themselves suggested that artillery was still unknown in the Vales, but he noted promising signs of technology. A few people wore spectacles. Stores sold printed books and musical instruments and tailored clothes, while food stalls offered a wide variety of crops. He saw very few beggars. The sewer system was underground and drinking water was piped to communal outlets. He had seen many towns on Earth less favored. He could still hold out hopes that Nextdoor had a London or a Paris somewhere.

That evening he peeled yamlike tubers for the cooks, fetched firewood, washed clothes, and helped to lay out the evening meal. The fare was sparse, but tomorrow should bring better fortune. The day's rehearsals had gone well. Old friends in Suss had promised to attend the opening night.

That evening, sprawled on the grass outside their hut, the players for the first time had leisure to discuss their new recruit. Understandably, they wanted to know just who he was and where he had come from and what he was planning to do. He explained as well as he could that he was a visitor from a very far country and did not know why the gods had brought him to Sussland. He would eagerly help in any way he could in return for his daily bread and a roof over his head. Eleal's tale was being regarded with justifiable incredulity, but Dolm vouched for him. The discussion went on a long time as those voluble, arty people passed a rare free evening doing what they enjoyed doing most—talking.

In the end the decision was made by the formidable Ambria. Edward would not be discussed outside the group, she decreed. The name "Liberator" would not be mentioned. He would be a traveling scholar from Nosokland, which was sufficiently distant that no one would question his mangled grammar and peculiar accent. "Choose a name!" she commanded.

Edward shrugged.

"D'ward's a *nice* name!" Eleal said. Everyone laughed.

It was certainly not uncommon, Piol remarked, being the name of a minor Tion avatar, god of heralds and envoys.

"Then D'ward Scholar he shall be!" Ambria decreed. Talk turned to other topics.

Probably only Edward knew how she came by her infallibility, for he had been trained in leadership. He had watched her read the group's wishes and put them into words, sensing where her followers wished to go before they themselves knew. Then she had led them there. She displayed no doubts. A man could learn from her.

Thus D'ward Scholar became one of the Trong Troupe.

He, in turn, accepted them. They were a strange group, but they had many admirable qualities. They were devoted to their art, cheerfully enduring poverty and hardship for its sake. They had a strong mutual affection and they rarely bickered. They knew one another's strengths and weaknesses, and worked within them. Politics and commerce they ignored, their religion was simple, their god benevolent. A world of such people would not be a bad place.

The following morning he again walked the streets with his placards, and he chose some odd parts of the city in which to advertise drama. He had observed waterwheels outside the walls, but the factories were not mechanized. Nevertheless they were true factories, employing dozens of people, with clear divisions of labor. He discovered something that he thought was a small blast furnace, although it was not in use. He saw both coal and coke. This was a culture waiting for an industrial revolution.

In the afternoon he went with Dolm Actor to purchase firewood, which was apparently an artistic necessity. Suss was one of the better towns of the Vales, Dolm said—proud to be the home of a major god and anxious to live up to his standards. Its citizens were devoted to freedom and democracy, which often meant social chaos. New laws must be approved by an assembly of all the citizens, leading to riot, destruction of property, and even deaths, but such mishaps were regarded as the price of liberty. In their own eyes Sussians were a sturdy, self-reliant people; their neighbors thought they were crazy anarchists. Of course, Dolm explained with a chuckle, Joalvale lay over the next pass and in reality Sussia was part of Joaldom. Edward decided that further understanding must await mastery of the language.

That afternoon he joined the whole troupe in a late lunch, another skimpy repast of fruit and vegetables. The first performance of the *Varilian* in Suss would begin just before sundown, and everyone was in a state of nerves. Again they had gathered on the grass outside the shed. The shade was welcome, the sun ferocious. Insects buzzed around the sweaty people, biting painfully whenever they had the chance. Tempers were touchy. It was no secret that the finances were exhausted. Only a favorable reception of the play lay between the band and disaster.

Edward was just as edgy as they were. His feet and legs ached and his sore tooth was hammering a red-hot chisel into his jaw. He feared he had another attack of diarrhea pending, when he had not properly recovered from the last one. An able-bodied scrounger might be acceptable if he were willing to help, but he could not expect the troupe to care for a useless invalid. He knew that the unfamiliar diseases of this world might kill him sooner rather than later.

Conversation turned to the evening's proceedings, with Ambria distributing responsibilities.

"And what will D'ward do?" asked Klip Trumpeter, a pimply adolescent. More than anyone else, he seemed to resent the freeloader—possibly because his own value to the troupe was questionable at best.

"D'ward will help pass the hat," Dolm said, dark eyes gleaming with amusement. "I think he will do very well at that."

"He will collect gold!" Eleal proclaimed. Everyone ignored that absurdity and went on with their various discussions.

Edward was sitting across from the charming Uthiam, not entirely by accident. She was married, but he enjoyed looking at her. "Tell me, please," he said. "Query . . . T'lin?"

She looked surprised, doing lovely things with her eyebrows. "T'lin Dragontrader? Eleal's friend?"

He had learned now that names were trades. What exactly this T'lin traded in, he was uncertain, except that it was something to ride on. He nodded.

She shrugged. "He comes and goes. A bit of a rascal, I think, but he seems fond of Eleal. If you believe her story, he helped rescue her from the temple in Suss. We run into him two or three times a year."

He got all that on the first try, except for the last bit, which he asked her to repeat. Two or three times a year? How long was a year? Could he bear to wait that long, or must he risk appealing to Tion?

Uthiam said, "Why do you want T'lin Dragontrader, or is that a rude question?"

"I think he may be able to help me."

She gave him a thousand-ship smile. "He must know the Vales as well as anyone. Stay with us and you'll meet him sooner or later."

"You're all very kind. I wish I could be more useful."

"You are useful! Have you ever done any acting?"

One schoolboy production? "A little."

Heads turned.

"Would you care to say a few words?" asked Piol Poet. The little man was genuinely interested, his eyes bright. He wrote the plays; he was the scholar, a likable old gentleman.

"You would not understand them, sir."

"But we may see if you have talent!"

Only if they had very sharp eyes, Edward thought. But a good laugh would help cheer them up and could not hurt him. He finished chewing a mouthful of the carroty root with the ginger flavor. "All right." He rose to his feet. If he were being honest with himself, he would admit that what he really had in mind was a test of some of his wild-eyed theories.

Other quiet conversations ceased. More heads turned to watch him. Reviewing his very limited repertoire, he chose the Agincourt speech.

"I'll give you a speech by a warrior named . . . " *Henry* would sound female to them. "Kingharry. His men must fight many more men." He struggled to put his thoughts into words. "He begins with scorn for those who want to leave. He says that they can go if they want to. He has too many . . . no . . . he has *enough* men that their deaths will hurt their land if they lose, understand? And then he tells of the glory that will be theirs if they win against such great odds."

"Sounds like Kaputeez Battlemaster's speech in the *Hiloma*," Trong pontificated.

Edward left the shade, out into the scorching sunlight. He detoured by a stack of properties to arm himself with a wooden sword, then took up his stance before a group of shrubs, his knees starting to quiver with stage fright. He must just hope that Shakespeare would sound as impressive to them as Piol's poetry did to him. He was going to perform in a foreign language before an audience of professionals? He was crazy! He reviewed the opening lines, wiped sweat from his forehead. *Idiot show-off!* Then he turned to face the watchers under the trees, the eyes, the expectant silence. He noticed the secret smiles. He took a deep breath. Mr. Butterfield, the English master, had always told him to speak to a deaf old lady in the back row. He spoke to Piol Poet, who was slightly deaf and well to the rear.

"What's he that wishes so?" he said sharply. *"My cousin Westmoreland? No, my fair cousin: If we are marked to die, we are enow to do our country loss."*

He saw the frowns, the shock as they realized that this was a language like none they had ever heard before.

"I am not covetous for gold . . ."

He began to raise his voice. He had caught the poet's interest already—Piol's eyes were wide.

"We would not die in that man's company that fears his fellowship to die with us! This day is called the feast of Crispin . . ."

Dolm was smiling. Eleal was agog. Trong, old ham, was frowning. But he had them! It was working! Creighton had known.

"Then shall our names, familiar in his mouth as household words,

Harry the King, Bedford and Exeter, Warwick and Talbot . . ."

The excitement was rising. He could feel their empathy, their professional response. Not his minuscule talent, not the roll of the bard's poetry, not challenge and bluster—no, there was other magic at work here. Fallow would have laughed him to shreds had he blustered like this, but ham was what the troupe enjoyed, so he gave them ham. He postured and flailed and roared the deathless words.

"And Crispin Crispian shall ne'er go by,
From this day to the ending of the world,
But we in it shall be rememberèd:
We few, we happy few, we band of brothers—"

The troupe was totally caught up in the bravado, and so was he. He stalked the field of Agincourt before them, a juvenile warlord reviling the potent French multitude, defying death in the name of fame. He was one with his audience. The troupe's joy flowed out to him, he ate it up and sent it back to them in glory.

"And gentlemen in England now abed
Shall think themselves accursed they were not here,
And hold their manhood cheap while any speaks
That fought with us upon Saint Crispin's Day!"

He waited, puzzled that no one had picked up the cue. The greatest inspirational English ever penned faded away into the alien trees. Suddenly he was back in the dusty orchard before the ramshackle hut, and the troupe was on its feet, cheering and applauding and screaming for more.

Laughing with relief, he bowed in acknowledgment.

His gut had stopped hurting and so had his tooth. He felt tremendous.

Creighton had called it *charisma.*

Generals, politicians, prophets, and sometimes actors.

∼ 55 ∼

ELEAL HAD KNOWN ALL ALONG THAT D'WARD WOULD BE
a wonderful actor, and she was delighted by the family's reaction
to his performance. As soon as she saw Trong going off by
himself, she ran over to him and said, "Grandfather?"

The big man jumped and looked at her as if he had never
seen her before. Then he went down on one knee and—much
to her astonishment—hugged her tightly. His beard tickled. She
noticed how rough and coarse his face was, scarred by years of
makeup.

"Darling Granddaughter! I missed you! It is wonderful to
have you safely restored to us."

Well! He might have said so two days ago!

"I missed you, too. And one day you must tell me all about
my mother."

He turned his face away, registering extreme pain. "It is a
tragic tale, child."

"I expect it is, but we don't have time for it now. I have a
suggestion."

"Indeed?" His astonishment seemed somewhat excessive.

"Indeed!" Eleal said. "I think D'ward would be much better
as Tion in the *Trastos* than Golfren Piper is."

She had feared he would dismiss the idea out of hand, but
the old man considered it seriously. "He has a very strange accent, Eleal."

"But Tion has very few lines to say, and I know D'ward could
learn to say those clearly. Besides, would it even matter? Do you

think the audience would notice? He would be so convincing!"

Trong smiled, which he rarely did. In fact she could not recall him ever actually smiling at her before. "Perhaps he would! But it would hardly be fair to Golfren."

"If he didn't mind, would you?"

"Well, I don't know. Tion is usually shown with fair hair, and D'ward is dark. And the Youth never wears more than a loincloth. D'ward may have a very hairy chest, and that would not look right."

"He can use a wig and he doesn't have any hairs on his chest." He did have marvelous eyelashes, though.

Trong flinched. "Oh. Well, I will think about it."

"Thank you, Grandfather!" Eleal said, and kissed him. He was still kneeling, staring after her, as she skipped away.

She had thought that the priests of Ois had stolen her pack, but apparently Ambria had saved it. So she had its familiar weight on her shoulders as the troupe set out for the amphitheater. She had a proper built-up boot again, too, which made walking much easier. She sidled next to Golfren, and waited until she had him to herself.

"Golfren?"

"Eleal? Up to your tricks again?"

"Certainly not. I mean, what tricks? I just wanted to ask your opinion of something."

He smiled down at her, eyes twinkling. Golfren had nice eyes, but they were not nearly as bright a blue as D'ward's. D'ward was altogether more handsome.

"I smell trouble. Ask away."

"Don't you think it would be nice," Eleal said carefully, "if we could give D'ward a small part in one of the plays? So as he could feel like one of the group?"

Golfren cleared his throat. "Well, that depends. What part did you have in mind?"

"Oh, I was thinking he would make a very good Tion, in the right sort of play."

"You were, were you? Well I think he might—in the right sort of play."

"I knew you would agree with me," Eleal said.

Piol was talking with D'ward all the way, and Eleal did not get a chance to talk with him until after they had arrived at the amphitheater. She changed quickly into her herald costume. As this was not Narsh, she did not need extra clothes to keep warm. She went in search of Piol, and found him in the middle of a circle of props, spread out on the grass.

"Piol Poet?"

"Yes?" he muttered abstractly. The trouble with Piol was that he so often had his mind on other things.

"Don't you think D'ward is a wonderful actor?"

Scratching his stubbly beard, the little man said, "Mm?" and then, "Hmm? Yes, I do." He glanced at his list and then peered all around.

"Good! Don't you think it would be advisable to give him a small part in one of the plays?"

"Mmm? But which part?"

"I think he would make a great Tion in the *Trastos!* Golfren thinks so too, and Trong agrees."

"Can you see Karzon's sword anywhere?"

Eleal sighed and picked up the sword, which was lying right by her feet. She poked at Piol's tummy with it. "Why not let D'ward play Tion when we do the *Trastos?*"

Piol spoke to his list. "What? Who? But Tion has to play his pipes!"

Sussians preferred plays that made Tion seem like the most important god in the Pentatheon, of course, but this year Piol had ignored tradition, as he so often did. He had written Tion's part for Golfren. Golfren looked splendid in a skimpy loincloth, but he couldn't act. So Tion mostly just stood by while the other gods argued. D'ward could do that just as well as Golfren, even if he didn't have golden curls!

At the end, when the doomed Trastos Tyrant fell into despair and called on Tion to help him—when the audience would be expecting Tion to make a big speech—Golfren came in and played his pipes instead. It was a big surprise. It had gone over well in Mapvale, fairly well in Lappinvale. What Narshians thought didn't matter.

"No he doesn't!" Eleal said crossly. "You just wrote it that way because you don't trust Golfren not to butcher his lines!"

"We can talk about it some other time. Take this flask over to the spring and fill it, will you? And stop threatening me with that sword!"

"No, listen!" Eleal poked him again. "Tion inspires Trastos with courage to go and fight even though he knows he's doomed. Of *course* you could give Tion more lines to speak instead of the silly piping, so the audience would know what it meant. A rousing speech like the one D'ward did tonight, but in Joalian, of course, and why are you laughing?"

"Me, laughing? I wasn't laughing! I was thinking about the soldier in the *Varilian.*"

That was Golfren Piper's other role, and he was just terrible in it.

"What of it?" she demanded warily.

"We could turn him into a general."

"D'ward could do that very well, too," she said. "But we can't change the *Varilian* now, in the middle of a run. And it really wouldn't be fair to steal all Golfren's parts. No, I think D'ward should play Tion in the *Trastos.*"

"I'll think about it." Piol knelt down to look in the makeup box. "Golfren might not mind losing his lines, but he loves to play his pipes. Fetch that water."

Fortunately Eleal had a spare string for her lute. "This is a tragedy we're talking about, not a masque! Now admit it—the only reason you have Tion play his pipes to encourage the tyrant is that Golfren can't act. Well, why not have Tion play his pipes to summon Gunuu?"

Piol finished counting greasepaint and closed the box. He reached for a pile of . . . He looked up. "Who?"

"Gunuu, god of courage," Eleal said airily. "An avatar of the Youth, of course. He's not very well known hereabouts, I admit, because his temple's down in Rinooland or somewhere, and there are some arguments about where he fits in the Pentatheon." She had accosted a pair of priestesses in the street that morning and asked them all about courage and who was god of courage, and she must know a lot more about Gunuu at the moment than Piol Poet did.

"What sort of arguments?" Piol was interested now.

"Oh, one school of thought considers him an aspect of Astina, as she is goddess of warriors. But no one will argue that in Suss. So Tion pipes and Gunuu comes on stage and speaks! A god can summon one of his own avatars, can't he?"

Piol stared at her as if she was crazy. "I never heard . . . Visek preserve me! Side by side?"

"Why not?" Eleal laid down the sword. "I think D'ward would make an ideal god of courage, don't you? He's a born actor!"

"And you're a born playwright!" The old man was staring blankly into space already. Recognizing the signs of genius at work, she crept quietly away to let him concentrate. She was glad to have that settled! Not that she'd been in any doubt how the conversation would turn out. It was written in the prophecy: *D'ward shall become Tion, D'ward shall become Courage.*

The amphitheater was a natural hollow on the cliff edge outside the walls. It was not as large as the one at the temple, but Eleal thought it had better acoustics, and there were two shacks in the bushes for the cast dressing rooms. The arena at the temple had only one dressing room.

Members of the troupe moved around with the money bowls as the audience trickled down the path. Later she overheard Gartol Costumer wondering how D'ward had managed to collect twice as much as he had. The play began at sunset, with Klip blowing a fanfare on his trumpet. The first act was played in twilight. The bonfires were lit during the intermission and again players went around with the bowls. This time everyone was interested to know how the play was being received, and again D'ward had collected the most.

In the second act Eleal made her entrance as the herald and said her line. She had played in Suss for the first time in her life! As she walked off into the shadows, wielding her staff so her limp would not show, someone began to clap, and then the whole audience followed, and that really did sound like the biggest applause of the evening. She had a strong suspicion that it had been D'ward who had begun that clapping, but she couldn't be sure, and of course she was too proud to ask.

At the end, as the audience trooped out under the moons, the actors offered the bowls again, and then some people did put real gold in D'ward's, exactly as Eleal Singer had predicted. He had not even had a part in the play, but he had such a nice smile!

56

THE NEXT DAY THE TROUPE MOVED TO MORE RESPECTA-
ble quarters and the meals improved considerably.

Before that, though, Ambria announced that she was going to the temple. Her expression suggested that everyone ought to go to the temple. There were a few grumbles, but most people nodded to show they thought this was a good idea. Eleal knew that she should go, to thank Tion for returning her safely to her family, certainly D'ward should. Obviously he did not want to.

"I shall not," he said firmly. "And I should be very grateful if you would not mention the Liberator in your prayers. Do you need someone to stay behind and look after your baggage?"

Ambria disapproved, but she could hardly force him to go to the temple against his will, and even she was not proof against his smile. Piol announced that he had some work to do, so he would stay behind also. Everyone else went.

Nothing special happened. Eleal thanked the god for rescuing her from Narsh, and from the reapers, and restoring her to her family. She did not mention D'ward, although it was very hard not to think about him while she was praying. And nothing special happened! She limped when she departed just as much as she had limped when she arrived. Perhaps she was being presumptuous in hoping that her efforts would be rewarded with a miracle—or had she not finished her task? She had not actually brought D'ward to Tion's temple.

Later the troupe moved into the Suss hostelry, which was a very good one. Piol Poet disappeared. Eleal found him in the attic, writing busily. She was confident then that he was working on a new speech for the *Tragedy of Trastos*. She left him alone and later, when Halma was looking for him, she said he had gone to the market.

It was wonderful to be back with her family again. They all told her how much they had missed her; she thought they appreciated her more now. Perhaps she even appreciated them more. That very afternoon, to her complete astonishment, Trong took her aside and sat her down and told her all about her mother, Itheria Impresario. It was a very sad story, and they were both weeping before it was finished.

An hour later, when Eleal was helping Ambria hang out washing, the big woman said, "Did Trong speak to you?"

Eleal nodded. She should have guessed whose idea that had been.

"Don't be too hard on him," the big woman said gruffly, standing on tiptoe to peg things on the highest rope. "He has never forgiven himself for letting you fall out the window when he was supposed to be looking after you."

"What has that to do with my mother?"

"Well, nothing, I suppose. He shouldn't have made us keep that a secret from you. It is still very difficult for him to talk about."

"But," Eleal said loyally, feeling her eyelids start to prickle all

over again, "if it was a god who, er, I mean . . . Well, if she fell
in love with a god, then that really wasn't her fault, was it?"

"You mean it was the god's fault?"

Um! "Well, yes. It must have been."

"That's what Trong finds so hard to talk about. Be careful
with that blouse, now!"

D'ward was becoming quite fluent in Joalian and everyone was
very careful to speak clearly and correctly around him, so he
would not pick up the terrible local growl. He asked Eleal to
give him reading lessons, too, and of course she graciously con-
sented to set aside some time for this. He wanted to find a copy
of the *Filoby Testament* and practice on that, but she explained
that it was written in Sussian, and would be bad for him.

"How about some of Piol's plays, then?" he asked.

"No!" she said firmly. "They're in *classical* Joalian. If you try
speaking that in the streets people will think you are very odd."

He smiled. "That speech I recited from *Kingharry* was like
that."

So they went with Uthiam to a secondhand bookstore. Eleal
picked out a famous romance, but D'ward refused it and instead
chose an *exceedingly* dull book about the moons and stars. Teaching him to read with that awful thing was not nearly as much
fun as she had expected. He seemed amazed to learn that Trumb
went through his phases in only four and a half days, making
solemn-faced jokes that Trumb wasn't really a big moon,
therefore, only close to the Earth. He was even surprised to learn
that the fortnight came from Ysh, who took exactly fourteen
days to go from eclipse to eclipse. He spent *hours* studying Kirb'l
and became almost surly in consequence. He claimed he had
not known that there were three hundred sixty-four days in a
year! At times, the Liberator was definitely *strange.*

She was not the only one to have noted his smile. Olimmiar
Dancer was making a perfect fool of herself, following him
around like a lapcat and blushing every time he looked at her,
until Eleal wanted to scream. The married women were almost
as bad. If their husbands noticed, they did not comment. Every-

body knew that D'ward was an honorable man.

Piol produced his ode to courage and Trong started rehearsing the *Trastos,* although the *Varilian* was still drawing full houses every night.

Eleal sat down with D'ward to help him learn his speech. He had trouble working out exactly what it said, of course, and then he seemed very unhappy with it.

"It's all, er—what do you call a thing that says something everybody knows already?"

Eleal wasn't sure, so they called over Golfren, who said the word was "platitude."

"This is all platitudes!" D'ward announced.

Golfren read over the speech. "Yes, it is. But isn't most poetry like that? It isn't what it says that matters, it's the way it says it."

D'ward pondered, then laughed and agreed.

He was absolutely horrified when Gartol Costumer produced his costume.

"You mean I have to go out in front of hundreds of people wearing only *that?* But there will be ladies present!"

"It's traditional," the old man said, "and the ladies will love it."

D'ward looked very shocked and turned red.

He was interested in all sorts of things—politics and customs and geography and business. Especially, though, he was interested in the gods. One day Eleal actually overheard him ask Trong which were the good gods and which were the bad gods.

Trong, of course, was horrified. "The gods are good and know not evil, my son!" he said, which was a line from *The Judgment of Apharos,* although D'ward would not know that.

"So where does evil come from?"

"Evil comes from mortals, when they do not obey the gods."

"Then you approve of what women must do in the temple in Narsh?" D'ward sounded more puzzled than impertinent.

Trong growled, "Certainly!" and stalked away.

The very next day, D'ward took Piol Poet off to a corner of the dining area and started writing something. It so happened that Eleal was helping Uthiam hunt for an earring she had lost, and while she was looking under a nearby table she chanced to hear some of what was being said. Piol seemed to be listing all the gods and goddesses he could think of, and D'ward was writing them down. Actually, he only wrote down some of them, and later he left the list lying around where anyone could pick it up and read it. There was no pattern to the ones he'd chosen: *P'ter, D'mit'ri, Ken'th, D'ward, Alis.*

He'd spelled most of them wrong anyway. And his handwriting was terrible.

Another day, when they were rehearsing in the park under the bridge and D'ward was sitting with Dolm in front of some bushes, Eleal just happened to pass by on the other side of the bushes.

"I know T'lin Dragontrader," Dolm was saying, "but only by sight. He's probably spying for someone, maybe both sides, maybe four or five sides. Most traveling merchants do. The Vales are always conspiring—Joalia, Thargia, Niolia, and all their vassal states."

"How about traveling actors?"

"Of course. When we return to Jurg in the fall, Ambria files reports with the Niolian ambassador."

Eleal had not known that! She moved to a more comfortable position, a little closer.

"Political spying?" D'ward said. "Do the gods play the same sort of game among themselves?"

"Likely they do, some of them."

"I suppose one tries everything in a few thousand years?"

Dolm chuckled. "I expect so. I was required to report to Zath if I ever learned anything that might interest him—a war brewing, or a plague, for example. I only had reason to do it once, and that was in Narsh last fortnight."

"How did you? Do you write reports to gods?"

"I had a ritual, of course."

"Explain that, please."

How typical of D'ward, not to know what a ritual was!

But Dolm did not laugh. "A ritual is a procedure decreed by a god. A priest will sacrifice a chicken in a particular way for a foretelling, another way for a blessing or a healing, right? It works because the god has arranged it so."

"So it's sort of like writing a name and address on a message? When you do certain things in a certain order, the god knows he's being called and what's expected of him?"

"I never thought of it that way, but yes, it must be."

How like D'ward to see things in a way nobody else did!

Dolm continued. "I had been given a ritual to summon the god in person. Obviously that is not something one undertakes lightly, especially when one's personal god is Zath. Parts of the ceremony had been made deliberately unpleasant, but of course that is to be expected." He laughed nervously. "Fortunately he approved of my presumption, and I must admit that he rewarded me well."

"May I ask how?"

Dolm sighed. "With rapture, mostly. But he also cured the wound I had inflicted on myself as part of the ritual. Otherwise I would have bled to death."

D'ward asked the question that was making Eleal want to burst: "What does Zath look like?"

There was a long pause before Dolm answered. "Hard to say. He wears a reaper gown with a hood. I never saw him properly, not really."

"This was what Eleal saw?"

"She saw the ritual, at least. I'm sure she'd run away before Zath arrived, or she would not be around now. I never met anyone one quarter as snoopy as that child!"

How *dare* he call her a child!

D'ward had not finished with his questions. "Why did you call Zath that time?"

"Because of what happened in the temple. Trong sacrificed to Ois. The priest was extremely surprised by the portents. Minor rituals like that are normally routine, so I knew the goddess was taking a personal interest. Thinking she objected to my evening activities, I reported to my master. Zath knew what was happening, though. He said Eleal was the problem, and I could leave her to the goddess."

There was a silence, then, broken only by Trong's rantings in the distance.

Dolm chuckled. "You look worried. What else do you want to know?"

"This story about Eleal's mother."

Eleal bristled. It was not polite of them to discuss her when she wasn't there! Or not supposed to be there, at least.

"Is it a common event—a god raping a mortal?"

"Not *raping!*" Dolm protested. "She would have submitted very willingly. It's not exactly common. But I don't think it's truly rare, either. You know the athletes from the festival here always spent a night at Iilah's grove? There's a common belief that at least one husky young man will always have an interesting experience that night."

"It sounds like rape to me, if the victims can't resist. And when it's a god and a woman—do the women always kill themselves?"

"No. But men or women, they're never much good for anything else. They never speak of it, but how could they ever be happy again, after having known the love of a god? Excuse me. I've got to go. My cue's coming up."

D'ward just sat there then, by himself, thinking. Eleal crept away.

He was accepted as one of the troupe. Even Klip could not dislike him. If he had a fault, it was that he would persist in regarding Eleal as a mere child. For example, one afternoon when he was in the kitchen, helping Uthiam Piper make supper—he was peeling blueroots, Uthiam baking bread . . .

"I am worried about Eleal," he said, and again that was very rude of him to discuss someone who was not there.

Uthiam laughed. "Why on earth are you worried about her?"

"Well, I'm grateful to her for what she did for me, of course. I should certainly have died without her help. I am very grateful to all of you, also, but I was brought here against my will.

Somehow I must find a way to go home again and . . . attend to certain important duties."

"We shall miss you. We enjoy your company. You more than pay your way with the collections—I wish I knew how you did that! But what has this to do with Eleal?"

"She seems to think she owns me! I can't stay with you forever, and I don't want to hurt the child's feelings."

Child? Eleal fumed.

"I am sorry for her," D'ward continued. "She is so convinced that she will be a great actor when she grows up! Can she? With that game leg? She won't be able to compete in the Tion Festival or—"

"You needn't worry about that small hussy," Uthiam said. "I would back her against the entire Sussian militia any day. In fact, if you were to peek around that door, there, right now, I suspect you would find a pair of very sharp ears, attached to the sides of Eleal Singer's head."

Eleal took off along the corridor as if Zath himself were after her.

Following six well-received performances of the *Varilian,* the Trong Troupe announced *The Tragedy of Trastos.* In the smallest print on the playbills, D'ward Scholar was mentioned in the role of Gunuu, god of courage. Rehearsals had not gone well. D'ward seemed very wooden and not at all the fiery young man who had played Kingharry for the troupe.

"Bigger, bigger!" Trong told him, over and over. "It's almost dark, remember! You're standing in firelight, not sunlight. Exuberate! Wave your arms! *Declaim!*"

But D'ward continued to play the part in the same dull way, almost as if he hoped they would cancel his appearance.

Even on the morning of the first performance, Trong was doubtful. Piol insisted it would be all right on the night, and even if it wasn't it would not spoil the show.

Eleal was sure it would be all right.

It was more than all right. It was spectacular.

★　★　★

Eleal had no costume to worry about in the *Trastos* because she sang her gods' messenger part offstage. She did it very well, but she won no applause. Nobody was being applauded. The collection at intermission had been pitiful. In backstage whispers, the actors agreed they had never met a harder audience. The trouble might be that Trastos was a historical villain in Suss, so Sussians did not enjoy seeing him portrayed as a tragic hero. Piol had bent tradition too far.

D'ward's scene came near the end. Eleal slipped out through the bushes to sit on the edge of the crowd and watch. The doomed Trastos, having defied the gods' command to abdicate in favor of a democracy and then challenged the rebels to send forth a champion to meet him in single combat, had now learned that this champion would be his own son, Daltos Liberator. Trong proclaimed his despair in a long soliloquy, crumbling by stages to the grass. He ended lying prone, howling out the cue: "Gods, send me courage!"

Golfren entered, wearing the golden loincloth that identified him as Tion. Even in Narsh, the audience had reacted a little to this dramatic confrontation. The Sussians sat in stony silence to hear what the god might say to rescue the evening from disaster.

"I will send you courage!" Golfren announced, and began to play. Eleal heard a few angry whispers near her. Golfren, too, sensed the crowd's displeasure, for he shortened his solo, raising the music swiftly to the rallying call that was D'ward's cue.

"I am Courage!" D'ward Scholar strode into the light of the fires, tall and lean, wearing an identical costume and holding a symbolic lantern high. How handsome he was! Surely every woman in the amphitheater must have felt her heart quicken at the sight of him! Surely every man would identify with his youthful bravado? The spectators gasped to see a god and one of his own aspects on stage together.

Piol had written better poetry, Eleal thought, but she had never heard any of it better spoken, and in a fine Joalian accent, too:

Courage alone is bone to shape our flesh.
Without such spine of mettle, man remains
Earthbound, a carrion worm perceiving death
In every shiver of a grassy blade.
Look up, look up! Behold the beck'ning stars!
Spurn not the gods who loaned you life to be
The wherewithal of deeds, not end itself.
Affection, reputation, pride and joy
Are but frail branches sprung from sturdy stem
Of valor, which defies the storms of fate,
Onslaught of age, the petty and the base,
To raise a crown above the common line
And stand one sunlit hour as mark and gauge
Of what may sometimes be . . .

And so on, in forty or fifty lines of rousing verse. It built to a satisfying climax with a local Sussian reference or two. All the time old Trong was recovering, rising with the poetry—to his knees, to one knee, until at the end he was erect and defiant, brandishing his sword at the stars and roaring out an echo of the final line, inspired to die bravely.

The audience was on its feet also. The hollow rang with cheers. D'ward had to come out again and repeat the entire thing twice. Then he and Trong had to take a special bow, while the audience screamed hysterically and threw gold coins.

Never had Eleal seen such a triumph! Later she limped around through the crowd with a bowl. Money clinked into it like rain until it became unpleasantly heavy. The others' bowls were filling up as well. She saw smiling faces everywhere. There was a huge throng around D'ward—mostly women, she was annoyed to notice—and she hoped he was managing the conversation successfully. Probably none of it was very subtle. She could not even get close to him.

Eventually she sidled up to Trong, to hear what was being said by all the admiring citizens clustered around him. Many of them were old friends she recognized from past years, who might have a kind word to say about her own debut. One of the others was an ancient priest from the temple, conspicuous in his splendid yellow robe. He seemed to be somebody special, for everyone was deferring to him.

Then Klip came lounging by, empty-handed.

"Here!" she said, thrusting the weighty bowl at him. "Some more loot!"

Klip whistled as he took it. "You've done well, Eleal!"

The old priest turned around. "Eleal? Is your name Eleal, my daughter?"

She curtsied. "I am Eleal Singer, Your Holiness. You heard me earlier, in my role as the gods' messenger. I have an onstage part in our other play where I—"

He must have sharp ears to have overheard Klip. He had very sharp eyes, too. His hair was silver, his shaven, wizened face had a snowy texture. "And this remarkable young actor we witnessed this evening . . . D'ward?"

"D'ward . . . Scholar, Your Holiness." Staring into that needling gaze, she felt a sudden uneasiness. "He's from Rinoovale."

"Is he, indeed?" The old man glanced around at his companions. "Excuse us a moment." He laid a spidery hand on Eleal's shoulder and urged her back a few paces, away from onlookers. He bent over, putting his face very close to hers, and he smiled in a grandfatherly sort of way. "There is an Eleal mentioned in the *Filoby Testament*. There is a D'ward mentioned there, too. What can you tell us about this strange coincidence, child?"

CURTAIN

57

EDWARD WAS SCREWED—SCAMMERED, CORNED, FRIED, paralyzed, and plastered. Intoxicated, in other words. He had not been drinking. First there had been that explosion of adulation from the audience. Now he had been backed against a bush with worse thorns than a wait-a-bit by a gaggle of gabbling, animated women. Some of them were old enough to be his mother; some of them weren't. Some of them couldn't keep their hands off him; some of them weren't. He wasn't wearing much more than a lace doily and terrible things were starting to happen. "Thank you, thank you, that's very kind of you, well, I'd love to, but . . ." They kept peppering him with invitations to parties, dinners, dances until his head spun—he thought he'd already accepted at least three for Thighday. And somewhere deep down inside, under all the fizz, if he could only have an instant to think about it, lurked the certainty that he'd made an epochal blunder.

Rescue arrived in the shape of old Trong, who came barging into the melee, thundering apologies while parting the crowd like a charging bull. Assisting him was Ambria. Behind them came a bent, elderly man in sumptuous gold vestments. The admirers fell back.

"Here he is, Your Holiness!" Ambria declaimed. "D'ward Scholar. D'ward, we are greatly honored by the presence here tonight of the Holy Kirthien Archpriest." Ambria was never serene, but she seemed more genuinely agitated now than he had ever seen her—why?

Having no idea how to greet a senior clergyman in Sussland, Edward merely bowed low. When he straightened up and saw the razor glint of mind in the age-ravaged face, his head cleared with a rush. Epochal blunder! And there was Eleal, at the old man's side. She was so flushed that her face looked fevered in the firelight; she was hopping up and down on the grass, up and down, up and down . . . Worse than epochal?

A word from the Archpriest worked wonders. Trong and Ambria shepherded the spectators back, aided by a couple of younger, lesser clerics. Edward was left alone with Kirthien Archpriest and Eleal. Sweat dried cold all over him.

"D'ward Scholar?" the old man murmured. "That is, of course, merely your stage name?" His withered lips wore a smile, but his eyes were as deadly as snakes'.

"It is, er, Your Holiness. I have reasons for not divulging my identity." He took another glance at the effervescing Eleal and knew that she had blown the gaff. She was precocious, but she would be no match for that sly Kirthien.

The priest chuckled softly. "Your performance tonight was a revelation to us, my son."

"Er, thank you, Your Holiness." Oh, damn! damn! damn! Why had he ever been such an idiot?

"Such virtuosity can only be a blessing from the Lord of Art." Kirthien was playing with his prey. "It behooves you to give thanks to him in person, my son. You have visited his temple recently?"

Edward stammered. "I do intend to go there . . . come . . . very shortly. Tomorrow, or . . . Soon . . . Thighday?"

"You will be welcome to ride back with us in our carriage—now."

That was an order.

"Er . . . "

"Oh, yes, D'ward!" Eleal cried, clutching at his hand. "You must come and give thanks to Tion and he will cure my leg!"

"What?"

"His Holiness says so!" She was beside herself with excitement and hope, terrified that he would not cooperate.

Kirthien tut-tutted. "Now, child! I made no promises! I merely said that I thought there was an excellent chance that the noble god would look with favor upon you for your assistance to the Liberator."

"Please, D'ward! Please? Oh, please!"

"I must change just a minute excuse me I will be back directly . . ." Edward ran.

He dodged past more of his starry-eyed admirers and hurried along the path to the shack that served as the men's dressing room, as fast as he dared go in bare feet.

Why had he been such a muggins? He should never have taken part in the play. It had felt like a way of repaying the troupe's kindness to him, even good camouflage, making him seem like one of them. He had not intended to create a sensation. The audience's enthusiasm had struck him in a tidal wave and swept him away. A rank novice had upstaged Trong Impresario, an old trouper with considerable talent and more than thirty years' experience—but only because that novice had the charisma of a stranger. Did the old priest know of that vital distinction, or had he merely made a shrewd guess? It didn't matter now, because he had obviously extracted the truth from Eleal.

Was Tion Robin or the Sheriff of Nottingham? Did he play for the Service or the Chamber? Edward was about to find out. If he did not submit to the archpriest's orders, then the old man could summon all those efficient-looking gold-plated guardsmen. Suss was too small a town to hide in. There were only four passes out of the vale. The population was fiercely loyal to its patron god and would not harbor a fugitive. All in all, the chances of escaping from Tion now were nonexistent, even without allowing for the workings of magic. The astonishing thing, really, was that Edward had evaded detection for so long.

He reached the shack. He should have brought a lantern. A three-quarter Trumb lit the sky, but the trees were casting heavy shadows.

As he threw open the door to the black interior, someone

spoke behind him: "By George, you really let the bally cat out of the bag, didn't you?"

The voice was unfamiliar, but the words were in English.

He spun around, stubbed his toe on a rock, and almost fell into a bush.

"Who? . . . "

There were two of them. One was a youth of his own age, or perhaps slightly younger. He was slim, golden-haired, and wearing even less than he was—wearing, in fact, nothing but an inexplicably self-assured smile.

It was the woman who had spoken, though. She was tall by Sussian standards, and her smock revealed thin arms and bony shoulders. He could make out almost nothing of her face.

"Monica Mason," she said. "Delighted to make your acquaintance, Mr. Scholar. May I have your autograph? I suspect it will shortly acquire rarity value."

He resisted a mad impulse to fall on his knees and kiss her feet. He found his voice somewhere. "Delighted to meet you, also, ma'am. You are with the Service, I presume?"

"Of course. I am usually known as Onica, by the way. What the hell were you doing, making an exhibition of yourself like that?"

"It was indiscreet."

"Indiscreet? Indiscreet, the man says!" She moved closer, and the moonlight gleamed on a hard, mannish face, framed by longish dark hair, hanging loose. She was wearing the standard local smock as if it were a coronation gown. "There are reapers in town, you dunderhead! Even if there weren't any in the audience, they're going to hear about you soon enough. And if they don't, then Tion will!"

"Tion already has! I mean his high priest or someone did. He knows who I am. He wants me to go back to the temple with him."

She snorted. "I came here to rescue you, not bury you. That is, if you want rescuing?"

"Want? Of course I do! Creighton was killed by—"

"I heard! The dragon trader told us. Well, if you want to come with me, then you'd better get some clothes on. Running around in that getup isn't going to help. You look like a bloody cherub sprouted in a dark cupboard."

Clothes . . . He pulled his wits together, stifling a swarm of questions buzzing around in his head. He turned to the blackness of the shed. "I need a lantern."

"Never mind! Even a pinafore would be better than that. Grab whatever you can. Move!"

She shoved him. He stepped into the dark and promptly stubbed his toe on a stool. The youth came in after him and raised a hand. Instantly a faint glow illuminated the plank walls, the rough benches strewn with clothes, the footwear lying around the floor.

He dived for his smock and sandals. "Gosh! Is this mana?"

The boy just smiled.

Edward repeated the question in Joalian, but still received no answer. Pulling his smock over his head, he went out. "Where are we going?" Home, Home!

Mason was a rangy black shape against the moonlight. "Anywhere we can, I suppose. Zath has his dogs loose, and as soon as that priest gets word back to the temple . . . He can probably notify Tion directly from here, actually. He's not on a node, but it's not far. He's bound to have some ritual or other."

Edward fumbled into his sandals. There was nothing else he needed. Naked he had come into this world; he had acquired no possessions yet. The woman turned and he began to follow . . . Then he remembered Eleal. His mouth went dry and his heart froze in his chest.

"Wait! What happens if I go to the temple?"

She stopped and looked around. "Can't say. Tion may turn you over to Zath. You're not serious?"

"The girl, Eleal. She saved my life! She stayed and nursed me when I was ill, although she knew the reapers were hunting me."

"You don't . . . What of it?"

"She's a cripple. The priest says that Tion will cure her limp."

Mason snorted again, a very unladylike noise. "And you have a huge honorable schoolboy lump of guilt, I suppose? Well, it's your neck. I'm leaving, and leaving pronto, because I value my skin. One reaper I might just be able to handle, if I saw him in time. Several reapers I can't, and God knows I wouldn't have a hope against Tion." She did not move, though.

Oh, hell! He clenched his fists in agony. "Would Tion cure her? I know he can. Would he?"

"Impossible to say. He's mad as a hatter. They all are. A few hundred years of omnipotence boils up their brains."

"He's one of the Chamber?"

She shrugged. "Probably not, and he can't be very happy having Zath's killers all over his manor." She frowned. "Tion fancies himself as a collector of beauty—pretty girls, pretty boys. He has unorthodox tastes in what he does with them. You would most likely find yourself in the temple guard, I'd think. He favors that role for tall young men."

"My preferences wouldn't matter, of course?"

"Not in the slightest. He's quite capable of turning you into a woman, if that takes his fancy, but he can do whatever he likes with you. You'll probably enjoy it, although I can't guarantee that, even. He's better than some, but I shouldn't want him as a friend."

Judging by her companion, who wandered around so shamefully in the altogether, she had liberal tastes in friendship.

"But Eleal saved my life!"

Mason tapped her foot on the path. "Make up your mind. Tion may very well appoint you a god, you know. That's what's prophesied. Whether that comes after the hanky-panky or instead of, I don't know."

"Make me a *god?*"

"There is no god of courage—hasn't been for a couple of hundred years. Gunuu was one of Tion's but he switched allegiance. You must know about the *Testament* by now, surely?"

"I haven't read it. What does it say?"

He could hear voices. Someone was coming, probably looking for him. The woman had heard them also. She glanced around as she spoke. *"D'ward shall become Tion. He shall give heart to the king and win the hearts of the people. D'ward shall become Courage.* That's it. Come on, laddie! Time to go."

Eleal! Blasted, meddling Eleal! Giving him the part of Gunuu had been all her idea. She had arranged the whole debacle. She must have found that passage in the copy of the *Testament* they had left back in Ruatvil. That was how the old priest had guessed. But . . .

"I fulfilled that prophecy tonight, in the play!" Bless you, Eleal!

Mason uttered a harsh bark of laughter. "Damn my eyes! I suppose you did. Actually, that's quite a relief, old man. We were worried about that one. Good show." She took a couple of steps and then looked back. "Are you coming or not?"

Time! He needed time to think. He turned to the youth, who merely shrugged, seeming amused but not about to offer any helpful suggestions. He had not spoken a word so far.

"Good luck in your new career, whatever it is," Monica Mason said. "Give my love to Zath, or Tion, whichever gets you first." She disappeared into the shrubbery. The youth went with her.

"Eleal saved my life!" Edward wiped his forehead. With a crippled leg, she could never have the stage career she craved, could never enter Tion's Festival. She had braved the deadly reapers to stay and nurse him through his fever. He had always thought that honor enabled a man to choose between good and evil. He had never seriously considered that a decision might lie between two evils. Be a god? Be plaything to an omnipotent pervert?

That damnable Gypsy witch, Mrs. Boswell, had defined the conflict exactly: *You must choose between honor and friendship. You must desert a friend to whom you owe your life, or betray everything you hold sacred.*

Fallow had not prepared him for this.

The approaching voices were louder, just around the last bend.

"Wait!" Edward said. "Where are you going to take me? What does the Service want of me?"

There was no answer. He could hear Mason and her young friend moving through the bushes, the sound growing fainter as they retreated. He shouted, "Wait!" and ran after them.

All that nattering about courage and then he ran away.

58

THEY SLIPPED OUT OF THE THEATER AREA, APPARENTLY unseen. Trumb's green brilliance suffused the landscape, but red Eltiana and blue Ysh added a strange mix of tints to the shadows. There could be reapers . . . Over the last week, Edward had almost forgotten the reapers, and now he was too tormented by thoughts of Eleal to worry about them. Mrs.—or Miss—Mason seemed to know exactly where she was going. She did not head for the city gate, but struck off down an unused, overgrown track, heading roughly in the direction of the river. He stumbled blindly along between her and the youth. Half a mile or so away, the temple dome shone points of colored light back at the moons.

Eleal was a likable kid. Her extreme nosiness was more funny than annoying. She was brave, amusing, dedicated. He owed his life to her, and now he was walking out on her. She could have what she wanted most in the world, and he was denying it to her. His betrayal might ruin her entire life.

Mr. Goodfellow had healed broken bones, which would have healed anyway. Eleal's trouble was more than that. *"Could* Tion cure a deformed leg, ma'am?"

"Call me Onica. Of course he could, easily. Didn't Creighton explain? Tion's a stranger, and strangers have charisma. We absorb mana. It makes us immortal, or almost so, and in large quantities gives us supernatural powers." She fell silent to work her way through a tangle of thorny shrubs.

Edward followed carefully. The boy just pushed through as if they were long grass.

Yes, Edward had worked it out—and even seen glimmers of it in himself after he had played holy man in the campground. Obviously the effect disappeared if the stranger returned to his home world. Creighton had possessed no "authority" back on Earth, but as soon as he had returned to Nextdoor, he had been able to smite a reaper with a thunderbolt. Mr. Goodfellow had been a stranger on Earth, an immigrant from Ruatvil.

"I think I picked up some tonight—a sort of tingle? Can I work miracles?"

She shook her head. "Unless you're on a node, it's pretty much impossible to collect enough to produce physical effects."

The campground where he had faced down old Graybeard had been a node, and he'd acquired real mana there. He had used that power to learn the language so swiftly and to cure Dolm's guilt. All the same, his tongue could find no cavities in his teeth now. What should be surprising about minor repairs? The guv'nor had lived somewhere in this world for thirty years without aging a day.

Even the charisma itself was dangerous. Edward Exeter could be the greatest actor in the world if he wanted. He could pluck women like daisies. He could enter politics and be a dictator in no time. He could raise an army and conquer the world. Now he knew why Creighton had wanted older recruits—they might be able to handle this sort of power without being corrupted by it. How long would Edward be able to resist adulation on that scale? How long before his moral standards collapsed like a wet soufflé? At last he understood why the guv'nor had wanted to break the chain and prevent him from becoming the Liberator.

But Eleal! . . . What sort of rotter was he to walk out on her like this?

They were past the bushes. He fell into step with Onica.

"What constitutes worship? Blood? Degradation? Public prostitution?"

She stalked on without looking at him. "Sometimes. They don't all go that far. The general principle is that sacrifice must hurt. The believer must voluntarily do something he doesn't want to do—give money or perform unpleasant acts. The greater the pain, the greater the crop of mana. Adoration works too. Tion's better than most in that regard. He bribes his worshipers with roses. He probably gains more mana from one hard-fought singing contest on his node than Zath does from any of his distant murders."

"Human sacrifice is the most powerful source?"

"With one exception. Look out for the burrower holes here."

They were closer to the temple now, and well below the city. Its roofs were a jagged blackness against the sky. Good-bye, Suss! Oh, Eleal!

"What does a god of courage do?" he asked miserably.

"He gives supplicants courage, of course. It isn't difficult to make young men behave like suicidal maniacs." Onica's voice held traces of the adenoidal accent of Lancashire. "The fact that they're still worshiping there on a node that's been unoccupied for two hundred years shows that most of the effect is wishful thinking. As I recall Gunuu's rituals, they're quite honest. The worshiper offers blood and is granted courage, but it's conditional on abstinence. As soon as he takes a woman, the deal is off. That must bring in lots of return business in the course of a long campaign."

He remembered what Piol had told him about the monastery at Thogwalby. "The god of strength works the same sort of swizz, doesn't he?"

"Garward?" The woman chuckled. "Yes, that's a potent sacrifice! All those young men in training, right on his node, forbidden even to think about their groins. Every night the mana must just pour in. Insomnia to the glory of god! They've been at this for centuries, remember. They've worked out all sorts of twists. Why? Are you seriously—"

She stopped and listened. "Blast! We're being followed!"

"How can you tell?" He could hear nothing.

"Come on!" She began to run down the slope. He loped along beside her, stumbling more often than she did. Either of them might break an ankle any minute. The youth went out in front, jogging steadily. His lack of shoes seemed to make him more surefooted, although he must have feet like hooves to run on this terrain.

"Who's after us?" Edward panted. "Tion? Or Zath?"

"Zath. Reapers. I can smell them. Look, make up your mind, Exeter! Do you want to come with me to Olympus, or don't you? Go to the bloody temple if you want to bare your neck for Tion. Or bare anything else, for that matter."

"Would he really make me god of courage?"

"He might. It's prophesied. Strangers are in short supply, and he needs to reclaim that attribute."

Eleal! Eleal was the problem. Tion might cure her leg out of gratitude, or Edward himself would be able to as soon as he had collected enough mana. A god did not have to be evil, surely? He could do good. A few years on Nextdoor, like the guv'-nor . . .

But the guv'nor's case was different. There was a war on now. Edward had a duty to King and Country. Even his debt to Eleal must take second place to that call. He certainly couldn't trust Tion.

Could he even trust the Service? He stumbled wildly, caught his balance. "Never mind what I want. What does the Service want with me?"

"Save you from Zath. Cameron's son."

Mana or not, she was panting harder than he was. How much farther?

"Suppose you do. Then what? Creighton told me you were divided over the *Filoby Testament.*"

"Obviously. Oh darn it!"

A peculiar, rumbling explosion rent the night. Edward shied

to a halt as he registered two huge green eyes glowing at him from the darkness.

"What in Hades is *that?*"

Onica had gone on to the monster and was embracing its huge head, provoking more belching rumbles. "This is Cuddles. She's a dragon. Quick! They're closing on us."

She scrambled up into the saddle. "Up here, behind me. Hang on. Cuddles, *Zomph!*" She held out a hand for him.

As she hauled him aboard, the saddle simultaneously shot skyward. He grabbed at the woman's arm and a pannier, was almost thrown as the huge brute launched itself forward. He caught a glimpse of two black shapes and cried out at a sudden pain in his leg like a jolt of electricity. He started to overbalance, then the spasm passed and he could grip again. A nasty pins and needles remained, but was already fading. The rush of wind in his face told him they were racing over the ground, although the ride was as smooth as the Bodgleys' Rolls.

"All right?" the woman yelled.

"Fine. Reapers?"

"Not quite within lethal range, fortunately." The wind caught her words and flung them past him. "They can't catch us now. You can relax."

He had been that close to death and he was expected to relax?

He shouted, "Righto!" and passed the word to his insides: relax! That was not so easy when he was perched on the rim of the saddle with a bony plate digging into his back.

Dragon? He had thought the word referred to something like a horse—T'lin Horsetrader. This thing was more like the stegosaurus in *The Lost World,* bigger than a full-grown rhino. She had a ridge of high plates along her back, one of which had been cut out to make room for the rider. A couple of wicker panniers were strapped to the one behind the gap. Dragon was a fitting name for the beast, though—she even had long winglike frills stretching back from her shoulders.

The monster raced along a flat, treeless terrace. Rugged hillocks and cliffs flowed by, pale in the moonlight, casting multitoned shadows. There was a gully ahead. Onica's hair kept flying in his face, and conversation was impossible. Cuddles hurtled down into the gully and up the other side with a stomach-churning lurch. They were heading east, passing the temple at a lower level.

Three or four gullies later, Onica yelled, "Hang on now. *Whilth!*"

The dragon swung to the left and headed straight up a fifty-degree slope. Edward toppled back, steadying himself against the panniers. He was deucedly uncomfortable. Onica had the advantage of a flat seat and stirrups.

When they reached the level again, she said, *"Varch!"* Cuddles dropped to a slower pace. No reins or handlebars—she was entirely controlled by voice commands and must be at least as smart as a dog.

In a few minutes Onica told her, *"Zappan! Wosok!"* Cuddles stopped and crouched down. "Off!"

Edward assumed that meant him, and gratefully scrambled to the ground. She slid down beside him. They were in another gully, a smaller one. It was dry and shadowed.

"Come on!" She hurried up the slope.

He strode beside her, his longer legs giving him an advantage.

The boy strolled along at his side. Edward turned to him and met the same inscrutable smile as before. He forgot what he had been about to ask.

"Well?" the woman said. "Which is to be, Exeter? The temple, or Olympus? If you want the temple, you can walk from here."

He could see it, not half a mile away, and the city beyond. "I want to go Home. To England. We're at war with Germany."

"I heard about that. We'll see you get Home, then, if that's what you want. Yes, we're of two minds about the Liberator, but if that's your decision, then I'm certain the committee will consent."

They crested the rise, coming to flat farmland. Onica headed for a clump of palmlike trees.

"Do you mind explaining what we're doing?" he asked politely.

"Wondered when you'd start wondering. I want to go west, to Lameby. I'm hoping the opposition will be deceived and give chase. We can watch the road from here."

A low stone wall ran through the grove. She sat down on it and wiped her face, puffing. "May be a long wait. They'll have to run back up to the town and find mounts."

"What sort of mounts?" Setting himself beside her, he tried to visualize a midnight chase of dragons.

"Moas."

"I thought moas were one-rider animals?"

"They are, but I suspect reapers can get around that. They probably have moas of their own, anyway."

They were in shadow, and now he could see the dirt track that was the main highway across Suss, a couple of hundred yards away. It was deserted at this time of night. The countryside slept peacefully under the light of three moons, which was much brighter than the moonlight he knew. Only a week or so ago, he had come along there with Dolm and Eleal.

Again he turned to say something to the youth sitting beside him, and again that cryptic smile distracted him.

Onica said, "Tell me what happened after T'lin escaped from the reapers."

"I arrived . . ." Edward told what he knew from his own blurred memories and what Eleal had recounted.

When he had done, she said, *"Hrmph!* We thought you'd been knocked off, of course. I came to investigate. Arrived last night, detected reapers still around. That made me wonder if you might be alive after all, keeping under wraps somewhere."

"How did you find me?"

"Sheer chance. I saw the playbill, saw a D'ward listed. Good job I made the connection before Zath's thugs did, you bloody idiot."

A change of subject was called for. "Tell me about Olympus."

"It's in a little side canyon. There's hundreds of those, of course, but that one's a beautiful spot. We try to keep it an outpost of real civilization—it's not unlike Nyagatha, actually."

"You know Nyagatha?"

"Dropped in there with Julian in '02. Met you—solemn, stringy kid, brown as walnut. Could have been a native, except for those blue eyes. You'll feel right at home in Olympus. We don't fly a Union Jack, but we do dress for dinner."

Mm! It sounded as if the Service was not unlike Holy Roly's Lighthouse Missionary Society, bringing enlightenment to the heathen. The guv'nor had supported it, so it must do some good.

He asked about dragons and received a long lecture on their habits and strengths. Mason was obviously an enthusiastic dragon-lover and made them sound like the finest riding beast in the Universe. Eleal had raved about them, although without thinking to describe what they looked like. When he had learned much more about the lizards than he wanted to, he managed to ask something more relevant.

"What about Gunuu? Why is there no god of courage?"

"How much do you know about the Great Game?"

He could say, "It means the struggle between England and Russia to control Afganhistan and the Northwest Frontier, which has been going on for more than a hundred years," and he would sound like a complete muffin. In the Vales there was a similar political rivalry between Joalia and Thargia, the major powers of the Vales, which he had privately classed as equivalents of Athens and Sparta, with Niolland, off to the north, roughly corresponding to Corinth. Obviously that was not what was meant either.

He said, "Nothing."

Onica grunted. "Immortality gets boring. The strangers compete among themselves. Earth has five great powers, right?—England, France, Russia, Germany, and Austria. So have the Vales, except here they're called Visek, Karzon, Eltiana, Astina, and Tion."

So the teams did wear colored jerseys! "Yes?"

"The priests' doctrine of the Pentatheon is a rough approximation—the Parent, the Man, the Lady, the Maiden, and the

Youth. Those are the parts, but the actors change from time to time. Each one has a supporting cast of avatars. They're all strangers, like us—from Home or other worlds. There's plenty backstabbing goes on within the teams, but mostly the Game is played between the five. They change alliances all the time."

"Sounds like a feudal system."

"Very much so," Onica said approvingly. "Especially since it all rests on the backs of the peasants, whose worship provides the mana. A couple of hundred years ago, Gunuu got subverted. He announced that he was an avatar of the Maiden, not the Youth—Gunuu Astina, not Gunuu Tion. He ordered his priests into blue instead of yellow, and so on. Tion wasn't willing to lose a profitable source of mana, so he retaliated. Normally the Game's played by Queensberry rules: Natives are fair game for anything, but stranger doesn't usually make a direct attack on stranger. That's a waste of mana and can be dangerous if your opponent turns out to have more power than you expected. In this case, Tion got nasty, very nasty."

Edward glanced at the youth, who shrugged sadly. He still had not spoken one word, and yet his reactions suggested he understood English.

"Pour encourager les autres?"

Onica chuckled. "Exactly! Since then Gunuu's node has been unoccupied. To recruit a substitute stranger, Tion would have to visit another world, and he's not likely to take that risk."

Creighton had commented on the problems of recruitment.

"He could send a helper, an avatar?"

"It's done, but then the new boys may have loyalty problems, what?"

"So, now, when people pray to Gunuu, where does the mana go?"

"Most of it's wasted. If they pray to Gunuu Tion, then Tion will get some of it. If they pray to Gunuu Astina, then the Maiden will."

"They play rough, don't they? Just before I arrived, Garward's monks sacked Iilah's grove at Filoby."

"Sounds fairly typical—the rough work would be done by

locals. Iilah herself would not be hurt. If a lot of nuns were raped or killed . . . well, they're only natives, you see. Garward's a fool. He'll pay for that, I'm sure."

"Pay to whom?"

"To his master Karzon, of course. Let's see . . . The Thargians are brewing a war. The warriors will seek portents from their patron goddess, Astina. The omens will be bad. Karzon will complain to Astina; she will demand justice for Filoby, because Iilah's one of hers. Karzon will pull strips off Garward's hide until she is satisfied. There may even be a change of resident at Thogwalby. Quite typical."

Quite disgusting! The guv'nor's support for the Service was starting to seem more understandable.

Edward squirmed. The wall was only slightly less uncomfortable than his perch on the dragon had been. How could the bare-arsed boy sit there without even fidgeting? He seemed quite content, listening to what was being said with calm amusement.

Something that sounded like a miniature pipe organ began singing in the branches overhead.

"What the dickens? . . ."

"We call them nightingales. They look more like squirrels, though."

Damn! Why did this world have to be so interesting? "It was Iilah who created the *Filoby Testament,* I suppose?"

Onica covered a yawn. "Apparently not. Even the big players rarely meddle with foretelling. Prediction involves holding a mirror up to memory, to recall the future. That can be dangerous! One can forget who one is and how to let go. The situation may become permanent. It also costs an incredible amount of mana. None of them likes to squander mana. I told you Garward's an idiot. The story is that he'd seduced Sister Ashylin— he's always in among the nuns there—and for some reason he gave her the gift of prophecy in return. He botched the ritual. The first time she invoked it, it drove her out of her mind with prophecy. It completely drained Garward himself, serves him right. She went mad and died. He almost died."

After a moment she added, "The future doesn't interest them. Most of them are centuries old. Nothing can harm them. The only thing they fear is boredom. Boredom kills them all in the end. That's why they play the Great Game. . . . *Look!*"

Two dark figures were racing along the road, coming from the town, going far faster than a man could run, or even a horse. The moas' long legs were a blur of ten-foot strides. The hooded riders crouched on their backs were barely distinguishable at that distance, and yet infinitely sinister in the green moonlight. Like silent motorcyclists, they disappeared along the Rotby road.

Edward suppressed a shiver. He glanced at his other, silent companion, who was frowning angrily. Then he met Edward's eye and smiled again. . . .

"Looks like they took the bait," Onica said. "We'll give them a few minutes, just to be sure they keep going. Then we head west."

"There's a bridge at Lameby? Then where?"

"The road goes on over Rothpass, to Nagvale." She hesitated. "You definitely want to go Home? You don't want to stay on Nextdoor and try to fulfill the prophecy?"

"No, ma'am. I definitely want to go Home."

She eyed him curiously. "You're an odd fish! A boy of your age, offered a whole new world to explore, a chance at fame and power . . . yet you refuse?"

He resented being called a boy, but Onica Mason must be a great deal older than she seemed.

"I'd love to stay," he admitted. "I'd love to see more of the Vales, and meet the people who knew my father. At any other time, I'd jump at it. Now—there's a war on. I must go Home and do my bit."

"Does you credit, I suppose," she muttered. "You'll have time to change your mind if you want to, because I can't take you straight to Olympus. Cuddles can go across country, but not with two riders. I did not expect to find you living, Mr. Exeter. I didn't bring a spare mount. I didn't bring warm clothes for two. You'd freeze your arse up there." She gestured at the towering peaks of Susswall.

The conversation was not heading in favorable directions.

"You can go over *that?*"

"Dragons can. They don't like the heat down here, and Nagland's even hotter. Furthermore," she added, "to take a dragon into Nagland would be like riding one down Whitehall."

"Conspicuous?"

"Quite. Rothpass is ranked as easy. By Valian standards, that means you can walk over it if you have the legs of a goat. I'll take you to the summit, though, and set you adrift there. I'll go over the hills to Olympus and report. You go down into Nagvale. The first village you come to is Sonalby. Ask for Kalmak Carpenter. He's one of ours, in the religious branch. The code question is, 'What do you get when you cross a wallaby and a jaguar?' "

"And what's the answer?"

"The kids' answer is, 'A fur coat with pockets.' If you get that, then you've found the wrong man. If he says, 'Sunrise over five peaks,' then he's sound."

Straight out of *Kim!* "And what do I do with Kalmak Carpenter when I've got him?"

"Mostly keep your mouth shut. He's a local, so he doesn't know what you know, but he's trustworthy, a good man. Stay with him until we send someone for you."

"How long?" he asked, trying not to show his doubts.

"Couple of weeks. Travel's slow here. I'll have you Home inside two fortnights, Exeter, promise." She twisted her awkward mouth in a smile. "A month, that means."

What could he say? "Fair enough."

She glanced at him quizzically.

He shrugged. "They all say the war'll be over by Christmas."

"So keen to kill? How long till Christmas?"

That she had to ask was a shock, a reminder of how very far away England was.

⚘ 59 ⚘

"WELL, THEY OBVIOUSLY DIDN'T SENSE US," MASON said. "Let's go."

Edward rose from the wall with relief. "What happens if they turn back and follow us?"

"Down here, they'd catch us easily. This is moa country. They can't handle heights, though. We'd have to try to get to the hills." She walked on for a few minutes, then added, "But we wouldn't make it."

"You know, you're full of cheerful information."

She chuckled. "If there's only two, I may manage to handle them."

He wondered how the members of the Service came by their mana. It might be an impertinent question.

The three of them walked in silence back down to the dragon, and again Edward had to squeeze himself into the gap between Mason and the bony plate. It was about as comfortable as riding on handlebars.

Once on the road, though, Cuddles ran smoothly. They sped by the temple, detoured around the town, and rushed on through the night, heading west.

He tried to keep watch behind. He felt worn-out by this interminable day. A few hours' sleep and he would be ready for anything. Talk was too difficult, so he just sat without speaking, wishing he could dismount from his uncomfortable perch— wishing, too, that he had not been such an unmitigated bounder as to walk out on Eleal when she needed his help.

★   ★   ★

After half an hour or so, Onica pulled the dragon in behind a copse of trees and made her lie down so the riders could dismount. There they were hidden from view but could look back along the dirt track crossing wide meadows of moonlit grass. They would see the reapers if they came.

"Just a short break," she said, stretching. "Hungry?"

"If you are going to eat, I could nibble something."

"Like a roast ox?"

"With potatoes and gravy, please."

She rummaged in one of the panniers and produced a small bundle wrapped in a cloth. She sat down and opened it, revealing some lumps of a hard bread. Edward was more than happy to sink to the grass and stretch out, finding new joints to put his weight on. He bit into one of the crusts. It was nutty and fresher than it looked, with a pleasant spicy flavor.

The golden-haired youth squatted down and took one also.

Edward said, "How the devil? . . . "

The boy smiled at him, chewing.

"What?" Onica asked.

"Nothing. Forgot what I was going to say. Tell me about Zath."

She grimaced. "What do you want to know?"

"Well, I don't like having an enemy who tries to kill me for something I haven't done and don't intend to do. Suppose I wrote him a note—"

"He'd never believe you! Zath's the worst of them all. I told you the native theology is only an approximation. The Man has always been god of both creation and destruction, symbolized by his hammer. Zath was his persona as god of death, but no one ever assumed the role—who would want to? About . . . oh, about a hundred years ago or so, someone did. Whether he asked Karzon for the post or it was all Karzon's idea, I haven't the foggiest. Doesn't matter. Zath invented the reapers. He may have stolen the idea from Indian thuggee."

"Their murders give him mana?"

"In spades. Human sacrifice died out a long time ago on

Nextdoor, just as it did at Home, but it generates huge amounts of mana. He's enormously powerful because of it, although his technique's very wasteful—the deaths don't happen on a node, and they're mostly a long way away from Zath himself. It's just that there are so many of them. In doctrine he's only an aspect of Karzon, but in fact he's by far the stronger now. The Five are worried about him, worried he may decide to promote himself to full Pentatheon membership."

"Can't they gang up on him?"

She laughed grimly. "Honor among thieves? Who bells the cat? Mana is power and power always has friends."

He looked at the youth, who grinned, shrugged, and went on eating.

Mason fell silent too. She seemed to be thinking hard, so Edward respected her silence. He had decided that Onica Mason knew what she was doing. She was a very competent . . . whatever she was.

Cuddles was grazing without standing up. She could probably do so for quite a long time before eating everything within the reach of that serpentine neck. Trumb was setting behind the peaks. Yellow Kirb'l had appeared, low in the south. He considered asking for an explanation of that rogue moon's motion but decided he was too fagged out at the moment to take in a lecture on astronomy.

Onica reached for the cloth. "Finished? Time to be on our way."

"Yes, thank you, ma'am." He stood up and peered back along the road. He could see no sign of the reapers. As they walked back to the dragon, he blurted: "Did you know my father?"

"Yes."

"I'd like to hear about him some time. I feel I hardly knew him."

She clambered into the saddle, keeping her back to him as she answered. "I knew him intimately. Does that shock you?"

"Of course not!" It did, though. He had never imagined the guv'nor having a lover. The information saddened him, emphasizing that his knowledge of his parents was that of a twelve-year-old. He had never really known them, and never would. They had died because of Zath and the *Filoby Testament*.

Onica held down a hand and helped him up with a surprisingly powerful heave. He wondered how old she was.

"He was a fine man, widely respected. I was very much in love with him. We drifted apart later. It was long before he met your mother, of course. All right, Cuddles, old girl. I know you're tired. *Wondo!*"

Did that long-ago affair explain why Monica Mason had come to aid Cameron's son? But why had she gone visiting her former lover at Nyagatha? That sounded like bad form, or was he just naive? There were too many questions to ask, too many pitfalls and unforeseeable hurts lurking in the possible answers.

He lost track of time. Uncomfortable as he was, he began to find the motion of the dragon soporific. He tried to keep watch behind them, but in the moonlight he probably would not have been able to see the reapers approaching until it was too late to do anything about them. Trumb and Ysh had set; now golden Kirb'l ruled the sky. The night was taking on a sense of nightmare, one of those awful dreams that never end.

Then Onica shouted something and pointed.

Houses. Lameby.

She skirted the hamlet, cutting across fields. Cuddles turned out to be as skilled as a horse at jumping fences, although Edward found the landings exceedingly unpleasant. Then they were on the road again, and it angled down into a narrow ravine, a dry streambed. A steady, low-pitched roar must be the voice of Susswater.

"Damn!" Onica said. *"Zappan!"*

The dragon stopped, claws scrabbling in gravel.

Silence, except for the bone-jarring rumble of the river, not even a whisper of wind, here in this little gorge . . . Walled on either side by steep cliffs, the track disappeared around a sharp bend about fifty yards ahead. The gap showed a glimpse of mightier, moonlit cliffs in the distance, and the far end of a bridge. Like the one he had seen at Rotby, it was suspended from heavy chains, but here there were no towers. The anchors must be set in the rock of the canyon itself. The near side was hidden around the corner.

"Trouble?" he whispered.

"At least two of them," Onica said. She sighed. "It's a logical place for an ambush. I should have thought of it."

"We can go back?"

"And then where? Cuddles needs rest, even if you don't. I think we'll try the direct method. Saint George and the dragon will now perform! Get down."

"Ma'am, I—"

"Get down!"

The command was spoken quietly, but it must have been backed with mana, because his feet hit the dirt an instant later. He staggered.

"Here goes the charge of the Light Brigade," Onica said.

"No, wait!"

"You can't help. Keep your fingers crossed, Exeter. Remember Kalmak Carpenter. *Zomph!"*

Cuddles shot forward, claws spraying stones. She hurtled like an arrow along the road, leaned into the curve, and disappeared.

He choked back a shout of anger. He stood there on the gravel, feeling like a pampered brat. The smirk on the youth's face did nothing to help his feelings. Bloody young exhibitionist, parading around in the nude!

"Well, come on!" he snapped. "Let's try to help!" He began to run, and the youth loped along at his side without a word.

The worst part was that he heard nothing at all—no screams, nothing. Cuddles came into view again, streaking across the bridge like a runaway lorry. Her claws must have made a considerable racket on the timbers, but the roar of the river below muffled it completely. At the far end, the dragon did not turn to follow the road, but went straight up the cliff face like a gigantic fly. She had no rider. In moments she vanished over a ledge. He caught one more glimpse of her, higher up, and then she had gone.

He stopped in dismay. The river rumbled, his heart thumped madly.

He wondered if he was the victim of some horrible hoax and rejected the notion as madness. *Something* had spooked that dragon!

If Onica were alive, she would come back. If she had died, she would not have accounted for all the reapers.

Now what? Eleal had explained that ordinary weapons were useless against reapers. Onica might be lying on the road, hurt and in need of help. If any of the enemy had survived, then they might well be able to sense him as Mason had sensed them—he did not know the extent of their powers. He bent and fumbled in the gravel until he had found a couple of rounded rocks that would fit his grip. He put one in his pocket and stood up. He would not likely have time for more than two shots.

What was the reapers' range? He racked his brain to recall that brief glimpse he had caught earlier. Fifteen yards? Hard to say in the dark, just two black shapes in the night. He had better allow twenty, at least. A cricket pitch was twenty-two yards long.

He turned to his cryptic companion, who was watching him with amused contempt.

"Are you going to help or just stand there displaying yourself?"

This time he got an answer. He had spoken in English, but the reply came in Joalian:

"You go ahead, D'ward dear. I'll be very interested to see what happens."

With a snort of disgust, Edward started forward. He walked as quietly as he could, although he knew the river would mask any sounds he made. The youth sauntered along beside him.

Edward ignored him, keeping his eyes on the corner ahead, rolling the stone in his hand, forced his breathing to stay slow. The corner was not a knife-edge, just a very sharp bend. He moved close to the wall, crept forward more slowly. One step at a time now . . .

He saw a body. And a dark-robed form bending over it. *Now! Quickly!*

He sprinted forward. The reaper looked up, surprised, then rose, brightly lit by moonlight. He raised an arm. . . .

Edward pivoted and bowled his best fast ball. For a moment he thought he had left it too late—a spasm of pain shot through his arm.

He hadn't, though. The reaper had no chance to dodge a missile moving at that speed. The rock took him between the eyes with an audible crunch. He went down, as if he had been hit by a sledgehammer.

Edward stumbled to a halt, rubbing his tingling hand and fighting waves of nausea. He did not want to think what that rock would have done to a human face. He had probably killed a man, or at least maimed him horribly. Worse, if the reaper was not dead, then he could still be dangerous. Dare Edward go closer to finish him off? Could he kill an injured man in cold blood? There were other bodies, but no one standing or moving.

He hurried forward. The first two were both reapers, and the one he had struck down was still twitching. The next was another reaper, sprawled in a contorted way that suggested he was very dead indeed.

Onica lay at the beginning of the bridge. She was dead, too. Her face was a lurid color in the green light, and twisted as if she had died in agony. A black trickle of blood had flowed from her mouth. He closed her eyes as he had closed Creighton's.

First Bagpipe, then Creighton and the Gover man—now Mason, too! How many deaths must he trail behind him?

Sudden realization made him leap to his feet. He turned to face his companion, the youth with the golden curls, the one who wore nothing but the light of the joker moon, the one who had not ridden on the dragon but had turned up at every stop. He had appeared at the theater with Mason, but she had not brought him. Mason had not even known he was there.

The two stood and looked at each other, the youth smiling, Edward fighting against tides of fury and despair, racking his brains. Out of the frying pan! *I demand to see the British Consul! Bring in the gunboats!*

What was the proper form for greeting a god? A local chieftain could be accorded respect, within limits, but Tion was not a secular authority, nor even a high priest or witch doctor. He was a brigand, a parasite, a first-class fraud. A native would undoubtedly throw himself in the dirt at this point, but no Englishman should grovel like that to anyone, and this young bugger ranked lower than a Sarawak pirate. *Grovel?* Edward wanted to smash that pretty face to pulp.

"I suppose you're Tion?"

The boy uttered a high-pitched laugh. "And you are the Liberator! Do you like this body? It was a present from Kirb'l." He turned around to display it. "He's a maniac, but he does appreciate my tastes."

"A present?"

"Or you could say I won it in the festival. I win one every year—my prize! Do you like it?"

Was there any good answer to that?

"It's a fine representation of the young Apollo."

Apparently Tion understood the reference, for he flashed white teeth in a smile of pleasure. "Thank you! You're quite nice-looking yourself, you know. I say so, and I am the ultimate authority on such matters."

Fury! He must be mad as a March hare and dangerous as a hungry shark. With his superhuman power, he had turned up like a *deus ex machina* and then done nothing at all! "Why didn't you save her?"

The god pouted. "Why should I? She was only one of those meddling, idealistic nobodies from the Service! They won't last. It's been tried before. I've been around a lot longer than the Service, and I shall be around when they're all dead and forgotten."

"I'm sorry she's dead!"

"Well, you shouldn't be!" The Youth sounded peeved. Then he smiled. "We mustn't leave the evidence lying around, though. It's unsightly, having bodies all over the place. Drop them in the river."

"I won't take orders—"

"Yes you will," Tion said quietly.

Before he knew it, Edward had bent to take hold of Onica's feet. He tried to let go, but his hands refused to open. His feet started to move, and he began dragging her out onto the bridge. There the roar of the river was deafening. A cold, misty wind blew along the canyon. The planks were slippery.

"Damn you!" he shouted. "She deserves a decent burial at least!"

"No she doesn't. This should be far enough."

Sick at heart, Edward pushed the body out through the chains and watched it dwindle away to a speck before it vanished in the surging foam of Susswater, far below.

He found himself hurrying back to the corpses, and then he stopped resisting the compulsion. He did not care about the reapers, but he felt shamed at having treated the woman so, even if he had had no choice. Tion strolled beside him, making no effort to assist. Manual labor must be beneath a god's dignity.

"This one she ran down with the dragon," he remarked. "But too late to avoid his power, of course. And you got the last of them, dear boy! Nasty vermin. You are a very good thrower, aren't you?"

Edward almost choked on his anger. "Why didn't you save the woman?"

"Because I chose not to, of course. She was trespassing. So were the others. I warned Zath to keep his trash off my lawn. Giving powers like that to natives is quite disgusting."

When Edward came to the man he had felled, though—trying not to look at the bloody wreckage inside the hood—he discovered that the victim was still moaning.

"This one's not dead!"

"A purely temporary state of affairs, dear boy. Go on."

Unable to refuse, Edward dragged the man to the bridge and

disposed of him as he had disposed of the bodies. He felt more nauseated by that than by anything else that had happened. He was really a murderer now. The Vales' equivalent of Inspector Leatherdale would be justified in swearing out a warrant for the arrest of D'ward Liberator.

The last reaper followed the others. When morning came, travelers crossing Lameby Bridge would see no evidence of the massacre.

"There, that's better!" Tion sighed. "And I suppose I must let you be on your way, tempting though you are. Mustn't upset any of the prophecies! The pass is clear, you'll have no trouble. You did frightfully well to dispose of that reaper without mana—but you are altogether the most *interesting* thing to come along in centuries, dear boy! I can't imagine how you're going to settle that horrible Zath, but I do so hope you succeed! I can't wait to see how you do it."

"You heard what I told Mrs. Mason—I'm not fulfilling any prophecies! I am going Home."

The Youth shrugged disbelievingly. "Beware the Service, D'ward Liberator. Remember Verse 114!"

Edward Exeter must be the only man on Nextdoor who had not read the *Filoby Testament*. "Which one's that?"

"Oh, let me think. . . . How does it go now? *Men plot evil upon the holy mountain. The servants of the one do the work of the many. They send unto D'ward, mouthing oaths like nectar. Their voices are sweet as roses, yea sweeter than the syrup that snares the diamond-fly. He is lured to destruction by the word of a friend, by the song of a friend he is hurled down among the legions of death.* Horrible prose, but you see what I mean, darling?"

If he was telling the truth, that did sound ominous. *Holy mountain* must refer to Olympus, because there was no other holy mountain. It was odd that Tion had made the connection, but he had known of Apollo, too.

"Well, that completes the night's business," Tion said. "It's been a most entertaining evening. Bye-bye!"

"Wait!"

The Youth cocked an eyebrow, almost as if he had been waiting for the word. "Yes?"

Edward braced himself to plead with this monster. "If you enjoyed the show, let's pass the hat. The girl who's mentioned in the *Testament,* Eleal—she deserves the credit for staging it. She's only a child. She has a crippled leg."

Tion switched on a smile that was too sudden to be genuine. "You want me to heal her for you?"

"Would you, sir?" It was hard to be respectful to this seeming-boy who had so callously let four people die, but Mason had said he was not as bad as some of the other strangers. "She'll go mad with joy."

"That's trivial, D'ward! Nothing to it. Delighted to do you a favor."

There was bound to be a catch, though. Cautiously, Edward said, "Thank you, sir! I'd be very grateful—and she'll be ecstatic!"

"You can't have omelette and roast goose, of course."

Trapped!

Tion's smile grew broader.

Edward wiped his forehead. He owed his life to Eleal, but to repay that debt would force him to stay here on Nextdoor, and inevitably he would find himself fighting in the wrong war. His war lay on another world.

What would his father have done?

Zath and the Chamber had killed his parents . . . but he had only Creighton's word for that.

Zath had killed Creighton. What sort of chap did not try to avenge his friends? But he had only Eleal's word for that.

He could cause Eleal's limp to be cured and thus repay her for saving his life . . . but he had only Tion's word for that.

Tion was smiling gleefully. "You understand what I mean?"

"You mean I can't have my cake and eat it, too."

The boy smiled sweetly. "I mean, if we're into doing favors . . . You have an Eleal problem, I have a Gunuu problem, that unmanned aspect. You'd make an excellent god of courage, D'ward, you really would." The childish face glowed with innocent appeal. "Even a beginner ought to be able to raise that much mana in a fortnight or so. To pay me back. I mean, that would only be fair, wouldn't it?"

"A fortnight? Just a fortnight?"

Tion pursed his cherub lips. "Perhaps a little longer. It's hard to say. . . . I'd have to see how you perform." His pale eyes shone very bright.

Speak ye one word in elfin land . . . If Edward bit, he would be hooked, somehow. Perhaps forever.

Where did honor lie in this morass? Where were courage and duty?

King and Country! There were no doubts about those. They took precedence over anything else.

"I cannot accept a favor from you on those terms, sir. I withdraw my request."

Tion sighed, but he did not seem surprised. "Good-bye, then, D'ward Liberator! I wish you luck—god knows you'll need it, and I speak with authority." He shrieked with childish glee and faded away.

Edward was alone.

He didn't even have Eleal to look after him now. *Oh, Eleal!* Would the dragon find her way home to Olympus? Would she return in search of her mistress? He could not control her if she did. The only course of action open to him was to head on over the pass and find Kalmak Carpenter.

Having nothing else to do, he walked over the bridge and began climbing the trail on the other side.

He was going Home! That was what mattered, he told himself. Duty called. Onica's death gnawed at his conscience. So did his despicable betrayal of the child who had saved his life, but there he had made his own choice and it was too late to back out now.

Nextdoor was a snare and a temptation. He must answer his country's call. Zath was not his proper foe. He would go Home and enlist to fight in the war he was meant to fight in.

There a man at least could know who was right and who was wrong. There a man fought with bullet and bayonet, not hideous sorcery. There a man could hope for honor, trust in courage, believe in a cause.

END OF ROUND ONE

To Come

Round Two: *Present Tense*
Round Three: *Future Indefinite*

In Round Two of "The Great Game," Edward Exeter goes Home and discovers that even there he cannot escape the workings of the Filoby Testament.

ACKNOWLEDGEMENTS

I have been granted willing assistance by many people. Some merely confirmed a single fact, others slaved over the manuscript for me word by word. To list them in anything but alphabetical order would be invidious, but to all of them I extend my sincere thanks:

J. Brian Clarke, Janet Duncan, Michael Duncan, Jean Greig, Betty Hutton, the Public Library of Wiltshire County Council, Jean-Louis Trudel, and John Welch. All responsibility for the text, however, is mine.

The Embu and Meru are authentic tribes of Kenya, although I have taken some liberties with their history.

I have no desire to offend anyone's religious sensibilities. To the best of my knowledge, there never was a Lighthouse Missionary Society. This is a work of make-believe. Even on its own terms, the "gods" it depicts are divine only in the eyes of those foolish enough to worship them.